"Theresa Scott's historical romances are tender, exciting, enjoyable, and satisfying!"
—*Romantic Times*

PASSION'S CAPTIVE

"You have pleased me. And you'll continue to please me, until I tire of you." It was an order.

Sarita's jaw dropped. "You—you worm! I will continue to please you!" she repeated in a high shriek. "You—you—!" Words failed her. "Let me tell you something, O high and noble chief!" Her eyes blazed. Her hair in tangles, her back straight, she faced him, proud and undaunted. "*You* do not please me! You will *never* please me!"

Fighting Wolf had to admire her courage. "You're fortunate we're not in my village. Some of my people, hearing such talk to their war chief, would demand your death."

Sarita grimaced at him. "Go ahead and kill me! You've taken everything else from me! Why not my life, too!"

"Death is no victory over a woman like you. At least not for a man like me. I'd rather have you crying out your passion for me. I want you in my bed, whenever I desire you. A much better revenge, don't you think?"

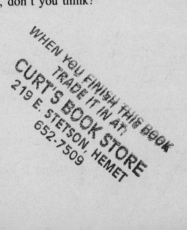

Van Couver Island

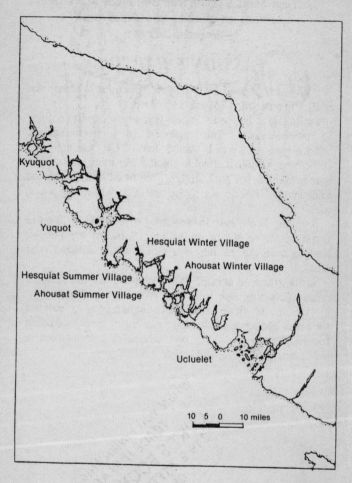

Kyuquot

Yuquot

Hesquiat Winter Village

Ahousat Winter Village

Hesquiat Summer Village

Ahousat Summer Village

Ucluelet

10 5 0   10 miles

Location of villages is fictionalized.

SAVAGE BETRAYAL

Theresa Scott

LEISURE BOOKS   NEW YORK CITY

In memory of Jana Kwiatkowska

A LEISURE BOOK®

March 1994

Published by

Dorchester Publishing Co., Inc.
276 Fifth Avenue
New York, NY 10001

Printed in the United States of America.

1

"Enemy or not, you will marry the Ahousat!"

Her father's order rang in her ears even now, as Sarita picked blueberries on the peaceful hillside. With those few words, her life had shattered.

She stripped another handful of the luscious blue-gray fruit off the delicate, lacy branch. She dropped the berries into her cedar basket, then straightened. Rubbing the small of her back, she looked over at the other women scattered about the clearing. Several women, commoner and slave alike, worked quietly at their task, bending over the heavily laden bushes. There was Spring Fern, her slave, busily picking a rich harvest of berries. Perhaps she could help calm Sarita's unhappy brooding.

Sarita looked around her. A gentle sea breeze, tangy with a salty smell, rustled the bushes growing on the slanting ground. Stark, fire-blackened skeletons of dead cedars dotted the clearing—remnants of a long-forgotten forest fire. Higher up on the hillside the thick, green growth of cedar and fir reclaimed the land. All around the brush-covered clearing, the soft purple flowers of fireweed scattered bursts of color against the light green and yellow of the dried grass. It was a tranquil scene—in vivid contrast to Sarita's thoughts.

"Spring Fern," she called, "Come over here and pick with me!" She watched as the slave gathered up her basket and slowly trudged the distance between them.

Usually, picking sweet blueberries was one of Sarita's favorite chores. Today, however, her hands trembled and her thoughts raced. She couldn't concentrate on her picking and when she looked into her basket, she noted that many blueberries were crushed. Picking with care, however, was of little concern. Her mind was on Fighting Wolf.

She wiped a purple-stained hand across her forehead. It was so hot on this early summer day. Below her she could see the quiet village laid out in the morning sun. Tiny dots, people, went about their daily activities. Occasionally, the muted sound of someone's laughter drifted lazily up to the workers on the hill. She, however, would never laugh again, she told herself bitterly. There would be no laughter in a forced marriage to Fighting Wolf.

Standing on the side of the hill in the small clearing, Sarita could look down at the village spread out along the beach embankment. In each long, wooden house lived several families. This was the summer village. In the fall, the houses would be disassembled, the side planks taken down and packed away. Then, everything and everyone would move to the winter village. Everyone, that is, except me, she thought angrily. By then she would be living amongst the hated Ahousats.

The reflection of the sun's intense rays on the bright water far below temporarily blinded her. The shallow arms of a bay formed a gentle half-curve separated by a wide expanse of water. It was almost as if the arms stretched futilely towards each other to keep out the rolling grasp of the sea. They afforded some protection from the huge ocean, but in the rare, wild, summer storms were forced to surrender to the raging gray waters. Today however, the sea was silver, like a gently rolling sweep of shimmering mercury.

Sarita turned back to her blueberry bush. She picked carefully now, the big, plump berries falling easily into her hand. Popping a berry into her mouth, she chewed it quickly, tasting nothing as she pondered the events of earlier that morning.

"Have you given any more consideration to Fighting Wolf's offer of marriage, my daughter?" her father had asked her.

When Sarita answered him with stubborn silence, he continued patiently. "He's a very good provider for his family. He'd make a good husband. In addition, his family is as wealthy and as well-known as ours." He paused. "Wealthier, in fact. They have large clam beds, hunting territories, many slaves. They are a powerful and ambitious family."

"Oh?" Her tone conveyed her disinterest.

"You would seek long and hard to find a better match for our two families."

Sarita lifted her chin defiantly and her eyes flashed. "That may well be, Nuwiksu," she sniffed haughtily, "but I find Fighting Wolf not to my liking. I don't know him and I don't see how I, a Hesquiat woman, can love and respect someone from the Ahousat tribe. They've been our enemies for many years."

Her father began to lose some of his usual calm manner. "You will obey me, daughter! Think seriously on this matter. You've tried my patience long enough. You've rejected every eligible young man in this village and the next!"

His voice rose in anger. "No other father is so patient! Most young women have long been married by your age, betrothed from the time of their puberty ceremony! I've been exceedingly patient with you . . . but no more!"

Sarita watched as, with great effort, her father brought himself under control. "Too much rests on this alliance. As you say, we've been enemies of the Ahousat for several years. But I," he announced, "have had enough of war and killing."

He paused, his angry gaze upon her, and Sarita had flinched inside. "You will marry Fighting Wolf in five days!"

"Nuwiksu!" Sarita had cried then. "No!

Please—!''

"I've already agreed to the marriage. I'd hoped you'd see the wisdom of it and accept it. I see now that you won't. No matter."

"Nuwiksu—" implored the distraught girl.

He waved away her pleas. "You'll accept your husband-to-be gracefully. Enemy or not, you will marry the Ahousat!''

With this grim pronouncement, her father had stalked off, leaving his daughter standing with head bowed and tears coursing down her cheeks.

Sarita's thoughts returned to the present. What would she do now? she wondered woefully.

It was true that she had rejected every eligible suitor in the village and a few others besides. But she wanted a man to love and respect, one who would cherish her as in the romantic tales the storytellers chanted on long winter evenings. That wasn't so wrong. She wanted to love and be loved in return. Now, being married off to an enemy, she had no chance for love. How could Nuwiksu do this? she lamented hopelessly.

As Spring Fern approached, Sarita stood lost in thought. The slave noted her mistress' lithe figure in the woven cedar bark dress. Shining dark brown hair, highlighted with gold, hung loose to Sarita's waist. High cheekbones and a straight nose made her face striking. The delicate arch of her eyebrows graced scintillating golden eyes that danced with an inner fire. Her cheeks were lightly tanned, touched by the rosy blush of good health.

Sarita's full lips parted to show even, white teeth as she smiled briefly at Spring Fern, noting her heavily laden basket. "Oh, Spring Fern," she sighed. "What am I to do? What am I to do?"

Spring Fern bent and carefully placed her burden on the ground. She straightened, looking at Sarita with compassionate eyes. Given to Sarita when both were but children, Spring Fern was sensitive to her mistress' moods and needs. She knew Sarita was truly upset.

"About what, mistress?" she asked carefully.

Sarita quickly told her slave of the earlier conversation with her father. Picking the succulent berries, she asked solemnly, "How could Nuwiksu do this to me? He's giving me to the enemy!"

"Perhaps this Fighting Wolf isn't so bad," consoled the slave. "Your father loves you very much. Surely he wouldn't give you to someone who'd harm you." She managed to keep the doubt out of her voice. As she spoke, her nimble fingers speedily gathered the fruit.

Sarita shook her head sadly. "We've been fighting the Ahousats for a long time. No, I know they're our enemies."

Spring Fern had to agree. "Yes, for as long as I can remember, we've been at war with the Ahousats."

Sarita went on, as if she hadn't heard, "They've always wanted our fishing streams, our clam beaches. Countless times they've raided us in the night like the thieves they are! They kill our men and steal our women and babies. Fighting Wolf is their war chief. He's the one who leads them in their bloody fights. He's the worst of them all! And he's the man my father would have me marry!"

Spring Fern heard the agony in her mistress' voice. She answered quietly, "I don't understand it myself." She sighed. "It seems it's always the way of men to make war . . . and the way of women to suffer from war. Your father is a good man," she added reassuringly. "Perhaps he wants an end to all the fighting and killing. If your father gives you to Fighting Wolf, the Ahousats won't raid us any more."

Sarita didn't answer, she just stared at her slave, a sudden question forming in her mind. She burst out, "But it was Fighting Wolf that approached my father about marriage."

Spring Fern shrugged. "Oh? What difference does that make?"

"It means," said Sarita excitedly, "that Nuwiksu didn't approach Fighting Wolf and offer me in marriage. Fighting Wolf came to my father and asked for me. Don't you see? Fighting Wolf asked for me! It was only then that my father agreed to the marriage."

The two women stared at each other for a moment, pondering the meaning of this revelation.

"Now, why?" mused Sarita. "Why would Fighting Wolf offer for me? What possible advantage is there for him?"

"Perhaps the Ahousats are losing the war with us," suggested Spring Fern. "Maybe he wants to make peace. He knows that if he marries you, your father will no longer fight against him."

Sarita snorted. "The Ahousats aren't losing. They're winning against us! Why would the winners chose to marry into the losing side? It doesn't make sense."

"Maybe Fighting Wolf is tired of war," sighed Spring Fern. "I know I'm tired of talking about it." She caught Sarita's eye and grinned as she added, "Maybe he's heard how beautiful you are and wants to marry you for that reason."

"Hmmph," sniffed Sarita. "I suspect a man like Fighting Wolf, trained only for war, doesn't concern himself with things like beauty. He would have no softness in him. Besides, he probably has his pick of beautiful women."

When Spring Fern raised a brow inquiringly, Sarita explained, "Women taken as slaves in the many raids he's led."

"Oh."

Sarita continued her musing, "No, there must be something, some reason, why he offered for me." She paused in her picking. "Spring Fern, I don't like it. I don't trust him."

"Your father does," shot back Spring Fern.

"Does he? You say that because he's agreed to give me to Fighting Wolf," stated Sarita slowly. "Or is Nuwiksu forced into this alliance as much as I am?"

Spring Fern could see no end to Sarita's specula-

tions. She decided to distract her mistress. "My cousin
is visiting me. She comes from Yuquot." Spring Fern
watched as Sarita turned to her pensively, still preoccupied by thoughts of Fighting Wolf.

"Yuquot?" Sarita asked dazedly. She gave a start,
coming out of her reverie. "Any news from that town?"
she asked, feigning interest.

Spring Fern smiled. "My cousin says there have
been many changes in Yuquot since the *mumutly*, the
white men, came there, many moons ago. They came in
their big ships . . . ships longer than your father's longhouse, and with big tall trees on them." Spring Fern
paused, catching the spark of interest in Sarita's face.

Satisfied that her mistress' curiosity was aroused,
she continued, "My cousin says the *mumutly* are crazy
for sea otter furs. They'll trade anything for the furs,
even for old robes no one wants to wear any more.
They'll even take old sea otter blankets, good only for
sleeping on! And it's hard to believe, but for those
ancient furs, our people can get hard metal fishhooks.
We can get weapons like knives and daggers. We can
trade for kettles, pots, and jewelry too. Very valuable
things! The traders have beautiful blankets,
too . . . some red ones and the prettiest blue ones,
woven from soft cloth. Fit for a chief," sighed Spring
Fern. She herself would never have such fine things, but
perhaps Sarita would.

Spring Fern continued, "My cousin even said,"
and here she lowered her voice in a conspiratorial
whisper, "that some of the *mumutly* traders have a new
kind of weapon, things called 'mus-kets'. But she
didn't know how they worked."

Sarita was becoming interested in what her slave
was saying. She knew little about Yuquot, only that the
small village had sprung into prominence since the
recent coming of the white men. Yuquot was to the
north of Sarita's village, some two days' travel by
canoe. "Is it true," she ventured, "that there are now
many more people living in Yuquot than ever before?

Did your cousin mention that?"

"Oh, yes," nodded Spring Fern. "She says there are many more people now. Too many. She'd like to leave, but she can't." Sarita guessed the cousin was also a slave.

"Everyone who wants to trade goes to that town now. People from up and down the coast travel for days so they can get the hard metals or weapons. My cousin said the chief, Maquinna, owns the *mumutly* traders and will not let them sail their ships to any other village. He told them they're safe at Yuquot; they won't be eaten. Everywhere else lurk dangerous cannibals!"

Amused, Sarita asked, "And they believe him?"

"They must. They don't trade anywhere else." Spring Fern chuckled. "My cousin tells me that when the *mumutly* first came to Yuquot, Maquinna and all his people thought the *mumutly* were Salmon people."

"What?" exclaimed Sarita, intrigued. "Whatever do you mean?"

"Well, you know stories are told that deep under the sea there's a great house where the Salmon People and the Herring People live. We must honor the Salmon and Herring People, and give them gifts, otherwise they'll become angry and dangerous; they may even leave and we'll go hungry."

"I know that," interrupted Sarita impatiently.

Spring Fern continued hastily, "When the *mumutly* first came to Yuqout, they stood on the decks of their big ships with the tall masts. Our people paddled out in canoes to get a closer look. There was a fat man, very red-faced with a big nose. 'Oh, he is a coho salmon, ready to spawn,' one man said. Another *mumutly* had a very hooked nose. 'He must be a dog salmon, that one,' said someone else. Still another had a hunchback. 'See the humpback salmon,' exclaimed somebody else in the crowd. So it went. Every *mumutly* on the ship looked like a fish of some kind. And after all, they were floating on the sea, where the Salmon People come from." She paused. "Of course it didn't take long to find out they were just men."

Sarita was fascinated. "What else did your cousin say?" she asked.

"Hmm, well. When the *mumutly* first came to our shores, they gave out gifts to all the people. Everyone received a round, flat, hard thing with tiny holes poked in it. No one knew what to do with such strange things, but everyone was too polite to ask. Some people used them for good luck charms. Others thought they were pieces of polished wood. Most used them for souvenirs but a friend of my cousin's used one to wipe her breasts when her baby wouldn't drink all the milk. Nobody really knew what to do with the things. The *mumutly* called them 'pilot bish-kit.' One day, a Yuquot man watched in astonishment as a *mumutly* popped a bish-kit in his mouth and ate it!" Spring Fern paused dramatically. "And so, to this day, pilot bish-kits are eaten." The women laughed together at the story.

"Those *mumutly* sound like strange creatures," marveled Sarita. "Fish who eat wood."

"Very strange indeed," agreed Spring Fern. She continued, "At this first meeting, a high-ranking chief was given a hatchet with a leather thong on the handle. He hung it around his neck and paraded around with his beautiful new 'necklace' for all to see! Can't you just imagine him strutting about with a heavy axe weighing him down?" Both young women burst into giggles at the picture.

Suddenly Sarita looked around. The other women were far down the hillside, winding their way back to the village. The sun was slipping towards the horizon. "Oh, we must hurry! We've been so busy talking, we've hardly picked any berries!"

Laughing, the two hurried to join the others. For a brief time Sarita had relaxed, forgetting that in five short days she was to be married off to the enemy.

It was dusk. Sarita's thoughts returned again and again to her conversation with her father as she sauntered along the beach under the watchful eye of her aunt. Rain-on-the-Sea often hovered quietly nearby, but Sarita had grown accustomed to chaperonage, and accepted it.

Unlike most noble girls her age, Sarita had not been kept within the dark confines of her longhouse from the time of her puberty ceremony until the day of her marriage. She had long ago persuaded her father to let her roam freely about the village. Crab Woman, her father's first wife, had proven an unexpected ally. Declaring that she would not "spoil and coddle" her highborn stepdaughter, Crab Woman had insisted that Sarita perform the same chores as other women did, be they commoners or slaves.

Much to Sarita's surprise, she found she liked doing the different tasks. It was certainly better than sitting around a dingy longhouse, learning house-keeping chores and waiting to be married off. Sarita was far too active to take kindly to such a life, and her father had wisely recognized that fact. He gave Sarita considerably more freedom than other young women were permitted by their families.

On one point, however, Sarita had found her father adamant. On those few occasions when she was not surrounded by other women he had demanded that Sarita be chaperoned. So whenever she left her home alone, Rain-on-the-Sea, his widowed sister, walked along to protect her niece from the young men who tried to talk with her. Sarita appreciated that Rain-on-the-Sea was tactful in her watchfulness and never imposed upon or embarrassed her young charge. The young men still attempted conversation despite the aunt's vigilance.

Seeing her eldest brother, Feast Giver, far down the beach, Sarita quickened her pace. He and several small figures were hunting for the tiny crabs that hid under the large rocks on the pebble beach. The children were laughing and jumping on him, trying to persuade him to overturn a particularly big rock.

Sarita was proud of her brother. He was a tall man,

muscular, with ebony eyes. Sister and brother shared the same lightly tanned skin, but Feast Giver's hair was jet black. He was their father's heir and a chief in his own right. Perhaps he could explain why their father was marrying her off to a hated Ahousat.

As with most men of her village, her brother was dressed in a knee-length kutsack, tied at the left shoulder. Of course, as with all the younger men, Feast Giver was beardless. Many times, Sarita had watched him pluck his beard hairs with two small clam shells as tweezers. One time, she remembered, she asked him if it hurt. He had only patted her on the head and laughed, assuring her the pain was worth it.

On his head he wore a cone-shaped cedar hat, the badge of his chiefly status. A graphic design of whale hunters chased their giant prey around the brim. That design was especally appropriate, thought Sarita. Feast Giver was one of the best whale hunters in the village. Only chiefs could hunt the leviathans, and it required much skill to harpoon the huge gray whales from the bow of a canoe. Feast Giver always took several men with him, but the actual killing was his responsibility and his right.

"Catlati, are the children teaching you how to catch crabs?" Sarita asked innocently. "Pay attention. Once you know how to catch the tiny crabs, it will be no time at all before you can go after the big gray whales!"

Her brother looked up at the sound of her voice and his face broke into a grin. "Sarita," he exclaimed. "I've been looking for you. I want to talk with you."

He tried to walk over to her, but two little boys clutched at each leg, making it impossible for him to walk. He unwound the tiny arms from around his legs, only to have others replace them. "Help me, Sarita," he joked. "I've been attacked by a giant octopus!" Sarita laughed, watching him gradually free himself and slip away from the grabbing children. Reluctantly, they let him go.

Leaving the children behind, he drew Sarita off to

one side, out of their aunt's considerable hearing range. But before he could say a word, she burst out, "Catlati, please tell me why Nuwiksu is marrying me off to that Ahousat! I thought the Ahousats were our enemies! Does Nuwiksu love me so little that he would give me to our enemy?" Sarita cried.

He was taken aback at her outcry. "That's what I wished to speak with you about," he began. "Your marriage to the Ahousat is very important, but I can see you're very upset about it."

Sarita nodded. "More than that. I don't want to marry him. Not at all!"

He looked at her seriously, wondering how to begin. "You know Nuwiksu loves you," he assured her. "Are you not his favorite daughter?" Seeing her tentative nod, he continued, "Nuwiksu's been watching for an opportunity to make peace with the bloodthirsty Ahousats for the last two years."

Sarita looked at him in surprise.

"Yes," confirmed her brother, "he has. He's convinced your marriage to Fighting Wolf will be the best way to achieve peace."

"Oh? And why should Nuwiksu want peace?"

"You know as well as I do that many of our women and children have been stolen by that tribe. Many of our warriors have been ambushed and killed in the night."

"I know, believe me, I know."

"We're losing too many people. We must have an end to the war or there'll be no Hesquiat people left," he said bitterly. "That's why Nuwiksu accepted the marriage suit of Fighting Wolf."

Sarita looked down at the ground. So she had been right. Nuwiksu was losing the war and wanted peace. But that still did not explain why Fighting Wolf wanted the marriage.

When Sarita remained silent, her brother continued, "You are Nuwiksu's last hope for peace. He told me he was getting desperate until Fighting Wolf suddenly offered for you. Nuwiksu accepted gladly."

He added softly, "Sarita, he's hoping to spare the lives of our people."

That brought Sarita's head up. "And so I should do my duty. Is that it, catlati? I should go to my enemy husband quietly and spare our people's lives?"

Her brother was silent. Sarita noticed he did not contradict her. She could barely suppress the pain, the violence, in her voice as she said to him, "It's my life we're talking about. My life!"

Their eyes met and he looked away. "It's the Hesquiat people's lives, too," he answered quietly.

Defeated, her shoulders sagged. "And what of Fighting Wolf? Why does he want this marriage?"

Her brother shrugged. "Probably a strategic alliance. If he allies himself with us, he can fight some other tribe. He knows we won't attack him any more, once you're married to him."

It made sense, thought Sarita.

"The best thing for you to do is to accept this marriage. It seems our Nuwiksu is determined to go through with it." He paused for a moment. Finally he pointed out, "You'll be in a position to help our people. *If* you can gain—and give—this man love and respect."

"Love and respect!" she flared. "How can I love and respect a man who kills our people and sells our women and children into slavery? How can I overlook that?"

Her brother had no answer. He could only stand helplessly in the gathering dusk. Reaching to touch her arm, he quickly dropped his hand and shrugged, knowing nothing would comfort her. Not while her anger and agony were so fresh.

Sarita sorrowfully turned away, bitterness and despair washing over her.

2

The village of Ahousat sat nestled at the foot of several high mountains, their tall forest-covered peaks thrust into curling white clouds. Twenty longhouses were stretched across a narrow field of yellowed grass that fronted a gravel beach. On this sunny day, small waves danced in from the broad green sea, teasing the shore. Behind the houses, a forest of graceful alder and tall cedar trees rustled in the summer wind.

Canoes lay on the beach, resting at crazy haphazard angles, waiting for the tide to come in and once more restore their dignity. Up and down the beach raced small children, shrieking and chasing each other. Nearby their mothers watched with benevolent brown eyes while smoking salmon on racks over the open fire pits.

Summer was the time to dry salmon, pick berries and preserve foods for the oncoming winter when rain would keep the people bundled up in their cedar cloaks and cedar homes.

In the darkened interior of one longhouse set off from the others, a large group of men huddled around a smoking fire. The lean, brown, muscular men squatted or hunched in various positions as they listened intently to the tall warrior speaking in their midst.

Fighting Wolf, war chief of the Ahousats, addressed his warriors with his customary air of imperious command. His wide shoulders tapered to a

lean waist and narrow hips that were hidden by the
cedar robe he wore tied cavalierly at one shoulder. He
stood with muscular legs planted firmly on the floor, his
bearing confident and majestic.

Shoulder-length, blue-black hair framed the hard
planes of his face. The cleft in his chin was the only
gentle feature in an otherwise rugged, masculine face. It
was his eyes, however, that held the combative audience
of fighters in thrall. Jet black eyes, glinting with anger,
surveyed his fellow warriors . . . eyes that captivated,
then dominated the battle-scarred veterans.

"Men," he exhorted. "Many times you've fought
for me and for our people. Many times you've gone
forth in battle against great odds. It is because of you,
your bravery, your ferocity, that we are the strongest
people on this coast today."

Here he was interrupted by cheers and loud
exclamations attesting to the truth of his words. "Yes,
the name 'Ahousat' strikes fear and terror into our
enemies." More cheers. When silence was restored, he
continued, "I am asking you to once again take up arms
against our enemies, the hated Hesquiats."

Some groans were heard. Fighting Wolf frowned
briefly. "This time, however, I can promise an easy
victory." Mutters of interest ran through his audience.
"This time you will have a chance to revenge yourselves—" the mutterings increased, "—on the
murderers who killed your beloved chief, my father,
just twenty-six moons ago. On the murderers who
slaughtered many of our beloved brothers and sons."

He paused for effect. "You, Otterskin, you lost
your brother in that raid." A grim-faced man nodded.

"And you, Comes-from-Salish." A barrel-chested
man straightened, his full attention on the dynamic
speaker. "Your only son was blinded when that
cowardly Hesquiat speared him with a lance."

The father glowered. "I'll follow you, and gladly,
whenever you care to lead a war party against those
Hesquiat dogs!" He spat on the dirt floor for emphasis.

The serious looks on the men's faces told Fighting Wolf he had not only their bodies to command, but their hearts as well. "I'll need brave men like you when we raid those bastard Hesquiats. For two years, I've waited for the right time to take our revenge. That time is now!"

Lusty cheers broke into his impassioned speech. He waited patiently until they died down. "This time we'll use cunning as well as weapons to bring the Hesquiat worms down. They'll be like the dirt beneath our feet when we're done with them."

Shouting and stamping interrupted him once more. "Their names will be spat upon by our neighbors up and down the coast. Our friends will have nothing but contempt for the name 'Hesquiat,' for the name 'Thunder Maker,' for the name 'Feast Giver.' Hah! The only feast he'll give will be for the dogs." Gruff laughter greeted his sally.

"We'll take their women and children as slaves, the only status a Hesquiat deserves. We'll laugh at their shame!"

This time the shouts were interspersed with eager whoops. Time to calm them down and tell them his plans, he thought. "No longer need we torment ourselves over the treachery of the Hesquiat killers. No longer need we fear another brutal slaughter like the one that took my father's life."

Hoarse murmurings and low rumblings could be heard as the warriors remembered the humiliation inflicted from the vicious Hesquiat raid. Fighting Wolf spoke in a calm, deadly voice now. "They killed our warchief, the greatest Ahousat war chief we've ever had. And why? Merely because we killed one of their chiefs. An insignificant chief, at that! No, we can't allow our beloved chief's death to go unavenged!" Thoroughly angry now, the men were ready to kill every Hesquiat still alive.

"Listen closely, men. I want these plans completely understood. This is what we're going to do . . ." and he smiled to himself as his warriors leaned closer to hear his long thought-out plans of revenge.

"So you're planning a wedding with the Hesquiats?" began Birdwhistle conversationally as the warriors gradually dispersed from the meeting.

Fighting Wolf looked at him. Since childhood the two had clashed, competing over everything from the number of salmon caught to the number of enemy killed. As he sauntered through the doorway of the longhouse into the bright sunlight, Fighting Wolf answered casually, "You heard the plans, cousin. Any objections should have been raised at the meeting."

Falling into step, Birdwhistle responded, "Oh, I've no objections." As they walked along, he toyed with the sea-otter fur on his kutsack, the cedar robe he wore. "I was just wondering what this Sarita looks like."

Fighting Wolf shrugged. "What does it matter? That's not my concern. All I care about is that her father agreed to the wedding."

"Did you get to see her?"

Fighting Wolf shook his head. "No. The marriage negotiations were carried out between my messenger and his. I sent a relative to ask Thunder Maker for his daughter. My instructions were to convince the Hesquiats that peace would come from such an alliance. Thunder Maker sent back his answer, by his own messenger."

"Sounds like you two don't trust each other." Seeing his companion's sardonic look, Birdwhistle added hastily, "But at least Thunder Maker agreed to the marriage."

"All too readily, I thought."

"How so?"

"He seemed most anxious to give her away. He didn't reject my offer the usual two or three times before accepting. Any respectable father would have said 'no' the first time I asked. But not Thunder Maker. He agreed to the marriage on the first request. He didn't even demand any expensive gifts for the bride. Practically shoved her at me," said Fighting Wolf.

"Ho, ho, cousin," laughed Birdwhistle, "It sounds like she's someone he wants to be rid of." His eyes twinkled. How amusing to see the proud Fighting Wolf stuck with a flawed bride. "Probably hunchbacked."

"Or ugly," added Fighting Wolf with disgust.

"Or has already been married two or three times. You know how some upper-class fathers marry their daughters off every few years to a new husband. Each time it's to a man more exalted than the last. Maybe that's what Thunder Maker's doing. You should be flattered he thinks so highly of you, cousin," smirked Birdwhistle.

Fighting Wolf frowned. "I'd prefer a virgin." Then he added lightly, "Perhaps she's just an uncontrollable nag."

"Or missing a few front teeth." Birdwhistle chuckled at Fighting Wolf's mounting dismay.

With great enthusiasm, Birdwhistle launched into an eloquent, unflattering description of Fighting Wolf's bride-to-be. How pleasant to goad the younger man.

At last Fighting Wolf wearied of the game. "Cousin," he said, "if she's as bad as you think she is, I promise I'll give her to you . . . as a symbol of my esteem." He snickered.

Birdwhistle eyed him warily. "No, no. I insist you keep her. After all, it was your idea to get 'married.' "

"Ah yes. Married," laughed Fighting Wolf. He clapped his cousin on the back as they shared a private joke on their way to the beach.

Fighting Wolf walked through the village. The afternoon sun slanted through the clouds and illuminated the Ahousat village longhouses that stood so proudly.

A longhouse was as wide as seven men laying head to toe and twice that distance in length. The height of the house was equal to two tall men. A frame of long cedar ridge poles ran the length of each side, and was supported by sturdy posts at the four corners. Two stout posts framed the main entrance.

A carved sea lion figure-post stood at the back of the house. Poles as high as two men, and carved in human design, supported the central beam. Long cedar planks made up the siding of the house, and a gabled roof of rafters, covered by cedar planks, kept the inhabitants dry through the long, rainy winters.

From inside the house, smoke holes were made by shoving roof planks back with poles. During winter storms, large stones and logs anchored the roof and kept its cedar plank covering from blowing away. At various places along the back side of the house were small doors; escape hatches should enemy raiders come sweeping into the village.

As he neared one of the longhouses, Fighting Wolf heard his name called. There, leaning in the doorway, stood Limpet. She took her name from the small, pointed-shelled sea animals that clung firmly to rocks at the tideline. Limpet was a woman who, it seemed to Fighting Wolf, had dedicated her life to making herself his mistress.

Crooking a finger at him, she gave him a lazy look over one shoulder as she sauntered seductively into her longhouse. Grinning to himself, Fighting Wolf watched her full hips sway against her tight robe, slightly torn at the hem. He took his time following her into the darkened building.

Within the house, along the inside walls, each of the several resident families had their own cooking fire and sleeping benches. Often, planks or cedar chests filled with the family's belongings were piled high to mark off each separate apartment. The highest ranking chief in the house lived in the right rear corner with his wives, children and slaves. The next ranking chief lived in the left corner and lower ranking chiefs, or nobles, and their families occupied the remaining two corners. Along the sides, or middle of the house, lived commoners and their families, usually relatives of the ranking chief.

Smoke from the many firepits hovered in the interior of the long building. Rows of smoked fish hung from the rafters. The smoky aroma mingled with the rancid smell of oil-filled fish bladders, but the strong odor went unnoticed by the inhabitants.

Inside the longhouse, Fighting Wolf went to the middle section, Limpet's living area. He noted the haphazardly piled cedar boxes that marked the boundaries of her apartment. Torn and ragged cedar mats hung against the walls, ostensibly to provide decoration. Instead, they added to the air of impoverished tackiness.

Moth-eaten furs clung desperately to the wooden plank bed perched precariously one handspan above the dirt floor. The circular firepit in the center of her living area burned with a sooty fuel of some sort that gave off small puffs of smoke, causing a gentle haze that stung the eyes and suffocated the nose.

Old fishbones, broken clamshells, discarded tools of antler and the twisted remains of a woven cedar basket, long since deceased, lay scattered across the floor, giving the place a well-lived-in appearance.

Limpet smiled languidly at him. Fighting Wolf was amused that she thought she was irresistible to him; she was always giving him come-hither looks.

The men of the village took great delight in telling each other tales of her ardent advances and novel approaches to lovemaking.

The most famous of the stories told of the time when she and Sea Turtle, one of her favorite young lovers, decided to go line-fishing for salmon. Getting into a tippy old canoe, they paddled slowly towards the fishing grounds. As the day was hot, and they felt lazy, they only got as far as the middle of the bay in front of the village before they decided to set out their fishing lines. After waiting for a while and getting no bites, Limpet became amorous and began to seduce Sea Turtle right there in the old canoe.

All went well until the lovers forgot they were sporting in a canoe, which is an unstable craft at the best of times.

The energetic, lusty efforts of the two started rocking the canoe. Faster and faster it rocked. Soon a large crowd had gathered on shore. People were pointing and staring, chuckling amongst themselves at this latest exploit of Limpet's.

Suddenly, the rocking canoe lurched to one side. Sea Turtle was seen poised dramatically against the bottom of the canoe, Limpet's arms and legs flailing madly around him, then the canoe slowly rolled over. The boat completely capsized, throwing the intrepid lovers into the cold water. They came up gasping and sputtering, sodden hair dripping over their eyes, blindly groping for the canoe, sure they were going to drown.

The crowd on shore roared with delight. Ah yes, a good tale and one still talked about among the men . . . out of Limpet's hearing, of course!

Today, it seemed Limpet was outdoing herself in her sultry approach. Having lured him into her lair, she leaned back sensuously against the ratty fur-covered plank that doubled as a couch in the daytime and a bed at night. It was precariously hitched to the side of the building and wobbled a bit when she moved. Limpet intended to get the bed repaired but so far had been unable to convince Sea Turtle to fix it.

"I've been waiting for you all afternoon, Fighting Wolf," she said with what she hoped was a delectable look. He merely smiled, waiting to see what she was up to.

She leaned forward and began to undo the knot of his kutsack. A wicked smile curved her lips. After much fumbling and cursing under her breath, she finally got the knot undone, and lay back, propping herself against the wall. This was uncomfortable, so she slid down onto the furs, her eyes never leaving his.

"Would you like to learn something new?" she

asked. She wriggled her back invitingly into the bed.

He leaned over her. "Like what?" he asked playfully.

But she wasn't listening. She suddenly grimaced and lay still, frozen. Hastily, she pushed him off as she fumbled about behind her. "I have it!" she cried, holding up a fishhook triumphantly.

"This thing is sharp," she complained, rubbing her shoulder blades awkwardly with one hand. "Damn that Sea Turtle! Can't he be more careful where he puts his fishhooks?" She stared at the sharp pointed bone barb for a moment, but not one to let small things bother her, she tossed it casually to one side.

Then as if nothing had happened, she pulled Fighting Wolf down on top of her again. "Now, where were we? Oh, yes. I was going to show you something new." She puckered up her lips.

Fighting Wolf reared his head back, staring at her. "How strange you look," he commented mildly.

"This is called 'kissing,' " she said throatily. No need to tell him she had learned it from Sea Turtle who had learned it from a slave woman who had learned it from a fat white man trading kisses and furs at Yuquot.

Gently touching her lips to his, she pressed carefully, holding his head steady between her warm hands. Feeling him press back, she continued the pressure.

"Mmmm, this feels good," she murmured. Relaxing, she kissed him slowly and languorously, until they were both breathing heavily. "You learn quickly," she acknowledged, coming up for air. She grew bolder. Pushing her tongue between his lips, she met the hard resistance of his teeth. She swirled her tongue around his lips, thrusting firmly against his teeth several times, finally prying them open. Running her tongue around his mouth, she wrapped it around his and then slid away. A soft moan escaped her. Breathing quickly now, she reached for his hand and placed it on her breast.

Fighting Wolf felt her warm lips on his. He rather liked what she was doing, and as he felt her tongue thrusting against his teeth, he decided he liked what she was doing, very much. He began to respond to her excited efforts to arouse him. His tongue darted aggressively into her mouth. They were both panting. He heard her moan with delight.

Her next moan, however, was one of pain. A sudden, loud *thwack!* shook the apartment. Limpet's bed had collapsed. It had threatened to do so for a long time. Her moan was due to her soft lower lip being bruised by Fighting Wolf's hard white teeth.

Lying stunned and nearly suffocating under his weight, Limpet thought quickly of how to save the seduction scene. Tightening her grasp around his neck, she pretended not to be affected by the sudden thump they had just undergone and kissed Fighting Wolf enthusiastically, if somewhat sloppily.

Fighting Wolf, however, had had enough. The sharp jolt when they fell, though he landed on top of the soft Limpet, had destroyed his sensuous mood. The pleasurable touch of her lips on his own aroused him, but the collapse of the bed annoyed him severely.

Disentangling his arms and legs from hers, he finally managed to free himself from her tight grasp. He rose to his feet in one smooth fluid motion and paused for a moment, staring down at Limpet. Suddenly the absurdity of the situation struck him. His lips twitching spasmodically, he sought desperately to stifle the strong urge to laugh that swept over him. Finding himself sputtering uncontrollably, he staggered quickly out the door clutching his mouth and stomach.

Limpet heard him coughing all the way down the path.

Struggling up, she cursed the collapsed bed. In the next breath she cast rude aspersions on Sea Turtle's parentage, or lack thereof. Never mind, she consoled herself. She would get the damn bed fixed and try again!

It had been an active day—one spent checking and repairing weapons, patching canoes, and drilling men,

until all was in readiness. As Fighting Wolf strode
through the village, he thought idly of the unknown
Hesquiat woman who was preparing herself to become
his mate.

He laughed cynically. No woman had appealed to
him since his wife and baby son died in childbirth a
bitter three years ago.

He cast his thoughts back to when his wife was
alive. She had been a gentle, quiet woman. Theirs was
an arranged marriage, as was proper for men and
women of the noble class. During their short marriage,
Fighting Wolf prospered. He increased the number of
his slaves through warfare, was extremely successful in
getting sea otter furs, and gave huge potlatches. Now he
was a wealthy, respected man.

As husband and wife, they grew to like and trust
each other and were looking forward happily to the
birth of their first child. His life with her was calm and
placid, but he often felt something was lacking, though
he couldn't quite place what it was. He loved her in his
own way, he thought to himself.

Then one day he returned, exhausted after a long
whaling hunt, to find she had died giving premature
birth to their son. At times he would miss her and the
quiet contribution she had made to his life but there was
always a twinge of guilt . . . he wondered why he didn't
miss her more. She had gone from his life the same way
she had entered it: quietly.

The loss of his son was, in some ways, harder to
accept. Naturally, he wanted an heir, but more, he
wanted a child to love. Life had looked so bright when
they had been expecting the baby. True, death came
often to babies on the west coast, but he had had such
high hopes . . .

Turning his thoughts from the painful reminiscing,
he resumed his tirade against the Hesquiats. He hugged
thoughts of revenge close to his heart these days, he
mused. It seemed there was little room left for love.

He thought of the forthcoming "marriage." A

woman of the hated Hesquiats would not appeal to him, nor warm his cold heart, he was certain of that. He could not honestly want to honor a woman of the tribe that had killed the father he had loved and respected so much.

Coming just a year after the loss of his wife and child, the murder of his father had been a devastating blow. None knew just how deeply he felt the death of his father—he tried to keep the pain to himself.

Fighting Wolf remembered the many happy times spent as a young boy, with his father. They would go fishing together, paddling far out to the fishing grounds. He especially liked going seal hunting, pretending it was one of the great whales he chased, instead. One day he confided his dream to his father, who laughed.

"Concentrate on the seal. Later I'll show you how to harpoon whales." He was as good as his word.

How well Fighting Wolf remembered the excitement of his first whale hunt. Long before the hunt, his father had taken him to a private bathing spot, a small cove some distance from the village. From that time onward, the cove was his to use for whale hunt rituals, and later, for war chief rituals. Fighting Wolf knew it was an honor to use the bathing spot because a large supernatural shark lived in an underwater cave nearby. Nobody but his father was brave enough to bathe there—all the other men were afraid the shark would eat them. It was very powerful medicine for a mere boy to bathe there.

For eight months in succession he had prepared for the whale hunt. He and his father prayed to the Four Chiefs for a favorable hunt. The Four Chiefs were: Above Chief, Horizon Chief, Land Chief and Undersea Chief. Over the Four Chiefs, of course, and all living things, was Qua-utz, or God.

For the first four months he bathed in the fast-flowing river. For the second four months, he bathed in the sea, at the secret cove his father had shown him, rubbing himself with stiff-needled spruce branches until his skin stung. He listened carefully to his father's lectures on whaling. Only certain noblemen were entitled to hunt whales and Fighting Wolf, even as a young boy, was very conscious of his special heritage. He paid close attention to the whale hunt rituals his father taught him.

Then came the day of the great hunt. Even now he could remember the excitement of the chase, smell the sea as it sprayed across the bow of the canoe, feel the roll of the large whaling craft under his feet, tense with the excitement of the men around him, all of them keyed up for the great thrust.

A whale was sighted. Paddling noiselessly, the eight man crew approached the leviathan. Fighting Wolf's father waived his prerogative to strike the giant gray whale first. Instead he indicated his son should have first chance.

The great, broad, dark back loomed off to the right of the canoe, so close Fighting Wolf could count the barnacles on its back. Fighting Wolf stood poised, deadly harpoon in hand, waiting for the critical moment.

Just as the beast began to sink under the waves for the second time, his father gave the signal. Immediately, the youth lunged with all his strength and stabbed the cetacean in the side, just behind the flipper. The boy quickly crouched down, as the cedar rope attached to the deadly barb of the harpoon paid out.

The wounded creature's thrashings roiled the water; the steersman, at the stern of the canoe, used every bit of his skill to maneuver the craft away from the dangerous smashing flukes of the tail. The canoe shot out of harm's way. Suddenly out of the water surged the huge bulk of the wounded whale, breaching violently to dislodge the stinging harpoon. The wounded animal fell back with an enormous splash, cold water drenching the occupants of the whaling canoe.

Now the titan dove into the depths of the sea, another attempt to lose the harpoon. The beast stayed submerged for a long time. But the hunters expected such tactics. They were not about to lose track of their prey. Four large bladder floats, spaced at intervals along the cedar line, followed the giant as it sounded, the fourth float never dunking beneath the waves. The men quickly retrieved the floating harpoon lance and affixed a second barb to it.

When the whale surfaced again, Fighting Wolf struck a second time. This was a signal to the harpooner's aide to plant his barbs in the beast. By now, the giant was tiring; several harpoons and lines of floats blossomed from its back. Hanging on tightly to the protruding lines, the men forced the beast to tow the canoe.

The cetacean continued to dive, but was wearying rapidly. It surfaced once more. The canoe maneuvered closer. The first paddler leaned over and cut the main tendons of the whale's flukes. The tail hung uselessly in the water. The man sliced again, deep into the flesh behind the front flipper. Hamstrung now, the great animal rolled over, spurting blood everywhere, and with a loud, fetid gasp, died.

One of the men dived into the sea alongside the whale and, taking his knife, cut holes in the lower jaw and in the upper lip, quickly tying a cedar rope through them. Once the giant's jaws were tied shut, the men planted more floats around the carcass to keep it from sinking.

In great triumph, they towed Fighting Wolf's first kill back to the village where it was to be cut up and apportioned out to various families.

Fighting Wolf remembered the exultant pride he felt, pride in himself and his father. In his own mind, that great hunt marked his coming to manhood. In later years, on succeding hunts, Fighting Wolf again recaptured the sense of triumph, the essence of what it was to be a whale hunter.

Fighting Wolf shook his head at the memories. His father taught him many things, often sharing his worldly wisdom and seeking to instill an inquiring mind in the young boy. He also encouraged a sense of responsibility in the boy, knowing the Ahousat people must one day look to Fighting Wolf to lead them in war.

Yes, his father had been a good man, cut down in the prime of life by the underhanded Hesquiat bastards . . .

How wise his parent had been, Fighting Wolf could now appreciate. In his last year, his father had particularly warned Fighting Wolf to be wary of the white traders. Fighting Wolf accepted that advice, and, as war chief, maintained a deep interest in the recent activities of the white traders from the tall, white ships. Headquartered at Yoquot village, a three-day paddle to the north, the traders' influence was still felt at Ahousat.

The traders opened the whole west coast to a much larger world and good leadership was needed among the Indian peoples to protect their interests.

The traders protested that they only wanted sea otter furs for which they would gladly exchange swords, knives, metal buttons, tools and ornaments. Fighting Wolf was very glad to exchange the furs for knives, but what he really wanted were the "mus-kets." He had managed to get several of the weapons on his last trip to Yuquot. Such strategic planning kept the Ahousats better armed than their neighbors.

Fighting Wolf was not so sure that sea otter skins would keep the greedy traders satisfied for long. He had observed them closely when he visited Yuquot, and he saw how arrogantly they treated the Indian people; how they laughed when the people were standing on the big ships waiting to trade their hard-earned furs.

He saw, too, how they looked at the women, these men who had been away from their own women for many moons, and he did not like what he saw. One of the traders, a rather portly fellow, with a red face and even redder hair, was constantly licking his lips and touching his crotch whenever a woman came near him. The sight disgusted Fighting Wolf.

From the inhabitants of Yuquot, he had heard that after every tall ship left the harbor, many of the village people became very sick for a time, some even died. He did not want his people exposed to those sick white people. He was content to make the voyage to Yuquot when he had furs to trade. No need to encourage the tall ships to stop at Ahousat; he would keep his people away from the whites.

Amazed at the time he had spent reminiscing, Fighting Wolf arrived at his longhouse and stepped into the darkened interior. Blinking his eyes, he adjusted them to the sharp contrast after the bright sunlight outside. Reoriented, he glanced around at the bundles and chests that marked his apartments off from the others.

Sitting quietly in a corner, his sister, Precious Copper, was weaving softened cedar strands into a winter cloak. She raised her eyes to his and asked in her musical voice, "Did your meeting go well, brother?"

She gazed briefly at his face, then dropped her eyes to her work. She sighed quietly. Fighting Wolf had become so bitter since the death of his wife and infant son three long years ago, she thought to herself. Sometimes it was almost as if he didn't care about anyone or anything. After the death of their father a year later, his feelings had turned to rage. Fighting Wolf had always been close to their father and he still had not recovered from the older man's death.

Many times Precious Copper had found herself hoping that a young woman from the village would catch her brother's eye; that he would want to marry again and put his losses behind him, to the past where they belonged. But her brother was content to visit several different women; he had not established a stable relationship with any of them. Nor had he forgotten the deaths of those he loved.

Precious Copper knew he had approached the Hesquiats about marrying one of their women. She thought it strange that he would marry an enemy, but she was glad of his decision to marry. He was not acting like a man about to take a bride, however; he continued to visit his various paramours and parried her questions whenever she inquired about her new sister-in-law to-be.

She suspected something was afoot. There had been several meetings of all the warriors, but no word leaked out as to what was discussed at the councils.

Fighting Wolf looked fondly at his only sister. Her straight, black hair hung in two heavy braids on either side of her delicate face. A high forehead with finely arched brows gave her face a studied dignity. Her small nose and finely drawn lips were set in a sweet face, made even sweeter when she smiled by the dimple in each cheek.

"The meeting went well enough," he answered laconically.

Seeing that this approach would gain her nothing, Precious Copper switched tactics. "I'm looking forward to greeting my new sister-in-law soon. I think you're very wise to bury the hatred we've had for the Hesquiats for so long."

Noticing the wide grin he shot at her, she continued, "What are you laughing at? You know I hate war. I truly hope this marriage you've arranged with the Hesquiats will stop all the senseless killing."

She bent to her work again. "My brother, I'll truly try to make your new bride feel welcome . . ." She looked up, sincerity shining on her face. "Even if she is a Hesquiat."

He stared at her before answering. When he did, his voice was cold. "Don't involve yourself in my business." Seeing Precious Copper recoil from his tone, he added more warmly, "You'll meet the woman soon, but you may regret your kind offer to make her feel welcome."

He flashed her a smile as he made that enigmatic statement, then turned and strode out through the doorway, leaving a dazzling blaze of sunlight that lit up the room, then disappeared as the skin swung back into place.

Precious Copper thoughtfully went back to her weaving. She felt a chill of foreboding. Something was definitely afoot. But what?

Precious Copper was getting too concerned about his personal life, Fighting Wolf reflected as he strode down to the beach. Time to marry her off and let her concern herself with a husband and children.

In the past, he'd been too busy with his own pursuits to tend to the business of arranging her marriage. He sighed. He'd talk to his uncle, Scarred Mouth, the senior ranking chief of the village. He recalled the old man had mentioned two recent requests from neighboring tribes for her; he'd mull them over and choose the best one.

She'd be angry, though. Every time he'd brought up the topic before, she'd fought him, saying she had not seen anyone she could love. Women! Why did they confuse love with marriage? The two were separate. Everyone knew that one married for wealth and status—at least the noble class did.

Still, she was his sister and the only close family left to him now that the others were dead. He'd hate to see her unhappy. And if anything happened to her . . . he didn't allow himself to complete the thought.

Yes, he decided, when the trouble with the Hesquiats was settled, he would marry her off to a good man who would love and care for her, not just for her wealth.

Glancing up at the sky, he speculated that it was going to rain soon. He hurried down to his canoe to prepare for the forthcoming raid.

As he strode down the path to his canoe, an

attractive, willowy girl with flashing eyes intercepted him. She greeted him eagerly. "Fighting Wolf, where are you off to in such a hurry? Visit with me awhile. Better still, why not come to my longhouse and I'll prepare you a meal?" Her dark eyes sparkled and her shining black hair gleamed, even in the dull light of an overcast sky.

He realized he was hungry and politely accepted her invitation. As they walked slowly to her longhouse, Rough Seas regarded him coquettishly and said, "I hear rumors that you're marrying a Hesquiat. You don't have to look so far for a bride. I'm right here."

Fighting Wolf answered lightly, "Why take another husband? You just got rid of one."

"Ohh, him!" she pouted. "He was too boring. All he wanted to do was fish, hunt, trade and potlatch. He was always trying to show others what a great chief he was."

"That's what all men do," answered Fighting Wolf dryly. "That is, men who care about their families and want the best for them."

"He had no time for me," she stated petulantly.

"I thought it was the other way around," laughed Fighting Wolf.

"What do you mean?" she asked innocently.

"The men," he prodded. "The many lovers you took while he was gone fishing or hunting or trading. Remember?"

"Oh, them," she sighed. She smoothed the irritated frown from her brow. "He didn't care about them."

Fighting Wolf thought that was probably true. Jealousy was frowned upon by Nootka men and women. It was the jealous spouse who was scolded by friends and relatives, not the wandering wife or philandering husband. It was foolish to fight over a woman; a jealous man never became wealthy if he was worrying about who his wife was sleeping with. A wife was cautioned not to get upset over her husband's amorous affairs. Men were like that, anyway.

She watched him covertly. "Would it bother you if your wife had lovers?" she asked.

"Not particularly," he answered indifferently. "No one would catch me making a fool of myself over a woman." He grinned. "Why do you ask?"

She shrugged, but did not answer his question. She turned her dark brown eyes on his and batted heavy eyelashes. "I've given up all my lovers," she remarked.

"Oh?"

"Yes. I wanted you to know that. I—I wouldn't want any other man if I could have you."

"Really?" He laughed. "I suppose that's because you've already sampled every high ranking chief, married and otherwise, in the village."

She shrugged again. "They don't thrill me like you do, Fighting Wolf."

"Is that so? I only thrill you because I don't come every time you call me." She flushed and he knew he'd accurately guessed why she was attracted to him.

"Oh, Fighting Wolf. Look around you," she gestured at the surrounding longhouses they were passing on their walk. "How many eligible women are there here for you?" When he didn't answer, she went on, "There's none. Except me. I'd make the perfect wife for you." His silence encouraged her; she rushed on, hoping to convince him, "Both our families are wealthy. Our names are spoken with respect. I've even had practice as a wife. What more could you want?"

Fighting Wolf looked at her askance. "As to wealth, marriage to you won't bring me any extra wealth. The bride price I'd have to give would equal the repayment gift your family would have to return . . . neither of us would profit from the exchange. So don't try and bribe me into marriage." He paused. "As you said, we both come from powerful, illustrious families. There's no problem there."

"Then where is the problem?" She wanted to shriek at him, but managed to control her voice.

"The problem," he said calmly, "is that I don't want to get married at this time."

"Oh?" she sneered. "What about the Hesquiat?"

Mentally cursing himself for forgetting the impending "marriage," he answered coolly, "The Hesquiat woman is none of your concern."

Feeling his withdrawal, she implored, "Fighting Wolf, I love you. Surely you know that. I'll even be your second wife. For no other man would I suggest such a thing."

"I appreciate your sacrifice," he chuckled. "But there's really no need."

"Ohh, how can you be so cruel as to laugh at me?" she demanded. She was relieved to reach her longhouse and step inside, away from prying eyes. "What's so wonderful about this Hesquiat woman, anyway?" she asked sullenly. "Why won't you take another wife?"

"It's not that I won't take another wife," he said calmly. "I will. It's just that I do not wish a second wife right now." His voice turned grim. "One is enough."

Hearing his solemn tone Rough Seas felt renewed hope. "I understand," she said.

"You do?" he asked, surprised.

"Yes, I do. Oh, Fighting Wolf, why didn't you tell me?" She threw herself into his unsuspecting arms. "How generous of you."

"You're talking nonsense, woman," he stated sternly, trying to disengage her arms from around his neck.

"I understand now," she said, laughing up into his eyes, her good humor miraculously restored. "You're doing it for our people. You're only marrying that Hesquiat for political reasons. You don't love her!" Rough Seas' voice rang with triumph.

"Oh, Fighting Wolf, I'm so glad! She'll never come between us, I swear!" She threw her arms around his waist and cuddled close to the bemused man.

He stared straight ahead, thoughtful.

She looked up at him again. "I can understand

such a marriage. I can only respect a man who would go to such lengths to save our people.''

Of course, she thought to herself, I'll make sure it's a marriage in name only. She released her grip, then took his hand. "Come," she enticed, leading him towards her bed. "Let's celebrate our new understanding!"

3

The summer village where Sarita lived totalled eleven longhouses of various lengths. Her father's was the biggest longhouse, appropriate for his standing as chief of the village. Thunder Maker's family, his four wives and their several children, occupied the best corner of the house. Across the way, in the second choicest space, lived Feast Giver and his servants. The two corners near the door were occupied by two lower ranking chieftains and their families. The middle of each wall was the space allotted to commoner families who were distantly related to, and wished to work for, Thunder Maker.

Sarita kneeled on a cedar mat in her father's quarters. Packing her best woven-cedar robes into a wooden chest, she was preparing for the move to her betrothed's village. The wedding was two days away.

Spring Fern, acting as maid this time, was helping her pack. As the two worked, they chatted quietly together in the cozy confines of the family's living space.

The cedar kutsacks that Sarita lovingly packed into her wooden chest had been made from cedar bark soaked in salt water and beaten into a soft fibrous thread, then woven into the ankle-length robes the women always wore. She included several small cedar aprons to be worn under the dress. Men went naked under their kutsacks. Sarita carefully folded several elbow-length capes that tied at the neck. The capes were worn out-of-doors. Lastly, she placed three conical rain hats on top of the garments. She would not be caught unprepared when the torrential west coast rains poured down from the heavens.

She frowned pensively as she reached for one of her beautiful hair ornaments, a delicately colored white and pink dentalia shell hair clasp.

Her thoughts dwelled on her upcoming marriage. She did not want to marry this Fighting Wolf. The last few days had given her time to think about what she did want. She knew she wanted a husband she could love and respect and one who would love her in return. A husband who was in love with his wife would not take other wives to his longhouse. Nor would he marry a woman just for the wealth or property she could bring him.

Her parents' marriage, she remembered, had been loving. That was when Sarita was small, before the tragic death of her mother one dark night when she was paddling back from visiting a nearby village. A sudden storm arose; violently lashing waves overturned the canoe. Her mother's body was found washed up on the beach the next morning. For a long time her father had been inconsolable and had neglected his small daughter and son.

Though only eight years of age at the time, Sarita thought the pain of losing her mother would never go away. But with time, it had . . . or at least it had dulled. Now she could think peacefully of her mother.

Two years after her mother's death, her father remarried. His new wife, Crab Woman, brought property and a political alliance with a nearby village to the marriage, but no love. Lacking affection and love from her, he had taken another wife into his longhouse and then a third. He now had four wives living in his longhouse, but very little peace.

Yes, thought Sarita to herself. She knew about loveless marriages. She had watched her father battle with his wives. Their unhappiness and discord often

kept her away from the family's hearth. Many nights
she pressed her hands to her ears to keep out the shrill
cries and vicious words said during an argument among
her father's wives. It was only after her father bellowed
for quiet that a seething peace was restored. The
squabbles occasionally involved intended or imagined
slights to one wife's children, but most often were over
Thunder Maker's attention, or lack of it, to one or
another wife.

Sarita honestly could not blame her stepmothers
for fighting. She would not want to share her husband
with other women. No, that was not for her. Not for her
the jealousy and unhappiness. Not for a young,
beautiful woman like Sarita. She wanted a man to love
her, and her alone. Not one who would take other wives
and then cease to love her or her children.

She sighed. Now those wishes were past dreams.
She was to be married to the enemy. What hope did she
have that he would love her, and only her? As for
herself, she shuddered to think of loving an enemy of
her people. Well, when he took other wives—and chiefs
were expected to—she certainly would not care. Let him
marry as many women as he wanted, then she would be
spared his foul attentions.

A new thought occurred to her. If she did not like
him, or living in his village of hated Ahousats, she
would leave him and return to her father. Other wives
did that.

Her favorite stepmother, Abalone Woman, had
done that very thing. Abalone's first husband had been
a cruel man and she had suffered his behavior for a long
time. Then one night his malicious taunts exploded in a
vicious beating. The next day Abalone left him and,
bruised and battered, returned to her parents' house.
Shortly after that, Sarita's father noticed the quiet
young woman. Her spirit had not been crushed by what
she'd been through; her resiliency and gentle manner
appealed to him. He asked to marry her. Her family
gladly accepted the suit of their chief and Sarita's
second stepmother moved into the longhouse.

Dragging her thoughts back to her own troubles, Sarita felt the gooseflesh rise when she thought of living amongst the Ahousats. To be surrounded by enemies, dependent on a man who fought and killed her people, made her tremble inside. Perhaps she should take Spring Fern with her, she deliberated. Then she would have company and comfort in the village of her enemies.

She turned to Spring Fern, who was kneeling beside her as they folded garments. "Spring Fern," she asked. "Do you wish to come with me to my new village?"

The slave locked her deep brown eyes with Sarita's golden ones. "Yes," she replied simply. "Please take me with you."

The urgency in her voice startled Sarita. "What's wrong?" she asked in concern.

The pretty slave looked down at the floor for a moment. "I was so hoping you would take me with you. You see . . ." her voice trailed away.

"Yes?" prompted Sarita.

"It's just that I—I'm afraid to stay here by myself."

"What do you mean? You're not by yourself. You're surrounded by people here."

"Pardon, mistress, but that's not what I mean. I—I'm afraid of some of the men. Without your protection—"

"Oh." It was beginning to become clear to Sarita.

"You see," burst out the slave, "I'm very much afraid to stay here without you! That big slave your father recently traded for, Rottenwood, keeps staring at me I'm afraid of him and I fear he may ask your father for me as—as a wife! Your father seems to like the work he does and might humor him. I could never live with that man." She was in tears now. "Please take me with you!" she cried.

Sarita patted the sobbing girl gently. "There now," she soothed. "No one's going to marry you off to some slave just because he stares at you. I'll take you with me when I leave this village. Then you won't have to worry about that old Rottenwood anymore.''

Spring Fern clutched Sarita's arm and sniffled into her robe. "Oh thank you, mistress. Thank you! I do so want to come with you!" Spring Fern wiped her eyes, and tried gamely to smile at the other woman.

Sarita stroked the soft ebony hair and said, "It'll be so reassuring to have you with me when I'm in a strange village, surrounded by strange faces." She paused, seeing that Spring Fern was regaining her composure. "Go now, wipe your eyes and fetch my other dentalia shell clasp from my cedar jewel box."

Spring Fern hurried away to do as bid, leaving a quiet Sarita staring off into space. Would that all her problems could be solved so neatly, the young noble-woman mused wryly.

The day before the wedding, the village was bustling with activity. Thunder Maker's slaves were emptying his fish traps of the beautiful silver salmon that would tempt the guests' palates at the lavish feast Thunder Maker was hosting. Several female slaves were picking berries and digging roots to add to the table. The commoners who lived on Thunder Maker's bounty were out digging clams as soon as the tide was low enough. Everyone was working hard to make the feast and wedding a great success. The more Thunder Maker impressed his unfriendly guests, the safer the village would be from further Ahousat depredations.

Thunder Maker's chief wife, Crab Woman, was overseeing many of the details, and Sarita tried to stay out of her way. Crab Woman had a sharp tongue for most people, but especially for Sarita. Crab Woman could never forget that Sarita's beautiful mother had been so very loved by Thunder Maker. Her eyes narrowed every time she saw the favors and gifts Thunder Maker lavished upon his eldest daughter. Her own children seldom got such fine presents. In retaliation, she never let Sarita forget for an instant that it was she, Crab Woman, who ruled the longhouse.

Today she was amusing herself by badgering Sarita about her betrothal to the enemy.

"And the cost . . ." Here Crab Woman rolled her eyes, having come upon Sarita just as she had finished packing away her robes. "The cost of this wedding is going to be enormous. Your father will be poverty-stricken by the time it is over. Who knows what the rest of us will have to eat this winter, but Nuwiksu's dear daughter must have a lavish wedding. Oh yes," was Crab Woman's malicious refrain on this hot afternoon.

"And such a fine bridegroom," she hinted slyly. "Old, with rotten teeth, and I hear he likes to beat his wives."

"What?" gasped Sarita.

"Oh yes," answered the older woman. "I've heard such things about him." She shook her head as if in pity. There, that should scare the girl. She chuckled, then added deprecatingly, "Of course he's merely a war chief, second in command in his village. Your father is head chief here."

Sarita caught her meaning. The old bat was gloating because she'd married the highest ranking chief while Sarita was being married off to a second ranked chief. I don't care, thought Sarita to herself.

"And it doesn't really count for much to be a chief of the Ahousat dogs," the old woman added for good measure.

Seeing Sarita's face flush under the light tan, Crab Woman hugged herself in delight. "The bride price the Ahousats pay for you should be huge. Oh, not because you're worth it," she snorted. "But so the Ahousat bastards can show their good intentions of peace toward us." She spat, then complained, "All that means is your poor Nuwiksu will have to come up with a costly bride repayment gift to give back to the bastards when you have your first child." She spat again, contemptuously. "If you have a child."

Happily she continued her tirade, "I don't know how your poor Nuwiksu will ever come up with enough slaves and furs to give him. I told him! But no, he has to put a good face on these things, even if it means the rest of his family suffers. So much expense, and all for a useless girl like you!'' She glanced scornfully in Sarita's direction.

"And another thing," she harped, "you'd better be a virgin! All this family needs is a scandal to bring down your poor Nuwiksu's good name. Which is exactly what will happen if your new husband finds you're no virgin!''

Humiliated, Sarita got to her feet and ran out of the house, her face flushed with anger and shame. One thing she would not miss, she raged, was Crab Woman's spiteful tongue. Of course she was a virgin, Sarita railed to herself. What a thing to say!

Crab Woman was correct in one respect, thought Sarita after she'd regained her composure. It could prove difficult for her father to come up with the bridal repayment gift.

Traditionally, the groom's family paid a bride price, and at the birth of the first child the bride's family returned a gift of approximate value. This was known as the bridal repayment gift. Sarita knew her father would need at least a year to come up with the repayment gift, especially after giving such a costly wedding feast. He couldn't save the articles and slaves he received as the bride price, to repay later, because he was obligated to distribute those goods amongst his loyal supporters.

Suddenly Sarita realized how tightly bound she was by the betrothal agreement. If she left her husband, there would be little likelihood her father would welcome her back. He'd be too concerned about paying back the massive bride price. Feast Giver was right, she mused, more rested on this alliance than she had first thought.

A wide-chested, medium tall man, his dark bronze skin dappled in the afternoon shade of the trees, stood poised on the river bank. One of Thunder Maker's many slaves, he waited patiently for a large salmon that was slowly nosing its way into the cone-shaped fish trap set into the stream. Rottenwood gazed unseeingly at the fish under the clear water.

Rottenwood had not always been his name. Once, he had been free, and had had a free name.

He cast his thoughts back to that fateful day, the memory as clear as if it had been yesterday. The young boy, Crouching Fox, walked swiftly away from his parents' camp, anxious to try out the new bow his grandfather had carefully and lovingly made for him. The dark forest he entered was quiet and, in the hush, he searched carefully for a quail or a large grouse to surprise his family with. Several times he had gone hunting alone in the forest, but never so far from camp as he did this particular day.

Suddenly he froze. There, not more than one good arrow shot away stood a four point buck. Slowly bringing his bow up, he aimed the arrow straight at the buck's heart. The boy's gaze did not stray from the deer standing so still and majestic, its nose sniffing the air, alert to impending danger. The boy's heart beat rapidly as he let fly the arrow. He didn't realize he had been holding his breath until he released it in one long gasp. Excitedly, he watched the deer crumple to the ground, all in silence.

Crouching Fox took only a step towards the deer when suddenly a large hand covered his mouth and a piercing pain ravaged his skull. He sank forward onto his knees and from there sank into sweet, merciful, dark oblivion . . .

Upon awakening, he shook his head slowly and painfully, only to find himself bound and gagged and laying next to a smoking camp fire. The mouthwatering scent of venison tantalized his nostrils. Nearby lay two other, trussed-up small figures, while several men hovered in and around the camp clearing.

Over the next several days, the boy learned he had been captured by the notorious Wishram slave-catchers,

who worked the territories along the Columbia River,
searching for women and children to sell in the slave
market at The Dalles. From there, the boy was bought
by a man from Neah Bay and taken far from his home
and family.

It was the Neah Bay man who gave him the
insulting slave-name of Rottenwood. It was a joke . . .
the boy was soft and useless, just like rotting wood.
Crouching Fox determined to himself to prove the
foolish man wrong, and over the next few years he
learned every skill he could. The dull master could not
see beyond the name he'd given the young slave and
decided to trade him up north to the wife's relatives.

The two embarked on the long canoe trip. For
several days they canoed north, across open water and
then following the coastline, until they finally arrived at
the bay of Hesquiat village. The Hesquiat chief,
Thunder Maker, saw the strength in the young man's
build and hoped to make a good worker out of him.
Rottenwood found that Thunder Maker could be a
good master, and one appreciative of an industrious
slave. Rottenwood therefore did his best to impress
Thunder Maker with his working abilities, but he never
forgot that he had once been free.

Always he thought of escape and knew that one day
he'd be free again. But he had to be very careful. Slaves
who escaped and were caught again were usually killed
as an example to the others. Now he was so far away,
and so many years had passed, that it would be very
difficult to return to his people, even if he could find
them. Yet, he knew one day his chance for freedom
would come and he would take it. Slavery was too
humiliating for a man who had once been free.

A quick, darting movement under the water
brought Rottenwood out of his reverie. The large, silver
salmon lunged into the trap and Rottenwood quickly
scooped him out. He grinned in satisfaction. The plump
fish would feed many guests at the feast.

Some time later, the cedar net bag filled with

salmon and slung over his back, Rottenwood made his way slowly back to the village. As he was passing by the river path, he chanced to look up at the hillside where several women were picking berries. Ducking behind the branches of a tree and shielding his eyes with his hand, he gazed up at them. He was too far away to hear any of their conversation, but close enough to hear the drift of low laughter every few minutes.

One graceful form in particular caught his eye. The beautiful slave girl, Spring Fern, was leaning over some blueberry bushes, intent on reaching some of the juicy fruit hidden deep in the bush. A slight tremor shook Rottenwood's body as he gazed at her. He had watched for her many times, deeply smitten by her beauty. His manhood stirred as he thought of making love to her. His heated gaze devoured her. A strong desire to hold her, touch her, swept over him and he vowed to himself that, somehow, he would make her his.

As if feeling his eyes on her, Spring Fern turned in his direction. Seeing nothing, she turned back to her berry bush, a cold shudder passing over her delicate frame. She wondered why the day had suddenly turned so chill.

"I feel cool all of a sudden. Do you?" Spring Fern asked the slave women next to her.

"No," answered Cedar Bundle.

"Oh." The two women picked berries in silence for a while. "The blueberry harvest is certainly bountiful this year," said Spring Fern conversationally.

"Yes," agreed her companion. "Back home, though, there were many more berries than these." She sighed heavily.

Spring Fern heard the sigh, and guessed what caused it. Gently she asked, "Are the people in your longhouse treating you any better?"

Cedar Bundle didn't answer for a moment. "No," she finally admitted in a tremulous voice. She pretended to be very interested in a patch of the luscious fruit. Finally, she could hold back no longer. "I hate being a slave!'' she burst out.

Spring Fern nodded. ''It's a very difficult life. I was born into slavery and I still find it hard to accept. For someone like you, it must be terrible.''

Cedar Bundle responded, ''It is terrible—for me and even worse for my two little sons. For me, it means being ordered around by women who, back at my old village, wouldn't have been fit to invite to my longhouse. For my sons, it means fetching water and wood. For them, it means the loss of their rightful names, their wealth and property. Their father . . .'' Cedar Bundle choked on her words.

Spring Fern put down her burden basket of berries, and patted the distraught woman. ''It's better to talk about it, if you can,'' she encouraged.

''I must tell someone,'' sobbed Cedar Bundle. ''It's just that their father was such a good man, a high-ranking chief, beloved by his people. I loved him, too. When the Hesquiats came and raided our village, they killed him. I ran to him and threw myself on his body, weeping. My two little sons followed me. That's how we were taken so easily. If only I had thought to hide my sons—''

''Now Cedar Bundle,'' Spring Fern said, a hint of sternness creeping into her voice. ''Don't blame yourself. Your sons would have been taken anyway. The Hesquiats would have searched everywhere until they found your boys. You know a chief's wife and children are especially prized as slaves.'' She added, ''Perhaps it's a good thing you were taken with them. At least you can protect them while they're in this village.''

''Protect them?'' repeated Cedar Bundle bitterly. ''I can't even protect myself!'' Sensing Spring Fern's unspoken understanding, Cedar Bundle continued, ''It's so humiliating. I was always a faithful wife to my good husband. Now I'm preyed upon by any and every man who wants me. I've no protection from them at all. Never before have men talked to me or touched me like that. I don't know what to do.''

Spring Fern nodded sadly. "Slave women are considered fair game for any man who wants them. It's only because my mistress, Sarita, is so protective of me, that I've been able to avoid those lechers."

"You're very fortunate," answered Cedar Bundle, wiping her eyes. "What will you do when she goes to the Ahousat village?"

"She's taking me with her." Ignoring Cedar Bundle's dubious look, Spring Fern added, "But I know what I'd do, if Sarita weren't around to protect me."

"What's that?"

"I'd find one wolf to keep the other wolves away. I'd find the smartest, strongest, highest ranking man I could. I know that commoners and noblemen won't marry slaves, but I could still be a concubine. That status would certainly give me protection."

Cedar Bundle stared at her. "But what about marriage? Back home, unmarried women who slept with men were considered loose women." Seeing Spring Fern start to object, she added hastily, "Oh, I know everyone does it. But they're all married. Most of my noblewomen friends were seldom happy, so my friends would have affairs. I knew they did, but I never did."

Spring Fern looked sternly at Cedar Bundle. "Your situation is changed now. The old rules don't count. You're no longer a noblewoman, your sons are no longer the heirs of a great chief." Cedar Bundle opened her mouth to say something, but Spring Fern held up her hand. "Hear me out. You are a slave. A slave! Now you must do what you can to protect yourself and your sons. What alternative do you have? It's either be raped by several men or be one man's concubine. Those are your choices."

Cedar Bundle was silent for a long while. At last she said humbly, "Thank you for sharing your wisdom with me, my friend. I must think about what you've said."

She picked up her burden basket and started slowly back to the village. Spring Fern watched her go, head bent, shoulders bowed, and wondered if she'd been too hard on her friend. No, she thought at last. Someone had to tell her. What Spring Fern hadn't told her was that Cedar Bundle's life was at stake. Some slave women died from the brutal treatment they received. Spring Fern knew enough of slavery to realize that Cedar Bundle had to make a choice, and soon.

Spring Fern couldn't let Cedar Bundle walk away, defeated. "Cedar Bundle," she called. "Wait!"

Lugging the almost full burden basket, she caught up to Cedar Bundle. "What are you going to do?"

Cedar Bundle smiled slowly. "Do? As you said, what choice do I have?" Seeing the sad look on Spring Fern's face, she added, "I'm going to take your good advice."

"You are?" Surprise crackled through Spring Fern's voice.

Cedar Bundle nodded. "It won't be easy, though. I've been so upset and afraid of men lately. I'd given up noticing men because I didn't wish to encourage anyone. I've also avoided any man who showed an interest in me." She smiled ruefully. "There's a certain man who's been watching me. I suspect he's attracted to me, but I've avoided him. Maybe if I encourage him—"

"Oh, do that," implored her friend. "Perhaps if you seem interested in him, he'll seek you out and keep the other men away."

"I think he would," agreed Cedar Bundle. "He's a nobleman. He seems to treat his family and slaves well. I've never seen him strike or beat anyone, even when he's angry," she mused.

"Hmmmm, it's a good thing you'd given up noticing men!" teased Spring Fern. They both laughed as they sauntered back to the village.

4

The day of the wedding dawned. Gray seas rolled across the horizon, white sea gulls wheeled overhead, their raucous cries striving to alert the inhabitants of the sleeping Hesquiat village. The sky was overcast, threatening to rain at any moment onto the verdant plain of the village and the weather-beaten, gray long-houses.

In Thunder Maker's longhouse, the commoner and slave women had been up for hours, preparing the last details for the huge wedding feast to be held later that day.

Crab Woman dropped the heated rocks into a bent cedar box filled with water. She would first boil the large chunk of venison and then allow it to cool before it would be fit to eat. Spying Thunder Maker strolling towards the door, she called, "Husband, those Ahousat dogs will eat well today!"

Thunder Maker walked over, a pained expression on his face. "Please. These people are now our allies. I won't have you insulting them." Then to mollify her, he added, "I'm glad we've plenty of food to offer the Ahousats. They'll see we Hesquiats don't come begging to them for this alliance."

Crab Woman snorted. "It's the other way around. The Ahousats beg us to make peace with them!" Her husband raised an eyebrow but didn't comment. After all, his wives weren't privy to the men's talks and she had no way of knowing how wrong she was.

"Tell me," began Crab Woman, "Why are the Ahousats so insistent on giving us the bridal price the day after the feast?"

"It is strange," answered her husband. "Usually they'd present the bridal gifts—the slaves and furs—on the first day so we could turn them down two or three times over the next few days. Then, of course, we'd politely accept them on about the fourth day of celebrating."

"Strange!" snorted Crab Woman. "Anyone knows they should be presenting those gifts on the first day!"

"You can't wait to get your hands on all those gifts, can you?" teased her husband. She nodded, her eyes glistening with anticipation. "Well, you'll be pleased to hear that Fighting Wolf is bringing some gifts with him. The majority of the bride price will arrive the next day. He needs more time because he's giving so many presents that his heavily laden freight canoes must travel slowly."

"I knew it!" shouted Crab Woman. "I knew he'd pay us a high bride price! That's how desperate he is to make peace with us!"

Her husband chuckled as he left the longhouse. The only reason he'd gone along with Fighting Wolf's suggestion to wait for the bride price was because that's how desperate he, Thunder Maker, was to make peace with the Ahousats. One more day of waiting would make no difference.

After he left, Crab Woman stepped back from the steaming box and wiped her sweating brow with the back of a greasy hand. Where was that lazy Sarita anyway? She should be awake and helping with the food preparations. It's her wedding day, she should help, thought Crab Woman as she stomped off to awaken her stepdaughter.

Rudely interrupted from a sound sleep by Crab Woman's loud entrance, Sarita quickly gathered up a soft blanket, and headed for the nearby river. She followed the narrow path to the women's bathing spot, relieved to see that this morning no one was there.

Slipping out of her cedar robe, she stood on the riverbank, shivering in the cool morning air. Breathing deeply of the fresh water fragrance, she waded out into the slow-flowing river. Her tan skin looked almost translucent in the early morning light. She stood poised, her high, firm breasts set above a narrow waist that flared out to graceful hips. Her long, slim legs were partially hidden by the water.

At last, taking a deep breath, she plunged into the cold water. Gasping from the shock of the freezing liquid, she paddled around in the slow current until she felt numb. Scrubbing herself quickly, she raced for shore. Grabbing the soft blanket, she vigorously dried her hair and body.

Dressed once again in her cedar robe, she felt refreshed and invigorated. She was now ready to face marriage to Fighting Wolf, she told herself. Humming quietly, she walked briskly back to the village.

Later, sitting on a cedar mat in the longhouse, Sarita listened patiently to Spring Fern's chatter about the upcoming ceremonies.

Spring Fern's practiced hands enthusiastically combed Sarita's long hair, still damp from her river bath. In the dark interior of the longhouse, Sarita's soft mane gave off the dull gleam of auburn highlights.

In stark contrast to her dark hair, she wore a beautiful cream-colored kutsack. To make the garment, cedar bark had been pounded to exceptional softness, then bleached for many days until the color of spring dogwood flowers. Interwoven into the pliant bark was the soft, white wool of the mountain goat. The wool attested to Sarita's noble status, and also gave the robe a luxurious texture.

She wore a low-slung girdle of shiny, black sea otter fur around her waist. Shining copper earrings dangled gracefully from each delicate ear and a necklace of white dentalia shells alternated with shining copper beads encircled Sarita's long, elegant neck.

The robe reached to the white dentalia anklets she wore, leaving bare her long, narrow feet. Over the robe, Sarita donned a brilliant blue trading blanket cloak, a surprise gift from her father. He was determined to marry off his daughter in the finest of clothing and to spare no expense for her wedding ceremony.

Sarita stood quietly as Spring Fern carefully darkened the arch of first one thin eyebrow, then the other. Spring Fern stepped back to appraise Sarita's completed costume. Nodding approvingly, she brushed an imaginary speck of dust off one shoulder.

"Your husband-to-be won't be able to take his eyes off you, you're so beautiful," she said admiringly to Sarita. She added, "I've heard rumors that the Ahousat is sending great canoes full of gifts to our village."

"Maybe when he sees me, he'll send for even more canoeloads of gifts," snickered Sarita.

Spring Fern chuckled. Then she said hesitantly, "I wonder if he'll 'kiss' you."

" 'Kiss' me?" echoed Sarita. "What's that?"

"Oh, surely you know," answered a blushing Spring Fern.

"No, I don't know. Tell me what you mean!" commanded Sarita shortly.

Sometimes Sarita could be too authoritative, thought Spring Fern. Still, as mistresses went, she was better than most. She sighed aloud. "It's just that . . ." She paused.

"Yes?" said Sarita impatiently.

"Well," continued Spring Fern hesitantly, "I've never actually done it—"

"Done what?" shrieked Sarita, ready to throw her heavy wooden comb at the girl. "Will you tell me!" she demanded.

"All right, all right," said Spring Fern hastily, putting her hands up to protect her face. Sarita rarely got angry but when she did, Spring Fern did not care to be on the receiving end.

"It's when a man and woman touch their lips together." Spring Fern waited for her mistress' reaction.

"Touch lips together?" repeated Sarita incredulously. "Why ever would they do that?"

Her slave shrugged. "It's considered very romantic among the *mumutly*, the white men."

"Oh?" asked Sarita suspiciously. "How do you know this?"

Spring Fern giggled. "Not from experience, I assure you," she answered. "Do you remember my cousin who lives in Yuquot?"

Sarita nodded.

"She told me about this. My cousin says that ever since the *mumutly* came to our shores in their big ships, the people at Yuquot have been doing this thing—kissing. First the *mumutly* men would kiss the women, then later, the women would kiss their own boyfriends or lovers or husbands. It's very easy, my cousin says," concluded Spring Fern doubtfully.

Seeing Sarita's disbelief written all over her face, Spring Fern continued hastily, "I've seen some of the slaves do this thing. I think it's because the women first given to the *mumutly* were slaves. They spread the practice. Now I hear many people do it, even noblemen. I guess they learned it from the slave women, too," she added slyly.

Sarita shuddered, thinking of kissing an old man with bad teeth. "I'm sure Fighting Wolf is too old to do that kind of thing," she reassured herself aloud. Then she gazed thoughtfully at her friend for a moment. "Spring Fern," she asked casually. Too casually, thought Spring Fern. "Have you ever made love with a man?"

Spring Fern returned her gaze. She shook her head. "No, I haven't."

"Hmmm," responded Sarita. "I wonder what it's like?'"

Spring Fern shrugged. "From what I hear, some women like it and some don't. Most of my friends have no say in the matter," she added bitterly.

Sarita nodded. Spring Fern's friends were slave women. Sarita mused, "I'm sure that having a choice makes a difference. Especially if you love the man," she added dreamily.

Catching herself, she said harshly, "Well, I don't love Fighting Wolf. I don't even like him. I haven't even seen him. Crab Woman says he's old and has rotting teeth. He's probably ugly and scarred up from all the fights he's been in and all the raiding he's done! Oh, how could Nuwiksu give me to an ugly, old killer like him?" she cried.

"Oh, mistress, don't despair," consoled Spring Fern. "I know it seems terrible right now, but maybe things will turn out well. You won't be alone," she reminded. "I'll be going with you."

Sarita hugged her friend. "Yes, and I'm so glad you'll be with me. I hope you're right; I hope things will work out." She recovered herself. "There's one thing I will do, and Fighting Wolf won't stop me," she said fiercely.

"What's that?"

"I won't let him attack my people. There'll be no more raids on the Hesquiats. If I can't persuade him personally," here Sarita gave a small, feral smile, "then I'll interfere with any such plans he has!"

Spring Fern agreed enthusiastically. "Your marriage will count for something! Even if you aren't happy in it, at least you'll be protecting your family and those dear to you."

Sarita and Spring Fern looked at each other with new satisfaction. "I'll make sure the Ahousat knows he must treat me, and my people, with respect!"

Spring Fern gazed at her beautiful mistress and did not doubt the Ahousat would indeed treat his wife and her people well.

Suddenly loud shouts and high-pitched yells from outside the longhouse interrupted them. Sarita and her slave ran to the door and peered out.

"They're coming! They're coming!" rang the excited cries of the village children. Flying up and down the beach, the boisterous imps danced their news, their excitement and gaiety contagious.

Sarita walked towards the beach, shading her eyes with one hand as she looked out to sea. Far off in the distance, she spotted several small black dots on the water. They'd arrive soon. In spite of herself, she trembled in anticipation. Shaking herself sternly, she dashed back into the longhouse, followed by her slave.

"Don't let them see you," cautioned Spring Fern. "You're not supposed to put in an appearance until the feast tonight."

Sarita took her slave's order with good humor. "I won't. I'll watch them from inside the doorway. They'll never know I'm here." The two women chuckled together, shivering in excitement at seeing the dreaded Ahousats.

The villagers slowly drifted down the pebbly beach to watch the arrival of the Ahousats. As if in league with the visitors, gentle sea winds blew away the cloud cover, letting the sun shine hot and brilliant onto the waiting populace.

The Ahousats' large war canoes circled the cove and their deep chanting voices carried over the water. The crowd thrilled to the sound. After circling the bay several times, the first of the groom's great war canoes ground into the gravel of the shallow waters just off the beach. Four men jumped out and, heaving in unison, pulled the canoe further up the beach.

People in the assembled crowd commented on the gifts that were no doubt piled under the cedar mats in the large canoes.

Fighting Wolf stepped out. He was draped in a full-length, shiny, black sea otter robe, his glistening blue-black hair twisted into a hundred long, thin braids all over his head. Tiny white feathers of eagle down were scattered over his hair. Across his forehead were painted

wide wavy black lines; a solid red covered the lower half
of his features. His face was dusted with powdered
black mica; silver and gold sparks glinted off his visage
where the sun slanted across. His arms were painted red,
and large copper rings encircled his ankles. He looked
magnificent.

The men accompanying him also wore painted red
and black facial designs. Each nobleman's hair was
secured in a large topknot tied by a green spruce bough.
Eagle down was strewn over the locks of the high
ranking men. The commoners were dressed in bulky
cedar kutsacks, their hair loose, faces painted a solid
red.

The visitors debarked from the canoes and stood
defiantly facing the Hesquiat crowd. The two groups
stared at each other, neither willing to initiate a friendly
gesture. Fighting Wolf, planted at the forefront of his
men, gazed impassively back at the staring assemblage.

The watching throng of men and women began to
shift anxiously. "Why are there so many men?"
murmured someone. "There must be over a
hundred . . . and no women."

"Probably afraid to bring their women,"
speculated another. "We haven't really stopped fighting
them. If this alliance doesn't work—"

"Probably don't trust us," came a third opinion.
"Afraid we'll take their women away from them!"
Several chuckles greeted this sally.

At a gesture from Fighting Wolf, the visitors began
shaking the rattles that miraculously appeared in their
hands. Singing to the beat, the Ahousats began the
shuffling dance steps that took them slowly up the
beach. Swaying and chanting, they made their way
towards the longhouses, stopping in front of the largest.

A lean, wiry Ahousat man of indeterminate age
stepped forward, a stout, carved stick grasped in his
hand. His wrinkled face screwed up, he confidently
addressed the waiting crowd.

"Good people of the Hesquiat tribe," began the

Speaker. "You are very fortunate to have our noble prince, Fighting Wolf, ask for the hand of Sarita, daughter of your chief Thunder Maker. Fighting Wolf is a great war chief. Few warriors have killed as many enemies as has our prince. He is feared far and wide for his prowess in battle, for his cunning raids on our enemies, and for his strength in fighting off raiders foolish enough to attack our village."

The listening Hesquiats stirred uneasily. "Why's he dwelling on war talk?" muttered Feast Giver, standing next to his father. "Doesn't he know this is a marriage he's come to attend? This marriage is supposed to bring an end to war. His words are too inflammatory."

Thunder Maker shrugged his large shoulders carelessly. "There're many things about this marriage proposal that are strange," he answered. "We've little choice but to see it through, for all our sakes. The alternative is war. I'm afraid our people will be completely slaughtered by the Ahousats if we don't marry into them. I don't like it, but there's nothing I can do about it."

He paused. "Look at him," he added, pointing at Fighting Wolf, who was standing next to the Speaker. Strong legs parted in an arrogant stance, the war chief haughtily surveyed the villagers crowded around.

"He doesn't look like a kind man, but what can I do? I just hope our dear Sarita can defang such a wolf," sighed Thunder Maker, almost to himself. Turning back to the Speaker, he strained to catch the man's words.

"Fighting Wolf comes from an illustrious line of wealthy and prestigious noblemen," the Speaker was saying. "The vast fishing grounds near our village belong to him and his lineage. He has many slaves who work under him. He is able to provide much meat and fish for his household and he still has great quantitites left over to give in potlatches—potlatches that far surpass anything your poor chief can give." Here a gasp went up from the audience. Thunder Maker would not take such insults lightly.

Indeed, Thunder Maker was frowning darkly at the Speaker. That man, as if oblivious to the reaction, proceeded.

"Not only does Fighting Wolf have many slaves, but he will soon have even more! His wealth will be increased many fold and his name will be known and feared up and down this great coast of ours."

"Arrogant bastard," muttered Feast Giver to his father. He received a grunt in reply.

"Whaling is one of our prince's special accomplishments," continued the indomitable Speaker, shifting his cocky stance. "Our esteemed prince has killed more giant whales than any other whale hunter, including your Hesquiat chiefs. Because of special, secret rituals, our noble prince is blessed by the gods. Every year they favor him with drift whales."

Drift whales were those that died at sea and washed up on the beach. The chief owning the beach owned the whale as well. He was said to have "called" the whale to his property.

"Last year, our war chief called four whales to his beaches. Yes, four!" Here another gasp went up from the audience. Four whales was truly a large number of whales to have drift up on shore, by anyone's standards.

"And," continued the intrepid speaker, "this year he will call in even more!" Many in the crowd could be seen shaking their heads, some with disbelief openly written across their features.

"But our illustrious prince does not need whales to feed his people. He has clamming beds that supply his family with much meat, and his slaves are always hunting for deer in the forest to supplement the fish caught in his fishtraps. Truly our people are very fortunate to have such a wealthy man as Fighting Wolf! You worms are indeed fortunate to be marrying into such a noble family."

Covert glances were cast at Thunder Maker to see his reaction to the slurs the cagey Speaker was casting. Thunder Maker was glowering.

The Speaker continued, boasting of Fighting Wolf's illustrous ancestors, the great deeds done by his family, their territorial possessions and anything else he thought would intimidate the critical crowd. Much time passed, the Speaker droning on and on. Finally, his voice growing hoarse, he was forced to end his oration.

He made his parting comments to the audience. "Fighting Wolf can afford to give a huge bride price for your insignificant daughter. He can give so much you Hesquiats will never be able to come up with enough wealth for the bridal repayment gift! You are too poor!"

By now, Thunder Maker's hold on his temper was gone. He had heard enough insults. Only Feast Giver's urgently whispered reminder of how badly they needed this alliance with the Ahousats restrained his fury.

With a final croak, the Speaker directed the attention of everyone back to where the canoes lay on the beach. Some of Fighting Wolf's men separated themselves from the others and headed down to where the canoes waited. The men staggered up the beach carrying armloads of gifts to present to the bride's family. Although the bulk of the gifts would be arriving the next day, Fighting Wolf brought several canoes filled with blankets, furs and other gifts as representative of his family's great wealth. The men set the bales of goods down on the pebbly beach, near Thunder Maker's longhouse and above the high tide mark, so that the incoming tide would not ruin any of the precious items.

Thunder Maker stomped over to inspect the proffered gifts. He did not have to pretend the vehemence with which he angrily rejected this first offering. At his signal, his men carried all the prizes back down to the waiting canoes.

The rejection of the groom's gifts was a traditional part of the marriage transaction. Over the next few days he was expected to dismiss the bridal price three or four times before finally accepting. Thunder Maker took exquisite satisfaction in refusing, expected though it was. He regretted he could not reject the full bride price today; that treat would have to wait until tomorrow. He brightened.

Turning on his heel, he marched up to the long-houses, too angry to watch the visitors load the gifts back into the canoes.

He would show those cocky Ahousats! He had some difficult games to challenge them with. They wouldn't be so arrogant after a few failures, he thought angrily. These were games that Thunder Maker owned through inheritance, and only he and his family had the right to display them at wedding ceremonies. He was very proud of the privileges and knew the Ahousats would be hard-pressed to win them.

The crowd followed him up the beach to the open space in front of the longhouses. People chatted and visited with each other, happy to have exciting entertainment on such a fine day. Dressed in their finery, everyone looked their best. A festive air prevailed.

At a gesture from Thunder Maker, his men leaned two strong poles against each other, then anchored them firmly in the sand. The poles were tied together at the fork where they met, at approximately the height of three men. A cedar rope, greased in bear fat, dangled just off the ground. To claim the prize, a contestant must climb to the top of the slippery rope.

His eyes narrowing, Fighting Wolf quickly scanned his men. He must choose carefully; he wanted to impress the Hesquiat dogs with Ahousat superiority.

At his signal, two lean, healthy specimens of manhood, Otterskin and Birdwhistle, stepped forward.

Otterskin was one of Fighting Wolf's most trusted fighting men, a man who could be relied on to do his best. Seeing that the poles were stoutly supported by two men, Otterskin carefully eyed the dangling rope. Giving a quick jump, he anchored himself securely on the slippery rope and entwined it once around his fist. Now to climb it. He paused for a moment, then jerked

himself sharply upwards to wrap his free arm around
the rope. To his utter dismay, he quickly slid downward
and landed in a heap on the sand. Shaking the sand off
his now greasy body, he strode ruefully over to the
sidelines.

It was Birdwhistle's turn. Fighting Wolf's cousin
glided forward and was under the rope in one smooth
movement. Looking up at it for a brief moment, he
suddenly juped high from his standing position. He
entangled the rope around both his hands and wrapped
it over his heels in one even movement. Carefully, one
hand over the other, he slowly ascended the rope,
always keeping the rope looped over one heel.

The crowd groaned with him as he slowly gained
the top of the greasy rope. A collective sigh went up as
he debonairly touched the top and swung gracefully to
the ground. He glanced out of the corner of his eye to
see Fighting Wolf's easy grin. Good!

He exclaimed loudly to the bridegroom, "These
games are no challenge! They're for children, not
Ahousat men!" Fighting Wolf laughed and Birdwhistle
strode forward to collect his prize, a beautifully carved
and decorated miniature cedar box.

Thunder Maker was glowering darkly. These
Ahousats were insolent! That game should have
challenged at least four or five men. Well, the Ahousat
slave-faces would not find the next game quite so easy.
Signalling briefly to one of his men, he gave the order to
start the next contest.

To Thunder Maker's great disappointment, the
Ahousats continued to easily win the games set out for
them. The crowd cheered but Thunder Maker couldn't
watch as, again and again throughout the afternoon, the
Ahousats upset the Hesquiat plans for humiliating
them.

Finally he could stand no more. The last game was
one he had saved for just such an occasion. He
whispered directions to Feast Giver.

Ten Hesquiat men stepped forward and formed

five pairs. The members of each pair faced the other across a space of two arm's lengths. Feast Giver walked among the men, quickly handing burning brands of pitch to each. The fiery torches formed a flaming gauntlet that would challenge the staunchest Ahousat warrior. The acrid smell of smoking pitch tainted the air, and the crowd murmured happily. Here was a test to put those arrogant Ahousats in their place!

Grimacing slightly, Fighting Wolf nodded quietly to one of his henchmen. Comes-from-Salish stood proudly in front of the gauntlet. He flexed his leg muscles by squatting on his haunches several times in succession. A fine figure of a man, he was middle-aged, broad-shouldered, with an innate sense of dignity. He was also that rare man: a freed slave.

Originally a Salishan slave bought from the Neah Bay people, he had proved himself to be an exceptionally loyal and heroic man. One day on a sea lion hunt, far out to sea, a mad bull attacked the canoe the slave and Birdwhistle were in. Risking his own life, the slave saved the nobleman. When they returned to the village, Fighting Wolf was so impressed by the slave's courage in saving a sometimes cruel master that he freed him and gave him a new name. From that time onwards, Comes-from-Salish had proven a strong fighter and the most loyal follower of the chief who freed him, Fighting Wolf.

Comes-from-Salish was aware of the many pairs of eyes upon him. Ostensibly exercising, in reality he was waiting for the torches to burn down before attempting his run through the line of fire.

At last, judging that the flames were reduced to the point where they would do him the least harm, he took several paces backwards from where the line of grinning men began. He paused for a moment, centering his thoughts on the feat he was about to perform.

The crowd was still, their anticipation hanging in the air like a live thing. Suddenly, he took off at a run, head down, in a mad dash for the tiny tunnel of safety between the fiery walls.

The watching throng gave a collective gasp, then began a voluble commentary on Comes-from-Salish's performance as he ran.

"He's twisting and turning!"

"Of course, fool! He doesn't want to get burned!"

"Look at him run! See! Someone just tried to trip him!"

"He runs well . . . for an Ahousat!"

"Ouch!"

"Little Eel, get away from those torches! I won't tell you again!"

Dodging the men, Comes-from-Salish twisted his body away from the burning brands as he ran. Crouching low, he darted and wove his way through the line. Someone thrust a burning brand at his face. He ducked just in time, almost thrown off balance. He kept running. At last he was through!

Taking a deep breath to still his heavy panting, he coughed on the acrid smoke and almost dropped to his knees in the sand, still panting heavily.

Several Hesquiat and Ahousat men rushed forward. Slapping him heartily on the back, on the arms, they cheered his prowess. Two men lifted him to their shoulders and marched him through the crowd.

"What a run!"

"Never seen anyone do it like that!"

"Congratulations!"

"What a performance!"

"No wonder we're losing the war . . . if all Ahousats are as brave as you!"

"Shut up, fool!"

Fighting Wolf coolly surveyed the people rushing to congratulate Comes-from-Salish and smiled to himself. A good day's work. These Hesquiats had seen for themselves how powerful the Ahousats were. Now, if his other plans went as successfully . . .

Thunder Maker approached the Ahousat guests and politely invited them to his longhouse for the feast his wives had spent long hours preparing.

Fighting Wolf led his delegation into the longhouse. Once inside, he insisted, before anyone was yet seated, "Thunder Maker, my father-in-law to-be, I ask, as a gesture of our goodwill towards each other, that you let my men sit interspersed with yours around your great fire. By sitting next to each other, we will learn more and have a better basis for our new friendship."

Thunder Maker frowned at the highly irregular request, but, wanting to placate his future son-in-law, he nodded to Crab Woman to carry out Fighting Wolf's suggestion. At last everyone was seated and Thunder Maker stood, holding an arm up for silence.

"My people," he began, "today I welcome my new son-in-law to-be and his respected nobles and friends. I am giving this feast to announce the forthcoming marriage of my daughter, Sarita, to Fighting Wolf of the noble Ahousat tribe. Tomorrow I will potlatch these Ahousats in my daughter's honor and they will see what a truly great family they are marrying into.

"It is with great pride that I tell you that the food for this feast was produced on my own lands, on my own fishing grounds, and gathered by my own slaves. Because this is such a special occasion, I have brought out my family's great feast dish. You see before you 'Always Bountiful.' That is the name of this great carved dish, heaped high with salmon. Now, please help yourselves to the food. We have plenty and are very glad to share it with you all." Thunder Maker sat down, and let the hall fill with the talking and laughter of hungry guests as they went about the business of eating.

In the center of the eating area, set between two small firepits, sat "Always Bountiful," the illustrious feast dish. Truly a work of art, it was a large cedar dish about five feet long, carved in the shape of a killer whale, and painted with family crests and designs along the sides. The elaborate dish was piled high with dried sockeye salmon. Guests helped themselves liberally to its offerings.

The first course served was dried herring eggs, a great delicacy. The eggs were gathered in the spring when schools of the small fish spawned on submerged fir tree branches the Indians prepared for that purpose. After collecting the eggs, the people dried them and stored them away for feasts.

Small, carved, wooden dishes were set out. They held the ubiquitous whale oil that no Nootka meal was complete without. Every morsel was dipped in the rich oil. In between courses, young men brought around bowls of water so that each guest could wash and dry his hands.

The next course was smoked salmon. Platters heaped high with the delicious alder-smoked salmon were presented to the guests and each one helped himself.

A delicious vegetable course followed. Roasted camus bulbs seasoned with wild herbs were greeted with delight by the participants.

The last course, boiled venison, sliced and served cold, was well received, though not consumed quite as readily as the preceding courses. The guests were feeling very full. It did not pass unnoticed, however, that Fighting Wolf's men ate only small amounts and very slowly. Fighting Wolf himself declined to stuff himself, even though war chiefs of his status were expected to have very large appetites.

During the feast, indeed, it was all Fighting Wolf could do to eat even a small amount of food. The bile rose in his throat several times when he thought of how he was sharing food with his father's murderers. His anger threatened to surface when he thought of his beloved parent falling prey to these men. Only with a strong act of will could he push back his anger. Soon he would allow himself the luxury of revenge on these low creatures. Soon. For now, he would keep a calm facade while in the enemy's lair . . .

The noise of the feasting drifted outside. Tonight

the usual night sounds were silenced. The croaking frogs were mute, the singing crickets stilled, and small animals tread warily near the boundaries of the village.

A large, yellow moon shone down on the bay, casting its long, ghostly light over the sea and over the land, creating eerie giant shadows everywhere. Far out to sea could be seen swirling mists, waiting to surround the unsuspecting canoe traveller.

A shadowy figure glided quickly along the darkest wall of Thunder Maker's longhouse. The figure paused. Moments later, the fur flap over the door opened briefly and a smaller shape stepped out into the night.

Spring Fern needed a breath of fresh air. She wandered quietly out into the night, away from the longhouse, breathing deeply of the scented stillness. The cool moist air blowing in from the ocean felt good against her heated skin. All the loud noises and partying had given her a headache and she longed for quiet. She had felt Sarita's tension all evening and the waiting was wearing her down, too. In a little while it would be over. Sarita would be married and she and Sarita would be on their way to the Ahousat village. She wondered idly what was in store for her there.

The harsh snapping of a twig caught her immediate attention. Turning quickly back to the longhouse, she found her way blocked by a dark, looming shadow. With a gasp she stepped back, prepared to run.

"Don't be afraid, little one," came a quiet, deep voice.

"Who is it?" she asked tremulously.

"Rottenwood."

"Oh," she gasped. "You quite scared me, Rottenwood. I—I was afraid for a moment." She suddenly stopped, realizing she didn't really know Rottenwood, and she had no reason to relax in his presence, despite his reassurance.

As if reading her thoughts, he spoke again in that quiet voice, "I was enjoying the night air. I feel restless tonight with so many Ahousats in the village."

She nodded, unaware that he had to strain his eyes to see her response. "I don't like it either," she admitted. "Soon, however, I'll be used to them, I suppose. I'm going to their village with Sarita, you know." This last said with a toss of her head.

She heard the quick intake of his breath. "No, I didn't know," he answered blandly. "Are you pleased to be going there?"

She shrugged. "It is all the same to a slave, isn't it?" she said ruefully, with just a trace of bitterness.

It was his turn to nod in the dark, her turn to strain her eyes looking for his response.

They stood there quietly for a moment in a comfortable silence. Quietly he reached out one large hand and brushed a long curl of her hair away from her face. "You're very beautiful," he whispered, moving slightly closer to her.

"D-don't, please," she trembled in the cool night air, but not from the cold.

"I wouldn't hurt you, little one," he murmured. "Don't you know I've wanted to talk with you, to hold you for so long?"

"Wh-what do you mean?" she asked uncertainly. "I don't really know you. I've never encouraged you in any way." She began to grow indignant.

He let out a quiet chuckle. "No, you certainly haven't encouraged me. But you have seen me watching you, haven't you? I've admired you for a long time," and here he inhaled the sweet fragrance of the lock of hair he'd been toying with. He continued on, "It makes me sad to know you'll be leaving so soon. I'd hoped to have more time."

"More time?" she echoed.

"Yes," he answered, in that same deep, reassuring voice, "I was hoping for more time to get to know you, to court you in a proper fashion."

"Court me?" she echoed stupidly. Then regaining control, she sneered, "Slaves don't court. Slaves have no choice when and if it comes to choosing a spouse."

"Nevertheless," he answered, unperturbed, "I want you for my wife, and I had hoped that, given time, you would want me. Now that you're going away, I'm deeply disappointed."

Spring Fern stood quietly, in a daze. At last, she sighed, a quiet, desperate sigh.

"If only we did have a choice, if only a slave could choose—"

"Would you choose me?" he broke in on her thoughts.

"B-but I hardly know you," she answered, stalling.

"Well," he answered sardonically, "it doesn't seem like we'll have any time to find out anyway. Will we?" Still toying with her hair, he now reached over to run his fingers lightly down her arm.

"N-no, I guess not," she answered doubtfully.

Chagrined with the way the conversation was going, Rottenwood leaned over and lightly brushed his lips against hers. Feeling her tremble, he pulled her closer and pressed more firmly. She tried to push him away with both her hands pressed against his chest, but after a moment relaxed with a small sigh. Slowly, hesitantly, she put her arms softly around his neck. Embracing her tenderly, he rained gentle kisses on her cheeks, forehead and eyelids. Spring Fern grew warm under his touch and gave in to the marvelous sensations his lips were evoking. She felt his mouth rove slowly down her throat to the hollow at the base of her neck. Moving languidly against him, she sighed luxuriously.

Suddenly, louder noises from the party inside the longhouse crept into their consciousness and they broke slowly apart, staring at each other.

Rottenwood reached for her again, but she raised a palm to hold him off.

"P-please," she begged feebly, "I—I must go in. They'll miss me." She quickly ducked around him and darted back into the longhouse, leaving him staring at the swaying flap of fur that marked the door.

He spat angrily into the sand, and stalked off

towards the beach. Perhaps a brisk walk would cool his raging blood, he thought resentfully.

Once down on the beach, his silent figure moved restlessly in the bright moonlight. He could hear the sounds of revelry coming from Thunder Maker's long-house, but now he no longer had any desire to sit with the slaves and join in the festivities. His uneasiness intensified, but he didn't know why.

He thought of Spring Fern. He'd seen her and touched her for such a short time, and yet it meant so much to him. Had those warm kisses meant anything to her? he wondered wistfully. She'd looked so lovely in the moonlight and her kisses had tasted so sweet it made his heart ache with longing for her.

With a grunt, he kicked at a piece of rotting kelp on the beach and strode onwards. As he approached the Ahousats' canoes, lying in wait half on the sand, half in the water, he sat down to clear his head of his recent turmoil. Thoughts of Spring Fern, and the hiss of the waves lapping hungrily at the canoes, lulled him into a peaceful state, his anger forgotten.

In the longhouse, people were commenting about how little the visitors had eaten. Despite Ahousat protests of satiation, the host's men muttered amongst themselves. How could the guests be full? They hadn't eaten that much! They were trying to insult Chief Thunder Maker's generous hospitality. Guests should show better manners than that!

Hearing the murmurings of discontent and anxious to head off any confrontation, Thunder Maker sought a diversion. He decided to bring out Sarita, with some of her female attendants. She had not yet met her husband-to-be and Thunder Maker felt that now was the time to introduce her to her new people. At his gesture, Crab Woman heaved herself to her feet and marched over to their private apartments to fetch Sarita.

Sarita sat quietly with her women about her. Tensely awaiting her father's summons, her thoughts

raced on and on about her husband-to-be. She tried to
reassure herself by telling herself over and over that this
marriage was what her father and brother, who dearly
loved her, wanted for her, and of the peace it would
bring between the two peoples. Surely they would not
arrange something harmful for her. Would they?

At Crab Woman's curt order, Sarita rose and tried
to still her trembling frame. She gave one last nervous
touch to the neckline of her cloak, unconsciously
twisting a lock of her shining seal-brown hair, then
finally took a deep shuddering breath. She gathered her
courage and followed Crab Woman over to where the
revellers were eating and talking loudly.

All conversation suddenly ceased as, head held
high, Sarita entered the room, followed by her ladies.
She briefly scanned the room, then went quietly to her
place and sat down gracefully, head still high. Her
women positioned themselves around her, grouped like
a bouquet of summer flowers. After a moment, conversation resumed and Sarita felt herself relax now that she
was no longer the center of everyone's attention.

Amidst the background buzz of talking, Sarita
surreptitiously looked about, trying to guess which man
was her husband-to-be. Suddenly from across the room
she was confronted by the darkest, most piercing, jet
black eyes she had ever beheld. Set in an arrogant face,
the eyes held hers imprisoned for a timeless moment
until she finally forced herself to look away. Shaken
inside, she tried to calm her suddenly rushing emotions.
Lifting a cup of water to her lips, she sipped slowly and
finally set it down again as she felt her heartbeat
returning to normal.

Who was this man whose captivating gaze had
slashed   across   her   vision?   He   was   dressed
magnificently, like—like a groom should be. Surely he
wasn't Fighting Wolf! He didn't look anything like the
man Crab Woman had described. This man was young,
handsome and she was certain he had all his teeth. Yes.
There, the flash of his smile for the space of a heartbeat.

He had a full set of gleaming white teeth.

Turning her head as if to whisper to Spring Fern, Sarita glanced quickly out the corner of her eye to see what *he* was doing. She caught her breath as she realized his eyes were still on her. Mind awhirl, she tried to concentrate on the conversation around her, but all she could think of was the man whose dark gaze held her captive.

Fighting Wolf had been quietly fuming, dwelling on thoughts of revenge, when he noticed Thunder Maker's signal to his wife. With unconcealed interest, Fighting Wolf watched her disappear behind a screen, only to reenter moments later followed by a retinue of women led by one of the most beautiful women he had ever seen. Dressed in a blue trade blanket cloak that only partially covered her cream-colored wedding costume, she outshone any woman he had seen in a long, long time.

Unable to take his eyes off her, he followed her progress to her seating place and still could not pull his eyes away. Long gleaming hair spread over her shoulders and hung down to her waist. The large expressive eyes, set in a flawless face, caught and held his for a moment before she looked haughtily away. Her dignified posture, her calm control, all served to overwhelm him with her presence. No one else in the room existed for him. Trying to cover his shock with a look of unconcern, he still could not tear his eyes away from the beautiful woman.

Who was she? She had the noble bearing of a chief's daughter. Could this lovely woman be his bride-to-be, Sarita? For a brief moment, intense regret flooded him. Then he recovered. It didn't matter who she was . . . she'd soon be his.

Fighting Wolf at last managed to drag his eyes away from the tempting vision of Sarita. He surveyed the room, watching his men. Dressed in their bulky robes, some sat and talked convivially with their hosts, others argued loudly. Nearby hovered several serving

women and slaves who waited on the guests. The
women laughed and giggled in their higher-pitched
voices.

The meal over with, many of the men were lying
around, relaxing. His own men, noted Fighting Wolf,
looked more alert and responsive than the indolently
sprawling, satiated Hesquiats. Fighting Wolf shifted
impatiently in the heavy elk armor he wore under his
robe. The armor, three hides thick, was the prerogative
of a war chief and Fighting Wolf had decided to wear
his tonight, despite the discomfort.

It was time. Giving a quick nod to Otterskin on his
right and Comes-from-Salish on his left, he tensed his
muscles and sprang up.

Simultaneously the air was filled with loud
screeches and victory yells as the vengeful Ahousats
pulled out weapons from under their robes and turned
viciously on their unsuspecting Hesquiat foes. Caught
completely unawares, most of the Hesquiats were
weaponless. They moved slowly, as if unable to comprehend the full extent of the Ahousats' treachery.

Fighting Wolf was immediately embroiled in a
struggle with an unarmed Hesquiat. Fighting Wolf
quickly dispatched the warrior and turned to see Otterskin give a ferocious laugh as he stabbed an openmouthed Hesquiat man. Blood spurted and the man's
horrible gurgled cry added to the mad pandemonium.
Another vicious stab by Otterskin and the victim was
silenced forever.

Women rushed around screaming. Confusion
reigned. One woman was shouting hysterically at the
men, another sobbing uncontrollably. Panic-stricken
women ran into the middle of fights only to be beaten
back. Other frantic women darted about, searching
desperately for children and clutching wailing babies to
their breasts. The utter fear of the women could be seen
on all their faces as they cried, watching husbands and
sons, sweethearts and lovers, fall to the brutal enemy.
Men's shouts and hoarse screams added to the din.

Spring Fern, seeing from the first what was happening, shook Sarita's shoulder to get her attention. Their only hope of safety lay in escape. Suddenly an enemy warrior swung brutally at her with his war club. She ducked instinctively. He missed. She raced to an escape hatch on one side of the longhouse. Slipping through, she ran as fast as she could into the nearby forest and crouched, gasping, under a thick net of bushes. Hidden in the dark, she resolved to wait until the last raider departed.

Birdwhistle was fighting off two determined Hesquiats, the struggle going against him until Comes-from-Salish leaped to his defense, striking one of the Hesquiats from behind. Quickly disposing of his man, he turned again to aid Birdwhistle, who by now needed no help. He had already killed the other adversary.

Fighting Wolf was shouting encouragement to his men. His loud voice could be heard reminding them of their reasons for revenge and promising them many captives.

Searching through the fighting men, he quickly spied Feast Giver, fighting off one of Ahousat's best warriors. As he watched, Feast Giver quickly stabbed the man in the side of the neck and jumped back as the man crumpled in a bloody heap. Feast Giver bellowed a victorious war cry.

That was all the provocation Fighting Wolf needed. Rushing over, he attacked Feast Giver, clubbing him from the side. The blow glanced off his head and one shoulder. Caught unawares the young Hesquiat twisted to one side, but lost his balance. As he fell to the ground he stabbed at Fighting Wolf with his knife. His target stepped back smoothly and missed the blow aimed at his thigh.

Now Fighting Wolf had the advantage and he used it. Kicking Feast Giver's knife from his hand, he disarmed him. Then he lunged on top of the man, knife out, ready to stab. Fighting Wolf felt the fury over his father's death erupt and cascade over him.

As he was about to bring his knife down for the second time, a large hand grabbed him from behind and spun him off Feast Giver's prone body. Defending himself, Fighting Wolf lunged at his attacker. The man, large and strong, swung a warclub at Fighting Wolf's head, but missed. At the last moment, he was pushed off balance by Fighting Wolf's tackle around the knees.

Completely caught up in defending himself from the brutal attack, Fighting Wolf had no time to see Crab Woman surreptitiously approach the almost unconscious Feast Giver. Looking hastily around to see that no one was paying her any attention, she grabbed him roughly about the shoulders. Gripping underneath each arm, she staggered with the heavy body over to a haphazardly stacked wall of cedar chests. Grunting heavily, she pulled the inert body around the wall, hiding it from view. Looking around, she spied several cedar mats. Grabbing some, she tossed them over the body to hide it from searchers. That done, she ran back out into the melee.

The warrior was on his knees, Fighting Wolf wrapped around him. Seeing the man aim his war club again at his head, Fighting Wolf quickly stabbed him in the back several times. Blood was streaming down the man's back as he bowed forward and fell on his face, never to stir again. Pushing the heavy body off himself, Fighting Wolf got slowly to his feet, panting. The suddenness of the man's attack had caught him off guard. Turning quickly to confront Feast Giver once more, Fighting Wolf was surprised his opponent was nowhere to be found. Puzzled, he had no time to wonder what happened before he was distracted by Thunder Maker, his archenemy.

He stalked over to where Thunder Maker was trying vainly to hold off two bloody Ahousat attackers. A guttural order from Fighting Wolf and the men slunk away to engage other enemy victims.

Facing the hated Thunder Maker, Fighting Wolf bared his teeth in a snarl and demanded, "Defend yourself, cur! I will defeat you in revenge for my father's death, you offal!''

He thrust one of his own daggers into Thunder Maker's hand. He would let no man say it was not a fair fight.

Thunder Maker circled his opponent warily. He saw the deep hatred in the glistening eyes, the breadth of the panting chest, the taut body in fighting stance, anger barely controlled. And he knew fear. More than that, he knew he looked into the face of death. He could hear the screams around him and he knew his time had come.

He lunged at the younger warrior, stabbing at him with a powerful blow. He missed. Fighting Wolf's low laugh taunted him as he ducked the blow and returned one of his own. Thunder Maker felt a sharp, burning pain in his right shoulder, but knew he could not stop the fight. It was to the death.

There were few sounds of battle now. Most of his men lay dead, their bodies littering the floor.

Desperate, Thunder Maker switched his knife to his functioning hand, the left one. At such a disadvantage, he must kill the younger man soon. Feinting to one side, he quickly jabbed from the other. Fighting Wolf was expecting such a trick and jumped easily out of the way. In a surprise move, he lunged for the older warrior's legs and tripped him. Thunder Maker fell heavily to the floor. Bringing his knife up and under the old man's chin as he lay prone, Fighting Wolf was surprised to look into eyes that held no fear, only resignation.

Grabbing the knife out of the old man's hand, he grinned down into his face. His voice carried in the silence and all eyes turned to him as he sneered, "Old man, do you think you'll die this day?"

No answer, just the resigned eyes staring back at him.

"No, old man, you won't die today. And I'll tell you why I, Fighting Wolf, war chief of the Ahousats, will let you live." Here he snarled his hatred at the old man. "I let you live, old cur, because I want you to see and taste the humliation every day of your life of what I've done to you. Look around you! Your warriors are dead. Your son—''

Suddenly realizing Feast Giver's absence, Fighting Wolf ordered Comes-from-Salish, "Bring me his son!"

Turning back to the chief on the floor, he growled, "I'm taking your women with me as slaves . . . including your daughter. I wouldn't want you to wonder where that worthless bitch is!" He laughed cruelly.

Still no answer from the old man, just his steady gaze in reply. Fighting Wolf jabbed the knife a little closer, the point of his dagger cutting the thin skin of his enemy's neck. A drop of blood, winking in the firelight, ran down the blade.

Comes-from-Salish strode up, an unconscious Feast Giver in his arms. "Get some rope and tie him up with the old man," commanded Fighting Wolf.

Quickly and competently, the warrior tied the chief back to back with his son. The two half-sat, half-slumped in the middle of the feast remains, their dead warriors at their feet.

"Listen well, old man," snarled Fighting Wolf. "Your name will be reviled and loathed up and down the coast. No one will attend your potlatches. No one will make alliances with you. You can't even protect your own name or family. Look at your people. Destroyed! And by my hand! Do you know why, old man?"

His face twisted with hate, Fighting Wolf held the knife even closer. Another crimson tear slid down the blade. "Because you led the raid that killed my father. My father, old man, was a better war chief than you or your son could ever hope to be!"

Standing up, he looked down at his victim and spat in his face. "Humiliation, old man! That's what you'll live with every day for the rest of your worthless life!" Contemptuously, he turned his back on the old chief and his unconscious son, and walked away.

Fighting Wolf gloated to himself in savage glee.
The old man would indeed live a life of humiliation
from this day forth!

Looking around quickly, he noted with satisfaction
that several women were herded into one corner of the
longhouse. He saw, with even greater satisfaction, the
blue blur of a trade blanket that told him the woman he
wanted had been captured.

At the first wild yell, Sarita sat in a bewildered
daze, but only for a moment. The touch of Spring Fern
at her shoulder galvanized her into action. Her breath
caught in her throat as she watched a warrior swing his
club at her slave. Seeing the girl run for the escape
hatch, relief swept over Sarita.

But she had paused too long. The brutal warrior
that had swung at Spring Fern now turned on her.
Instead of clubbing her to death as she expected, he
reached one brawny arm around her waist and dragged
her off with him. Kicking and screaming, she tried to
dislodge herself from his iron grip. Ignoring her efforts
as he would a mosquito's, he carried her over to one
dark corner of the longhouse.

There, hugging crying babies and sobbing children,
several women crowded together. They stood in groups
of twos and threes clutching one another for solace, and
grim-faced, watched the bloody spectacle.

Sarita was shoved roughly into the pitiful group.
Darting away, she was seized in a tight grip and a loud
laugh rang in her ear. Thrust back into the group of
women, she drew her blanket tightly about her as if for
protection. She glanced around. Armed with knives and
warclubs, several burly Ahousats guarded the women,
effectively preventing any escape. Sarita huddled in
hopelessly with the other victims.

It seemed such a long time that she stood with the
women, staring dully out at the battling men. She
watched, sickened, as Fighting Wolf fought with a
warrior of her father's. With a snarl, the war chief
grabbed the man's hair, jerking his head down. Sharply

bringing his knee up, he smashed the man's face, then stabbed him through the ribs and laughed as the Hesquiat crumpled to the floor.

Another Ahousat was bending over a stout Hesquiat he had walloped over the shoulders, and then beaten over the head. The body lay still, unmoving in that scene of frantic activity.

Sarita recognized the man who had run the flaming gauntlet. Comes-from-Salish grabbed another man's head and quickly bent him over backward as he plunged a knife into the man's vitals. Hearing a groan, he bashed his victim over the head with his war club and watched in satisfaction as the man sank lifelessly to the floor.

Sarita continued to stare with lifeless eyes at the hazy scene, her horror growing with the mad slaughter. She searched slowly for some sight of her father or brother. Far off to one side, she could make out the body of her brother, then the bulky figure of Crab Woman as she dragged him off to safety. The old woman's heroic efforts shook Sarita from her terror-induced lethargy.

Peering through the haze, she searched frantically for her father's stout frame, but couldn't see him anywhere. She felt a cold hard lump in her stomach. Surely he was not dead! She quickly searched through the captives. Perhaps he had been captured. With a despairing heart, she realized the enemy was taking only women and children as captives. The men they were killing.

At last she spotted Thunder Maker, just as Fighting Wolf attacked. Breathless, heart pounding, she watched their short, vicious battle to its humiliating conclusion.

Sarita became aware suddenly that the sounds of battle around her were gradually dying. There were only the moans and groans of the wounded and dying, broken occasionally by the piteous cries of mourning or captive women. The battle was over, and her father's people had lost. It was a bitter moment for Sarita. And one she knew would haunt her the rest of her life.

She gazed, stricken, at her father and brother trussed together in the midst of the carnage, heard the cruel words Fighting Wolf spoke. He was right . . . her father's and brother's names were irredeemably destroyed. Truly a fine-honed revenge to let them live, she thought. They would have gladly chosen an honorable death with their warriors.

Exhilarated, Fighting Wolf surveyed the battle scene. All around him lay the dead and dying enemy. Squinting through the smoke at the captive women and children huddled in the far corner, he snapped, "Take the prisoners down to the beach and load them into canoes. Make sure our retreat is covered. Then let's get out of here." His men hurried away, happy to carry out both orders.

In disbelief, Sarita felt a sharp point—a knife?—prodding her in the back. Dazed, she moved passively along with the other women. Looking at the decapitated bodies sprawled all over the floor, people she'd known all her life, a great sorrow mingled with anger and the bitter taste of defeat welled up in her. Thunder Maker's people had been ignobly conquered and there was nothing she could do. All was lost.

Shoved out into the night with the others, she felt the cool breeze on her skin. It revived her spirits somewhat. Also, it was a relief to be away from the scene of deadly confrontation.

She looked around at the weeping women, as if seeing them for the first time. Some of them clutched their children to them as they walked slowly towards the beach. Many had no children. Sarita noted that the captured women were the young, attractive ones of her village. She shuddered as she wondered what was in store for all of them.

Once down on the beach, the terrified women milled about like frightened deer. Waiting to be loaded into the war canoes, they were poked and prodded by the laughing victors. Men stood around the captives, holding up the grisly heads and gesturing obscenely at the women. Some of the warriors took great delight in mauling those women standing at the fringe of the crowd.

Sarita, clutching her blanket tightly around her, was crowded into the middle. She was protected from grabbing hands but could feel many eyes upon her.

Suddenly the women around her were pushed to both sides, leaving a wide path. Fighting Wolf strode forward, stopping in front of her. He stood, grinning down at her, his piercing black eyes staring straight into hers. His hard gaze disconcerted her, but she would not let him know it.

He stood there arrogantly, looking at her for a long moment. At his belt hung several daggers, and his beautiful sea otter robe was smeared with blood. Hesquiat blood. Sarita clutched her blanket closer and stared up at him with angry, hate-filled golden eyes. "Murderer!" she hissed.

He laughed, his deep voice echoing in the stillness and sending a shiver down her spine. He reached out one strong hand and took her shoulder. Spinning her around, he pushed her roughly towards his canoe. Stubbornly, she dug her heels into the sand. Anything to thwart him, she thought. There was a long pause, then Sarita thought she heard a low chuckle.

Suddenly, she was seized and thrown over one hard shoulder. She struggled and kicked, but the blue cape she wore interfered with her movements. A massive hand swatted her buttocks, and a deep voice ordered, "Stop struggling, woman!"

Fighting Wolf took several strides through the water, then dumped her ignominiously into a canoe. Glad to pull away from him, she crawled to a seat in the canoe, drawing her blue cloak closer and glowering at him, before haughtily turning her back.

Once seated in the middle of his war canoe, she stoically watched the scene on the beach.

Fighting Wolf chuckled to himself at the girl's

rebellion. Later he would have time for taming her, he thought with anticipation. Surveying the beach, he urged his men to load the captives into the canoes quickly. Most of his men were standing by the canoes, ready to jump aboard after the women were loaded. A few last Ahousats hurried down the beach, clutching booty.

A slumped, brown body dressed in slave rags caught the war chief's eye. The man lay draped over the bow of Comes-from-Salish's canoe. Fighting Wolf raised an eyebrow interrogatively. Comes-from-Salish looked sheepish.

"Caught him hanging around the canoes. Thought it best to take no chances. We hit him over the head. Didn't want to kill him since he's a strong-looking slave," the former slave muttered gruffly.

Fighting Wolf recognized Comes-from-Salish's pity for the unconscious slave and, feeling magnanimous in his victory, answered casually, "Well, well. I'll consider him my bridal repayment gift." He chuckled. "Just make sure the man stays out of my way. Any trouble from him and you'll be held responsible."

"Yes, noble chief," answered Comes-from-Salish solemnly. Then he grinned. "There's lots of work for this slave to do. He'll earn his keep, don't worry." He gave Rottenwood a hard kick in the ribs. The captive lay still, unconscious. He felt nothing even when he was lifted and tossed into the bottom of the canoe.

Ten of Fighting Wolf's men still stood on the beach. They were armed with muskets and were covering the others' retreat. A few straggling Hesquiats chased the Ahousats to the beach, only to be scared off by scattered shots.

Finally, all the canoes were loaded with captives and warriors. The remaining ten pushed the laden craft into deeper water, jumped in, then whirled to aim their weapons at any would-be rescuers.

A few brave survivors managed to race for their canoes, avidly pursuing the raiders. Fighting Wolf grinned, watching them. It was soon clear to his men why he was so amused.

The Hesquiats stopped at the waterline, milling in confusion. Out in deep water lay the Hesquiat war canoes, half-sunk. Paddles and equipment floated easily on the outgoing tide. One or two hardy men splashed into the water, frantically trying to retrieve the submerged dugouts. The rest stood on shore, shouting foul curses at the rapidly disappearing Ahousats.

Fighting Wolf laughed exultantly. His strategy was a success! His revenge was complete! Turning to his men, he grinned broadly, his eyes touching briefly, triumphantly, on Sarita huddled in the center of the canoe.

"A good day's work!" he yelled, holding up a bloody, dripping head by the hair. His victory yell echoed across the water to the warriors in the other canoes. With a resounding answering shout, his men bent to their paddles with a will and raced swiftly for home as full darkness descended.

5

Stiff and chilled, Sarita sat huddled in Fighting Wolf's war canoe. She stared straight ahead, unseeing, at Fighting Wolf's broad back as he sat in the prow of the boat.

Despair overwhelmed her. She felt numb and dazed, barely able to comprehend the enormous change in her life in such a short time. Her mind crowded with images of the marriage feast, and she could concentrate on little else. Again and again she saw her father and brother tied and helpless, heard the cruel words Fighting Wolf spoke, saw the headless bodies of her father's warriors.

Once she briefly glanced over at the other canoes to the bundled shapes of the captured Hesquiat women. They looked as broken and listless as she herself felt.

Desperately she tried to focus her mind on her present danger, but scenes from the slaughter kept intruding. At last the awful visions were interrupted by a fitful sleep.

In another canoe, Rottenwood groggily shook his head. The hammering on the back of his skull would not go away. Shaking his head again, he moaned and tried to sit up, feeling sick. Gradually, the nauseous feeling in the pit of his stomach disappeared. He became aware of the gentle rocking motion of the canoe.

At last able to sit up, he looked around, squinting into the darkness. The shadowy coastline they were passing was unfamiliar territory. Noting a big, dark land mass to his left, he realized the Ahousats were pursuing a southerly course. He glanced about repeatedly to memorize landmarks.

One of the Ahousats, seeing he was awake, thrust a long, carved oar into his hand and harshly ordered him to paddle.

Realizing his life hung in the balance with these ruthless new captors, he obeyed with alacrity. As he paddled, his strength began to return. He followed the rhythm set by the Ahousats. Many times his eyes darted surreptitiously to the coastline as he paddled. Should he escape, he must be able to find his way back to Hesquiat . . . and Spring Fern.

Thoughts of escape were far from Sarita's mind. Scrunched up against the cold, she shifted uneasily as she dozed. Her cape had fallen to one side and she was shivering in the cold night air. Fighting Wolf moved cautiously to where she was slumped, lifted her cape and gently covered her shoulders. The tender gesture surprised him. Why should he care if the daughter of his enemy was cold? Setting his jaw, he ignored the astonished glances of his men and moved back to his position at the bow. Keeping his back to the sleeping woman, he refused to examine his bewildering actions too closely.

Hours passed in silent paddling. The dark of night gave way to pink streaks of light at dawn. The sky behind the shadowy land mass soon glowed with mauve and orange clouds as the sun rose to herald a clear day. Sea gulls wheeled overhead, their raucous cries greeting the brilliant orb.

Fighting Wolf stretched his long limbs as he yawned. He straightened himself from his cramped position in the canoe. It had been a long night. He could see Ahousat village in the distance. As they paddled closer, he spotted his longhouse, off to one side. A few children played in front, despite the early hour. He stretched again, languorously, like a tawny cougar. Ah, yes, it was good to be home after a successful raid.

Sarita awakened gradually. Looking at the strange men through sleep-ridden eyes, feeling the gentle rocking of the canoe, hazy memories of the previous night leapt into sharp focus. She straightened as gruesome scenes flooded her mind with painful clarity.

But her body's clamorings interrupted the rush of thoughts. Her back ached from sleeping hunched over. Her bladder was full. She was cold and hungry and still tired. Desperately she tried to ignore her bodily complaints and rally her defenses for the upcoming ordeal. She would soon be in the village of her hated enemies.

Glancing across the water at a nearby war canoe, she noticed Rottenwood for the first time. He looked vaguely familiar. Hadn't she seen him in her own village? She wondered what he was doing with the dreaded Ahousats.

Casting a peek at her fellow captives, she noticed the women looked even worse than they had last night. Many were sobbing openly and clinging to each other, their worst fears surfacing as they came closer to the enemy's village. Their hysteria was contagious and Sarita felt a surge of panic well up inside her. Taking several deep breaths, she fought down the treacherous feeling. These despicable Ahousats would never see her fear!

Clenching her hands tightly into fists, her nails dug painfully into soft palms. She stared straight ahead, showing no hint of turmoil, but inside she was seething with apprehension. As a prisoner of the Ahousats she anticipated little kindness and much hard work. But what she really dreaded were the advances she was sure the men would make. She'd seen how the men of her village treated newly captured, pretty slave women and she was terrified and angry at the same time. She would not, absolutely would not, tolerate such treatment of her person, she resolved. After all, she was a chief's daughter. Her admonitions served to quell the fears threatening to engulf her.

She would prove herself worthy as her father's daughter and not degrade her family's name. She choked back a sob as she realized anew that her family's name was already degraded—foully degraded—for she was a slave.

The word echoed through her mind as she struggled to come to terms with her horrendous situation. Spring Fern was a slave, Cedar Bundle was a slave, Rottenwood, too, but Sarita?

Never, ever had she ever imagined herself in such circumstances, though she'd heard tales of slavery ever since childhood. Somehow it had never touched her personally, though. Oh, she knew that noblewomen were sometimes captured and forced into slavery, but it had always happened to someone else. Not her. The image of Cedar Bundle crept into her mind. Hadn't she been a noblewoman at one time? Sarita shook her head. Now was not the time for such disturbing thoughts. Surrounded as she was by enemies, she needed her wits.

She glanced about quickly. The tight, tired faces of the warriors could not hide the triumphant grins they slyly cast at the women.

The cutthroats, she thought bitterly, gloating at our humiliation. Her chin lifted higher. The sooner these dogs realized she would brook no abuse, the sooner they would leave her alone. Determined, she set her beautiful mouth in a grim line.

Her gaze came to rest on Fighting Wolf's broad back. Here, here was the man responsible for her predicament! Hot anger welled up inside her and she longed to jump at him, to rip him apart with her bare hands. She hated him passionately. Fury at her humiliating losses washed over her and she was blinded to all else. She clenched her jaw, and closed her eyes. She must control her fury. Her very life depended on it. But later, later, she would seek revenge against this vicious animal who had destroyed her family and name.

Suddenly Fighting Wolf turned, as if feeling the

heat of her gaze on his back. Their eyes met and he was startled at the fury he saw in her golden eyes.

Looking into the depths of those jet black eyes, she wanted to snarl curses at him, but some primitive instinct for survival stopped her.

"Just you wait," she whispered to herself instead. "I'll escape your clutches and return with my father's warriors to kill you!"

As if he'd heard her, he smirked insolently, and leaned forward to touch her face. She jerked her head away and looked off to the side in stony, seething silence.

"Looks like this Hequiat slave has a temper," he sneered to his men.

Coarse chuckles greeted this remark before everyone's attention turned to the village they were rapidly approaching.

Welcoming songs and chants congratulating their triumphant return echoed through the early morning air. Women and children rushed into their small canoes and paddled out eagerly to meet the returning victorious heroes.

Sarita watched as an attractive, sloe-eyed young woman approached Fighting Wolf's war canoe and reached out to grasp his arm. She whispered intimately to him in a low voice. Sarita glanced away, but not before she met the woman's darkly speculative gaze. Through her lashes, Sarita watched as the woman reached up with both arms to hug Fighting Wolf.

Such a display lacked breeding, thought Sarita with distaste, turning away before she could see the war chief disengage the woman's arms from around his neck.

Why should Sarita care if he already had a wife? She should have known he'd have other wives, she snorted to herself. Now that she knew what he was really like, she could see he deserved such a fawning, low-class woman as this one appeared to be. How very common, she sniffed to herself.

Shifting her gaze to encompass the village, she saw

that it was much bigger than her home village. A wide,
swiftly running river bordered one side.

The village itself was nestled in a lovely setting,
Sarita noted. Tall mountains rose in the distance and
stood over the village as if they were alert sentinels. Had
she been coming here under other circumstances, she
might have learned to love such a beautiful spot, she
thought wistfully. Then she hardened her heart. It
would do no good to dwell on what might have been,
she told herself. She must now deal with reality, and the
reality was that she was coming to this place as a slave.
But not for long, she vowed to herself silently. This
place—beautiful or not—would not hold her for
long!

The entire Ahousat village turned out to witness the
return of the warriors. Many did not realize their war
chief had been raiding until victory chants rang in the
still morning air. Most of the crowd remained on shore,
leaving only the more zealous to paddle out and greet
the raiders.

The group amassed onshore numbered about two
thousand souls, of which one-quarter were slaves. The
nobility owned the slaves. Of the slave population, one
hundred and fifty-three belonged to Fighting Wolf. Most
he had won in raids and warfare, some he'd purchased in
trading. A large part of his wealth was measured in these
slaves, and by Ahousat standards he was a very successful
man. He had several excellent canoe makers, and some
slaves who were soldiers. They accompanied him on raids
and added greatly to his prowess in war. The remainder
hunted, fished, or picked berries for him—doing whatever was necessary at any given season. Their surplus
labor added to his wealth.

Management of this small army of captives fell to
Fishtrap and his wife Periwinkle. Fishtrap, a
commoner, was a distant relative of Fighting Wolf's,
and lived permanently under the war chief's roof. A
middle-aged man, he had lost an eye years ago and
despaired of ever being able to make a decent living for

his family. What had begun as a charitable gesture on
Fighting Wolf's part had turned into a very satisfactory
arrangement for both when it was discovered that Fishtrap was a natural organizer. He was able to deal fairly
with the people around him and to assign tasks to the
slaves in a manner that brought out the best in each one.
Fishtrap's thoughtful management, combined with his
wife's firm authority, made Fighting Wolf's household
of slaves run very smoothly indeed. Also, Fishtrap's
loyalty to Fighting Wolf was unquestioned, a fact the
war chief appreciated as he was often gone for long
periods of time on warring raids or whale hunts.

Fighting Wolf's slaves resided in his longhouse, a
circumstance usual in Nootka villages. A few villages
had separate quarters for slaves, but Ahousat was not
such a one.

The slaves lived midway along both sides of the
house. Rather crowded conditions existed, but by slave
standards they were well-treated with good food to eat,
and adequate clothing. Some were even married or
cohabiting, but most were single men or mothers with
small children. Such were the conditions the unsuspecting Sarita could expect to live in.

As the returning war party approached the beach in
front of Ahousat village, the volume of the chanting
increased. The warriors enthusistically sang their victory
songs as they neared the beach, allowing the incoming
waves to push them to shore. Sarita, sitting in the
middle of the war canoe, watched the large crowd
warily.

Her first view of the villagers showed little different
from her own people. Surveying the crowd, she noted
hair coloring ranging from dark blond to midnight
black. Everyone wore cedar kutsacks, as did her own
people. Some of the men were naked, again typical of
the men in her own town.

A sudden lurch of the canoe as it scrunched into the
gravel threw her off balance. A strong hand on her
shoulder steadied her. She looked up to see Fighting

Wolf looming over her. Before she could push his hand
away, he had removed it and was jumping out of the
canoe.

He reached into the canoe and grabbed a bloody
head in each hand. Dangling them by the hair, he held
them up to the gathered crowd. People pressed around
him, anxious to see and touch the trophies. Several of his
men followed his example, cockily displaying the grisly
prizes. Singing their triumph, they told the eager crowd
of the victorious revenge over the low, sneaky
Hesquiats.

Listening to the chanted story of the raid and
betrayal, Sarita was not surprised to hear her father and
brother maligned. They were described as horrible
villains to the listeners.

At last, after the story had been told and retold,
with several embellishments, the crowd began to get
restive. Realizing they would lose their audience if they
didn't do something else entertaining, the warriors
began to prod the captive women from the canoes. The
women had been sitting, huddled into small, tight balls
so as to draw as little attention to themselves as possible.
Sarita could hear their moans and cries of fear as they
were pushed and herded onto the beach. Surprisingly,
no one approached her, so she continued to sit,
watching and waiting nervously.

The women were now standing on the beach,
clutching their children or each other in an effort to
calm themselves. The tight little group began to move
slowly up the beach to the longhouses, prodded by the
laughing warriors. The crowd was jubilant as they
watched the unhappy women struggling up the beach.
Some Ahousats were excitedly poking and mauling the
women, only to be pushed back by the warriors.
Fighting Wolf had given explicit orders that the captives
were to be taken straight to his longhouse and not to be
beaten or molested by the crowd.

The crowd, disappointed to be denied the fun of
killing a few worthless war captives, began to grow ugly.

Murmuring angrily, thwarted hungry eyes watched the tired warriors unload the bridal gifts and other booty brought back from the hapless Hesquiats.

From a nearby canoe, Rottenwood was pulled roughly to his feet and pushed over the side. He landed in the shallow water with a loud splash. This brought guffaws and merriment from the hostile bystanders. Dripping wet, he waded awkwardly out of the water. The laughter and tittering followed him. Realizing he had lost face anyway, he pretended to stumble, and was rewarded by more laughs. Legs wide apart, he stalked up the beach. The crowd chortled happily.

Wondering how far they wanted to see him go, he again stumbled, wincing in pretended agony. The crowd howled. Pretending great dignity, he marched forward, only to trip and land flat on his face, his arms stiff at his side. This last fall had the crowd doubling over in laughter, their previous anger forgotten. People hooted and hollered at him; he saw one woman with tears running down her cheeks she was laughing so hard.

Suddenly, to his astonishment, a few male slaves rushed forward to good-naturedly assist him further up the beach. They patted his back, cracked jokes and jovially welcomed him into their brotherhood.

Once away from the crowd, the slaves' mood turned serious. "You had a close call there, friend," one of them assured him grimly. "That crowd wanted blood."

"Well, they're not going to get *my* blood!" answered Rottenwood confidently.

"Oh?" answered his new acquaintance, amused. "You're fortunate you were able to think so quickly and give them someone to laugh at, instead of someone to torment. Perhaps you'll even be able to fool these oafs and survive as a clown or a comic."

Several of the other slaves leapt at this suggestion with enthusiasm and assured Rottenwood that it was a great idea.

"In fact," said another excitedly, "we still have a

trunk stuffed with costumes and theatrical props that
the last comic used!''

His first informant added casually, ''This village
recently lost their favorite clown.''

Rottenwood was silent a moment, digesting this
new fact. Finally he asked, ''What happened to him?''

''Oh,'' came the response, ''see that old man over
there, the one leaning on his cane?'' Rottenwood
glanced at the old man. ''The poor clown was killed for
telling a joke about that great, high-ranking old chief.''
Several nearby listeners stifled their snickers.

Rottenwood surveyed the decrepit figure more
carefully. The old man's skinny elbows and knees
protruded at angles from his tattered kutsack. He
looked suspiciously like a slave.

Rottenwood paused. ''No loss,'' he answered at
last, aware his new acquaintances were watching him
closely, ''as long as the joke was funny!'' A trifle weak,
he thought critically to himself but his audience
guffawed their delight.

Rottenwood laughed along with them. ''You didn't
fool me at all. I knew he was no chief,'' he assured his
new friends. There was another burst of laughter at his
patently false claim.

Sarita watched Rottenwood pick himself up off the
beach. She was amazed at his quick handling of the
situation. Well, she thought to herself, if he can do it, I
can do it. Not in the same way, of course. She sensed
that humor would not work as well a second time, but
she realized these people could be won over, if not to
like her, then at least to respect her.

A warrior tapped the pointed end of a paddle
against her spine. She stood up as gracefully as she
could in the wobbling canoe and stepped carefully out.
Standing on the beach, she wondered what to do next.
Unaware of the hauntingly beautiful picture she made,
head held high, she waited defiantly. Her clothes, still in
fairly good condition despite the overnight voyage, lent
a classical dignity to her regal posture.

Feeling Fighting Wolf's eyes upon her, she turned and looked directly at him. Their gazes locked for a moment. For a second time she felt his overwhelming presence. Mesmerized by his stare, she thought she saw fleeting admiration in those unfathomable dark eyes. Then it was gone, leaving only a calculating arrogance. His sensuous upper lip curled as he snarled at her to follow him.

Holding her head high, she swept after him, her body swaying gracefully. For a moment, the crowd was silent, watching the beautiful woman follow their war chief. Captive or no, there was no denying the majestic dignity evident in her every step.

As Sarita was halfway through the crowd, she began to hear a malevolent hissing that grew louder. The Ahousats must have guessed her high status from her mode of dress, realized a nervous Sarita. Crude shouts reached her ears as the crowd began to taunt her. Drawing her blanket tightly around herself, she maintained the same steady pace, her eyes focused on the massive, muscled back of Fighting Wolf. Seemingly oblivious to the crowd's hostility, she swept on, her bearing queenly.

Suddenly, children started throwing pebbles at her, followed by angry women casting bigger rocks. One small stone glanced off her cheek. A sharp pain stung her cheekbone and she jerked her head to the side.

Continuing bravely onward, she was suddenly surrounded by ranting, angry women and cursing men. Hurling insults at her, they began to tear at her clothes.

All at once, a deep bellow brought the angry mob to a halt. Fighting Wolf strode into their midst, scattering men and women into each other and disbanding the crowd single-handedly. Furious, he ordered them to their homes. Smarting under his words, the angry crowd slowly broke up and the villagers made their way sullenly back to their longhouses.

Sarita, already mortified by the angry words and malevolent outpourings of the crowd, was further humiliated by Fighting Wolf's defense. That it was he, her enemy, who had rescued her was almost more than she could bear. She resolved not to show him any gratitude as she marched proudly after him, head still high.

As they neared Fighting Wolf's longhouse, she chanced to see the shadowed form of Rottenwood, leaning against a tree. He had obviously been watching the confrontation. In a flash, so fast she thought she imagined it, he gestured sympathetically. Sarita was startled; she had expected no show of concern from him. Feeling a slight relief that she was suddenly not alone, she stiffened her spine and nodded infinitesimally in his direction. Then she followed the quickly disappearing Fighting Wolf to his longhouse.

Alone outside the longhouse door, she paused. The pressure on her bladder was tremendous. Looking quickly about, she stepped into a nearby bush. Moments later she returned and hurried into the longhouse. No one had noticed her absence.

Once in the darkened interior, Sarita waited until her eyes adjusted to the dim light. She noticed a neat, spacious apartment, lit up by a low-burning fire in the center. Along the walls were cedar plank beds covered in furs. Cedar mats carpeted the floor area. On the walls hung creamy cedar mats painted with black mythical animal figures. Designed to prevent cold drafts from chilling the occupants, the mats were very attractive as well.

Large woven baskets, decorated with designs Sarita had never seen before, were placed neatly in one corner, and obviously held many cooking implements. Several chests of cedar were piled up to section off smaller open rooms within the larger living area. Bundles of dried fish and pungent herbs hung from the rafters, as did many seal bladders full of oil. The floor, in those places where no cedar mats were spread, was clean, noted Sarita in surprise. It looked as if it had been swept with a large branch. Back home, her family tossed fish bones and garbage on the floor as a matter of course, as did all the other families she knew.

The whole living area had a homey atmosphere. Sarita was astonished to find it so. She had not associated a barbarian like Fighting Wolf with such neat, cozy living quarters. Then she remembered the wife she had seen hugging him, and admitted somewhat grudgingly that the woman did keep a neat home.

"I regret the insults you just endured," said Fighting Wolf apologetically. He smiled, baring gleaming white teeth.

"What do you care, Ahousat dog?" she spat, tossing her head. "It's your fault I'm here in the first place!" She absolutely refused to thank him for his defense of her in the face of that savage mob.

"True," he admitted casually. His voice held only amusement. He continued to stare at her, and she felt her face flush.

"What do you want, Ahousat worm?" she demanded.

He smiled slowly. "What would any man want of a beautiful woman?" His eyes roved over her body and Sarita stiffened at the fire that blazed momentarily in those jet eyes.

She snorted. "I will have nothing to do with the man who humiliated my father and brother and killed my people! I loathe you!" Fury raged in her golden eyes.

"Maybe so," he shrugged. "But, loathe me or not, you're still my slave to do with as I wish." The truth in his statement stung her. Before she could respond, he added casually, "So it was your father and brother I humiliated. You must be Sarita."

Her fury upon realizing he hadn't even known who she was knew no bounds. "You bastard!" she screamed and launched herself at him, nails curved into claws.

He caught her wrists in a tight grip and held her stiffly from him. Jet black eyes stared into golden cougar eyes. Inwardly he admired her courage, but said harshly, "Control yourself, woman! Here in my longhouse there are plenty of witnesses. The penalty for striking a chief is death!" He watched her warily.

She glared into his eyes. Her seething anger was a tangible thing. "Coward!" she hissed low. "Hiding behind your chieftainship. Are you afraid I, a woman, will kill you?" she taunted. How quickly she changed from physical to verbal attack. Still he held her from him.

Suddenly she realized he was touching her. "Let me go, Ahousat dog!" She began squirming and trying to release her arms from his sure grip.

"No," he said insolently and transferred both wrists to one hand. Then he pulled the struggling woman closer, his other hand splayed across her back. He marvelled at the outrage in those expressive golden eyes.

"Stop it! Let me go!"

"Not until I do this," and before she realized what he was about, she was pressed up against him, her head fell back and his lips descended.

"No!" she cried. But the sound was caught and muffled in her throat. Her useless struggles served only to arouse him, she realized. His hot mouth devoured her. Tossing her head from side to side, she tried to throw him off.

His only response was to release her wrists and bury his hand in her tangled hair. Easily, he held her head steady and continued his punishing kiss. His lips ground harder into hers until, frightened, she no longer tried to struggle.

What was happening to her? What was he doing? A surge of fear followed by a wave of lethargy swept over her and she leaned into his kiss. The next moment, she was startled at his response. His punishing mouth softened against hers and moved slowly across her lips. When his coaxing tongue suddenly demanded entrance to hers, she stiffened in fear. She pulled away.

"I've been wanting to do that since I first saw you." His reminder of their first meeting—at her "wedding feast"—brought Sarita back to reality.

"No! You're my enemy!"

He looked at her out of glazed eyes that quickly cleared. He pushed her away from him. She stumbled and barely caught herself from falling to the floor.

"Hesquiat bitch!" came the muffled curse. "You're my enemy, too!" How could he have forgotten so easily? How could he forget that her people had killed his own father? He stared at her coldly, recovering his self-control.

He was still staring when Precious Copper pushed back the skin flap on the door and stepped inside. She could feel the charged tension in the air.

"Well, Precious Copper, what do you think of my new 'wife'?" he sneered. "She's nothing but a slave. A worthless Hesquiat slave woman that I stole from her father. I've taken my revenge against the Hesquiat dogs that killed our father."

Sarita, stung by Fighting Wolf's scathing statement, barely noted the pretty young woman who had entered. Holding her head proudly, Sarita stared defiantly back at Fighting Wolf, then swung to face Precious Copper. She would not let these Ahousats intimidate her!

Precious Copper looked from her brother to Sarita and back again. "So I have heard, my brother. Our people are singing of your victorious raid on the Hesquiats even now." These two were brother and sister, realized Sarita. Then her attention was quickly caught by the deep chanting drifting through the village.

The singing reminded Fighting Wolf that he could not risk putting Sarita in the slave quarters—at least not while his people's hostility against her was so strong. Later, when the anger had died down, he would send her to live with the other slaves. If she went now she would surely be beaten, possibly killed.

His eyes ran over his latest possession. No, he had other plans for her. She was very beautiful, and he'd only had a brief taste of her in his arms. It might prove amusing to keep her near him for awhile . . .

"I've not decided what to do with her yet," he

drawled to Precious Copper, while his eyes moved insultingly up and down Sarita's lithe form before finally settling on her full breasts. They lingered there caressingly for a moment.

Sarita fought the impulse to cover her breasts with her hands. His black eyes flicked back to hers and she caught the mocking gleam in their dark depths. "Until I decide, she shall stay in my apartments."

Sarita could not suppress a startled grasp. Then she caught herself. This, then, was to be the start of her life as a slave. Well, she vowed, she would do her best to escape such a degrading lifestyle and she certainly would avoid this—this lecher! She shivered inside at the burning look he was giving her.

Pleased to see he had shocked Sarita, Fighting Wolf turned to Precious Copper and ordered, "I'm placing her in your charge. See that no one harms her when I'm away." Precious Copper nodded. In a more compassionate voice he added, "Feed her. She's hungry and thirsty and tired. We all are." With a final glance at Sarita, he turned on his heel and departed. The skin covering the doorway flapped in his wake.

Sarita warily faced Precious Copper, bracing herself for the confrontation she knew was to come. To her immense surprise, Precious Copper reached out a small hand and grasped Sarita's tightly. Sarita let herself be led over to the central eating area. Precious Copper gestured to Sarita to sit down, which she gratefully did.

The exhausted captive watched as her captor's sister prepared a small meal and then served it. In silence, Sarita hungrily bit into the dried fish. Never had food tasted so good, she thought. Thirstily, she gulped the water Precious Copper offered. While Sarita ate, Precious Copper busied herself withh household tasks. When Sarita was finished, Precious Copper gestured for her to rise.

Wearily, Sarita got to her feet and followed the smaller woman over to an alcove marked off from the rest of the house. Inside there was a cedar plank bed covered with sea otter furs. A cedar mat carpeted the floor. Walls were formed from piled cedar chests, reaching to the ceiling. The alcove was more private than the rest of the house, noted Sarita apprehensively. But at the moment, she was too tired to care.

"These are your quarters," said Precious Copper politely.

Sarita thanked her and walked over to the plank bed. Precious Copper silently left the alcove. Alone in the dark privacy of the small room, Sarita threw herself face down onto the bed and sobbed into the fur pelts.

Grief, anger, despair washed over her in waves as she lay there, crying pitifully. All was lost—her family shamed, herself a slave. And now she faced a terrifying future at the hands of the very man responsible for her tragedies! She sobbed and railed into the furs. Her angry and tormented cries were muffled by the thick pelts. At last, the great, heaving sobs lessened, and the streaming tears no longer poured forth. A weary calm drifted over her.

Once again aware of her surroundings, she could feel the soft sea otter fur against her face, inhale the faint animal smell still on the furs. A feeling of unutterable weariness overcome her as she lay there. Her whole life had been changed in such a short time. So much happened . . .

Much later, Sarita awoke to the delicious aroma of roasting meat. Feeling greatly refreshed, she stretched lazily, then scanned her surroundings. As her eyes settled on the unfamiliar objects in the small room, she at last remembered where she was. A rush of despair at her captivity swept over her momentarily. Resolutely, she pushed it aside. Rising slowly, she stretched languorously once more, then tiptoed over to the small opening, the only entrance to the alcove. She peeked out to see what was going on.

Precious Copper and two other women hovered about the central fire pit, busy cooking. One of the women poked a stick into the ashes of the fire, probably testing to see if the meat was done, thought Sarita. She guessed they were preparing the evening meal. If so, she'd slept the whole day away!

Gathering her courage, Sarita sauntered out of her hiding place and into the main room. Standing thoughtfully near the fire for a moment, she looked up to catch Precious Copper's gaze on her. Neither spoke.

Finally, Precious Copper's melodious voice broke the uncomfortable silence. "That's a beautiful dress you're wearing."

Sarita glanced down at her lovely kutsack, still in good condition, though a little wrinkled. She absently fingered a crease. "Thank you," she mumured at last. Then she said softly, "It—it was to be my wedding dress." She paused, swallowing the painful lump in her throat. "I—I thought I was to be married to Fighting Wolf."

Now the words were spilling out, tumbling over each other. "My father told me I was to marry Fighting Wolf. He and his men came to my village. My people welcomed them. My father entertained them. We feasted together. After the feast, everyone lay around relaxed and full of food."

Sarita brushed a shaking hand across her eyes. A bitter note crept into her voice. "It was then that Fighting Wolf's men sprang up. They fought with my people. They killed unarmed warriors. They wounded my father and brother. Fighting Wolf denounced my father, shaming him before all. Then," she paused, struggling visibly not to cry, "Fighting Wolf stole me and several other Hesquiat women away."

An awkward silence greeted the end of her sad tale. Sarita stood there, forlornly staring at the floor, her mind flooded with the scenes she'd just described. But she had not cried. She could not, would not, cry in front of these Ahousats. She glanced at Precious Copper, wondering if the woman even cared that her brother's treachery was exposed.

Sarita watched as Precious Copper's lips tightened.

What a fool she'd been to confide in Precious Copper! How the woman must be laughing at her! Sarita's pride rose and she straightened, looking Precious Copper directly in the eye.

At last Precious Copper spoke, her melodious voice giving no hint of inner turmoil. "Allow me to get you another cedar robe to wear. We can put your beautiful dress away in a safe place."

Twice over a fool! Sarita cursed to herself. Very well, if Precious Copper was going to ignore the treachery that had brought Sarita to this longhouse, Sarita would go along with it. She couldn't prod a conscience that didn't exist.

Seeing what she thought was an obstinate look cross Sarita's face, Precious Copper hastened to explain. "I make the suggestion to put away your dress only because, should you continue to wear such a beautiful garment, I fear some jealous woman will tear it off your back for her own use."

Sarita glanced down at her dress again. Precious Copper's veiled reference to Sarita's new status sparked a sharp retort. "It's what I'd expect of thieving Ahousats!" she spat.

She heard the quick intake of breath from one of the women attendants. Precious Copper stared at Sarita, then motioned to the women to leave. Once they had left, Precious Copper sat down on a nearby mat, indicating that Sarita do the same. Defiantly Sarita continued to stand. Precious Copper shrugged.

"When I first heard that my brother was to take a wife," began Precious Copper, "I was very pleased. His first wife and child died in childbirth three years ago. He's been alone for far too long."

"No wife?" echoed Sarita. "Then who—?" She stopped, embarrassed. That meant the sloe-eyed woman she'd seen hugging him in the canoe was not his wife. Sarita couldn't explain the sudden lift in spirits she felt at this news. "Excuse me," she muttered stiffly. "Please continue."

Precious Copper nodded genially, and went on.
"When I heard he was to marry a Hesquiat woman, I
was surprised." Seeing Sarita tense defensively, she
added, "But still pleased. I thought at last there'd be an
end to the fighting between my people and the
Hesquiats. I hated seeing my people at war. I hated
seeing widows and orphans weeping when a husband or
father failed to return from a raid. I wanted peace."

She paused and Sarita looked at Precious Copper
with new eyes. There was no mistaking the sincerity in
the melodious voice. "So, as I said, I was pleased. I
thought the warring would stop when my brother
married into the Hesquiats. Now," and here Sarita
could hear the heavy disappointment, "I see you and
hear you tell me about Fighting Wolf's raid on your
people, and I realize I was wrong to hope. He never
intended to marry you; I see now that he only intended
to avenge the death of our father." Sarita saw the sheen
of tears in the smaller woman's velvet brown eyes. "I'm
terribly sorry for what he's done to you and your
family. I deeply regret that my brother has brought you
such pain."

Sarita stared openmouthed at Precious Copper
after hearing this quiet declaration. She sank slowly to
her haunches on a nearby mat, her thoughts churning.
This woman did not hate her, nor was she proud of
what her brother had done!

Finally Sarita could trust herself to speak. "I'm
amazed that you feel this way," she answered Precious
Copper. "Amazed and pleased." Her quick mind was
whirling. "Knowing you feel this way, can I look to you
for help during my stay here?"

There was a long pause. "I'll do what I can to keep
you from being overworked," replied Precious Copper
cautiously. "But please understand that my brother is
war chief here. I cannot and will not go against him. I
don't know how long my brother intends to keep you
with him, but I'll do what I can to make your lot with
him easier."

Sarita also quickly realized that while she might expect help from Precious Copper during her stay in Ahousat village, she could not depend on any help in planning her escape.

Sarita smiled and nodded her head to Precious Copper, indicating her understanding of Precious Copper's position. Grateful to have an ally in the village, Sarita quickly decided it was advantageous to get along peaceably with Precious Copper for the present.

"Now that I understand that you don't wish to hurt me," Sarita said, "I'll take your advice about changing my dress. I would like to keep it, if possible, as it is so beautiful."

Precious Copper nodded. She left and soon returned with a plain, undecorated, dull-brown cedar robe. Handing the robe to Sarita, Precious Copper looked up into her eyes and smiled shyly. Why she's beautiful, thought Sarita, watching the dimpled smile light up Precious Copper's gamine face.

In the alcove, Sarita swiftly changed into the plain cedar robe and reluctantly folded her wedding dress. She rubbed her cheek on the soft material and wondered sadly if she'd ever wear the dress again. She knew that, for practical reasons, a slave had to wear plain, serviceable clothing. Still, she wished the unadorned, roughly woven cedar robe did not have to be quite so plain—and scratchy!

At least it would not draw unwanted attention to her appearance, thought Sarita ruefully. In this she was mistaken. Even the homely garment could not hide her beauty. She attempted a severe hairstyle, long brown hair, pulled back tightly and tied with a leather thong, was left to hang loosely down her back. But such a style only showed her beautifully molded face to even better advantage. The robe was short and hung only to her knees, exposing shapely calves and graceful feet. Short sleeves left her slim forearms bare. She was pleased that Precious Copper had supplied an ornament: a carved wooden bracelet, polished until the rich, brown wood gleamed. Slipping the bracelet over her wrist, Sarita stepped back into the main room to help Precious Copper with dinner preparations.

As she worked, she casually glanced about, looking for Fighting Wolf. She saw no sign of him. She didn't know whether to be relieved or disappointed. One of the women mentioned the victory party being held down on the beach. A large bonfire was blazing and some of the village women were cooking food for the celebration. Hearing chanting from outside the longhouse, Sarita concluded that Fighting Wolf was probably one of the celebrants. Well, at least she wouldn't be bothered by his presence for awhile, she thought in relief.

On the beach, the victory party was underway. A large bonfire of driftwood logs had been built and bright flames leaped high into the air. The roaring blaze was too hot to stand close to. Delicacies—clams, mussels, sweet berries—to tempt the most discerning palates were set out. Small boys darted about, first listening to boastful tales of the recent battle, then running off to play war with each other. Little girls dashed screaming for their mothers, the boys hard on their heels. Exuberant warriors related brave exploits to each other, the tales growing more fantastical with each telling.

The evening sun was dipping into the sea, sending the day's last golden rays over the earth. Fighting Wolf lounged casually near a large rock, facing the hot fire. He was listening to Birdwhistle finish a boastful, rambling account of how he'd sneaked up on a particularly vicious Hesquiat and stabbed him in the back. After a short silence, Birdwhistle turned to Fighting Wolf and asked casually, "What are you going to do with your female slave?"

"Which one?"

" 'Which one?' " mocked Birdwhistle. "Come now, cousin . . . The tall one. The one that wore a blue trading blanket cloak. The one that rode in your canoe. Remember?''

"Oh.'' Fighting Wolf shrugged indifferently. "You mean Sarita.''

"Hmm, so that's Sarita. I guessed it might be.'' After a pause Birdwhistle asked, "Well?''

"Well what?''

"Are you going to give her to me like you promised?''

"Cousin,'' chortled Fighting Wolf, "you have a very faulty memory.'' He paused, "I offered her to you, it's true . . . as a 'token of my esteem.' But,'' he sighed exaggeratedly, "you rejected my generous offer.'' He eyed Birdwhistle sardonically. "It's not my fault you said 'no' to a perfectly good gift.''

"But that was before I saw how beautiful she was,'' snapped Birdwhistle. After a stealthy glance at Fighting Wolf, he offered, "What about a trade?''

"Such as?'' answered Fighting Wolf, appearing interested.

"Well, such as that new freight-canoe I recently had built. I saw you admiring it the other day. I had the best craftsmen possible working on that canoe!'' boasted Birdwhistle.

"I know,'' came Fighting Wolf's dry reply. "You borrowed them from me.''

"True, true,'' responded Birdwhistle, undaunted. "Then you know it's well-made.'' He paused, watching Fighting Wolf carefully. "How abut a trade—my canoe for your slave? Straight across.''

Fighting Wolf seemed to ponder his cousin's words. "You'll never get a better offer,'' argued Birdwhistle. "You'd better trade her while she still looks good. It won't be long before she's as beaten and cowed as the rest of the female slaves. Then you won't get even a one-seater dugout for her.'' Birdwhistle spat on the ground, showing his contempt for such a poor bargain.

An image of Sarita, bruised and cringing, flashed

through Fighting Wolf's mind. He felt sickened at the thought.

"That canoe's new. Made from the best cedar tree I could find," added Birdwhistle convincingly.

Suddenly Fighting Wolf was tired of toying with his cousin. "Keep your canoe," he stated. "No trade."

"Wh-what?" Birdwhistle's look of disappointment almost made Fighting Wolf laugh.

"You heard me. No trade." With that, the war chief grinned disdainfully and turned on his heel. Watching him stride away, Birdwhistle's jaw clenched and unclenched in anger.

"Master! Master!" A slave came rushing up. "Your wife wants—"

"Shut up!" snarled Birdwhistle as he viciously backhanded the unsuspecting slave across the mouth. The man staggered from the blow, then caught his balance. He touched his hand to his injured face. Bright red blood dripped through his brown fingers. "Get out of here, you useless offal!" shouted Birdwhistle. The slave fled, glad to get away from his master's cruel temper.

Fighting Wolf strolled in the direction of his longhouse. The villagers stepped deferentially out of his way as he passed through the crowd.

He brooded on what had just passed between himself and Birdwhistle. His cousin was a fool to think that Fighting Wolf would part with such a beautiful slave woman so easily. Trade, indeed! Fighting Wolf snorted. No, he was not ready to trade her. Yet. Perhaps later, when he'd grown tired of her. For now, he found her . . . attractive. No, not merely attractive, he admitted. Devastatingly beautiful. He wanted her for himself. His heart swelled as he remembered how lovely she'd looked dressed in her wedding finery. She'd made a beautiful bride, indeed. Now she was no bride, would never be, he thought sardonically, but she was still beautiful. And she was his.

He quickened his pace, anxious to see how his new slave was doing under Precious Copper's tutelage.

6

Fighting Wolf was winding his way slowly through the crowd of people gathered around the bonfire, when his uncle approached him. Scarred Mouth, elder brother to Fighting Wolf's deceased father, was head chief of the Ahousats.

Scarred Mouth had been anxious about the Hesquiat raid. During the council when Fighting Wolf had introduced his plan for attacking the Hesquiats at a wedding feast, Scarred Mouth had spoken against the motion. He argued that his younger brother's death should go unavenged because the Ahousat people were weary of fighting. He asked the warriors at the council to reconsider. While the death of Fighting Wolf's father was indeed a great loss to the tribe, the loss of more Ahousat warriors killed in the revenge raid would be much worse, stated Scarred Mouth. Why not make a genuine offer of peace to the Hesquiats? Then the Ahousats would no longer have to defend themselves on that front.

At the council meeting, Fighting Wolf had respectfully pointed out to his esteemed uncle that few Ahousat warriors would be killed as the Hesquiats were not expecting treachery. Also, if a war chief's death was left unavenged, the Hesquiats would think they could kill an Ahousat whenever they wanted. Surely the venerable leader of the Ahousats did not want to have his people called cowards? To be the prey of any aggressive tribe on the coast? No, Fighting Wolf thought not. And so, hearing the young men's cries for vengeance, Scarred Mouth had reluctantly acceded to his bloodthirsty nephew's plans.

Fighting Wolf watched with eyes narrowed as Scarred Mouth approached, for this uncle never did anything without good reason. After all, his position as chief of the large tribe of Ahousats rested solely on his astute political maneuverings, and Fighting Wolf had reason to suspect that he was about to see more of his uncle's widely touted political abilities in action. Scarred Mouth, however, merely greeted Fighting Wolf with a bland smile.

"Nephew, I'm glad the raid on the Hesquiats went so well!" he said heartily. "Truly, you pulled off a successful attack and brought home many prizes. I saw a number of captive women and children—even a husky male slave!" He paused for a moment. "Did you have any real trouble with those Hesquiat dogs?"

"No, Uncle, I did not. Everything went according to plan. They were caught completely unawares," answered Fighting Wolf, not willing to tell his uncle any more than the man asked.

"Ahh, good, good," grunted his uncle. His nephew could be exasperatingly closemouthed at times. "And what of old Thunder Maker? Is he still among the living? Heh, heh."

"Why as a matter of fact, he is," answered the nephew smoothly. "Last time I saw him, he was humiliated, but definitely still alive." What was the old uncle up to now?

"Hmmm," responded his uncle. "It might have gone better for us if Thunder Maker was dead." Drat the nephew! Why hadn't he killed the Hesquiat leader when he had had the chance? Now Thunder Maker would lead a revenge raid and the fighting would begin all over again. Scarred Mouth sighed heavily.

"Dead? I don't think so, uncle," responded Fighting Wolf carelessly. "I wanted Thunder Maker's humiliation more than his death and I succeeded in that.

The woman you saw step out of my canoe this morning is his daughter. Now warriors up and down the coast will spit on Thunder Maker's name. They will say he can't even protect his own family!''

Scarred Mouth looked with interest at his nephew. "That woman is Thunder Maker's daughter? Huh! I didn't think the old man had it in him!'' he muttered almost to himself. "His daughter, you say,'' he marvelled anew. Well, his bloodthirsty nephew certainly seemed to have a good eye for women, he conceded.

Aloud Scarred Mouth said, "Well, well. Perhaps there is something in what you say, after all. You know, for a fine nephew like you, I could spread the word among some of my good friends—chiefs every one of them—up and down the coast that Thunder Maker cringed and tried to run away when you attacked him. No one thinks much of a coward!'' He gazed assessingly at his nephew.

Fighting Wolf's eyes narrowed. Here it comes, he thought. He remained silent, however, watching his uncle intently.

"Of course, in return, I'd expect a little gift,'' continued Scarred Mouth. "That useless Hesquiat woman you just mentioned, Thunder Maker's daughter, would be suitable, I suppose.'' He tried to gauge the effect of his words on the younger man. Fighting Wolf, however, was not easily read. "Surely she will not be of much use to you,'' Scarred Mouth added disparagingly. "She's far too thin to be a strong worker. And,'' he went on grandly, "my friends would be very impressed to hear how brave you were, how well you fought. They would flock to your potlatches . . .'' He was watching Fighting Wolf closely now.

The younger man was silent, pretending to consider his uncle's offer of influence. At last he drawled, "Many thanks, uncle, but I think I'll keep her for myself. Despite what you say, she looks to me like she'd be, uh, a strong worker. As to her thinness, at least she won't eat much, will she?'' Fighting Wolf had to grin at his own words. Everyone knew his uncle was tightfisted, and this would just exacerbate the old man's greed.

"Hmmph. well, it's up to you, boy. It's up to you. Just let me know anytime you want the word to get around, though. I do have a lot of friends," he added importantly, hoping this smug nephew would change his mind. Seeing that Fighting Wolf remained steadfast, Scarred Mouth decided to retreat. Hastily making his excuses, he was soon lost in the crowd.

Fighting Wolf turned to watch him go. In just one day, he marvelled, he'd been offered a new canoe and political influence in trade for a supposedly "useless" female slave! He chuckled to himself. Birdwhistle and Scarred Mouth must think him a blind fool not to see through their offers! All they wanted was a beautiful woman to warm their beds.

He continued chuckling as he walked in the direction of his longhouse, shrugging off a slight irritation that the woman they wanted he considered his.

At the longhouse, he entered silently through the door, leaving the skin cover to flap back and forth and announce his return. His apartment looked very welcoming.

Several clamshell lamps threw their soft light gently around the room. These lamps, large white clamshell halves filled with dogfish oil, had twisted cedar bark wicks in their centers. They were lit in every house as soon as dark descended, which at this time of year, summer, was well into the evening.

A cozy scene greeted his eyes. Precious Copper and several of her attendant women sat around the small fire crackling in the center of the room, the jumping flames casting a warm glow on all within. The women were chatting and gossiping quietly as they wove cedar strips into matting and clothing. Seeing Fighting Wolf enter, one of the women murmured in a low voice to her companions. The other women giggled, peeking at the war chief shyly.

Fighting Wolf's eyes narrowed as he searched for

Sarita among the women. She was not there. Unwilling
to ask her whereabouts of Precious Copper in front of
her curious friends, he strode over to his sleeping area
and lay down, thinking to get up and find Sarita shortly
after the nosy women left.

He awoke much later in the night when all was
silent about him. Small red coals glowed in the fire pit;
the clamshell lamps had burned out. The women had
retired to their respective beds, as had Precious Copper.
The large room was dark and only the occasional cough
from one of the families sleeping far down the house
filtered through to his alert ears.

Shoving the sea otter fur bedcovers to one side,
Fighting Wolf rose quickly. One thought dominated
him: to find Sarita. Picking up a clamshell lamp, he
glanced quickly around the large room until his eye
caught the small alcove in the far corner. Guessing she
was there, he padded over and looked inside. Indeed,
there lay Sarita, asleep on the wooden plank bed. Sea
otter skins covered her and the trade blanket cloak was
drawn tightly up to her chin. He lifted the lamp and
gazed down at her. Her face in repose looked so young,
a momentary twinge of pity washed over him at the
predicament he had placed her in. His harsh face
softened as he surveyed her sleeping form.

Placing the lamp carefully on the floor, he kneeled
down beside her, still studying the sleeping woman, but
now reverently. Reaching out one large hand, he
captured a wayward curl that fell across her jaw. He
brought the silky softness to his lips and held it there a
moment, then brushed it gently back from her face. He
reached out one strong arm and placed it carefully
across, but not touching, her body. He wanted so much
to hold her, but knew should she awake she'd cry out.
She continued to lie there, breathing rythmically in
sleep.

Bending quietly over her, he inhaled the warm
woman smell of her, perfumed with some floral scent.
Breathing deeply he touched his lips against her cheek

first, a touch as soft as swamsdown. Then he brushed his lips against hers ever so lightly. Her lips felt smooth and warm and he found himself lost in her gentle softness. Seeing that she continued to breathe evenly, he caressed another stray lock of hair gently back from her cheek before he slowly stood to his full height. He towered over the unknowing woman, reluctant now in this new mood of tenderness to wake her. Still savoring the last kiss, he turned away quietly and stole back to his bed.

In the dark alcove, beautiful golden eyes stared out into the darkness, a new knowledge dawning. It was a long time before sleep gently claimed them once again.

The high-pitched tweeting of robins awoke Fighting Wolf from his sleep. Yawning and stretching several times, he was finally fully awake. He cursed aloud as he remembered a gentle kiss, a soft caress in the dark of the night. In the bright light of day it seemed but a dream.

He knew now he had to have Sarita, to possess her fully in the one way a man can truly possess a woman. One kiss would not suffice. He would not rest until his body had tasted hers. Today, he thought in satisfaction, he would find out more about this desirable woman. Soon he would know all there was to know about Sarita, he chuckled to himself.

Fate, however, had other plans. When he was only halfway through a breakfast of smoked clams, word was brought that several war canoes had been sighted skulking around Ahousat waters. It appeared the Ucluelets, a belligerent tribe to the south, were scouting out new fishing grounds and encroaching on Ahousat domain.

Precious Copper hastily packed dried fish and water-filled seal bladders for Fighting Wolf to take with him as he quickly dispatched the remainder of his meal. While he ate, his men hustled to arm themselves and prepare the war canoes.

"Those Ucluelets have infringed on Ahousat territory far too often lately. This time we'll show them a good fight!'' exlaimed Fighting Wolf.

"Do be careful,'' cautioned Precious Copper.

Adrenaline pumping, Fighting Wolf raced for the door. Over his shoulder he called, "I'll be gone for as long as it takes to drive those cowardly Ucluelets back to their pitiful village!''

Sarita awoke late in the morning. She felt greatly refreshed and stretched languorously. Rising from the bed, she cast the sea otter blankets to one side, but still clutched her trade blanket close to her chest. She shivered slightly in the cool morning air.

Suddenly thoughts of Fighting Wolf's late night visit flooded over her. Holding her hands to her face, she felt her cheeks flush at the memory of his lips on hers. A tingle shivered up and down her spine as she remembered his gentle caresses. Then she got a grip on herself. The man was a barbarian! He had viciously tricked her father and stolen her away. She would not indulge in daydreams over him, not at all! Still, her step was light and she went about humming cheerfully to herself all morning.

Precious Copper was impressed with the new captive's good spirits. She had feared the girl would be moping about at first. Seeing Sarita in a cheerful humor caused Precious Copper to respond in like manner and the two young women got on very well that day. Precious Copper hoped it was a sign that the captive would adjust well to her new fate.

Sarita's good mood gradually wore off through the morning and by mid-afternoon she was beginning to feel apprehensive as to what the future held. She was finally able to shrug off her fears, however, resolving that she had only to cope with the Ahousats until she could make her escape. Equanimity restored, she concentrated on helping Precious Copper do the household chores. She found Precious Copper treating her rather as an equal, more like a visiting kinswoman of equal rank than as a slave, and admired the small woman's quiet tact. Sarita was not sure she would treat a captive as well, even under the odd circumstances of being almost a sister-in-law.

It was late afternoon when Sarita chanced to over-hear a discussion between one of Precious Copper's middle-aged attendants, Oyster Woman, and a lantern-jawed young woman, an attendant whose name Sarita did not know yet.

Sarita was careful not to appear to be eaves-dropping. "Are you expecting your husband back soon?" asked the lantern-jawed young woman.

The older woman shrugged. "Who knows?" she answered philosophically. "You know how long these expeditions can take. My husband's a warrior. He just does what they tell him. They left this morning and will probably chase those Ucluelets for several days at least. Seems they're always running off to fight someone," she grumbled. "And my old husband has a bad shoulder—"

"Yes, that is too bad," commiserated the younger woman. "I think, though, that Fighting Wolf wants to hurry home with his men as soon as he can." Here Sarita was startled to note the younger woman glance slyly in her direction. Feeling her face grow hot, Sarita turned away and pretended to be very busy with her weaving.

So Fighting Wolf would be away for a while, she thought with relief and just a small stab of regret which she hastily ignored. Good. That gave her some time to make her plans.

Her chance to plan her escape came the very next afternoon. Precious Copper asked Sarita to take two small cousins down to the beach to hunt for rock crabs. The two, a girl and a boy of about seven and ten summers respectively, were lively children. The girl was very active, running and jumping and teasing the boy who tried his best to ignore her antics with as much dignity as he could muster. He treated Sarita with casual disdain at first, trying to be manly, but soon forgot

himself under the continual assaults of the taunting girl.
Finally he lost control and aimed a punch at his younger
cousin. Sarita stepped between the two, and the child's
blows glanced off her forearms. She winced in pain, but
quickly recovered.

"Young men who are going to be chiefs someday
do not hit girls," she said sternly.

"How would you know?" retorted the boy, somewhat taken aback at her interference. "You're nothing
but a slave!" he exclaimed, repeating gossip he had
heard in the longhouse.

Sarita took a deep breath and expelled it slowly. "I
know," she said as calmly as she could, "because I am
the daughter of a chief. My father taught my brother,
who will be chief after him, not to hit girls and women
but to respect them. That's the way a wise chief
behaves," she stated firmly.

The boy, embarrassed, looked down at his feet as
he kicked the sand. "She started it!" he cried. Seeing
that Sarita remained unimpressed with this age-old
argument, he tried again, "Well, she did!"

Keeping her face serious, Sarita admonished,
"Nevertheless, as a future chief, you must learn to
ignore the picky little things people will do to you and
concentrate your attention on correcting the important
things. A chief would not let a small girl's teasing bother
him. He certainly would not hit her. He would speak
calmly to her and tell her to go away and play somewhere else."

The little girl, meanwhile, was hopping about and
sticking her tongue out at her cousin when she thought
Sarita wasn't looking. Sarita, however, had words for
her, too. "Duck Feather," she said to the girl, "a noble
girl does not behave so rudely. Is this what your mother
has taught you? She will be shamed by such a daughter
if you continue to tease your cousin and then laugh
when he gets into trouble. A true noblewoman likes to
play, of course, but not to hurt others by her actions."

Sarita thought perhaps she was being heavy-handed, but she would not let these children run roughshod over her. Besides, she remembered many lectures from her childhood and knew this was how high-ranking parents disciplined their children.

Somewhat subdued, the children made their way to the beach, following peacefully at Sarita's side. Seeing their friends hunting for crabs down near the waterline, they asked for, and received, her permission to run over and play there. Sarita sat down on a log nearby, content to watch them and contemplate her future.

There Rottenwood found her, on his way to repair a nearby canoe that lay a short distance away from where Sarita was sitting.

Bending over ostensibly to locate the small hole in the boat, he nodded politely to Sarita. She recognized him as the captured slave from her home village.

Seeing her return his nod, he quietly asked her, "Are they treating you well, mistress?"

"Yes," she sighed. "I'm very fortunate. Precious Copper, sister of the war chief that abducted me, has taken me under her protection and I'm living in her quarters. What about you?"

"No complaints," he shrugged. "I live in the slave quarters of that longhouse over there." He pointed to one of the houses. "I get enough to eat, they don't work me too hard—" He let the sentence trail off.

"Don't you get tired of being a slave?" Sarita asked. "I don't mean to pry, but I certainly don't like being at another's beck and call."

"Hah," he snorted scornfully, "you've only been a slave for a few days. Wait. It gets worse. Some nights you lie awake cursing your fate and you know you'd give the rest of your life to taste just one day of freedom!" he said bitterly.

"Oh?" said Sarita cautiously. "Do you wish for your freedom?" Seeing a frown cross his face at her careless words, she said hastily, "Of course you do, how silly of me." She added dejectedly, "I, too, long for my freedom."

Rottenwood's eyes narrowed, but he said nothing.

Realizing that the next move was up to her, Sarita began tentatively, "Do you think it's possible to escape from here?"

Looking around cautiously to make sure no one was watching or listening to them, Rottenwood answered slowly, "Might be." He paused for effect. "It depends—"

"Depends on what?" she asked eagerly.

"It depends on how desperately you want to get away. Slaves are killed for escaping, if they're recaptured, you know."

"Better to die in the attempt, than live as a slave," she responded bitterly.

He had to admire her courage. Maybe, just maybe, he could use her in an escape attempt. Realizing that someone might come along at any moment, he said quickly, "Are you serious about escaping?"

She looked him straight in the eye. "Very serious," she answered firmly.

"Then maybe we can help each other. I too, want to escape this place. If we work together, we are more likely to succeed."

"What can I do to help?" she asked eagerly. "I just want to get away from here and back to my people as soon as possible."

"It may take some time," he replied. "I have to get hold of a seaworthy canoe first. We'll need provisions, food, paddles, rain gear if it's rainy season, things like that."

"I can help with saving and storing food," she answered hopefully. "I can easily get dried fish and smoked meats, too. I'm also a good paddler," she added for effect, hoping to convince him that she would indeed be useful. "Not only that," she said cagily, "but I will listen in on conversations and find out when the warriors will be away from the village."

He looked at her for a moment, then a slow smile spread across his face, giving him a boyish look. "You may do after all,'' he teased.

"Of course I'll do,'' she said scathingly. "You just get the canoe!''

He chuckled, then became serious. "And what's in it for me? Why should I help you escape? You need my navigation, my paddling ability, my canoe, more than I need your help.'' He watched her closely.

She flushed, wondering what he was getting at. She remained silent.

Seeing that he could not prod an answer from her, he said carefully, "Don't you wonder why I, a slave, should want to go back to your village, to certain slavery there?''

Now that he mentioned it, it did seem odd, she thought. What was he getting at? Then she remembered Spring Fern had mentioned this man. "Spring Fern,'' she guessed shrewdly. "You want to go back because of Spring Fern.''

A flash of annoyance crossed his face for a moment, but he did not deny her answer. He pressed on, "Should our escape prove successful—and it will if you follow my instructions completely—I would ask for a certain reward upon returning to Hesquiat village.''

"What is that?'' she asked smugly, knowing he would ask for Spring Fern.

"My freedom,'' he answered curtly, watching her face.

Astonished, Sarita merely stared for a moment. She had misjudged the man. Then she answered slowly, "If we get to my village successfully, I give you my word as the daughter of Thunder Maker, chief of the Hesquiats, that you will have your freedom. I promise you this on my honor and my life.''

Realizing there was little he could do if she chose to go back on her word, he nodded. "Very well,'' he answered, "let's meet again.'' He pointed to a landmark and asked, "See that big rock further down the beach?'' At her nod he continued, "When the moon is full, and is rising over that large tree,'' pointing again, "come to the rock and we'll discuss our plans further. For now, it is enough that you hide away food and listen for any news."

Sarita did not like him ordering her about, but decided to say nothing. She needed his help too much. Seeing her quiet nod again, he stood up, "I'll leave now. It's best if we're not seen together. People will get suspicious."

Agreeing with the wisdom of his remark, Sarita answered quietly, "Yes. And thank you for your help, Rottenwood. If we get out of this alive, I will abide by my promise to you."

He smiled briefly and went off, wondering if she truly would keep her promise.

7

The days passed quickly. Sarita helped Precious Copper
with household tasks. It was fortunate, though perhaps
she had not quite appreciated it at the time, thought
Sarita ruefully, that Crab Woman had insisted that
Sarita learn to do all household tasks. Many noblewomen did not know how to do housekeeping chores,
always depending on their slaves. Had that been the case
for Sarita, she would have had a very difficult
adjustment to her new status as the household tasks she
was expected to do were not light work.

In addition to working in the longhouse, she was
expected to go into the forest with the other slave and
commoner women. There they would dig up roots and
bulbs for the evening meal. There were fern roots to be
dug, the odoriferous skunk cabbage root and clover
roots. People considered all these roots delicious.

Sometimes they also dug up the long spindly spruce
roots to be used not for food, but for weaving.

Occasionally, a few men would accompany the
women into the forest and carry back long strips of
yellow cedar bark that the women peeled off the tall
trees. Later, these strips of bark would have to be
carried down to the beach or to a quiet cove and
weighted down with large stones. The bark would soak
in the salt water for several days before being dried and
separated into feathery strands for weaving. Sarita was
involved in every stage of this textile production, from
gathering the bark to weaving it.

Then there were berries to gather. Several varieties ripened through the long summer; the juicy orange salmonberries, the red seedy thimbleberries, the plump pink huckleberries and blueberries, and the delicious blackberries. Tasty berries were the only sweets in the Nootka diet.

The only berries kept year-round were black salal berries. To preserve this favorite, salal berries were parboiled in wooden boxes, then poured into other long wooden frames. These were dried over a fire and finally sun-dried. The berry cakes were then stored away for winter.

Firewood had to be collected. The pieces of driftwood found on the beach made the best firewood.

Slaves were also expected to catch salmon and preserve them for the long winter ahead. One method was to dry them. Long strips of salmon were hung over the drying racks overnight, then smoked thoroughly before being piled into bales for storage.

Halibut and cod were sun-dried. On sunny, windy days the fish was filleted and hung on racks to dry.

Every night Sarita fell into bed exhausted. She had never worked so hard in her life! She was familiar with what had to be done from her training at home, but there she had mostly directed others in what to do; she hadn't actually to do it all herself.

By the fifth day, her blistered hands were forming calluses. Every muscle in her body ached. Her legs hurt from tramping up and down forest slopes. Her back seemed to be made of cedar wood, it was so stiff. But that evening she sat in front of the fire and started a piece of weaving before tottering wearily off to bed.

Whenever thoughts of Fighting Wolf crossed her mind, she shoved them mercilessly away. At first she was just too busy concentrating on all she was expected to do to think of him. But now that she was catching on to the intensive routine, she was able to daydream a little, and she found herself thinking of him more and more.

She wondered what he was doing, if he thought of her at all. Memories of his kiss still sent shivers down her spine but it all seemed so long ago. Try as she might, she had not been able to forget the touch of his lips to hers, and the memory tugged at her heart constantly.

Did I affect him so? she wondered. What shall I do when next I see him? She knew what she should do. She should run in the other direction but she was becoming too curious about him and the new feelings he had awakened in her.

She remembered his rugged face; he was really one of the most handsome men she had ever seen, and his eyes . . . ! It's too bad we hadn't really been married, she thought idly, then caught herself with a start. What was she thinking of? The man was her enemy! He had ruthlessly attacked her father and brother and herself. Feeling safer with this train of thought she shrugged off the softer feelings his memory evoked.

Her plans for escape had not proceeded very well. After her talk with Rottenwood, she had kept her ears open for news of the warriors' return, but no one seemed to know when to expect them back.

Dried food had not been that easy to secure as yet, either. Precious Copper kept a close eye on her charge, more for Sarita's safety than anything else, but still it did prevent Sarita from secreting away any dried food for the escape attempt.

She hoped Rottenwood was having better luck, but she had not been able to contact him. The moon would be full in four more nights and she would meet him then as planned. She would find out more then.

At last, the warriors returned home. On the way back from a berry-gathering expedition with some of the other women, Sarita glanced down the beach and recognized the war canoes. She had no trouble picking out the distinctive markings on Fighting Wolf's canoe. Her heart sank with dread.

She made her way slowly into the longhouse, a basket of huckleberries draped over her arm. Thinking

quickly, she decided her best strategy was to keep out of
sight. Maybe, just maybe, he would have forgotten
about her. You don't really want him to, do you? asked
a small voice in her mind. She chuckled apprehensively
to herself.

Quickly piling her berries with those of the other
women, she hurriedly made her way out the door of the
longhouse.

She headed towards a narrow trail that ran in back
of the longhouse. Normally, a slave would not be
allowed to go off by herself like this, but Sarita knew
that everyone was too busy welcoming the homecoming
warriors to watch where one insignificant slave went to.

She had followed this trail before and knew it
eventually led to a grassy knoll overlooking the village.
She needed time alone anyway. Time to sit and relax
with no one's eagle eye upon her and no one finding
more work for her to do.

She reached the knoll and knelt down on a patch of
the soft green moss that grew scattered amongst the
brown grass. A large rock partially hid her from the
village.

She peeked down at the village. Her perch
reminded her of another day, far in the past, when she
had been picking blueberries and had looked down on
her own village. Then, she had been the carefree
daughter of Chief Thunder Maker. She sighed. Now she
was living among strangers and doomed to a life of toil
and drudgery and, she shuddered, possible concu-
binage.

True, some of the women she worked with had
shown her kindness, especially Precious Copper.
Fighting Wolf's sister also took great pains to keep the
men away from Sarita. Several men, assuming they
could treat Sarita like any other female slave and force
themselves upon her, had approached her. They had
been chased off by the small whirlwind of fury that had
descended on their unsuspecting heads. Precious
Copper defended Sarita like an enraged mother bear

defended her threatened cub. Word quickly spread that
Sarita was protected by the diminutive girl, but no one
wanted to challenge Fighting Wolf's sister as they knew
they would have to answer to the formidable war chief
himself.

But who would protect her from Fighting Wolf?
mused Sarita. Precious Copper had already said she
would not go against her brother.

As Sarita watched the men disembark from their
canoes, she pondered what to do. She watched the tiny
figures walking up to the longhouses, but she was
unable to discern Fighting Wolf's tall form from this
distance. She saw wives and sweethearts greet their
returning men enthusiastically. Little children ran to
their fathers and hugged them tightly, laughing
excitedly.

Up on the hill, the warm afternoon sun felt good on
her face, and she felt herself relax. The quiet hum of
insects drifted lazily through the air. The fresh scent of
pine was fragrant in her nostrils. It felt so good to just
sit here quietly in the sun. She closed her eyes for just a
moment.

Sarita woke up to a sudden stillness all around her.
The sun was still fairly high in the sky, but some time
had passed. Realizing she had fallen asleep, she quickly
got to her feet. They would be looking for her down in
the village if she did not get back there soon.

She raced down the narrow path, her long hair
streaming behind her. The air felt good rushing against
her skin and the short run revived her senses. As she
neared the village she slowed to a sedate walk on the
tree-covered trail. She was sauntering around the last
bend when she suddenly froze in her tracks.

8

Striding towards her through the green shadows of the forest came Fighting Wolf. The dappled sunlight glinted off his shoulder-length black hair. His striking face was partially hidden in the shadows. A pale yellow kutsack covered his strong body and left his powerful bronzed arms exposed. Several vicious-looking knives and daggers dangled from the belt at his waist. Sarita was almost overwhelmed by the aura of sheer power and masculinity he emanated.

Her first coherent thought was to flee but it was already too late. He paused slightly and she realized he had sighted her. She forced herself to keep to an even pace. Don't let him see you're afraid, she repeated to herself. Meeting his piercing gaze with a calm that belied her inner turmoil, she slowly closed the distance between them.

Fighting Wolf, spying Sarita coming towards him, quickened his step in anticipation. At sea, while chasing the Ucluelets, he'd had plenty of time to think about his lovely slave girl. He remembered her proud carriage, her long dark hair, her lovely face. He had wondered then if she was really as beautiful, if her lips were really as soft, as fickle memory had portrayed.

Seeing her again, he was struck anew by her startling loveliness. Even in a roughly woven cedar robe, she outshone any woman he had ever seen. He found himself anxious to touch and fondle this girl-woman. He advanced towards her like a beast of prey, watching her every move.

Women always came easily to Fighting Wolf. His rugged good looks and strong physique alone were enough to satisfy the most discriminating female taste, and he knew it. He had no doubts that this woman, too, would soon be his—especially as she had no say in the matter. What Fighting Wolf wanted, he took.

His sharp eyes took in every detail of her appearance. Yes, she was beautiful. Memory had not lied. He felt a hunger for her rise in him.

This was the enjoyable part of his revenge: having the beautiful daughter of his enemy as his own personal slave. His lips curled contemptuously as he gazed hungrily at her lithe form. It had been many days since he'd had a woman. Strong desire coursed through his veins as he halted in front of her.

Though tall for a woman, she stood only as high as his shoulder. Her nearness was intoxicating and he could smell a soft floral scent emanating from her body. As he looked deep into her golden eyes, all thoughts but of her fled from his mind. He stood gazing down at her for a moment, unaware of the uncomfortable silence on her part. She attempted to scoot past him.

He shook himself slightly. He was acting like a lovesick boy! Best he show this woman who was her master, and right now.

"Where have you been?" he asked harshly. "I've been looking all over for you." Too late he realized she now knew he had been anticipating seeing her. On second thought, what did it matter? She was but a slave!

"I—I needed some time alone with my thoughts. Surely no harm could come from that," Sarita answered, mustering her dignity about her like a cloak. She would not let this Ahousat dog see her fear.

He relaxed his stance. "Never mind. I've found you now," he responded in an almost pleasant manner. He continued to stare down at her, smiling slightly. At last, he reached out with one strong tanned hand and toyed with a strand of auburn-tinged brown hair. He wound the lock around his finger.

Sarita shifted her feet nervously. Painfully aware of their solitude, she felt a rush of fear. He was so strong, what could she do if he were to decide to take her right here on an isolated forest trail?

She gazed up at him and he read the fear in her beautiful golden eyes. For some reason it wrenched him to see such a beautiful creature afraid of him. He was awed by her and found himself wanting her to return that feeling. Gone for the moment were all thoughts of revenge or enemies. No one else existed but this woman and he.

Those piercing ebony eyes held Sarita spellbound. She stood for a timeless moment, feeling lost to all else but the commanding eyes with the gentle light in them.

Never had she felt so consumed by a man's gaze, so helpless. With great difficulty, she dragged her eyes away from his, passing hastily over his sensuously sculptured lips. She was shaking inside.

Almost as though he could read her thoughts, he ran a long brown finger gently down her cheek and slowly pulled her into his arms.

Spellbound, she gazed up at him, placing her hands shakily on his chest as if to protect herself from him, or was it from the feelings he aroused in her? She knew he could feel her erratically pounding heart.

A small knowing smile quirked the corner of his mouth for a moment as he realized she was as overcome as he was. Then that vanished as he bent his head to taste gently of her sweet lips. The soft yielding of her lips was heady.

Sarita felt his lips touch hers. Her whole being was concentrated in the touch. Lost in his kiss, she spiralled into a whirlpool of sensation and delight.

His breath was warm against her skin and she inhaled deeply of his musky male fragrance.

Feeling him draw her closer, she pressed her palms harder against him, trying to hold him off. She must recover her senses. She couldn't let him have this over-powering effect on her!

Fighting Wolf felt her push against him and his

mouth became avid in its search for hers. She tasted so good, so female.

Trying to pull away from his firm embrace, Sarita's head was suddenly jerked back as Fighting Wolf wound her loose hair around one fist. Her neck was bared to his teeth that grazed threateningly up and down the tender skin of her throat. Now his mouth was back to hers and she felt the hard frame of his strong body as he pressed her against him.

His tongue played lightly with her mouth, sending shivers through her. He outlined her lips slowly, then tasted the corners. She trembled slightly, almost afraid of his power over her. Letting herself go limp, she felt little fluttery movements of his tongue push against her lips and teeth, gently prying her mouth open. Her head still held firmly, her mouth fell open open and his invading tongue pushed against hers, plundering the soft inside. The sensation was overpowering and she sagged weakly against him, her knees almost buckling.

Fighting Wolf was breathing heavily against her, desire for her blotting out where they were and everything else. All he knew was he wanted this woman in a way he had never wanted a woman before. And her response showed she wanted him!

Feeling her arms creep tentatively around his neck, he kissed her deeply, releasing his tight hold on her hair. Only he and the woman in his arms existed. Strong desire swept over him. He had to have her!

Breathing heavily, he pulled her body closer. His large hands pressed against her full bottom, molding her to him. They clasped together as if they were one.

Sarita was moaning deep in her throat, aroused as she had never been before. Feeling all soft and light, she felt she was melting into the trail, at one with the shadowy green forest. She felt cherished and loved and wanted, all at the same time.

Clutching him to her, she returned his kisses with an ardor she did not understand, but only felt.

Suddenly she caught herself. This man was her

enemy! Jerking back to an awareness of where she was
and what she was doing, she was horrified. Wrenching
herself free from Fighting Wolf's embrace, she stepped
to one side and darted past him, racing for the
longhouse. Her face was aflame with humiliation and
arousal. What had she been thinking of? The man was
her captor! Had even killed her people!

Mortified at her wanton behavior, she ran past the
longhouse and down to the beach, ignoring the stares of
curious passersby.

Back on the forest trail, a bemused Fighting Wolf
stood staring after her, though her flying figure had
long since disappeared. His heart pounded fiercely, and
the blood roared in his ears. His breathing gradually
returned to normal, and with it his imperial pride. He
was not about to chase a slave woman across the beach
in front of gawking villagers! His position as war chief
demanded at least that much.

Suddenly he threw back his head and laughed.
What made Sarita think she could escape him so easily?
His mocking guffaws echoed through the still forest,
but his quarry was too far away to hear.

Sarita went out of her way to avoid Fighting Wolf
for the next few days. Every time she saw him, she
quickly fled. Feelings she could not understand churned
within her whenever he was near. She tried to remind
herself that he was her enemy, to think of her family
and how they were now. She avoided him because she
felt disloyal to her family and to herself, but she was
beginning to find Fighting Wolf extremely fascinating.

Previously, she could have admitted to herself that
he was very handsome, and physically attractive, of
course. But now she was becoming aware of just how
intensely she was attracted to him. He was obviously
brave and well respected by his people, but she didn't
think this was what drew her. She could not define what
it was about him that intrigued her. A more experienced
woman would have known.

Sarita thought about him often through the days. She dreamed of him at night. She remembered, over and over, his passionate kisses, and longed for his ardent embraces.

At other times, however, he was her enemy, the man who had stolen her away and humiliated her family. She berated herself for feeling so attracted to such a vicious enemy, but she could not help herself. Try as she might to feel nothing for him, her wayward thoughts returned time and again to Fighting Wolf and those brief, sweet moments when he'd held her in his arms.

She did not know how long she could continue in such a state of confusion, but she hoped she could sort out her feelings soon. In the meantime, she'd avoid him.

Fighting Wolf had no such compunction about avoiding Sarita. He sensed, however, her confused feelings about him. The few times he had casually approached her since kissing her on the trail, she hastily retreated.

At first he'd been amused. Confident it was only a matter of time before he possessed her, he waited, like a patiently stalking predator. And he watched—to see what his prey would do next.

He found it diverting to let her think she could maneuver around him. Perhaps it was that she had been promised to him as a wife, he reflected. With any other slave woman he wanted, a mere word would have brought her to his bed, willing or no. But he was willing to let Sarita run from him, curious to see how far she'd go to avoid him before he demanded her presence. The thrill of the chase, he mused.

After four days of watching her hide from him, however, he was growing impatient. He decided to confront her. She was not going to get away from him. Besides, there were other interested males around. The woman obviously needed to learn who her master was—and soon. He took to prowling restlessly about the village, alert to the impending kill.

Although Sarita was living in Fighting Wolf's house, she took great pains to do errands that would take her far from where he'd be.

The first day, she went off with several of the women to help gather cedar bark. The next day, she took her pointed digging stick and industriously dug fern roots to be roasted for the evening meals. The third day, she willingly looked after several small children when they were far down the beach. Her chaperonage was greatly appreciated by the busy mothers. It was on the fourth day, in her desperation to distance herself from Fighting Wolf, that she ran into trouble.

It was a bright sunny day, the sky was cloudless. Sarita decided to take her digging stick and go off to a somewhat remote clamming beach she had heard about from some of the other slave women. She knew she could avoid Fighting Wolf there.

She followed the winding trail through the forest as it shadowed the coastline. Walking through the quiet forest was a rare treat. The soft carpet of pine needles deadened the sound of her footsteps and only the occasional shrill cry of a bird disturbed the silence.

The trail wound on for a long way, and as she walked, Sarita hummed happily to herself, glad of the solitude on such a fine day. She could see glimpses of the sparkling sea now and then where the trail curved near the shoreline. Soon she could hear the pounding waves on the gray sandy beach ahead. Quickening her pace, she hurried down the twisting path, through the tall, wheat-colored grass of the sand dunes that bordered the beach. She gasped as she caught sight of the long, hardpacked sandy beach that stretched off into the distance.

Running now, she dashed onto the gray sand, her bare feet squeaking in the hot, dry sand. Racing towards the pounding breakers, she gained the harder wet sand and sprinted as fast as she could to the water. Seeing the beautiful stretch of beach, hearing the pounding waves, she felt free for the first time since her capture.

Tossing the cedar basket and digging stick carelessly to the sand, she ran to the water's edge, stepping high and lightly in the cool clear shallows.

She jumped through the waves, showering cold droplets of water, little glistening rainbows, all over herself as she pranced through the shallow waves. Seeing no one about, her sense of freedom was exhilarating and she ran along the beach, breathing the bracing air and feeling the stretch of every muscle in her legs.

She ran as fleetly as a deer, thought the man standing hidden at the top of the trail. He gazed hungrily at the loping girl.

Sarita ran until she could run no more. Her breath was coming in deep gasps until she at last halted to stand in the clear, cool waves that teased her ankles. Pausing, she stared out to sea, inhaling the cool, ocean-scented breeze that tickled her nostrils and ruffled her free-flowing hair.

Breathing restored to normal, she glanced down the beach, back the way she had come. She could barely make out a dark dot on the sand, her clamming basket. Seeing tiny round holes in the sand reminded her of why she was at the beach. Good, she thought. Many clams live here.

Walking slowly back towards her basket and stick, she bent over occasionally to pluck a pretty colored shell out of the swirling clear water. Picking up the basket and pointed stick, she searched for the tiny air passages of the clams.

Small jets of water were the telltale sign that the tasty little creatures were at home. Sarita found a spot where every step she took forced several small geysers into the air.

Her digging stick was admirably suited to digging the elusive clams. Choosing one of the narrow little holes, she plunged the stick far down into the sand and twirled it energetically. The she kneeled over the small hole, using her hands to quickly scoop up the sand. In

this way, she soon chased down several of the small
white-backed clams to put in her basket. She gathered
gray striped clams, too. These were especially good
when steamed.

Occupied as she was, Sarita thought herself alone
until a shadow fell over her as she worked. Her head
jerked up in consternation. A large man, vaguely
familiar, loomed over her.

Then she remembered where she had seen him
before. On the morning of her arrival to Ahousat, he
had been one of Fighting Wolf's fellow warriors who
had danced about with a gruesome head dangling from
his hand. In fact, she remembered clearly now, it was
his cruel face she recalled as he had licked the bleeding
head of one of the victims. Her stomach churned at the
thought.

He stood there quietly, looking at her. She stared
back at him. A large man, he wasn't particularly
handsome. There was an underlying current of
controlled violence in his manner. His nose was large
and hawklike. Dark circles ringed his eyes. She saw that
his face was painted in typical fashion, alternating small
red squares across his cheeks. Both arms were painted
red too. His lavish toilette must have taken him a long
time to prepare, she thought.

Sarita grimly noted his noble status. He was
dressed in a yellow kutsack bordered with sea otter fur.
She knew instinctively she would have to be very careful
with this man.

He continued to gaze at her without speaking. His
silence was unnerving. Getting slowly to her feet so she
could run if she had to, Sarita faced him fearlessly.

"What do you want?" she asked evenly.

"You," he shot back.

She gasped. "Who do you think you are to say such
things to me?"

"I am Birdwhistle," he stated arrogantly, continuing to ogle her. "I'm a very important chief. Now,
enough of this. Come with me."

He reached out and grabbed one of her arms in a steely grip. She pushed at his hand with her free one, but he wouldn't let go. Struggling now, she wriggled her arm, attempting to dislodge his grip. Still he held her. He began to drag her across the sandy beach towards the rolling dunes. She struggled against him, kicking and writhing. He stopped, as if surprised that she was fighting him.

"Come along now," he said impatiently. "I don't have much time. Get over to those sand dunes. Now!"

Shocked at his arrogance and angry that he would treat her so callously, Sarita drew herself up to her full height, threw his hands off her arm, looked him straight in the eye, and said coolly, "I'm not going anywhere with you, Ahousat dog!" She glared at him defiantly.

Somewhat nonplussed, he said, "You're too proud for a slave. You should be honored that I want to lie with you."

Sarita's mouth dropped at his unmitigated gall. "I'm a chief's daughter," she answered as coolly as she could. "I am not here to serve you or any other man!" The nerve of him, she seethed.

"You're a slave," he responded cruelly. "You're no longer a chief's daughter—merely a slave! Perhaps," he cajoled, taking a different tack, "if you were to treat me well, I might take you into my longhouse as one of my cocubines . . . *if* you're nice to me. Otherwise, I might just leave you for anyone who wants you, at any time. Anyone, anytime," he repeated, growing cruel again. "Not a very nice life for a well-bred girl, is it?" he asked, smiling maliciously.

"That's not for you to decide," she returned desperately. "I'm sure Fighting Wolf would be furious if he knew you were here." Privately she doubted Fighting Wolf would care, but she had to scare this horrible man away.

"Hunhh," he snorted. "Fighting Wolf?" The disbelief in his voice shook Sarita. "Fighting Wolf would just laugh. Besides, I don't see him here. If he's so concerned about you, why does he let you go about with no protection?'' His eyes narrowed. ''No, my little clamdigger,'' and here he grabbed her arm again, ''no one cares what happens to you, so you might as well come with me. Willingly.'' So saying, he began dragging her off again in the direction of the sand dunes. Sarita noticed despairingly that the dunes looked closer than ever.

She continued to kick and struggle as they slowly made their way along. Birdwhistle was cursing avidly. Sarita managed to break his hold on her at one point, but when she dashed away, he quickly caught her. She was tiring rapidly but still valiantly defending herself.

Reaching the sand dunes, he pulled her roughly behind the first mound, away from passing observers. Desperate now, she screamed shrilly, but he slapped a calloused, salty hand over her mouth and growled warningly at her. When she continued her muffled cries, he snarled in her ear, ''Shut up, you stupid bitch!''

Biting his hand, Sarita managed to get off another piercing scream before his hand descended again. Furious, he threw her to the ground and fell on top of her. Fumbling at the neck of her rough-spun robe, he managed to untie it and drag it halfway down her body. Frantic now, she screamed again and pushed madly at him. He lifted his own robe and she could feel hot, hard flesh pressing against her thigh. She gave one last desperate, frenzied struggle.

9

Suddenly Birdwhistle was plucked off Sarita, and she watched with incredulous eyes as he sailed through the air to land heavily, his robe high over his thighs. Fighting Wolf stood there, chest heaving. Ignoring Sarita, he lunged for Birdwhistle and picked him up by the neck and shook that hapless man as if he were a puppy. Birdwhistle had no time to recover his wits before a sharp blow from Fighting Wolf's hard fist sent him sprawling, this time into unconsciousness.

Fighting Wolf continued to stand, panting, and staring at the ungainly figure of Birdwhistle. At last, his breathing calmed, Fighting Wolf turned and walked towards Sarita. As he got closer, he stopped and stared down at the dishevelled woman.

She sat clutching her torn kutsack tightly about her. Her hair was tangled and hung loose down her back. Fighting Wolf marvelled that she could look so delicately disarrayed after such a brutal attack. He held out a hand to help her to her feet. "Are you all right?" he asked solicitously.

Sarita, trembling, gratefully accepted his support. She shook her head, still too shaken to speak.

With one hand holding her robe closed, she glanced towards the trail. She only wanted to leave this place—and Birdwhistle! As if reading her thoughts, Fighting Wolf quietly guided her to the path that led back to the village. Realizing she was still weak, he escorted her, one arm gently around her.

At last she could speak. "Thank you for saving me from that—that beast. I tried to fight him off but he was too strong."

Angrily he answered, "What were you doing so far from the village by yourself? Didn't you realize the danger?" He paused. "Although," he added as an afterthought, "it's not your fault he attacked you. The man is vicious. He's raped many slave women."

Fighting Wolf wondered at his own anger. Surely he was not jealous over this slave? Nevertheless, he shuddered to think what would have happened to her had he not arrived in time.

Sarita heard the anger in his voice and thought it directed at her. She was grateful he had appeared when he did, so she thought it best to mollify him. "Yes, it was foolish of me to go so far alone, unprotected." She looked down at the sand for a moment. "I just wanted to get away from the village and all the people for a short while." She was not about to tell Fighting Wolf she had been trying to avoid him! She continued, "I was clamming . . . Oh! The clams! I forgot them!" She halted abruptly.

Scanning the beach quickly, she saw the clam basket, almost submerged by the incoming tide. Still clutching her kutsack around her, she ran as fast as she could towards the pounding breakers. Fighting Wolf waited patiently near the path, watching her run.

Swooping up the basket and her digging stick before it floated off, Sarita dashed awkwardly through the shallows, basket and digging stick held in one hand, the other holding her flapping robe together.

Laughing breathlessly, she approached Fighting Wolf. It was the first time he had heard her laugh and he found he liked the sound. He wanted to hear more of her laughter. "I forgot all about these silly clams!" she exclaimed, smiling up at him. She knew she was babbling foolishly, but she couldn't stop herself. She was still shaken from the attack, she realized.

Even white teeth gleamed against the tan of her

face, and her dark hair blew gently in the wind. She was a beautiful vision as she stood there.

"He won't—" she began.

"He won't bother you again," finished Fighting Wolf grimly. "I'll make certain of that." On a lighter note he added, "It's easy to forget about a few clams when one is being dragged off into the sand dunes." His joking seemed to calm Sarita's fears. He flashed his attractive smile, and his black eyes gleamed with amusement.

Sarita was enchanted. Taking advantage of his good humor, she asked, "How did you happen to be here when I needed help? Did you know what he was planning?" She pointed with her digging stick to where Birdwhistle lay.

Fighting Wolf frowned slightly before answering. "It seemed to me that you've been avoiding me lately." He gazed into her eyes as he said softly, "So I decided I'd follow you today to see where you went. I'm very glad I did."

"I'm glad, too," answered Sarita shyly. She suddenly felt awkward, standing there clutching a basket of clams and the remnants of her robe.

"Now," he said briskly, seeing her discomfiture. "Let's start back to the village. I'll escort you and keep any other assailants at bay." He smiled down at her as he extended his arm for support. "You do feel up to walking, don't you?" he asked solicitously.

"Oh yes," she answered truthfully. "I gladly accept your offer," she added pertly, smiling back at him.

They entered the cool forest, the pounding of the breakers echoing far behind them. The trail was too narrow to walk two abreast, so Fighting Wolf took the lead. After a few minutes of silence, he turned and said, "Are you sure you weren't hurt in that attack?"

Now that the danger was past, Sarita was beginning to shake as she realized how narrowly she'd escaped being raped and possibly killed. It took all her

coordination to force her trembling legs along the forest
path. But she assured him she was fine, that the man
had not injured her, only scared her badly. Satisfied,
Fighting Wolf nodded and turned back to the trail.
They walked in silence back to the village.

Approaching the village, Sarita watched Fighting
Wolf's back straighten. She guessed that now they were
back in his territory his status as a chief was of
paramount importance to him. Pointing to his longhouse, he said gruffly to her, "Go."

She stopped and looked up at him. "Thank you
again for your help," she said softly. Then, still
clutching her torn robe about her and grasping her
basket of clams, she ran quickly to the longhouse.

Once inside, Precious Copper took in the torn robe
at one glance. She rushed over and grabbed the heavy
basket from Sarita's arm and dropped the digging stick.
"What happened?" she cried.

Sarita described Birdwhistle's attack and Fighting
Wolf's timely rescue. Precious Copper shuddered.

"Please," she urged, "Don't go off by yourself.
It's for your own protection that I ask this. I don't want
anything like that to happen to you again."

Sarita looked into Precious Copper's dark brown
eyes and saw the sheen of tears. Surprised and moved,
Sarita reached out and touched Precious Copper gently
on the cheek. "I'll do as you ask," she said at last. "I've
no wish to be hurt, nor do I wish to worry you."
Precious Copper smiled tremulously and Sarita smiled
back.

The moment of friendship was broken when
Precious Copper said quietly, "I'll get you another
robe. That one is useless to you now." She walked over
to a stack of cedar chests and began rummaging through
one. Elbowing her way through the clothes, throwing
robes here and there, Precious Copper finally held up
one particular robe triumphantly. "Here," she crowed.
"I knew I had this robe somewhere!" She tossed it
playfully to Sarita who caught it nimbly.

At least the softer weave of this kutsack would be more comfortable to wear, thought Sarita. The dress was longer, too, though still very plain. Sarita smiled and thanked Precious Copper, then went to her alcove to change.

It was near dark, the evening meal over with. Sarita had not seen Fighting Wolf since he'd rescued her earlier that morning. She felt torn; half of her wanted to see him again, the other half wanted to avoid him completely. But it was not thoughts of him that made her pace the longhouse restlessly.

The other women sat around the small fire, talking quietly together as they wove cedar bark into cloth or played their favorite gambling games.

Sarita's thoughts were on her coming meeting with Rottenwood. Tonight the moon was full and he'd told her to meet him when it was high in the sky. She hoped he had some news about their planned escape.

As the evening wore on, one by one the women bid good night and went off to their sleeping platforms. Sarita nervously bid Precious Copper a good evening, then headed for her alcove.

She sat waiting quietly until the only sounds in the house were the snores and coughs of the other sleepers. Then, wrapping a warm cedar robe about her shoulders, she tiptoed out into the night.

The bright moon shone high above the horizon, its path a silvery gleam on the dark waters of the bay. Sarita caught her breath at the eerie beauty. The cool night air was pleasant on her skin and she inhaled deeply. Looking furtively around, she saw no movement to alarm her. Gliding carefully through the shadows, she made her way slowly down the beach to the large rock outcropping.

Fighting Wolf sat with his friends and watched a gambling game in progress. His thoughts were not, however, on the game before him.

Instead he was remembering how he had rescued Sarita from Birdwhistle's clutches. She'd been so grateful—and beautiful. He castigated himself for the strong attraction he felt for the daughter of his enemy.

He should merely use her and cast her aside when he was done, he told himself. But whenever he saw her, such thoughts fled and all he could think of was how he desired her. Never had he seen such a beautiful woman, nor he suspected, such a delightful one. He smiled to himself as he remembered her laughter at the clamming beach.

He couldn't blame Birdwhistle for wanting her. What man wouldn't want such a woman for his own?

Fighting Wolf chuckled to himself. Birdwhistle had tried to sneak back into the village without being seen. But his slow gait and the dark bruises around his neck had drawn jeering questions from his friends. He had whined his story, quick to point out Fighting Wolf's jealousy in defense of the worthless female slave. Birdwhistle's friends merely laughed louder, especially those whose wives he had seduced. Realizing he would get no sympathy from his gloating audience, Birswhistle had finally limped off to his longhouse to nurse his wounds.

Fighting Wolf roused himself from his reverie. His friends were still engrossed in their game. As he paused to sip a drink of water, he felt a gentle touch at his elbow. His eyes met those of Rough Seas. She smiled and ran one finger down his arm. "Is what I hear about Birdwhistle true?" she asked in a low voice.

"What do you hear?"

"That you beat him for toying with your Hesquiat slave. Such talk is all over the village, but I want to hear the story from your own lips," she said, continuing to stroke his arm and gaze at him with almond eyes.

Fighting Wolf stared back at her briefly, wondering why she would concern herself about the incident. "Yes," he shrugged indifferently. "I beat the bastard. He deserved it."

"Oooh, I'm sure he did," she purred. "But tell

me," and here her hand crept up his neck to play with the lock of long blue-black hair that rested there, "tell me, what exactly did he do to you?"

Fighting Wolf focused intently on the guessing game in progress. "It's not what he did to me. It's what he tried to do to my new slave. He tried to rape her."

"Oooh," she pouted. "Such a little thing to beat him for. Slave women get raped all the time. It's nothing new," she pointed out casually.

Fighting Wolf did not like the direction the conversation was taking. He did not want to examine his own actions or feelings too closely where Sarita was concerned, and he certainly did not want the inquisitive Rough Seas prodding him. He shifted uncomfortably as he turned to face her. "Why are you so concerned? Is Birdwhistle your latest lover?"

Rough Seas slapped his arm lightly and giggled. "And if he were, would you be jealous?" Fighting Wolf merely looked at her with undisguised exasperation.

"Nooo, I'm just curious." She answered his taunt hastily. "Nothing more." She watched him closely. "Anything you're involved with, I take an interest in, that's all." She smiled coyly at him to take the possessive edge off her words. She ran one long finger under his chin. "Surely you don't care about this worthless slave." She tensed imperceptibly. "Do you?"

He pushed her away from him. "You're too clinging tonight. Don't you have a lover to meet?"

She laughed, a low, hoarse laugh. "Of course not," she answered. "I told you I'm not taking any more lovers," she reminded.

"Oh yes," he sneered. "Saving yourself for me. I'd forgotten."

She rose to leave. "I can see for myself that this slave means more to you than I thought." He raised a questioning brow. She patted his shoulder lightly. "Never mind, dear Fighting Wolf. You'll get over her—especially after half the village has had her. It happens to all the prettiest slave girls, doesn't it?" She laughed mockingly. "Oooh, and Fighting Wolf," she cooed over one shoulder as she headed for the door, "should you need, uh, company tonight, I'll be up late." With that she was gone, leaving only a trailing fragrance of pine. Fighting Wolf grunted and kept his eyes on the game players, annoyed with the woman's obvious manipulations.

Fighting Wolf's thoughts returned to the present. Growing unaccountably impatient with his friends' constant chatter and yells of encouragement to each other, Fighting Wolf decided to leave also. He stretched lazily and got up from where he had been sitting. Nodding goodnight to several of his friends, he made his way out of the longhouse and into the night.

Sarita reached the rock and hid in the shadows of a crevice on the far side of the outcrop, away from the village. She shivered in the cool night air. Surely Rottenwood would be here soon. The moon was already high and she had been waiting quite a while. She was nervous out in the dark by herself. Too many spirits walked at night.

Suddenly she saw a shadow slinking along the tree line towards her. Had she not been watching, she would never have seen Rottenwood, so well did he blend in the dappled light and dark of the forest along the beach. As he darted out from the forest and ran to the rock out-cropping, she breathed a sigh of relief—it was indeed Rottenwood. For a moment, she had feared it was someone, or something, else . . .

She noticed suddenly that the night sounds had stilled. Frogs had stopped croaking and the crickets ceased chirping. All was quiet. Too quiet, she thought.

She greeted Rottenwood, anxious to learn his news and return to the longhouse. He acknowledged her greeting and leaned against the rock, a short distance away from her.

His deep voice was calm as he relayed his information. "Good news tonight," he began. Sarita watched him, senses alert. "I found an old canoe. Checked it over for holes but it seems seaworthy. I managed to hide it under some salal bushes and grass. No one will spot it."

"Wonderful," Sarita whispered excitedly. "Now we can make our escape immediately!"

"Not so fast," he warned. "I don't want to leave until most of the warriors, and Fighting Wolf, are gone from the village. There are no long hunts or expeditions planned until Dog Salmon Moon. That means everyone will be hanging around the village until then."

"Dog Salmon Moon?" gasped Sarita. "Why—why that's over thirty days away! That's too long to wait!"

"It can't be helped," said Rottenwood shortly. "After the whole village moves to the winter site, the warriors will go off to catch the winter's supply of dog salmon."

Sarita knew the dog salmon was the most important food for her people. Hunting the great whales was brave and daring, but it took place in early spring. The people needed meat through the long, rainy winter. It was the dog salmon, caught in the fall, that fed the people all winter and kept the children from crying with hunger.

"Our best chance for success," Rottenwood was saying, "is when the men have gone fishing." He looked at her solemnly as he continued, "You know we can't risk getting caught." Sarita shivered and nodded her head.

"When we escape, we must not be caught. Otherwise," lectured Rottenwood grimly, "we'll be dragged back here and slowly tortured to death—as an example to the other slaves." Seeing her shiver again, he knew he'd emphasized his point. "There can be no mistakes. None."

"Then we have no choice, Rottenwood," she whispered desperately. "We will have to wait until Dog Salmon Moon when all the men will be occupied with fishing. But we dare not wait any longer!"

She vaguely saw him nod in the silvered moonlight. "What about food?" she mused aloud. "Waiting until then will certainly give me time to hide food for our voyage." A new concern occurred to her. "Are you sure you remember the way back to Hesquiat village?" She faced him questioningly.

"Yes," he grunted, "I was awake enough on the trip to Ahousat to memorize certain landmarks that we passed. I'm sure I can find our way back." The confidence in his voice relieved her doubts. "It'll be best to go at night, under cover of darkness. Later, if anyone notices our absence, it will be too late. We'll be far away by then!" Sarita nodded again, excited at the thought.

Their plans made, she and Rottenwood agreed to meet once more before Dog Salmon Moon, to ensure everything went smoothly. He bid her a good night and slipped off silently into the forest again. She watched the shadows and was rewarded only by a quick glimpse of movement farther down the beach, near the village. He had made it back safely.

Clutching her cloak about her, Sarita decided to follow the same route back to the village. It was easier and safer in the forest than being exposed by the moonlight shining on the open beach. She dashed quickly from the rock to the dark line of the forest. Sighing with relief that no one had seen her, she skirted the dense bush swiftly and quietly.

She was close to the village and just about to sidle her way past a tall spruce, when a large hand reached out and grabbed her. Spinning around, she gasped in fright as she stared up into the furious face of Fighting Wolf.

"Where have you been sneaking off to, you little bitch?" he snarled at her. "So this is why I haven't seen you for several days. You've been skulking around to meet your lover!" His grip tightened viciously on both her arms.

Fighting Wolf was indeed furious, and with a red-hot anger. The slave he had been protecting all this time had been sneaking through the dark to meet a lover! What a fool he'd been, thinking she was so sweet and innocent! How his friends would laugh at him when they found out! He gritted his teeth and tried to control his fury.

Whimpering in pain and fear, Sarita looked up at him helplessly, tears shining in her beautiful golden eyes. She realized her perilous position. If she denied meeting a lover he would want to know why she was sneaking around. She couldn't tell him it was to plan her escape! Such an admission would mean death, if not for her then surely for Rottenwood. If she continued to let him believe she was meeting a lover he would think her fickle and probably withdraw his protection. Or use her himself. She trembled, paralyzed with fear as she stood staring dazedly at him.

Fighting Wolf felt the woman trembling, but his fury was not appeased. Why didn't she say something? "I saw a man slinking away into the night, you bitch! Who was it?" he growled at her.

When she wouldn't answer, he shook her roughly. "Tell me his name!"

She shook her head, staring at him all the while. "I c-can't," she whispered at last.

This admission brought forth an explosive laugh from the enraged man. "What do you mean you can't tell me? Don't you even know who you mate with?" His bitter laugh rang hollow in the night.

"Or perhaps you don't care!" he growled viciously as he threw her to the ground. "Get out of my sight, whore! I don't want someone else's leavings. Go on. Get!" The last word a cold note of finality to it. Like one would talk to a dog.

Fighting Wolf did not want her near him. He was so angry, he couldn't trust himself not to kill her.

Sarita hastily picked herself up off the cold ground, clutching her cape closely, and ran for the longhouse as though spirits were after her. She knew she had barely escaped with her life.

Running into the longhouse, she halted in the center of the living space, glancing wildly about and panting heavily. Unbelievably, everyone was still asleep. She'd been sure the whole village would have heard Fighting Wolf's shouted fury.

Whatever was she going to do now? she thought fearfully. Fighting Wolf despised her. Creeping to her alcove, she lay down on the furs and closed her eyes, willing sleep to come. But she tossed and turned long into the night, fear keeping her awake. She waited to hear Fighting Wolf's heavy tread as he retired for the night, but when she fell into an exhausted slumber at dawn, he still had not returned.

10

Sarita awoke the next morning and groggily climbed out of bed. She stretched, the twinges of pain unwilling reminders of last night's encounter with Fighting Wolf.

With her uncomfortable memories came a whole new set of problems. What was she going to do now? Fighting Wolf no longer cared what happened to her. Perhaps Precious Copper would protect her, but Sarita held little hope of that. She hoped she could survive long enough in Ahousat village to make her escape. She wondered, too, if Rottenwood had been recognized and caught.

As these worries buzzed around Sarita's tired brain, she fought down the feelings of panic that threatened to engulf her. Breathing deeply, she at last regained a measure of control.

Sarita dressed in her soft-weave cedar robe and walked with dragging steps into the central living area.

Several of the others were already breakfasting on appetizing chunks of smoked cod. Precious Copper smiled and greeted her, as pleasant as always. Sarita sighed in relief. Fighting Wolf obviously had not said anything to his sister. Perhaps everything would work out after all.

The other women ignored her as was often their wont. She set about getting her own breakfast.

She no sooner sat down by the fire, about to breakfast from a platter of warm chunks of cod, when she looked up to see Fighting Wolf approaching the

breakfast circle. He grunted surly greetings in response
to the cheerful feminine chorus directed at him. But it
was on Sarita that his direct gaze fell.

He reached for some of the smoked cod, then
parked himself across the fire from her. Ignoring
everyone, he stared aggressively at Sarita as he ate his
smoked cod. The tension in the room was so tangible,
Sarita felt she could have touched it.

Her appetite gone, Sarita sat twisting her hands
nervously in her lap. Fighting Wolf continued his
intimidating stare. Sarita could stand it no longer. She
rose and fled the main area.

Word spread rapidly through the longhouse that
Fighting Wolf had withdrawn his protection. Sarita saw
the other slave women talking and giggling behind their
hands whenever she approached them. A sick knot of
fear gripped her stomach.

Precious Copper seemed oblivious to the gossip
and kept finding indoor tasks for Sarita. Sarita guessed
that Precious Copper realized her brother had withdrawn his protection, but the petite woman was determined to help in spite of his displeasure. Sarita was
grateful for the kindness.

Time and again, Sarita would catch Fighting Wolf
staring at her, utter contempt in his black eyes. She
refused to cringe as if guilty and gazed back steadily at
him before turning away.

Sarita became aware, too, of how quickly word had
spread throughout the village that Fighting Wolf no
longer offered her any kind of protection. Several men
made insulting proposals to her, and some even tried to
maul her. Because of these incidents, she was glad to
stay close to the longhouse near Precious Copper's
guardianship.

One afternoon she went to fetch water from the
river. As she was carrying a cedar container full of the
cold clear liquid back to the longhouse, she had to pass
by several men lounging around outside. Fighting Wolf
was among them. Sarita knew from their vigorous head

shaking and wild gesticulations that they were discussing politics and war.

As she walked by lugging the heavy container in her arms, the men halted their conversation. The uncomfortable silence was broken by several rude suggestions. One man made a lewd gesture at her. Cheeks flaming, Sarita struggled onwards, giving no sign she'd heard their crude remarks.

She was almost past them when Birdwhistle grabbed her arm. Water sloshed over her hands and arms as she stared at him uncertainly. He was dressed in his usual finery and paint. Several of the men guffawed as he leaned over to whisper a vulgar proposition in Sarita's ear. Fighting Wolf merely stood there, watching her. A contemptuous sneer crossed his face as he leaned casually against the longhouse, his arms folded across his chest. He murmured a low comment to his friends, and Sarita cringed inside to hear the burst of ribald laughter.

Suddenly she'd had enough! Clearly realizing that no one would protect her from any oaf who approached her, she had no choice but to defend herself.

Smiling sweetly, as if considering Birdwhistle's filthy proposal, she leaned towards him. The other men were watching avidly. When she had their full attention, she quickly raised the container of cold water and upended the frigid contents all over the unsuspecting Birdwhistle!

A sopping wet Birdwhistle, his careful toilette in ruins, stood there gasping. Around him, the warriors were doubled over in laughter. Fighting Wolf was laughing the loudest of all.

Birdwhistle was enraged. Furious, he groped blindly for Sarita, but she easily eluded his grasping hands. Unfortunately, she did not elude a second warrior's hands. Fighting Wolf grabbed and imprisoned her, holding her firmly against him.

Sarita knew that what she had just done was a serious offense—could in fact carry a death penalty.

Striking a chief was no light matter, but she could not stifle the small glow of satisfaction she felt as Birdwhistle stood wet and dripping, his carefully arranged hair in bedraggled ruins.

For one moment, she twisted around and her golden eyes met Fighting Wolf's, then she turned back and faced the others proudly. She would not beg for mercy. She stood silent, proud and beautiful, awaiting the verdict of death.

A furious Birdwhistle was sputtering at the top of his lungs. "This woman must be killed," he screamed, "for daring to strike a high-ranking chief such as myself!" The tendons on his neck stood out like cords, he was so enraged.

His screaming pronouncement made the others laugh even harder. They asked each other why an important chief like Birdwhistle would want anything to do with such a lowly slave in the first place. Various comments traveled back and forth about how badly Birdwhistle had needed a bath.

These witticisms were interrupted by another piercing howl from Birdwhistle who was insisting vehemently, "This girl must be killed! How else can I save face? That she dare strike me! Me—a chief!" he sputtered in outrage. "I will settle for nothing less than her death!"

Sarita stood frozen. Bitterness overwhelmed her. It was too unjust that her attempts to defend herself against his unwanted advances should meet with her death. She felt Fighting Wolf's hands drop from her arms as he stepped to one side.

She was alone. Her chin jutting defiantly, the empty bucket on the ground at her bare feet, she faced the Ahousats. Some of the men stopped laughing as they realized Birdwhistle was indeed serious in his demands for Sarita's death.

"Really, Birdwhistle," came a laconic drawl, "will killing a worthless slave truly save your good name?" Fighting Wolf paused, all eyes upon him. "I think not.

Who would even care about her death?'' He shrugged
casually. "A feast, however, is more likely to save your
good name—a big, expensive feast. A feast that
welcomes the whole village. Who, then, would dare
malign you or your name? No one. Not after they ate
your food and accepted your hospitality.''

The sound of the calm voice, the excellent
suggestion, the murmurs of approval from his friends,
all combined to cool Birdwhistle's raging fury. Fighting
Wolf did indeed have a point. Who would care if one
useless slave girl lived or died?

Birdwhistle was finding it hard to remember why he
had thought the girl so attractive in the first place. She
had been nothing but trouble to him. A feast for the
whole village! Yes, the idea had merit. He could recover
his good name and save face much more effectively that
way.

Fighting Wolf's suggestion was greeted by the
others with conspiratorial winks and nods. Birdwhistle
thought he heard a snicker or two, but decided he must
have been mistaken. Hearing his friends' agreement and
encouragement mollified him.

Sarita glanced quickly at Fighting Wolf. Golden
eyes met piercing black ones for a timeless moment.
They both knew she owed him her life. She wondered
why he had bothered to intervene, when his contempt
for her was so obvious.

Snatching up the water container, she fled towards
the longhouse. No one stopped her.

The men continued to sit or stand around and
laugh about the incident. Finally Birdwhistle, shivering
theatrically, invited all who had witnessed the
ignominious fall of his good name to a feast to be given
two days hence. Bidding good-bye to his friends, he
slowly sloshed off in the direction of his longhouse.

After his departure, several sarcastic comments
flew back and forth about Birdwhistle's smooth charm
with women. Women were constantly throwing themselves at him, it seemed. And all those present could

attest to how effortlessly he seduced them. One well-fed wag suggested his friends would do well to emulate the skillful maneuvers of Birdwhistle. Then there'd be feasts every night in Ahousat village!

Fighting Wolf, joining in the general laughter, gave no indication of the true direction of his thoughts. But he wondered to himself about his championing of a woman who had such loose ways. She seemed to bewitch him! He smiled ruefully to himself. He only knew he could not stand by and let such an intriguing woman die as a sop to the oft besmirched name of Birdwhistle.

11

Sarita awoke. As she munched her breakfast of cold roasted fern root left over from the night before, she thought over the events of the past few days.

Things had been going much better lately—due to the incident with Birdwhistle, she suspected. She had shown the villagers that she would protect herself. Men seldom made bold approaches to her, and she enjoyed the respite from unwanted advances. She had hated being constantly on guard against lechers. It was a relief to be able to relax her vigil.

She remained concerned about Fighting Wolf, however. True, he had made no overt move towards her—had barely acknowledged her existence—but she could not dispel the fear that flickered over her whenever she felt his cold eyes upon her. And his eyes were cold. She could not dispute that. Whenever his glance happened to fall on her as she worked about the longhouse, or as she did chores in the village, always the cold contempt in those piercing ebony eyes unnerved her. She knew he thought her a loose woman, but what could she do? To tell him she had not been party to a romantic rendezvous would be to seal her own death. Or Rottenwood's. No, better to let him think what he would, and continue to avoid him as much as possible.

Her thoughts returned rapidly to the present as she became aware of Precious Copper speaking to her.

"Please take my little cousins down to the beach," Precious Copper was saying. "I promised to take Duck

Feather and her cousin for a swim." Sarita nodded, glad of the chore. She found the two active children a delight to be with. And since her lecture to the cousins, she'd found they minded very well.

Sarita went to her alcove to fetch her cedar cape. It was a sunny morning, but there was a slight chill in the air. She was surprised the children would swim so early in the day, but then children always wanted to swim and play in the salt water, no matter how cold it was. She remembered how, as a child, she loved to splash with her brother in the cool waters of the summer village bay. The nostalgic thought brought a soft sigh to her lips.

Sarita was unaware of how beautiful she looked this morning. The golden tan of her skin contrasted favorably with the darker brown color of her kutsack. She had tied her hair back with a strip of rawhide. The plain hairstyle suited her patrician features, emphasizing strong cheekbones and large, innocent golden eyes. Clutching the cape in one hand, she returned to the main area.

"Little sister," she heard a deep voice drawl as she reentered, "you'll have to find someone else to take our cousins swimming. This woman is coming with me."

Sarita swallowed nervously and looked suspiciously into Fighting Wolf's watchful ebony eyes. She didn't like the way he was looking at her.

Precious Copper's gaze shifted from her brother to Sarita. The girl's body trembled and a flash of fear crossed her face. Precious Copper sighed heavily, but there was nothing she could do to protect Sarita. "As you wish, my brother," she responded calmly, turning away to begin separating stacks of dried berries.

Fighting Wolf picked up a nearby basket, then headed for the door. He was dressed in a fur-trimmed, pale yellow cedar kutsack that emphasized the dark bronze of his skin. His thick blue-black mane of hair hung in gentle waves to his shoulders. Rings of polished copper encircled both his wrists and ankles. Around his waist was twisted a belt of sea otter fur from which hung the ever-present daggers. Sarita counted three of them, each with a sharp, wicked-looking blade. She noted also that he carried a small cedar mat tucked under one arm.

Fighting Wolf exited the longhouse without a backward glance, obviously expecting Sarita to follow.

She stumbled blindly after him. A shiver of fear ran through her as she puzzled over why he had decided to take her with him today. She did not trust that gleam in his eye. For too long he had looked at her with anger and contempt and she wondered what he could possibly have planned that would bring a new look to those hard eyes.

Once outside the longhouse, Sarita paused briefly, breathing deeply of the crisp morning air. Fighting Wolf jerked his head, impatient for her to follow him.

Slowly Sarita walked behind him, wondering why he was leading her to the beach. Did he want her to help him work on his canoe? Puzzled, she continued to follow at a slow pace.

She was still pondering what he had in mind when he threw the basket into a small canoe that bobbed up and down in the shallow waves. He waded into the cold water and held the canoe steady, gesturing for her to climb aboard.

Sarita thought briefly of dashing back to the longhouse. She discarded the notion, realizing he would easily catch her. Holding her body proudly, she stepped gracefully into the canoe and knelt on the bottom near the bow. She watched the strong muscles of his arms flex as he pushed the small craft effortlessly from shore. Then he stepped in, shifting his weight to keep the bobbing craft from tipping.

Kneeling on the small cedar mat, Fighting Wolf picked up two paddles that were laying next to his bow and several arrows. Wordlessly, he handed one of the paddles to Sarita. She faced the front, squatting on her heels in a comfortable paddling position. At the stern, Fighting Wolf paddled the small canoe, steering it out of the harbor and straight out to sea.

The two paddled in silence for a long while, their rhythm even as they skimmed over the waves. The sun was beginning to feel hot on Sarita's back, but she dared not stop paddling to remove her cloak. She would ask nothing from Fighting Wolf, nor would she let him see her discomfort.

They paddled north for what seemed an interminable length of time to Sarita. She noticed they kept a safe distance from the white churning breakers pounding the long gray strip of sand that marked the coastline.

Seeing the direction of her gaze, Fighting Wolf commented easily, "That's a continuation of the long sandy beach where you went clamdigging."

Sarita remembered that long sandy beach very well—and Birdwhistle's attack. She wondered if Fighting Wolf had deliberately brought up the sore subject, so she answered coolly, "I should warn you: it's dangerous to take me clamdigging. Ask Birdwhistle."

Fighting Wolf laughed. "Aah, but who will protect you this time?" he asked in a low voice.

When she didn't answer, he added casually, "Well, we're almost at the end of our voyage. Only a short distance to go."

"Where exactly are we going?" she inquired, her curiosity getting the better of her.

"To a small, private beach," he answered. She could hear the suggestive tone in his voice, but she kept her back stiff and unyielding. "A private beach that I discovered when I was young." Enthusiastically, he continued, "It has soft sand, and is sheltered from the wind. There's even a small, freshwater creek flowing at one end. It's a beautiful spot. You'll love it," he drawled and she wondered what he really meant. That she would love the beach or love what he was going to do to her, for by now she had very strong suspicions as to his intentions, once they arrived at the beach.

Her heart began to beat faster and her palms,

already damp from paddling, were sweating profusely. She knew the reaction wasn't all fear, but anticipation as well. She decided to brazen it out. "Now, why," she began, "would you care whether I like the beach or not? I hadn't been aware that you particularly cared about my likes and dislikes!"

Her impudence delighted him. "Aah, but I do care, Sarita," he answered in a soft voice. "Very much." The way his voice caressed her name sent a warning thrill up Sarita's spine.

Sarita didn't quite know what to answer. She continued to paddle stoically, ignoring him, but the whole time her mind was racing.

She wondered if, once they were ashore, she could run fast enough to get away from him and hide in the woods. Many tall spruce trees lined the beach behind the sand. Once she ran through the spruce trees, she knew the tangle of salal bushes and shrubs would make it difficult for him to follow and find her.

She decided that she must make the attempt. What she would do after he gave up looking for her and paddled away from the beach, she gave no thought to.

She only knew she did not want to be alone with a man like Fighting Wolf. A man who roused so many different feelings in her. On the one hand, she was desperately afraid of him and what he might do to her physically. On the other, she was strongly attracted to him, more so than any other man she had ever known. She could feel his magnetism even when sitting with her back to him. Damn! Why did the man always have such an effect on her?

She was brought out of her reverie by Fighting Wolf's next comment. "See the island just off that point in the distance?" he asked, his canoe paddle indicating the long promontory of land. Shading her eyes with her cupped hand, Sarita stared off into the distance. A long spit of gray sandy beach led out to a small rocky island, topped with trees. She nodded. "That's our destination."

They paddled in silence for another while, until they neared the point of land. Large breakers rolled in, almost covering the gray spit of beach they were approaching. Small waves pounded dangerously at the rocky island, crashing against the rocks, but Fighting Wolf steered away from the island. Maneuvering carefully, he guided the small craft towards the spit, until one large wave pushed them in very close to shore. Looking down through the clear, rippling, shallow water Sarita could see pretty shells lying on the sand.

Fighting Wolf stepped out of the canoe, then dragged it easily into shore. Sarita felt, then heard the canoe grate against the hard sand. She hopped out, the cool water refreshing as it swirled around her calves. Fighting Wolf lifted the small craft and carried it farther up the beach, nearer to the treeline. There the waves and incoming tide would not reach the boat.

While he was occupied, Sarita surveyed the beach. It truly was a lovely place. A wide expanse of fine gray sand stretched endlessly in the direction from which they had come. The dark gray sand near the water, the lighter gray dry sand of the upper beach, the brilliant green trees and the bright blue sky conspired to make the most beautiful scene imaginable.

She gazed in the other direction. The island and spit of beach where she stood formed a small cove matched with another island and spit of land. Twins, she thought.

Between the two islands the long, gray curve of beach gleamed in the hot sun. She could see nothing beyond the second island, but she wondered if sandy beach extended endlessly from there, too.

Taking the basket from the bottom of the craft, Fighting Wolf turned to Sarita. After her first survey of the beach, she had been hastily judging the distance from the shore where she stood to the blue-gray spruce trees lining the upper beach. She chewed nervously on her full lower lip as she debated making her escape now. Seeing him retrieve the basket, she turned to watch him, willing her eyes to stay away from the beckoning tree line. She could not let him guess her plan.

Smiling at her, Fighting Wolf handed her the basket, obviously expecting her to carry it. Sarita hoisted it to her back, the tumpline around her forehead. She groaned inwardly as she thought of her escape and shedding this load she did not want. Ostensibly following docilely behind him, she waited in an agony of impatience for the opportunity to make her break for freedom.

Fighting Wolf walked silently towards the second small island, heading for a small stream Sarita had not noticed earlier. The creek, some distance from the canoe, cut into the soft sand and bubbled and chortled its way along. Walking quickly, they reached the stream. Fighting Wolf took the basket from Sarita, laying it down on the warm sand.

Sarita stretched her cramped muscles luxuriously. The hot sun felt good on her upturned face, and the warm sand squeezing between her toes felt even better. She inhaled the tangy sea air, content for a moment.

Fighting Wolf watched her, a small smile playing about his mouth. Turning away, he surprised Sarita by walking towards the sea once again. She watched as he waded into the cool water, not once looking back at her. He obviously did not expect any trouble from her, she thought, irritated. Seeing that he was wading farther out into the shallow water, she suddenly realized this was her chance to escape. Spying the canoe, she quickly changed her plans. She would run for the light craft, push it out to sea and paddle away, leaving Fighting Wolf stranded. Yes, that was a better plan! Besides, if it appeared he was going to come after her and catch her before she reached the canoe, she could still run for the tree line.

With a last glance at his departing figure, now thigh high in the water, she turned and ran as fast as she could. The canoe lay a good distance away. Dry sand squeaked underfoot as she ran for her very life. Afraid

to look back, she kept running. Suddenly she heard a
shout. She ran even faster. Breathing hard, chest
aching, yet still she ran. Her hair had come loose and
the silky dark mane flapped freely behind as she sped
down the beach.

She ventured a quick peek over her shoulder.
Fighting Wolf was sprinting after her. Fear lent wings to
her feet. Her feet flew over the solid wet sand and her
breath came in gasps as she raced desperately for the
canoe. Another peek over her shoulder revealed
Fighting Wolf gaining on her. He was too close. She'd
never make it!

Abandoning all thought of the canoe, she swerved
for the treeline. She could hear him panting now, mere
steps behind her. With one last burst of speed she
lengthened her stride, alarm giving her added strength.
The heavy thud of his feet pounded the sand; he was
almost upon her!

Suddenly, hard arms wrapped around her knees
and a vigorous tackle brought her careening to the sand.
She kicked and struggled against Fighting Wolf, trying
futilely to regain her feet, but his arms were clamped
tightly around her knees, his face buried in her hip.

She heard a low chuckle and struggled with
renewed fury. He thought it was funny! She was
running and fighting for her life, and Fighting Wolf
thought it was funny! Screaming her anger and lashing
out with her fists, she managed to land a blow on his
muscular back. Hearing him grunt, she lashed out
again, but he caught her wrist in one strong hand.
Inching himself up, Fighting Wolf threw one leg over
her lower body, using his weight to hold her down while
he freed his grip from her legs. Grabbing her other
hand, he quickly pulled both arms over her head and
held her wrists in a brutal grip.

The nearness of his body was intoxicating. Well,
she would fight him and her own body too, if she had
to! Breasts heaving, held immobile, Sarita hissed into
his face, her golden eyes shooting sparks. Those golden

eyes reminded him of a furious cougar he had once cornered.

Sarita was beginning to realize that her struggles were getting her nowhere. He was much too strong—and she was too tired. Finally she lay still, panting, angry and watching his every move.

He leaned over her, grinning, until she stopped her fruitless struggles and was once more breathing normally. Then he bent and softly touched his lips to hers. The gentle touch sent Sarita into new paroxysms of struggle. Determined to get free, she bit at him, growling her fury. His free hand grasped her hair, a great handful, close to her head. Holding her head still, he ground his lips into hers, this time savagely.

A groan escaped her. Aroused now, he shifted his weight over her. He continued his relentless kisses, his mouth hot on hers. She kept her teeth clenched, a barrier to the sweetness within. Pushing at her teeth with his tongue did Fighting Wolf no good. She continued to clench tight. Changing tactics, his mouth burned its way down the side of her throat, coming to rest in the hollow of her shoulder. Sarita was starting to melt. Sensing her vulnerability, he renewed his attack on her mouth. Pulling her head back even farther, her mouth fell open and he forced his way in, a prelude to further invasion. Moving through her mouth, he took all the sweetness he could, savouring the taste of her.

Sarita felt his hard tongue probing her mouth. She tried to stop him, but he would not be denied. The sensations he was arousing in her body were so wondrous! For a moment, she went limp, caught up in his possession of her mouth and body.

Feeling her relax against him, Fighting Wolf reached for one of the daggers at his waist. Holding it close to her face, he watched as fear lit those golden eyes. Laughing harshly, he leaned back and slit her robe from neck to knee, tossing the knife to one side. She lay under him, nude, staring up at him hopelessly, her beautiful body at last exposed to his hot, relentless gaze.

He took in her body at a glance, intense desire coursing through him. The firm, full breasts intoxicated him and he set his hungry mouth over first one brown peak, then the other, sucking avidly. She tried to free her hands, intent on pushing him away. Laughing low in his throat, he loosened his grip just a little. She redoubled her struggles, only to find him tighten his grip again. He was merely playing with her!

The attack of his mouth on her breasts jolted her out of her sensuous lethargy. Warm tingling feelings shivered through her as his mouth devoured hers. Desperately afraid now of the sensations he was arousing in her, she fought on.

Lifting his head, he quickly undid his own robe and slid it off his body, all the while gazing at her through heavy-lidded eyes. His warm, nude body pressing against hers was unlike anything Sarita had ever known. She could feel the hard muscles of his torso and legs. She looked down at his swollen manhood, pressing against her stomach. Fear thrilled through her at the sight of it, erect and pointing at her. He followed her gaze and grinned upon seeing her reaction. He slanted his lips across hers again, but this time she was too late to stop his entry into her mouth. Swirling his tongue around hers, he knew she was ripe for the taking.

With his free hand, he began to caress her smooth body, running his hand down the length of her torso. He cupped her rounded buttocks and pulled her closer to him. She fit so well against his length. He gently stroked her thighs, now the outside, then the inside, his fingers feathering lightly.

Sarita had vainly tried to free herself, but once Fighting Wolf had started his lovemaking, she felt herself turning to water. The sensations running up and down her body as his hands touched her thighs and then closer, ever closer to the center of her being, weakened her struggles severely. She gave herself up to the wonderful intoxicating arousal that swept over her. The smell of him, manly, slightly salty, stirred her senses powerfully. The feel of him, the hard muscles pressing against her body, the strong grip of his hand on her wrists, all overwhelmed her, leaving her breathless and compliant. When she felt his hand gently caressing her between her thighs, the lethargy coming over her almost sent her into a swoon. Her legs had a will of their own as they parted, trembling, to his intruding fingers.

Fighting Wolf could wait no longer. He lowered himself onto her. He sank into her velvety depths, stopped momentarily by the delicate barrier of her maidenhood. Too aroused to be surprised, he realized fleetingly, possessively, that he was the first man to make love to her.

Pausing slightly until he felt her relax, he plunged in deeply, holding her close. He lay motionless once again. Her low cry against his lips was stifled as he concentrated on gently kissing her over and over again.

Sarita stiffened, feeling something hard follow where his hand had been only a heartbeat before. She felt him plunge strongly into her and she struggled briefly against him as she felt the sharp pain, but his hot kisses on her now swollen lips distracted her. His hands were everywhere, soothing, calming her.

Finally, Fighting Wolf began to move slowly, slowly, building faster and faster. It felt so good, he couldn't stop. He knew he could never be satisfied with one time with this woman. He wanted more, always more . . . "Sarita!" He breathed her name over and over.

His voice, whispering her name, made it sound like a word of love. Soon his strong, rhythmic thrusts into her seized her completely, and she gave herself up to the magical sensation of his posession.

He climaxed powerfully inside her, spilling everything he had to give into the woman he held.

Sarita felt his shuddering release within her, and Fighting Wolf's grip on her wrists loosened. She entwined her arms around his neck, pulling him close to her. She wanted to hold his warmth and strength to her always.

Fighting Wolf held Sarita as if he'd never let her go. He lay there, marvelling at what had just passed between them. Never had it felt so good, so right, to be with a woman as it had with this one. He did not know what to say. How could he tell her, his enemy's daughter, how moved he had been in her arms? How he had never found such beauty, such wholeness, with a woman before? No, he thought, better to say nothing.

12

Sarita lay with her eyes closed, her arms wrapped around Fighting Wolf. Suddenly she felt as if she ought to shield herself from him. But it was too late for that. She cringed inside, thinking of her wanton abandonment in his arms. Her face flushed as she remembered responding to his touch, his voice, his smell.

Then came the anger. That he would dare touch her, a chief's daughter, was too much! That he should take the only thing she had left, her body, her virginity, infuriated her. It should not have been this way. She should have been taken with love, by her husband, by someone who cared for her and who would care for their children. Not taken as a slave on the beach like this. How she despised him!

Furious now, humiliated by her own condemning thoughts, she yanked away from him and rolled to her knees, facing him angrily. "Ahousat bastard!" she spat. "Treacherous Ahousat dog! Is this the way you make sport of me? I hate you!"

He stared at her for a long moment. "You certainly didn't hate me moments ago," he drawled. "In fact, I could have sworn you even liked me a little bit!"

With a scream she launched herself at him, her fingers curved into claws, intent on gouging his eyes from their sockets. Fighting Wolf grabbed her hands easily, and rolled her over onto her back. He leaned over her.

"Ready to go again? So soon?" he drawled in that maddening way.

"Get away from me, you filthy beast!" she cried,
enraged. "I want nothing to do with you! You're a
despicable beast! A rapist! A bastard!" This last she
screamed into his face.

Hurt by her anger when he had been so profoundly
moved by their lovemaking, Fighting Wolf responded
aggressively. Raising his hand to slap her, he gritted,
"Don't you speak like that to me, slave!" She couldn't
talk to him that way, not after what they'd shared!

Then he saw it—the shiny glimmer of a tear in the
corner of her eye. As he watched, it rolled down into her
hairline and disappeared. All that was left was a wet
trail into her dark hair.

Fighting Wolf hesitated, his hand dropped. He
gazed at her, suddenly realizing she needed time to
absorb the new feelings they'd discovered. Very well,
he'd give her time. His insight into her anger surprised
him. He wasn't in the habit of letting the needs of a
woman dictate his behavior.

To Sarita's surprise, Fighting Wolf rolled off her.
He rose and walked a short distance away, staring out to
sea.

Caught off guard, Sarita watched him warily. Then
she slowly sat up, gathering the torn remnants of her
robe about her. Breathing heavily, she was uncertain
now, but still angry. What was he up to?

Fighting Wolf sat down calmly where he was and
Sarita remained kneeling in the sand. They stayed like
that for a while, he staring at the horizon, she staring at
him.

Gradually Sarita's anger drained away. Her
breathing slowed, she relaxed and began to consider the
situation rationally, or at least as rationally as she could
under the circumstances. What would happen to her
now that Fighting Wolf had had his way with her? The
wretch! She wondered ruefully if he had noticed her
body's responses to his. Well, that certainly wouldn't
happen again. How could she ever have found him
attractive? She snorted. Now that she knew what an

animal he was, she would have nothing further to do with him. That was certain!

Her snort drew Fighting Wolf's attention. He looked across at her and saw that she had calmed down somewhat. He gazed at her, his mind spinning plans. He was not ready to let her go, not yet.

"I will keep you with me for a while," he stated evenly. "You've pleased me. And you'll continue to please, me, until I tire of you." It was an order.

Sarita's jaw dropped. "You—you worm! You bastard! I will continue to please you!" she repeated in a high shriek. "You—you—!" Words failed her. "Let me tell you something, O high and noble chief!" Her eyes blazed. Her hair in tangles, her back straight, she faced him, proud and undaunted. "*You* do not please me! You will *never* please me! And furthermore," she hissed in a lowered voice, "I will not stay to be used like this! Not by you. Not by anybody!"

Fighting Wolf had to admire her courage. It was foolish, talking to him, a chief, like that, but it was admirable nevertheless. "You know," he said casually, "you're fortunate we're not in my village. Some of my people, hearing such talk to their war chief, would demand your death."

Sarita grimaced at him. "Threatening me now, are you, Ahousat dog?" she sneered. "Well, go ahead and kill me! You've taken everything else from me! Why not my life, too!" Furious golden eyes stared into piercing ebony slits. They were both very angry.

"No," he drawled at last, "Death is no victory over a woman like you. At least not for a man like me. I'd rather have you crying out your passion for me. I want you in my bed, whenever I desire you. A much better revenge, don't you think?" He raised an eyebrow questioningly.

Furious again, Sarita could only sputter at him. "You—you dog!"

"Really," he responded coolly, "Can't you think of a more original insult? You've called me that at least three times already."

She fell silent. She would do better to find out his plans than bandy words with him, she decided. Keep calm, she encouraged herself. Don't let him rile you. Let him think you're going along with his foolish notions. "What do you plan to do with me?" she asked sullenly.

"That's better," he answered. "You might as well accept the situation." His hard eyes softened as he gazed at her. He walked over and squatted beside her. He ran one brown finger along her jawline. "You're very beautiful," he whispered. "My plans?" he said at last. "My plans are to keep you in my longhouse, away from the slave quarters. As long as you please me, you'll be under my protection. And," he paused, looking deeply into the defiant golden eyes staring back at him, "I don't want you meeting any other men. None, is that clear? No more evening strolls," he said firmly.

Sarita nodded, head lowered. She didn't want him to guess her thoughts. The next time she met Rottenwood, she'd have to be very careful.

"We both know how miserable a female slave's life can be. I'll see that you need not worry about other men's advances. My sister will continue to protect you in my absence." Even to himself he sounded pompous. "I'll do whatever I can to ease your burden of slavery," he added huskily.

Before she could stop herself the words were out. "How noble," she spat. "When you're the one who put me into slavery in the first place!"

Fighting Wolf winced at her words. He grasped her chin gently. "Nevertheless, I'll try to make your lot easier," he promised. "You can make it easier on yourself, too. You must realize that. Accept what has happened. You can still have a good life with me, with my people."

Sarita shrugged off his hand. She was obviously still angry at him, so he decided to let her be for a while. Getting to his feet, he reached down a hand and helped her up.

Even clutching the torn robe, she was dignified. She stood straight and tall, looking at him with those beautiful golden eyes, her tangled dark hair blowing gently in the warm breeze. Yes, he thought, he was very pleased to have such a beautiful woman for his own. Slinging his kutsack across one arm, he took her hand firmly in his. They started off across the sand towards the small creek where they had left the basket.

As they walked, Sarita let herself think back over what had happened. True, she was still angry about his forcing her, but some of her anger was beginning to drain away.

For the first time, she thought about the lovely feelings and sensations she had experienced. Did it mean anything to him? she wondered. When he held her in his arms, was she important to him? Or just a body to be used for his own satisfaction? She suspected the latter of Fighting Wolf. For herself, she knew that the joining she had just experienced was one of the most intimate things a woman could do with a man. She felt that she had changed, or been changed, irrevocably—from a girl to a woman. And somehow, the knowledge that it had been this marvellously masculine creature walking beside her, tall, strong, his blue-black hair gleaming in the sunlight, who was responsible for the change, secretly pleased her.

She did not dwell long on such traitorous thoughts. She forced herself to consider more mundane things. She was alive. She had survived. Though very frightened, she had fought valiantly against the odds, and she had survived the ordeal. Her virginity was gone, true, but she still had her life, her wits, and the will to use them. Perhaps things might work out well enough for her, after all.

It struck her suddenly that, if Fighting Wolf did indeed protect her, then her position in his village would at least be tolerable. She knew, even if she wanted him to—and she certainly did not!—that he would never marry her. Chiefs did not marry slaves. Not even commoners married slaves. That much she was sure of. If he denied her protection, or threw her out after he was tired of her, the best she could hope for would be marriage to another slave. The worst—well, she wouldn't dwell on that. She shuddered.

Perhaps it would be best for her if she became his mistress, she thought nervously. At least until she managed to escape. Now, more than ever, she was determined to escape. But if those wonderful feelings overwhelmed her every time Fighting Wolf took her in his arms, Sarita suspected she was in terrible danger.

And never, when she lived under her father's roof, would she have considered an alliance such as she was now being forced into. As the proud daughter of a chief, she had been taught since childhood to cultivate the community's respect for her own and her family's name. To maintain that prestige, her family had, since birth, expected her to marry well, to a noble of high rank. Living without a recognized marriage, and possibly bearing children out of wedlock, were not the ways to raise one's name in the status-conscious society in which she lived. Despite her current position as a slave, Sarita could not forget the expectations of her family. How it rankled to think of herself brought so low.

The only answer was escape. She had to escape! Until then, however, she would have to go along with Fighting Wolf's wishes. He gave her no choice in the matter, and try as she would, she could see no other alternative. For the time being, she would have to submit to his demands. Her proud spirit recoiled at the decision.

She watched Fighting Wolf out of the corner of her eye. Tall and bronze, he strode along silently beside her. His kutsack was still slung over his arm. He had made no effort to dress. His nudity did not bother Sarita, however; since childhood she had seen that men often went about naked, especially when the weather was so warm.

Women, however, did not. She looked down at the
torn robe she was clutching. It really hid very few of her
charms, torn as it was, she now realized. Her breasts
spilled forth at the top, but at least her stomach was
covered where she clutched the robe closed.

The robe split open again. She might as well be
naked!

Sarita almost smiled as she thought of how
Precious Copper would now have to find her another
kutsack. She was certainly hard on her meager ward-
robe! Fighting Wolf saw the small smile curve her lips
and he smiled in return. She really was quite
adorable—when she wasn't angry!

They reached the small gurgling stream. Sarita
stood, watching uncertainly as Fighting Wolf squatted
on his haunches and uncovered the basket. He took out
several chunks of smoked salmon. Suddenly she realized
just how hungry she really was. She sat down as gracefully as she could, feeling the warm soft sand under her
buttocks. Fighting Wolf handed her a large chunk of
salmon.

She shook her head. "I don't want your food!" she
said defiantly.

He shrugged casually. "It's up to you," he
answered, apparently indifferent. "Remember, though,
we have a long trip back to my village. Will you have
enough strength for all that paddling if you starve
yourself?"

Sarita did not answer, but sat stubbornly looking
out to sea. She couldn't refuse to eat forever, she
realized. Besides, he'd probably love to see her weak
and starving, she thought vengefully. Then he could
pounce on her whenever he wanted to!

She reached for one of the salmon chunks. Fighting
Wolf pretended not to notice. She bit into the smoked
salmon, the meat flaking off in her mouth. She loved
the salty salmon taste; it had always been delightful to
her.

Sitting on the warm sand, munching the salmon,

surrounded by the wild natural beauty of trees, sea and sky, exhausted physically and emotionally by her recent struggles, Sarita felt a warm lethargy steal over her. She began to relax. They might have been the only two people in the world, she thought, as she sat there naked, munching on the delicious salmon.

Her companion sat eating quietly and she cast her eyes surreptitiously at him now and then when she thought he wasn't aware of her. But he was—very much aware. The sight of her sitting there, delicately flaking off pieces of salmon and popping them into her luscious mouth interested him immensely, despite his cool exterior. He found himself wondering what she thought of him, if she hated him for taking her as he had, or if she too had felt the strong emotions sweep over her as they had made love. Shaking himself mentally, he conceded he was thinking like a love-smitten boy.

Getting to his feet, he walked over to the stream for a drink of the cool, clear water. Seeing a large, white clam shell lying in the stream, he picked it up and filled it with water. He drank his fill of the water, then filled it up again. He walked back to Sarita with the cool drink and wordlessly handed it to her. She hesitated, then cautiously accepted his offering; the salty salmon did tend to make one awfully thirsty!

At last, they were both satiated. Discarded scraps of salmon skin lay scattered over the sand, mute testimony to their meal.

Fighting Wolf sprawled indolently on the warm sand, contemplating the sea. Sarita's lethargy had vanished and she felt the need to move. She got to her feet. Fighting Wolf turned to her. "Don't worry, I'm not running away!" she exclaimed disparagingly, then headed for tree line. He let her go.

Spying some berry bushes clustered under a large spruce tree, she trotted over and began picking the succulent fruit. The large pink huckleberries hung heavily on several lacy, green branches. She picked two handfuls and walked back to Fighting Wolf. Smiling, she knelt down beside him and shyly offered both palms, full of the sweet, ripe fruit to him. He gazed at her solemnly and then accepted a handful of the bounty. "It's too bad they aren't poisonous," she said sweetly, unable to resist taunting him.

He burst out laughing. He continued to chuckle as he swallowed the fruit. Suddenly he clutched his stomach and began rolling on the sand. "Oooh, my stomach," he moaned. "I've been poisoned!" He continued to roll around, groaning and making grotesque faces.

Sarita burst out laughing. She couldn't help herself. It was just so funny to see him pretending to be sick. And it was secretly what she had wanted to do to him—to hurt him in some way.

"There's only one known antidote to poison huckleberries," he said between moans. He thrashed around some more until Sarita's curiosity got the better of her.

"What is that?" she asked, playing along with him.

"A kiss from a beautiful maiden!" he answered, springing towards her. She shrieked and tried to get away, but he held her down. "Now, lovely maiden," he said, chuckling, "will you save a poor poisoned man?" Sarita shook her head. "Only one small kiss," he coaxed. Sarita laughed and kissed him gingerly on the mouth. "Not enough," he said. "More." This time she kissed him full on the lips and held it. "Aaah," he sighed. "Saved—" He went limp in her arms and they both laughed.

Reluctantly Fighting Wolf stood up, pulling Sarita to her feet. She felt shy all of a sudden. Fighting Wolf broke the awkward silence.

"I'm going for a swim," he said in his deep voice. "Will you join me?"

Sarita responded quietly, "Yes, I'd like that." She was still unsure of how to behave with him. Though he joked with her, he still held all the power.

Taking her hand, he led her towards the water's

edge, the dry sand squeaking underfoot. Once they reached the firm wet sand, Sarita broke loose and ran for the waves.

She felt like a little girl again as she pranced and kicked the cool water. The waves rolled in, their timeless rhythm swirling the water about her ankles. She thought of how these waves had danced into shore since the beginning of time and how they would dance into shore long after she and her children's children had departed this earth.

Then the pensive thought was gone and she was jumping over those same waves, playing a game with them, not letting them touch her toes.

She turned and watched as Fighting Wolf padded up to the water. Giving a small laugh, she ran farther out to sea, then turned quickly and began kicking water at him. The clear spray arched towards him. She lunged as the cold water hit him, the silver droplets of water beading and running down his bronze shoulders and chest. She laughed even harder as he growled low in his throat and pretended to lunge at her.

Backing farther into the deeper water, now waist-high, she kept splashing at him, this time with both arms. She squealed in mock fear when he really did lunge for her, diving into the shallow water and swimming under her.

Fighting Wolf grabbed her knees and jerked her under with him. Sarita gasped and struggled as the water closed over her head, sure he was going to drown her. He let her go at once and she darted away, only to be caught as he again tripped her underwater. She pushed vigorously at his head, trying to break his hold, but to no avail. Taking a deep breath, she bent under the water and tickled his ribs. That made him let go! She heard his laugh underwater and saw the air burst out of his mouth. Sputtering, he jumped up, laughing.

She squatted in the water, grinning as she watched him, wary of his next move. Seeing her watching him, he cunningly feinted in one direction and then lunged in the other. Catching her up into his arms, he cradled her, one arm under her knees, the other under her neck. Swinging her high and wide, he threw her out into the deeper water.

Landing with a loud splash, Sarita twisted underwater and swam straight for him. Grabbing at his knees, she caught him by surprise. Off-balance, he fell splashing to one side. She burst straight out of the water, giggling in delight at catching him off guard. He grinned back at her, calling, "Truce, truce!"

"All right," she laughed, flushed. "I'll let you go—this time!"

They chuckled together as they walked back to their picnic spot on the beach, the hot sun quickly drying their naked bodies.

13

As the day waned, Sarita hoped for an imminent departure but Fighting Wolf made no move to leave their private beach. She had no wish to be trapped overnight on a deserted beach with the man. He might make love to her again. She watched him nervously, then finally broached the subject. "Shouldn't we be getting back to your village? If we leave now we can arrive home before dark."

He looked at her incredulously. "Are you so anxious to get back to my village? I thought you enjoyed being alone with me."

She caught the glint of humor in his dark eyes. She stuck out her chin. "Is that so? Whatever gave you that idea? I just thought you'd want to leave early, that's all," she answered, her voice tapering off weakly.

Fighting Wolf was clearly enjoying her discomfort. "No," he responded casually. "I've decided we'll stay here for a while. Surely you have no objections?" he asked, raising one eyebrow.

"And if I did?" she answered as haughtily as she could manage. "What good would it do for me to raise them? You'd do what you wanted to, anyway!"

"True," he responded dryly. "You know me too well. You'll know me even better after we've spent more time alone," he added. That was not what Sarita wanted to hear. She stared at the sky, marshalling her thoughts.

The sun was starting to set, the great golden disk

hovered over the sea. The sky was awash in purple and gold, highlighted with pink streaks.

"How long is 'a while'?" she asked at last.

"Oh, a few days—two or three, maybe."

"Two or three! But—but don't you need to get back to your people? Your sister—?"

He looked at her, amused. "Such concern for me and my people is impressive," he mocked. "To what do I owe such concern?"

"You blackguard! It's not concern! I don't want to be here with you, alone, all the time!"

"Truly? And why not?" He reached for her and drew her, protesting, to him.

"I just don't, that's all!" She was trying to fend off his strong arms but he held her in a firm grip.

"Mmm, well, I want to be here with you," he answered in muffled tones as he buried his face in her fragrant hair. He kissed his way down her throat, touching lightly on her rapidly beating pulse.

She stiffened and said through clenched teeth, "Don't."

"Don't what?"

"Don't do this to me. I don't like it," she lied.

Suddenly he pushed her away. She was free. She pulled back, startled.

"Go get some firewood, woman! We *will* be staying here. Do as I say. Now!"

Sarita was too astonished at the sudden change in his manner to do more than stumble to her feet. She gaped at him openmouthed for a moment, then clamped her jaw shut and stalked off to find driftwood for a fire. As she gathered the wood, she mumbled to herself about the vagaries and peculiarities of men, and of one man in particular.

Why had he suddenly pushed her away? she wondered. Was it something she'd said? She went over her words in her mind. Aah. She'd said she didn't like his lovemaking. Had he known she was lying? Was that why he'd rejected her? Or did he think he was such a great lover? That was probably it. She'd offended him because she wasn't smitten by his amorous advances! She almost laughed aloud. If only he knew how much she liked what he did to her!

Peeking over, she watched as Fighting Wolf dragged several larger pieces of wood to one spot and then lit some cedar shavings with a strike-a-light. He'd acquired it in trade with the whites. Within a short time, a fire was burning cheerfully. Sarita marveled at how quickly the fire had started. What an improvement over the time-consuming fire drill.

Now that the sun had gone down, the night air was chilly. She carried a large armload of dry driftwood closer to the warmth of the fire. She reached for her torn kutsack and flung it over her shoulders like a cape. Glancing across the fire, her eyes met Fighting Wolf's steadfast gaze. He appeared to be over his fit of anger, she noticed.

"What do you want?" she asked rudely.

He only chuckled. Getting up, he fetched the basket and pulled out smoked salmon and dried salal cakes. He offered her some. She eyed him carefully for a moment, then took the food. She did not like being so dependent on him for food and resolved that tomorrow she would look for some roots and berries to contribute to their diet.

Their meal finished, Fighting Wolf spread out his kutsack, obviously preparing for sleep. "Come here," he said quietly, patting his garment. Sarita shook her head slowly, never taking her eyes off him. He watched her in the flickering firelight. Her golden eyes gazed back at him, defiantly, fearlessly. He smiled to himself. The woman was certainly a challenge. A refreshing change from the easy conquests he was used to. Still, he must not let her have her own way. That would be disastrous. He shifted tactics.

"Tell me about yourself," he said gently, hoping to soften her up with conversation.

"What do you want to know?" she asked. She was suspicious of his apparent gentleness. The man she knew took what he wanted, when he wanted it.

"Well," he answered. "Your name for one. Where did you get such a beautiful name?"

"From my mother," she answered proudly. "It was the name of her mother's mother. It's also the name of a beautiful, smooth flowing river near where my mother grew up. After she married my father she moved away from her village. She was very happy at Hesquiat but she always remembered that beautiful river. As a child, she would sit by its banks and daydream." Sarita herself looked to be in a daydream.

"A beautiful name for a beautiful woman," Fighting Wolf's voice, soft now, brought her out of her brief reverie. "But I think you were misnamed," he said.

"Oh?"

"Yes, definitely. You should have been called Raging River, Wicked Waterfall, or Rapid Current. I don't see you as a quiet, slow-flowing river at all." Sarita laughed, charmed by his gentle humor.

"And you," she responded curiously. "How did you get your name? It's very formidable."

"Thank you," he answered, obviously pleased. "When I was a small boy of about ten summers, the 'Wolves' kidnapped me and several other children. It was part of a winter celebration when a nearby tribe visited us. The other children were very afraid of the 'Wolves,' adult men who wore fierce wolf masks. I'm told that I was the only one who did not cry or act afraid. In fact I attacked one of the 'Wolves' and tried to organize an escape. The 'Wolves' were very impressed and my father was extremely pleased when he heard this. He gave a great feast in honor of my bravery. The name 'Wolf' had been in my family for generations. My name became Fights with Wolves. Later, because of my battle experiences, it was shortened to 'Fighting Wolf.' "

Sarita looked at him admiringly. She guessed he had left out several important details. Still, it was gratifying to hear a man modest about his achievements, especially in a society that expected men to boast of their prowess at all times.

Seeing her thoughtfulness, Fighting Wolf reached for her and drew her back against him. He held her gently in his arms and nibbled softly on one ear. Sarita relaxed, languorous from the warm fire, and the warmth of his hard body. She knew there was nowhere to run and allowed herself to concentrate on the feelings he was arousing. Encouraged by her stillness, Fighting Wolf pursued his suit more aggressively. One hand curved over her rounded breast, the other, wrapped around her waist, held her close to him. Now he was planting feather kisses on the back of her neck. The hand on her waist was dropping lower, covering her stomach in slow, swirling motions. Sarita stretched and pushed herself closer to him. Encouraged by her response, Fighting Wolf lay back carefully, taking her with him. With one smooth movement, he was leaning over her, looking into golden eyes. He smiled and murmured small endearments as he brushed his lips along her jawline and to her ear. Sarita closed her eyes and gave herself over to sensation. Her breathing was starting to come in short gasps. Fighting Wolf leaned over her, one hand gently caressing a breast, the other propping his body. The sensations running through Sarita were at once both relaxing and stimulating. She had never felt like this before. She was apprehensive of what came next. Remembering the pain from her first time, she started and tried to sit up.

"What?" breathed Fighting Wolf.

"The pain—"

"Aahhh now, no pain this time, little one. Only pleasure. Let me love you," he coaxed, his breath hot in her ear.

She thought of struggling again, of fighting him off, but knew she could not prevail against his superior strength. Meanwhile, Fighting Wolf's hands and mouth were convincing her already traitorous body to surrender. Sighing, she lay back and relaxed under his ministrations. His lips sought and found the ripe fruit of her breasts and his tongue swirled the hard nipples. Then he was kissing her fully on the mouth, his tongue playing with her mouth, licking, sucking, tasting, teasing.

Sarita was so caught up in these sensations she didn't notice at first that one hand was gently exploring against her soft entrance. With one knee, he pushed her unresisting legs apart. She tensed slightly, then relaxed. She felt a soft tickle as he nudged his way into her, ever so slowly. Finally, his length fully enclosed within her, he held her close to him. Then began the rocking motion that felt so good. Wrapping her long legs about his waist, she forced him closer. Her fingers dug into his buttocks; her small whimpers encouraged his pulsing rhythm. He drove into her, pounding into her with all the power in his big, muscular body. Suddenly she felt a wave of incredible sweetness sweep over her and engulf her entire being. Its beauty was so powerful that tears ran down her face.

"My darling, my darling," she murmured brokenly as he too, struggled and reached that sweet release he had long sought. Never, ever had anyone told her that loving a man could be like this! "I didn't know, I didn't know it could be so beautiful," she sobbed into his shoulder.

He raised his head to look at her, tears streaming down her face, and he knew she, too, felt as he did, that feeling that was beyond words, that feeling that he and she were one. Profoundly moved, he held her to him, murmuring over and over into her soft dark hair, reassuring her, "Hush, hush my love, it's all right." All through the long, cold night they slept in each other's arms.

14

Hesquiat Summer Village

Feast Giver moaned. He lay on the hard cedar planking that was his bed. Crab Woman looked up from tending the fire. Had she heard something? She shook her head. Nothing.

She went back to her task. Prodding some fern roots out of the hot ashes, she piled them carefully onto a cedar platter. She shuffled slowly over to where her injured husband, Thunder Maker, lay. He looked so thin. Ever since . . . No, she didn't want to remember that night.

Sitting down heavily beside him, she lifted his head off the bed. Sunken cheeks, hollow eyes stared out at her. His head lolled in her hands. She dropped it with a thunking sound back onto the fur-covered plank. She waved a steaming hot fern root at him. It was one of his favorite foods. The old man turned his face to the wall.

What was the matter? she thought helplessly. He was wasting away before his family's—what was left of them—very eyes. Ah well, perhaps that slave could get him to eat.

Signalling to Cedar Bundle, Crab Woman sat there stolidly until the younger woman approached. "See if he'll eat some of these fern roots. I can't get him to eat a thing. I have no patience with him today."

Cedar Bundle nodded and sat by the sick man. Ever since she had been given the job of tending the injured chief, Cedar Bundle had watched as he responded slowly, little by little, to her. She found she enjoyed nursing him, and she was the only person who could get the ailing chief to eat. Even his favorite wife, Abalone Woman, could not always get him to drink the nutritious soups and teas she prepared. More and more of his care fell on the willing shoulders of Cedar Bundle. And because she genuinely wanted to see him recover, she did her best to make his convalescence comfortable.

Crab Woman made her way slowly to where her stepson, Feast Giver, lay. All these sick people lying around were making her irritable.

Feast Giver's breathing was hoarse, his body in the same position as when she had last checked him. Just as she was turning away, she heard it. A moan. She walked back to his bedside.

For several days after the attack by the Ahousats, Feast Giver had fought a raging fever. Abalone Woman had done all she could to bring the young man back to health. She had an extensive knowledge of herbal remedies passed down through her family for generations.

The fever was past, but Feast Giver's injuries, though few, were very serious. A glancing blow to the side of his head was responsible for the young man's frequent lapses in and out of consciousness. A huge purple and black bruise covered one shoulder.

An internal injury, a stab would in his ribs, was only now slowly healing. To aid his recovery, Abalone Woman had insisted that he drink a cold, foul-tasting tea several times a day. Crab Woman had watched as Abalone Woman had prepared it. After pounding equal portions of Red Alder, Grand Fir and Western Hemlock barks, Abalone Woman had steeped them in hot water. Once the infusion cooled, she had directed Crab Woman to give it to Feast Giver.

Crab Woman loathed the messy job. If the unconscious man wasn't dribbling the medicine all over his face and her, then he was spitting it back at her! Really!

And after all she'd done for him!

Crab Woman leaned over the young man, listening for further moans. She saw the flutter of his eyelashes.

It was with a great struggle that Feast Giver awoke. He mightily resisted being drawn back into the black vortex from which he had barely escaped. At last he was able to see a large vague shape hovering over him. Focusing, he recognized Crab Woman, his father's chief wife.

"What—what happened?" he mumbled.

"Battle," came the succinct answer. Then in an earsplitting shriek, "Abalone! Come quickly! He wakes!" Feast Giver groaned, trying to shut out the loud noise. He closed his eyes briefly and opened them to see Abalone Woman, his father's second wife, waving Crab Woman away.

"What happened?" he asked again, the words clearer this time.

Before Abalone Woman could answer, he passed out. She looked anxiously at Crab Woman. "I don't like the way he keeps waking up, then losing consciousness. It's not a good sign. I'm afraid that one of these times he won't wake up."

Crab Woman sighed heavily. "Let's wake him up then. He's been lying around here too long, anyway."

"It's not that easy—" began Abalone Woman. She winced as Crab Woman called loudly to the unconscious man. Surely such a sound would drive the poor man's spirit away!

A harsh cawing pounded at Feast Giver's ears, penetrating his darkness. A crow? A raven? Why was a raven screeching at him? Feast Giver came out of his stupor, his glazed eyes settling on the large dark figure calling his name with such vigor. Crab Woman again. "Go away with that infernal noise," he muttered irritably.

"He's awake," announced Crab Woman triumphantly to her co-wife.

"Of course, I'm awake." Feast Giver's voice was

stronger now. He turned slowly to face Abalone Woman. "You were telling me what happened—" he prompted.

"Are you sure you're up to hearing this?" she questioned cautiously. She feared bad news would send her patient back into a swoon.

"Yes, yes," he answered impatiently. "Tell me what happened."

Abalone Woman hesitated, unsure. He had been ill for so long. "There was a raid. The Ahousats . . ." she began tentatively.

"Aah yes," he mumbled. It was slowly coming back. The fighting, the screaming, his sister's wedding feast, betrayal. He groaned anew. "Why—why am I not—?"

"Dead?" she finished for him. "Crab Woman dragged you to safety after you fell from the blow on your head. She hid you in a corner, underneath some cedar mats. But Fighting Wolf found you. He tied you up with your father, surrounded by our dying warriors. Fighting Wolf wanted revenge. He decided to let you live. His revenge was your humiliation and loss of your good name." Her voice broke and she looked away.

Feast Giver nodded. Everything was slowly coming back to him. He noticed Crab Woman was still standing nearby, watching. "Crab Woman," he called. He reached out and took her hand when she came closer. "Thank you for saving me from the Ahousats," he said earnestly.

The old woman shrugged and withdrew her hand. "It was nothing." Her small, bright eyes blinked several times.

"Nothing to you, perhaps, but my life to me." He tried to chuckle, but only a small gurgle came out.

"Hush," soothed Abalone Woman. "You must rest now."

"No," and his voice sounded firm again. "I must know. What of my father?" Feast Giver feared the worst. The old man would have fought to the death.

"Thunder Maker lies on his bed, wasting away from shame and humiliation. His physical wounds are not good but the wounds we cannot see, the wounds to his pride and his heart, are serious indeed," Abalone Woman said sorrowfully.

Feast Giver paused a long moment, considering. At last he asked, "And Sarita? My sister. Is she—?"

"She's been taken," Abalone Woman answered gently. "She was stolen by the Ahousats in the raid. Several of our young women were stolen," she added sadly.

Feast Giver struggled to sit up. He grabbed Abalone Woman's hand. She pushed him carefully back onto the bed furs. "Abalone, I swear to you I'll kill them. I'll kill them all! I'll find my sister and bring her home and I'll kill every Ahousat dog I can find!" He lay panting from the exertion of his outburst.

Abalone Woman looked at him sadly, suddenly afraid for him and for her people. So much death and destruction! Would it never end?

"Please," she said softly, "don't worry yourself with such matters. It's more important that you get well."

He nodded, already drifting off again. "I'll get better, Abalone. When I do, those Ahousats—" He was asleep, his breathing strong and even.

Feast Giver was as good as his word. From that day on, his health continued to improve. Gone, however, was the happy, joking young man that all knew and loved. In his place was a grim, determined man, seldom given to laughter. And when small children came to visit him, the children he used to laugh and play with and hunt for crabs with, he dismissed them and turned his face to the wall.

One day, Feast Giver rose shakily to his feet, determined to get out into the sunshine, away from the dark confines of the longhouse. Near collapse, he teetered to the door. Then he felt a strong body support him under the arm. "Take me out into the sunlight," he demanded of Abalone Woman.

They staggered to the beach, and Feast Giver sank down gratefully amidst the sand and small pebbles at the high tide line. He breathed deeply of the fresh clean air blowing off the sea. How warm the sun felt! He sat watching the rhythmic play of the sparkling waves in the bay, his fertile mind busy hatching plans.

While Feast Giver continued to improve quickly, Thunder Maker's recovery was much slower. Several times, Feast Giver went to visit his father, only to turn away after long silent vigils, numbed by the change in the old man. Like Abalone Woman, Feast Giver suspected it was a sickness of Thunder Maker's spirit more than of his body.

Feast Giver stopped by the old man's bedside one afternoon. A slave woman hovered in the background, a bowl of soup in her hand. "How do you feel today, Nuwiksu?" he asked quietly. Perhaps today his father would speak.

The old man looked at him for a long moment. "Not good, my son," he answered at last.

This was more than his parent had said to Feast Giver in a long time. Encouraged, Feast Giver continued, "Where do you hurt, Nuwiksu? I mean besides the wound in your shoulder," he added hastily. He knew that the cut tendons in the old man's shoulder must ache painfully and would take a long time to heal.

While he waited patiently for his father's answer, he noticed the slave woman set aside the soup and approach the bed. She began fussing with her patient. Feast Giver, annoyed, watched her needless ministrations, but said nothing.

A bitter chuckle drew his attention back to his father. "Where I hurt is here," and Thunder Maker folded his good arm and pressed his hand to his heart. "My people are gone. My daughter and young women are stolen. My warriors are dead."

Feast Giver watched his father intently, unaware of the slave woman's warning glances. His concentration

Thrill to the most sensual, adventure-filled Historical Romances on the market today...

FROM ⌊ *LEISURE BOOKS*

As a home subscriber to the Leisure Romance Book Club, you'll enjoy the best in today's BRAND-NEW Historical Romance fiction. For over twenty years, Leisure Books has brought you the award-winning, high-quality authors you know and love to read. Each Leisure Historical Romance will sweep you away to a world of high adventure...and intimate romance. Discover for yourself all the passion and excitement millions of readers thrill to each and every month.

Save $5.⁰⁰ Each Time You Buy!

Six times a year, the Leisure Romance Book Club brings you four brand-new titles from Leisure Books, America's foremost publisher of Historical Romances. EACH PACKAGE WILL SAVE YOU $5.00 FROM THE BOOKSTORE PRICE! And you'll never miss a new title with our convenient home delivery service.

Here's how we do it. Each package will carry a FREE 10-DAY EXAMINATION privilege. At the end of that time, if you decide to keep your books, simply pay the low invoice price of $14.96, no shipping or handling charges added. HOME DELIVERY IS ALWAYS FREE. With today's top Historical Romance novels selling for $4.99 and higher, our price SAVES YOU $5.00 with each shipment.

AND YOUR FIRST FOUR-BOOK SHIPMENT IS TOTALLY FREE!

IT'S A BARGAIN YOU CAN'T BEAT! A Super $19.96 Value!

⌊ *LEISURE BOOKS* A Division of Dorchester Publishing Co., Inc.

GET YOUR 4 FREE BOOKS NOW—A $19.96 Value!

Mail the Free Book Certificate Today!

Get Four Books Totally FREE— A $19.96 Value!

PLEASE RUSH
MY FOUR FREE
BOOKS TO ME
RIGHT AWAY!

Leisure Romance Book Club
65 Commerce Road
Stamford CT 06902-4563

was interrupted when the woman had the effrontery to lean over and whisper into Thunder Maker's ear. This woman does not know her place, thought Feast Giver angrily. But Thunder Maker, instead of reprimanding her sharply, merely waved a hand. "It's alright, Cedar Bundle," he assured the slave woman. "I feel better talking about what happened. I've been silent far too long."

"I understand," murmured Cedar Bundle, eyes downcast momentarily. "Can I get you some water?" she asked solicitously.

Thunder Maker nodded and turned back to his son. "My name is nothing now," he said bitterly. His speech halting, he described Fighting Wolf's vengeful taunts. "He's had his revenge!" the old man finished. "I am nothing. I have nothing—nothing worth living for."

Feast Giver was silent. The despair and self-blame in his father's words were overwhelming. If the old man really felt so useless, then, indeed, he would continue to waste away, thought Feast Giver.

The slave woman returned with the water just in time to hear Thunder Maker's last words. "Thunder Maker," she chided, as Feast Giver's jaw dropped. "How can you say you have nothing to live for? What about your son? He's not lost to you." In a gentler voice, she added, "He knows you're a wise chief; he looks to you for hope. We all do."

Feast Giver was about to chastise the woman for speaking out of turn, when his father sighed heavily. "What you say is true, Cedar Bundle. I am fortunate to have my son, alive before me. But sometimes the weight of my people's sorrows overwhelms me and I forget to hope."

All three were silent. At last Feast Giver roused himself. "We must retaliate for what the Ahousats have done to us. Those Ahousats bastards can't get away with killing our warriors and taking our women!" He ground out the words between clenched teeth.

"And will retaliation give you hope, my son?"

asked Thunder Maker, his eyes focusing thoughtfully on the young chief. "Will revenge right the wrongs done to us?"

"Of course!" snapped Feast Giver with confidence.

The older man shifted his gaze to Cedar Bundle, then back to his son. Almost inaudibly, Thunder Maker objected, "But so many will suffer." Feast Giver leaned forward to hear the words more clearly. Thunder Maker spoke up. "My son, you're all I have left. I don't want to lose you, too. Don't talk to me of revenge." He passed a weary hand across his brow. "Leave me now. I must sleep."

The slave woman dared a quick frown in Feast Giver's direction. Then bringing a cedar blanket over to the ailing chief, she covered Thunder Maker gently with the blanket. She nestled herself comfortably on the floor nearby, obviously intending to keep watch over the old man as he slept. Feast Giver decided against reprimanding her for her rude behavior—this time. He realized his father had probably encouraged her poor manners.

Shrugging to himself, Feast Giver walked away thoughtfully. He must convince his father that reprisals against the Ahousats were absolutely necessary—for him, for his father, for his people.

Feast Giver continued to call on his father. The old man began to show a gradual improvement. Perhaps it was the young man's visits, perhaps it was the conversation they shared that one day. Whatever the reason, Thunder Maker began to take an interest in those around him. No longer did he turn his face to the wall. Now he watched his wives as they moved about the longhouse. He drank the medicines prepared for him by Abalone Woman and in general began to get his energy back.

One day Feast Giver was at Thunder Maker's bedside. As usual, the slave woman Cedar Bundle was also in attendance.

"I'm tired of lying around this longhouse," snapped Thunder Maker. "Take me outside so I can breathe fresh air, smell the sea and watch children play," he ordered the slave woman. "I can't stand being shut in this dark house any longer!"

Feast Giver and Cedar Bundle carried the old man outside to the beach. There Cedar Bundle fussed about with him and propped him up with cedar mats. She made sure he was covered with a soft cedar blanket so the slight breeze would not give him a chill. As she as wrapping another cedar blanket around his shoulders, he yelled out, "Enough, woman! Stop your fussing! Leave me to my son. We want to have a man-to-man talk."

With a twinkle in her eye, Cedar Bundle gravely patted the chief's hand. "Now I know you're getting better—you're anxious to be up and around," she said softly.

Drawn out of his anger, Thunder Maker smiled at her and said gruffly, "Go, woman. You've done enough for me." He watched as she walked gracefully back to the longhouse.

"Ah son, she reminds me of your mother." Feast Giver looked at his father in astonishment. Cedar Bundle was not at all like the memories he carried of his mother. His father continued, "How I miss your mother, even after these many years." Thunder Maker sighed heavily, then added, "Now I have Cedar Bundle. She's a good woman." Feast Giver, for once, was speechless. His father mistook the silence for tact. "What have you been doing while I've been wasting away in my longhouse?"

Feast Giver cleared his throat and responded cautiously, "I've been talking with some of the young men, Nuwiksu. They want revenge for the Ahousat betrayal."

His father nodded. "I was afraid of that, my son. I suspected you would not give up your plans of revenge.''

"Nuwiksu, you know I think we must avenge ourselves. If it becomes known up and down the coast that the Ahousats can come and kill our warriors and take our women, then we'll have nothing.''

His father nodded. "Too true, too true. Ah, but how I hate to risk your life, my son. You're all I have left now. Your sister is gone. Who knows if she's even alive—''

The scowl on his son's face cut short Thunder Maker's words. "My sister lives,'' stated Feast Giver stubbornly.

"Perhaps, my son, perhaps. Nevertheless,'' pointed out Thunder Maker, "I have no warriors left. Even were we to carry out your plans, we don't have the men to do it. Too many Hesquiat warriors were killed by the Ahousats. Too many Hesquiat heads sit on pikes in Ahousat village.''

"We may have few men, but those we do have are strong and eager to fight the Ahousats,'' answered Feast Giver. "Nuwkisu, listen. I have a plan, but to carry it out, our men must be well-armed.'' His father was watching him speculatively. "Nuwiksu, I want new weapons from the white traders,'' said Feast Giver evenly. "I want the weapons the traders call 'mus-kets.' ''

He waited to see his father's reaction. "I'm listening, my son.''

"These mus-kets can kill a man with one shot. A hard ball is rammed down the throat of the weapon—it looks like a heavy stick—then the stick is pointed at whoever you want to kill. I've heard talk of these weapons and I want them.''

Thunder Maker nodded slowly. "I've heard such talk myself,'' he revealed. Then he added musingly, "We have enough furs to trade for a few such weapons.'' He eyed his son thoughtfully. "But I want you to promise me one thing. I'll give my consent to your revenge raid only on one condition.''

Thunder Maker waited; it was Feast Giver's turn to watch warily.

"I want your consent, Nuwiksu," answered the young man at last. "You know I don't want a break between us."

"Good," grunted his father. "The condition is this: before you lead a revenge raid, you must rescue your sister." He held up his good arm to prevent the outburst even now forming on Feast Giver's lips. "I'm afraid for her life if you raid the Ahousats while she's still there. They'll kill her—if she's not already dead."

Feast Giver felt torn. He loved his sister and wanted her safe, but he felt deeply the obligation to uphold the family honor. And already, too much time had passed . . . At last he spoke, but his voice was as heavy as his heart, "Nuwiksu, I'll do as you say. I'll lead a rescue party for Sarita. But once she's safely returned," he emphasized forcefully, "I will lead my raid for vengeance." He smiled, his lips cruel. "And now, about those mus-kets—"

15

The several days that Fighting Wolf and Sarita spent at the beach seemed to fly by. Gathering berries and roots, fishing, swimming, laughing, and playing occupied their days. Moonlight swims and making sweet love occupied their nights. It was a time together like no other; here there was no master, no slave, just two people who laughed and loved together. Sarita was content with Fighting Wolf and pushed all thoughts that he was her enemy from her mind.

For him, it was an idyllic time. He gloried in the sensuousness of it all: the warm sunny weather, the cool water, the beautiful scenery. But most of all, the lovely woman at his side. When they made love, it was as if they had been fashioned only for each other. Never had a woman felt so perfect for him. During the days, too, he found her to be an enchanting, intelligent companion, interested in many things. He was becoming deeply enamored of her. He determined that when he was back in his village, he would keep her for himself. She was his.

Sarita relaxed and blossomed during this carefree time. Here with Fighting Wolf, she felt strangely free. Here he was entertaining, amusing friend, not the intimidating warrior she had known in the village. She felt free to be herself, to laugh, to make silly jokes, to feel happy and to make love. It was truly as if only the two of them existed in the world.

Then one morning Fighting Wolf woke her with a

kiss and the simple statement, "It's time to go back."
Sarita had known that this bliss could not last forever;
nevertheless she was sorry that the end had come so
soon. She nodded and returned his kiss slowly,
wondering how things would be for them, for her, once
they were back at the village. She rolled away from him
and rose quickly, gracefully, her long, lithe body
shivering. She pulled her kutsack, mended now, over
her head and, smiling, reached out a hand to pull him up.

Together they ate a simple breakfast of fish, berries
and roots gathered the day before. Their few
possessions were packed away, including a new, carved
digging stick Fighting Wolf had made for her. Then
Fighting Wolf loaded everything into the waiting canoe.

Reluctantly Sarita turned and her eyes swept the
panorama of beach. Wisps of mist still rolled over the
beach, the tops of the trees were gray in the morning
light, the dark shadow of sand stretched off into the
distance—she wanted to memorize it all. She had been
truly happy here, and she did not know when she would
feel as carefree and happy again.

Fighting Wolf pushed the small canoe into the surf
and they were on their way. The morning mist was all
around them now, muffling the sound of their paddling,
touching their skin with long wet fingers, leaving kisses
of dew in their dark hair.

They paddled for a long while until Sarita finally
broke the silence. "What will happen to me once we're
back in your village?" she asked bluntly. The question
had been preying on her mind all morning. She wanted
to know. She had to know.

Fighting Wolf continued paddling as he pondered
what to tell her. At last he stated arrogantly, "You're
mine. I'll let no one take you. You'll continue to stay in
my living quarters."

A feeling of hopelessness spread over Sarita at his
words. Nothing had changed. All these feelings she had
discovered, her body's responses to his touch, her
happiness at being with him, were all as nought to him.

He merely thought of her as a possession, someone to be owned. Her back to him, she concentrated on paddling, ignoring the tears that slid down her cheeks and mingled with the wet kisses left there by the mist.

They continued silently on their way, the rhythm of the paddling hypnotic, taking them farther and farther from their beach idyll.

Fighting Wolf was pleased. She was everything, and more, that he wanted in a woman. The last few days had shown him that. Even now, when he knew she must be disappointed to be going back, she did not reproach him, or beg and plead. Yes, he would keep her. She was his.

He wondered idly how it would have been between them had they been married, had he not stolen her away. Then he shrugged. It was better this way. He had complete control over her and could have her beautiful body whenever he wanted. He did not have to put up with what *she* wanted. Except in lovemaking, of course. Then he wanted to know what pleased her. He chuckled to himself. Even now, after several days with her, he desired her. The thought surprised him. Usually by this time, having spent so much time with one woman, he would have been glad to be rid of her.

He tried to picture his first wife running nude through the surf, splashing him, playing and laughing with him, and failed utterly. Gentle and quiet as she was, she could never have let herself play like that. If it had been her he was with for the last several days, he would have been bored. Well, perhaps not bored, merely uninterested.

Sarita could see the village now. The fog had rolled away, the hot sun was high overhead, burning down on them. Again she was struck by the picturesque setting of the summer village. The tops of the high mountains in back of the village were still covered in swirling mists. The lower mountains stood out gray-green. The river to one side flowed swiftly, its gray waters meeting and swirling with the sea on one side. Small figures moved

on the beach. The gray, weather-beaten boards of the
longhouses contrasted with the tall, dry, yellow grasses
growing around them.

As Fighting Wolf and Sarita approached the beach,
several figures ran towards their canoe. A man, a
commoner from Fighting Wolf's longhouse, waded out
and grabbed the bow of the canoe and pulled it in to
shore.

The people on the beach yelled greetings to
Fighting Wolf, ignoring Sarita. He greeted each of them
in turn as he stepped out of the canoe. He strode up the
beach to his longhouse, leaving Sarita to follow. She
paced silently, carrying her load, mouth set in a tight
line, back as straight as it could be under the weight of the
basket. Fighting Wolf couldn't have made it any clearer
that she was a slave again, she thought sardonically.

As Sarita reached the grass growing above the high
tide line, her proud gaze caught a pair of flashing dark
eyes. Walking towards her came a tall, willowy woman
dressed in a pale yellow kutsack trimmed with sea otter.
Obviously of the noble class, her pretty face was marred
by the sneer that curled her lips.

Sarita recognized her at once as the woman she'd
mistaken for Fighting Wolf's wife, the woman who had
hugged him so effusively on that long ago morning of
Sarita's capture.

The sloe-eyed woman, one hand on her hip in a
belligerent stance, blocked Sarita's passage. Sarita
halted, noting nervously that they were alone. Eyes
blazing, the woman leaned close to Sarita. "Where have
you been, slave?" Contempt dripped from her voice.

Taken aback at the woman's hostility and
unreasonable question, Sarita didn't answer for a
moment.

"I'm talking to you, slave. Answer me! Where did
he take you?"

"I fail to see how that's any of your concern," shot
back Sarita. She would not let this woman, whoever she
was, bully her.

"Aah, but it is my concern. You see," purred the woman, "Fighting Wolf is mine. Mine! He belongs to me, Rough Seas." Sarita gazed back at her impassively. "We're to be married," stated the other woman, watching Sarita narrowly.

Sarita flinched, but quickly regained her impassive countenance. What a fool she'd been to think that Fighting Wolf might like her, perhaps even love her one day. All the companionship and lovemaking of the past few days might never have been, Sarita thought bitterly. Fighting Wolf had only trifled with her feelings and her body when all along he had this woman waiting for him!

"Stay away from him," warned Rough Seas. "He's mine!"

Sarita marveled that Rough Seas thought Sarita, a slave, could evade the attentions of the man who was her master, especially if he was determined to bed her. Noblewomen had no idea what it was like to be a slave, she thought sadly. Aloud she said, "If he's yours, why isn't he with you? Why's he spending time with me?"

"Bitch!" screeched the other. "So you don't deny you were with him!" Furious, Rough Seas slapped Sarita sharply across the face.

Sarita recoiled from the impact, the red imprint of a hand reddening one cheek. Angry now, she wanted to strike back at that malevolent face. Raising her hand, she dropped it just as quickly, remembering she risked death if she struck a noblewoman. How Rough Seas would love that! "You say he's yours," Sarita sneered instead. "He doesn't show it, does he? I'd say Fighting Wolf doesn't want you at all!"

The contorted face in front of Sarita looked ready to explode with fury, when suddenly Rough Seas stepped aside and hissed in a low voice, a vicious parody of a smile on her lips, "Bitch! Fighting Wolf wants me! He's going to marry me!" She lowered her voice to hiss, "And when he does, the next day you'll be dead!"

Then she was gone, fleeing back to her longhouse. Thoughtfully, Sarita watched her disappear. She did not relish having a vengeful noblewoman as an enemy!

"What did she want?" came Fighting Wolf's deep voice. Sarita turned, surprised. He'd come upon her so quietly. She realized Rough Seas must have seen him. Why hadn't she stayed to confront him? If Fighting Wolf was her betrothed, she would have, thought Sarita angrily.

"She wanted you," came Sarita's terse response.

"What did you tell her?" he asked. She noticed he was eyeing her reddened cheek curiously. She put a hand to it, and turned from his gaze.

"I told her she could have you!" lied Sarita coolly. Let him think what he liked. She wasn't going to let him know she had practically challenged that sloe-eyed woman over him.

Fighting Wolf burst into loud laughter and was still laughing as they entered the longhouse.

Sarita felt a sharp stab of regret as she thought of the jealous Rough Seas' words. She should have known a man as attractive as Fighting Wolf would have a woman or even several women. What a fool she had been to think she meant something special to him. That she might even be the only woman he cared for. What a fool! Now he was going to marry that—that cruel woman.

They deserved each other, she thought angrily. What a fine marriage they would have—the woman-chasing warrior and the jealous, would-be murderer. Between the two of them they'd probably happily slaughter half the slave population of the village! Well, she wouldn't be around for the great wedding ceremony, she told herself. Especially with Rough Seas promising her death the next day. One more reason to escape, she decided. Let Fighting Wolf work his charms on someone else. Sarita knew better—now!

16

Ahousat Summer Village

Sarita stole quietly to her bed in the alcove. She was the last person to leave the fire in the common living area. She had not seen Fighting Wolf all evening—he was probably visiting Rough Seas, she thought. Well, Rough Seas could have him! She, Sarita, certainly didn't want him! Tossing and turning for a long time, she finally dropped off into a restless sleep.

She started awake. What was it—a noise, a mouse? Her eyes searched the darkened room, all senses alert. Then a shadow detached itself from one wall and glided towards her. Fighting Wolf knelt heavily beside her bed. She held her breath, suddenly afraid. "Are you awake?" he whispered softly.

His breath stirred her hair. "Yes," she whispered back. "What do you want?"

He laughed, a low rasp. "Come now, I should think you'd know," he chuckled.

"Go to Rough Seas," Sarita snarled. "She's your woman."

"What do you mean?" He grabbed her wrist in his strong grasp.

She tried to break his hold. "Leave me alone, Ahousat dog," she spat.

"So we're back to that, are we?" he sneered. "I was good enough for you out on the beach, wasn't I? Wasn't I?" he demanded, crushing her wrist.

She winced, but no sound of pain crossed her lips. Angry now, she taunted, "Isn't one woman enough for you? Do you have to have two women, or maybe three, panting after you?"

He laughed, hearing the jealousy in her words. The grip on her wrist loosened. If she thought he was after other women, let her. He certainly wasn't going to explain himself to a slave!

"Shut up and move over," he answered, pushing his big body into her bed. "What I do is no concern of yours. You forget yourself, slave." While the words were harsh, his tone was gentle.

He began to caress her breasts. His lips soon followed his hands as he dropped feather-soft kisses over the silken-skinned globes. He growled low in his throat, "Mmm, you taste good, woman," as he continued to kiss and caress her.

Sarita, angry at his insults and casual expectancy that she would acquiesce to his touch, tried to push him away. Both hands against his hard chest, she shoved futilely. He laughed softly in her ear. "My golden-eyed cougar, you'll have to do better than that to keep me away."

He buried his head in her neck, rubbing his chin slowly against her soft skin. Then his lips began to kiss the sensitive flesh. Shivers tickled her spine at his mesmerizing touch. She thrashed her head back and forth, trying to avoid his ravaging lips, trying to break the tender spell he was weaving on her traitorous body.

The upper half of his torso leaned across her, holding her struggling body in place. As she continued to resist, he got angry. "Stop, Sarita. Stop fighting me," he commanded. When she gave no heed to his words, he roughly pushed her legs apart with his hand and gently touched her private parts. Gasping in shame and humiliation at this blatant outrage, she fought him in earnest now. But he too, was in earnest. Determined to conquer her, he spread her legs wide, and quickly thrust into her. His hard shaft burned its way into her

soft flesh. She cried out against him, but he was
oblivious to her cries now, riding her with powerful
strokes. His hands reached down and grasped her
buttocks firmly. He lifted her up into an arched position
to meet his savage thrusts. There was nothing she could
do to stop his aggressive onslaught. She felt like she was
laid out as a feast for his enjoyment alone.

She struggled futilely against him. Suddenly his
aggressive thrusts stopped and he began caressing her
gently. Slowly, slowly, he plunged into her, then slowly
withdrew. "Don't go," she whispered, her traitorous
body wanting to hold him to her.

"I'm here," came his soft reply. With excruciating
tenderness, he continued to ply his magic against her
love-drugged body. She felt herself slipping over the
edge. "No, no," she cried, trying to hold him off at the
last moment.

"Come with me," was his hoarse response.

Suddenly he stiffened and massive shudders shook
his strong frame. At the same time, hot spasms passed
through her. Wave after mindless wave shocked her
lithe frame until at last she lay spent, in a quiet torpor.

Fighting Wolf lay, unmoving, on top of her, the
rapid beats of his heart vibrating through her chest as he
held her tightly to him. He rolled off her and encircled
her with his arms. She lay relaxed in the cradle of his
arms, her head against his chest. Afraid to speak, not
knowing what to say, and afraid to destroy this fragile
peace between them, she drifted off into a gentle
slumber.

Sarita woke later. All was quiet and she knew it was
still nighttime. She was alone. As she lay in the dark,
memories of Fighting Wolf flooded over her. Shamed at
her response to his sensuous attack, she closed her eyes,
castigating herself. How could her body have betrayed
her like that? He had only used her as a receptacle for
his lust—and she had loved every moment of it.

He was gone, she told herself bitterly. Here, in his
own territory, Fighting Wolf was merely a womanizer.

He would use her until he tired of her, then cast her aside.

She lay through the long night, her heart aching. Sometimes she cried into the furs on her bed. Was this what her life was going to be like now? At the mercy of a man who could arouse her body at will? Who cared so little for her that he could take other women to his bed? A man who owned her body, and perhaps, her heart?

She must squelch any tenderness she felt. She would not let him know how much he had meant to her, how much his touch had moved her. Yes, she thought, that would be the only way to protect herself.

Fighting Wolf was taking great care to avoid Sarita. For the first time in his life he was feeling confused about a woman. He needed time to think. At the beach, things had gone well between them. Now, back in his village, he realized he was again slipping into the role of conqueror, and he wondered if that was what he really wanted to be. He remembered her laughter, her spontaneous jokes, and knew that he would see little of that part of her if he kept on taking her as he had the other night.

He could have her body, his greater strength proved that, and she lived under his roof, there was nowhere for her to go. But did he want only the shell of her? Or did he want something more? He was preoccupied as he went about his work that day.

The men were making preparations for moving the village to its winter location, back inland, away from the cold seas. This move meant dismantling all the planks on the longhouses and packing up possessions into cedar chests, baskets and boxes and carrying them the long distance to the winter site. And after the move, there was the dog salmon run. This harvest of fish was critical to his people and would supply them with their winter meat.

With Sarita by his side, life suddenly seemed happier to Fighting Wolf. She would be accompanying him to the winter village and he thought hopefully of the winter festivities he could enjoy with her.

Now that he thought of it, perhaps it would be best to go gently with Sarita. He wanted her to enjoy her life with him, too. Fighting Wolf was surprised at the direction his thoughts had taken. Ruefully, he wondered if he was getting old and soft.

The next night he came to her. She was lying awake, unable to sleep, a small lamp burning by her bedside. "Having difficulties sleeping?" he asked solicitously.

She sat up, glaring at him. "What do you care, Ahousat dog?" she said insolently. Let him use someone else.

She wasn't going to make it easy for him, he saw. He held his anger in check. "I care," he answered as patiently as he could.

"Hmmph," was her answer to that.

"Do you remember our time together at the beach?" he asked softly. She nodded, unsure of what he was up to. "So do I," he went on. "I truly enjoyed the time I spent with you." She looked at him, wanting to believe what he was saying, but not trusting him. "Did you?" he coaxed.

She nodded, almost imperceptibly.

"I don't want it to be difficult for you here," Fighting Wolf continued. "I want it to be for us like it was at the beach."

"Then let me go!" It was a cry from her heart and it caught them both unawares. Realizing what she had said, she knew she had to continue. Reaching for his hand, she looked into his eyes, imploringly, "If you raelly want it to be good between us, let me go. I want to be free. Only then can I feel free to be with you as a woman is with a man."

Shaken, he could only hiss fiercely, "No, I can't let you go. I will not let you go. You're mine."

She saw that she had gone too far. She dropped his hand. "Then we are back where we started from," she said dully.

He got up and paced, trying to think. "There will be no more talk of freedom," he said sternly. "You're mine, and you will stay mine. I will not let you go," he repeated succinctly.

Then, he dropped to his knees by her bed, where she was sitting. "Can't you see, Sarita?" he asked softly. "I don't want you to go. I want you to stay with me. To be happy with me. To make love with me."

She looked at him. Her golden eyes met his piercing dark gaze, unable to believe the imploring note she heard in his voice. "What about Rough Seas?" she asked speculatively.

Taken aback, he hesitated. "She's nothing to me. She imagines she's in love with me." His tone dismissed Rough Seas as a concern.

"Oh? That's not what she tells me."

"What does she tell you?"

"That you are to marry her!" Sarita waited for his reaction, confident she'd caught him in his lies.

To her astonishment, he threw back his head and laughed. "Marry her," he repeated, incredulous.

Sarita watched him warily. He looked at her, saw she was serious. Fighting Wolf strove to match her mood. "She would love to marry me," he said seriously. "She's asked me a few times. But I—I care little for her. It's you I care about."

Sarita began to relax, surprised at his admission of caring for her. "Will you marry her?" she pressed.

"No," he chuckled. "Not unless I suddenly decide I want a life of misery. For surely that's what she'd give any man foolish enough to become her husband."

"That—and the dead bodies of his concubines," Sarita muttered under her breath.

"What did you say?"

"Nothing." She smiled brilliantly at him, relief evident on her face. He gazed at her beauty, a warm feeling spreading through him.

"Fighting Wolf, how long can we go on like this?"

Sarita asked, serious once again.

"Like what?"

Her golden eyes bored into his. "I will be honest
with you. I—I care about you, too." She dropped her
gaze, momentarily regretting telling him her feelings.
Still, the way he was tonight, with the rapport between
them, she felt she could do no less than speak truly. She
raised her eyes. "How long could we be happy together?
Chiefs and slaves have no future together." There, she
had said it. Their biggest problem: the status difference.
She couldn't take the words back. Let him deny it if he
wanted to, but she—she had been honest.

He took her hand, "We'll be different. We can be
more than just slave and master here, in the privacy of
my house. I'm willing to let you be free here under my
roof. Not in the village, of course, but here in my
house."

She shook her head. "It's not as private as you
think. There are many that live here." She gestured
around them. "Many that observe you and talk about
you. You don't give them a second thought. They're
only slaves," she added, unable to keep the bitterness
out of her voice.

Fighting Wolf was silent, plans turning over in his
mind. "That's the best I can offer you," he finally
responded.

Sarita was acutely disappointed. Her position was
still the same. She sat silently, lost in thought. Beside
her, Fighting Wolf waited quietly, his mind busy. At
last Sarita roused her flagging spirits. He'd said he cared
for her. That was an improvement, she thought
ruefully.

Fighting Wolf yawned, effectively dismissing the
topic. He climbed into bed and nudged her warm body.
Soon they were in their own private world where they
showed each other just how much they did, in fact, care.

17

Precious Copper squinted her eyes as she scanned the fog bank rolling in on the bay. Yes, the day should be clear and hot once the mist burned off. She called to an old slave woman. "Frog, go prepare a basket of food for three people. We'll take it with us today. We're going on a short canoe trip." The old woman nodded wisely and bustled way to do her bidding.

Precious Copper walked over to where several of Fighting Wolf's canoes lay on the beach. She saw an older male slave crouched nearby, patching one of the canoes. He had served her family faithfully for years. "Slug, old friend," she said, "it's time for our yearly voyage to pick flowers. Do you know what I mean?"

He nodded. "Yes, mistress. Every year we go and pick those little white flowers you like some much. Been expecting you."

She smiled at him. "Today we go to that beautiful little island to gather the flowers. Make sure no one knows where we're going, won't you?" She added conspiratorially, "I don't want my secret to be known. For generations my family has been known for the lovely dye that only we can make. I don't want anyone to know where we get the flowers that produce such a rare color."

She paused and thought for a moment. "There'll only be three of us—you, old Frog and I. She'll help me pick the flowers. We'll leave as soon as Frog comes with the supplies."

"You want me to take a weapon with us, mistress? Might run into trouble. Never know," he said.

"No, we'll be safe. We'll only be there during the daylight hours. Cougars and bears will leave us alone, I'm sure."

" 'Twasn't the cougars and bears I was thinking about, mistress. Thinking more about the two-legged animals we might run into."

"Why, we've never had trouble before, Slug. Why are you worried now? Our people are stronger than ever."

"That may be, mistress, but I hear there's been raiders in this area lately. Don't want to cross them."

"Oh, surely they wouldn't raid so close to our village," she answered, trying to discourage his fears and hers. "We'll take a bow with arrows then, if you're concerned. I don't think we'll need them, though," she said, trying to make her voice firm.

He nodded, relieved at her decision, and headed over to another small canoe. "We can use this canoe, mistress," he called to her. "I'm going to the longhouse to get my bow. Be right back." He headed up the beach.

Soon, the beautiful young woman and the two oldsters were paddling out into the bay. Already Precious Copper could see through the wisps of fog. "Let's hope the blossoms are ready," she told Frog.

The old woman, scrunched up in the bow, was dipping her paddle carefully in the water on every second stroke of Precious Copper's. "Yes, mistress," she answered in her creaky voice. "I'm sure they are. You haven't been wrong yet. They've always bloomed, just for you," she cackled.

Silence reigned once again as the trio paddled onward. After a long while they reached the small island and pulled their canoe ashore.

The day had indeed turned beautifully clear and warm. Precious Copper and Frog began picking the mature white blossoms on the low bushes. Precious Copper looked over to see Slug stagger up from where he'd been sitting on the beach.

"I'll help you too, mistress," he called.

"No, no, Slug. You rest. You did most of the paddling to get us here." It was true that the old man should rest. It was not true he'd done most of the paddling.

"I am a bit worn out," admitted the old man, sinking gratefully to the gravel.

"You can guard us," suggested Precious Copper tactfully.

The old man reached for his bow and took up his position, looking out over the small cove of the island. Precious Copper went back to picking blossoms. When next she glanced at Slug, he was sound asleep. She chuckled to herself. These slaves were getting too old for such expeditions.

She looked at Frog. "Why don't you take a rest, too," she urged. The old woman eyed the snoring man doubtfully. "Go ahead," coaxed Precious Copper. "I'll wake you in a little while." The old woman nodded and tottered over to where the old man sat slumped over his bow, his soft snoring borne away on the gentle wind. Soon the two of them snuffled in harmony.

Precious Copper hummed to herself as she picked the blossoms. They really were lovely. Her timing was perfect—ideal for making the dye, the flowers were at the prime of their fullness. One day more and she would have been too late.

18

They swept down from the north—bearded, short, squat, dark men who threw terror into the hearts of the Nootka. The five brutal warriors were of the people known as the Kwakiutl.

Kwakiutl warriors were trained from childhood to be efficient killing machines. Raised as soldiers, the boys were shown little affection by either mother or father. They slept outside at night without blankets or covering to warm them. Physical training was arduous and efficient: they were carefully trained in running, swimming, diving and weapons. Taught to be cruel and treacherous, warrior sons were encouraged by their fathers to beat up other boys, to seduce girls and leave them crying. A boy in training to be a warrior had no friends, except perhaps other warriors. Even then, it was a cautious kind of friendship.

Kwakiutl warriors raided their Nootka and Salish neighbors for slaves to take back to their villages. They also raided to revenge the loss of relatives and chiefs in either war or accidental death. The Nootka were not always successful in avoiding these warlike neighbors and often fell victim. Even other Kwakiutl tribes were not safe from their brothers' predations.

The five men in the large war canoe skimmed quickly over the smooth surface of the ocean, heading for the small island they had sighted.

Their mission of vengeance had already met with success. They'd found several wayfarers to murder. The

dead would accompany the deceased Kwakiutl chief the
warriors had sworn to avenge. No longer alone, he
would have the company of the victims in his afterlife.
He would "pillow" his head on their bodies.

Like sharks, the five warriors had been cruising the
sea, searching for more unfortunates to satisfy their
battle lust.

"Now my uncle has a 'pillow' in death. He has the
companionship of those three chiefs we killed," stated
the leader. Taller than his companions, his headband of
grizzly bear claws bore mute testimony to his prowess
against his enemies. A string of grizzly claws also
draped his neck. The claws scratched his bare chest with
each movement of paddling.

The youngest warrior grunted assent. "Yes, Grizzly
Crusher, your old uncle should be happy now." He spat
over the side of the canoe. "He never was in life."
Seeing Grizzy Crusher frown, Devours Men added,
"Let's stay overnight on that island ahead. We can rest
tomorrow, then head back home." He kicked a bloody,
pulpy mass of hair lying in the bottom of the canoe. "I
want to show off these scalps."

"Going to add them to that fine cap you already
wear?" joked Grizzly Crusher. Devours Men grinned
and nodded as he fondly patted the cap of scalps
adorning his own jet locks. The cap was his favorite
possession. The men were in a good mood after their
successful raid, and talked easily amongst themselves.
Rather taciturn in public, they tended to be garrulous
among their own kind.

"We'll rest on that island," said Grizzly Crusher.
"But I'm not ready to return home yet. We still have
four days to find more companions for my uncle.
Maybe we'll find a slave or two to take back with us."

Devours Men shrugged. It was all the same to him.

They neared the island. Trees covered most of it,
right down to the waterline in some places. They steered
towards a small pebbled beach. The island seemed a
good choice for camping. It was large enough that they

could hide in the woods should any larger force happen to pass by, and small enough that they knew it would be uninhabited.

They pulled the canoe ashore and made camp near a small stream. Dusk was approaching, so they lit a small fire near the top of the beach. Here they would bed down for the night.

Because they were on a war expedition, they could only eat four mouthfuls of food a day, and drink four swallows of water. These they would have in the morning.

Devours Men staggered up from where he'd been resting. He strapped on his belt with the two vicious-looking daggers. "Anyone want to come?" he asked, taking a few steps along a narrow trail that led inland.

Cannibal shook his head and the toenail necklace around his neck rattled. Made of the nails from his dead enemies' big toes, the grisly ornament testified to the wearer's ferocity. "Not me," he answered. "I'm too tired from all the paddling and fighting. Better take someone else with you, though—you might get lost in the forest!" The others chuckled.

Devours Men made an obscene gesture and walked into the woods. Grizzly Crusher got lazily to his feet and followed him. He was curious to see what the island had to offer.

The two men followed the deer trail that appeared to lead across the island. They walked quickly and silently through the forest, glad of the chance to stretch their legs. The lapping of waves ahead caused them to quicken their pace. They had crossed the island. Silently approaching the beach, they stared in surprise at the scene before them.

Around a small campfire sat three people. Two were obviously old, but the third, ahh, the third was a beautiful young woman. The men looked at each other, their thoughts the same. They held a whispered conference. Crouching low, Devours Men melted into the bushes to the right, the hand holding his knife trembling with excitement. Grizzly Crusher took the

path to the left. The encroaching darkness aided them in
creeping closer to their unsuspecting victims.

Precious Copper sat quietly looking into the fire.
Old Frog asked anxiously, "Mistress, do you think
they'll miss us tonight? After all, we thought we'd be
home before dark."

"I'm sure it's all right," answered the young noblewoman. "We really couldn't help it. There were so
many blossoms that I just kept picking. I lost track of
the time!" Reassuringly, she added, "We'll leave early
in the morning and be back to the village before anyone
has a chance to worry."

"Hmmph," was all Frog said.

Slug sat slumped towards the fire, nodding quietly
as he dozed. Soon the soft sounds of his snoring drifted
across to the two women. Precious Copper giggled. "We
should stretch Slug out on a mat for the night." She
winked at Frog. "He's already fallen asleep."

"Hmmph," answered Frog, "he must be getting
old."

Precious Copper giggled again. Together the two
women staggered with their burden to the mat and
positioned him as comfortably as they could. His bow
lay on the ground on the other side of the fire. Frog
rested near the old man and watched as Precious
Copper crossed over to pick up the bow.

Suddenly a terrifying cry cut through the dusk and
two shapes dashed out of the forest. It was over in
seconds. Slug never woke up. His head was severed
from his body in one brutal stroke of the knife. Holding
up the old man's head and waving it around in circles
while blood poured from the neck, Devours Men
crowed triumphantly in Kwakiutl, "One more enemy
dies by my hand!"

Frog gave a low gurgle as Grizzly Crusher's dagger
drove through her back and heart. Her body slumped to
the ground, her old gray head bowed and still.

It all happened so fast that Precious Copper stood
as one paralyzed. Realizing she held the bow in one
hand, she grabbed blindly for the arrows lying on the

ground. If she could but reach one arrow—!

Too late—she was shoved aside as Grizzly Crusher simultaneously pushed her and kicked the arrows out of her reach. Then he stood there, alert, legs apart, watching her, a menacing smile on his face.

Precious Copper crouched low, holding the bow in front of her for meager protection. The two men were larger than she. Both wore beards and the one with the headband of grizzly bear claws had a hooked nose. The other was slightly leaner, looked younger and had a more aquiline nose. They were both grinning ferociously. She glanced quickly at Devours Men as he slowly approached. "Let's have some sport, brother!" he said in the Kwakiutl language.

Grizzly Crusher laughed, never once taking his eyes off the cornered woman. Seeing the two men between her and the trees, Precious Copper began to slowly back towards the water, where the canoe lay. She didn't have much hope of escaping these Kwakiutl, but she determined she'd fight to the death. She glanced quickly at Devours Men again, and barely had time to slash the bow acros Grizzly Crusher's face as he lunged for her weapon. He yelped and jumped back.

Devours Men laughed. "What's the matter, great killer? One little woman too much for you?" Grizzly Crusher's snarl was his only reply.

While Devours Men was busy taunting his fellow warrior, Precious Copper bent to pick up a handful of pebbles. Now she was armed with rocks. She would do as much damage as possible before she went down, she vowed.

The two men were circling her carefully. Grizzly Crusher feinted a lunge, she swung to face him and Devours Men grabbed her from behind, one arm around her waist, the other grasping her wrist. He shook it, trying to make her drop the bow. Struggling desperately, she brought one foot sharply down on his arch, then twisted as much as she could to face him.

Devours Men stopped grinning when she kneed him

in the groin, hard. Wincing, he grabbed his injured parts, all thought of holding her gone. Bent over in pain, Devours Men snarled with rage as Grizzly Crusher taunted him. "One little woman has disarmed the great warrior! Now who's having problems?"

Furious, Devours Men could only gasp hoarsely, "See if *you* can hold the bitch. I've a score to settle with her."

Grizzly Crusher began circling his diminutive quarry carefully. Feet apart, Precious Copper watched for an opening. She hefted the rocks threateningly. Taking aim, she threw them hard at his face. Grizzly Crusher raised his arms to shield himself.

Precious Copper ran for the canoe, never looking back. She managed to get the canoe into the water and was just pushing it into the waves when strong arms plucked her off the canoe and threw her onto the beach. Landing on her back, she scrambled quickly to her feet, again grabbing handfuls of rocks as weapons.

The two men were by now extremely wary of her. They held a hasty conference. "You take that side. I'll take this one. When I give the signal, tackle her," said Grizzly Crusher in his own language.

Precious Copper smiled grimly. Let the fools think she didn't understand their language. How were they to know that her grandmother had been Kwakiutl? Precious Copper had heard Kwakiutl spoken since she was a child.

Despite knowing they were going to rush her, when it happened she was caught off guard. All three of them went down in a heap onto the hard pebbled beach. Precious Copper clawed fiercely with her sharp nails at any arm or leg or torso she could find. She was rewarded by many yelps of pain and angry growls. Inevitably, however, she was subdued.

Panting, Grizzly Crusher stared at her as Devours Men, held her wrists behind her back with one hand. The other encircled her waist, effectively reducing her struggles.

Chest heaving, eyes flashing, body taut, she continued to fight as best she could. Gradually, her frenzied efforts weakened and she ceased her struggling. Even then, she defiantly spat at Grizzly Crusher. He smiled cruelly at her and sauntered over to fondle her breasts. He pinched one and Precious Copper struggled frantically to get away from his reach.

"She's very pretty," observed Grizzy Crusher. "She should fetch a great deal when we trade her—later. After we've had our fun." He leered at her.

Grizzly Crusher continued to play with her breasts. Precious Copper, seeing him relax, lunged for his bare arm and sank her teeth into it. She clamped her jaws shut until they ached. With a loud yell, Grizzly Crusher grabbed one of her braids and yanked viciously to make her let go. Fearing he'd rip her scalp off, Precious Copper released her grip on his arm. Furious, he raised his arm to slap her, but Devours Men swung her, still struggling, out of the way.

Devours Men was having difficulty holding her. "One blow from you and she'll be dead," he panted. "You're not going to ruin my fun with your bad temper."

"My bad temper!" growled the still-furious Grizzly Crusher. "She deserves punishment. Look at my arm!"

Precious Copper was pleased to see she had drawn blood. She smiled into his face, relishing his pain, then renewed her struggling.

"Bitch," he muttered, "I'll show you—!"

"Let's get her back to camp," interrupted Devours Men.

"What?" asked Grizzly Crusher in surprise. "Don't you want to have her here?"

Devours Men shook his head. "No," he answered ruefully, "I'm too tired. And she's too mean."

Grizzly Crusher burst out laughing. "A fine warrior you are," he chortled. "Worn out by a mere woman's struggles!"

"If you think she's so easy to hold, why don't you hold her then?" retorted Devours Men angrily.

Grizzly Crusher just shook his head, laughing, and started back on the trail to their camp. Devours Men followed, pushing the reluctant Precious Copper in front of him. All the way back to camp they were treated to Grizzly Crusher's jokes about the softness of some warriors these days, and of how certain warriors should stay at home with the women and children. It was when Grizzly Crusher began to cast doubts on Devours Men's masculinity that he was angrily growled into silence. After that, the walk through the forest was quiet.

Precious Copper's legs felt weak under her, from all the struggling she had done. She stumbled along the trail, dreading what was surely to take place once they arrived at camp. She didn't know how many men were there, but she doubted she'd survive what they had planned. Still, she would go down fighting. She was the daughter of a war chief and the sister of a war chief and she had proud blood in her veins.

All too soon the trail ended, and they burst onto the beach. Grizzly Crusher and Devours Men let out triumphant war yells as they approached the three men sitting around the fire.

"Look what we found!" cried Devours Men enthusiastically. He shoved Precious Copper into the circle of light thrown by the campfire. The other men exclaimed in delight.

"A spirit woman of the woods," joked Cannibal. "Let me see her." He walked up to Precious Copper and gripped her arm. "Tasty little morsel, isn't she?" he asked the others.

"No, Cannibal! She's not for eating! Can't you ever get your mind off food?" exclaimed Grizzly Crusher, exasperated. "You're not going to eat this slave. She's ours to play with," he clarified for the others.

Their conversation made perfect sense to Precious Copper who knew the Kwakiutl did indeed cannibalize their victims. She decided there was no advantage in hiding her knowledge of their language any longer, especially since she knew she wouldn't be able to escape them.

"Kwakiutl snakes!" she spat. "My brother will kill you for this!"

"Oho! The lady knows how to speak. I thought she only knew that Nootka gibberish," observed Devours Men. Then, playing the part of host, he turned to the others and said, "Who wants to go first?"

A chorus of lusty cries greeted his question and Grizzly Crusher finally had to shout to gain silence. "Enough!" he bellowed. "I'm the leader here, I'll go first."

The others growled sullenly at this announcement. "You, Man Hunter, take her arms. Cannibal, her legs. Hold her down."

"I still say we should eat her," grumbled Cannibal as he went to do as bid.

"Later," answered a now excited Grizzly Crusher.

If things weren't so desperate, Precious Copper would have laughed. She couldn't believe her life was going to end like this, with these vicious, unfeeling, bumbling fools. Instead she began to scream as loudly as she could. She kicked and scratched and fought. She writhed and twisted.

"She's so little. Where does she get all that strength?" marvelled Devours Men. She struck out at them with arms, legs, teeth, nails, anything she could. She screamed continuously.

"Shut her up," ordered Grizzly Crusher. "I can't stand that noise she's making!"

"What's the matter? Can't get it up?" taunted Devours Men.

In anger and frustration, Grizzly Crusher grabbed a burning brand from the fire and thrust it a mere handspan away from Precious Copper's face. She froze immediately. "That's better. Lie still or I'll burn your face, bitch," he said viciously.

Seeing the fire in front of her, feeling its heat, Precious Copper went limp. She'd done all she could. She could fight no more.

19

Once he had the guns, it had been easy to recruit the warriors, mused Feast Giver. He looked at his men, all young men in their prime, all well-armed with bows, arrows and daggers. And best of all, stacked carefully on the floor of the war canoe, sitting on a raised dais of cedar mats so they would stay dry, were the valuable mus-kets.

He had ten good men. Men who had been absent or away fishing when his enemy, Fighting Wolf, had struck such a devastating blow to his people. And the men were well-armed. Feast Giver had seen to that. Never again would he be caught off guard, never again so trusting, he vowed, his eyes narrowing.

He stopped paddling, letting his hand trail in the cool water. It was one of his favorite times of the day. Dusk was approaching and the sun was setting in one last burst of color before it sank into the sea. "It's getting dark," he said to his men. "Time to find a place to camp. We're close to Ahousat territory, but we'll risk it. We need a base before we scout out the village."

He noted the nods of assent in the growing darkness. They had paddled the whole day. The men were tired, but glad to be doing something to avenge their tribe's name. Tomorrow they would find Sarita and rescue her from the Ahousats.

Feast Giver sat up suddenly, seeing a light glowing off in the darkness. The faint outline of an island could barely be discerned in the dusk. "There, what's that?"

he asked, pointing to the orange flicker against the island's darker shadow.

A warrior known for his keen eyes responded, "A campfire."

"Can you see anything else?" questioned Feast Giver eagerly. "Can you see how many people there are?"

"Too far away to tell," came the quick response. "Need to get closer."

Signalling his men to be cautious, Feast Giver silently paddled forward. So quiet were they, that they were able to get very close. They followed the rocky shore, keeping close to a rocky point, and blending in with the darker shadow of rock. It was almost dark by now and Feast Giver hoped the campers would not be looking out to sea.

"Looks like four, no five, men," breathed the scout in Feast Giver's ear. "They seem be standing around something or someone."

Just then a sharp scream rent the air. "A woman's scream," said Feast Giver softly. "What—?"

"Looks like they're throwing her down onto the beach," whispered the scout. "She's struggling, hard."

At Feast Giver's silent signal, the men paddled quietly to shore. So far no alarm had been raised.

Feast Giver knew there was little likelihood that the screaming woman was Sarita. Still, it was obviously some defenseless woman in need of help. His men had been spoiling for a fight. Why not give it to them?

One of the Hesquiats commented quietly, "That looks like a Kwakiutl-style canoe." He pointed to a beached craft. Feast Giver nodded. This made the game even more exciting. The Kwakiutl were formidable opponents!

He whispered his plan of attack, and saw the understanding nods. The warriors silently paddled closer to where the rocks met the beach. One warrior got out of the canoe and crouched on the rocks, holding the canoe while the others quietly disembarked. Quickly tying a cedar rope from the bow of the canoe to an over-hanging tree branch, he took up his bow and arrows and followed the others.

Sneaking up on the Kwakiutl was easy. The enemy was far too distracted by the screaming, struggling woman. Feast Giver saw the largest man pick up a flaming torch and wave it menacingly in front of the woman. Whoever she was, she was putting up a lot of resistance.

"Now!" he yelled, breaking into a full-throated Hesquiat war cry. Arrows of death flew through the air, and several found their mark. Three of the Kwakiutl crumpled to the beach. The remaining two whirled to face the intruders and at the same time grabbed for their knives. Hopelessly outnumbered, Grizzly Crusher and Devours Men cockily went into a fighting stance, back to back, as the ten Hesquiat warriors rushed to surround them.

The Hesquiats grinned at each other as they waved their sharp daggers menacingly at the Kwakiutl. Aware they were being toyed with, the outnumbered Kwakiutl each chose a man and lunged for their opponent, preferring a quick death. The Hesquiats swarmed over them. In seconds it was over. The last Kwakiutl lay dead on the beach.

The victors wasted little time cutting off the heads of their dead foes to take back for trophies. One held up the grisly cap of scalps that Devours Men had adorned himself with. Grinning, the warrior swung the cap vigorously and gave a victorious yell. Several of the Hesquiat warriors busily wiped their bloody knife blades clean on the victim's bodies. Pleased with the easy victory, they now turned their attention to the lone woman.

Precious Copper had been prepared for the worst from her Kwakiutl captors, when suddenly an unfamiliar war cry pierced the silence. Her arms and feet were unceremoniously dropped. She was startled when three of her enemies collapsed to the ground beside her and lay unmoving. Then she saw the arrows protruding from their backs. Realizing her captors were under attack, she stayed still, not wanting to be hit by stray arrows. A short while later, the deadly shower of arrows ceased, so she reached for her torn kutsack and pulled it on. Her cedar cloak was in shreds, but she put that on, too.

Precious Copper tried to get shakily to her feet, but her knees buckled. Her trembling legs could not support her weight. Finally, after several attempts she got to her feet. Still feeling weak, she squatted on her heels to watch the two hated Kwakiutls battle for their lives. Although she knew she was still in danger from the newcomers, she felt a great deal of satisfaction watching her previous tormentors fight for their lives. Elated, she watched breathlessly as they were quickly dispatched. But then she stood transfixed in horror as her rescuers decapitated their victims. For a moment she felt faint, then rallied. She would need all her wits about her to face the newcomers. Standing straight in her ragged clothing, she waited stoically for whatever was to happen next.

A tall, light-skinned man of proud bearing approached. Obviously the leader, he was extremely handsome. His unusually colored dark brown hair curled down to his shoulders, held in place by a band of twisted cedar bark at the forehead. His eyes were a sparkling ebony, reflecting the firelight. Around his waist he wore several daggers and carried his bow over one shoulder. Dressed in the yellow kutsack of the upper class, he did indeed present a noble figure, she thought.

Feast Giver approached the small woman slowly, not wanting to scare her. Even in her torn and ragged clothing he could see she was beautiful. Her long black hair hung in two heavy braids on either side of her small, well-shaped head. Sparkling black eyes observed him fearlessly from beneath delicately arched brows. A high forehead gave her a look of intelligence. The finely shaped lips compressed in a straight line were not trembling, he noted.

Before he could say anything to her she spoke, quietly and with dignity. "What do you plan to do with me?" Precious Copper preferred to know the worst, immediately.

Taken aback, Feast Giver answered, "Why, you're free to return to your people. We have no wish to detain you."

She sagged in relief that they did not intend to take her captive, too. "My sincere thanks, noble sir," she answered weakly. "Thank you for rescuing me from those Kwakiutls. They captured me on the other side of the island and dragged me here."

Feast Giver answered politely, "My pleasure. Are you injured? Can I help you in any way?" He could see little by firelight, but surmised she may have been hurt.

Seeing his glance run over her, she hugged herself and assured him she was fine, only bruised. "You arrived just in time. I'm so very grateful to you and your men." She nodded in their direction. "My family will want to thank you and reward you for my rescue.

"I'm so relieved to be rescued from those wicked men. I shudder to think what they were going to do." Here she bowed her head and was quiet for a moment, striving desperately to regain her self-control in front of these strangers.

Mention of her family started an idea in Feast Giver's fertile brain. Perhaps she and her family, owing him a debt of gratitude, could help him find his sister. Aloud he said, as he saw her bowed head and shaking shoulders, "Mistress, my men and I are glad we arrived when we did. Please think no more of it. We were happy to help you."

"You're very gallant, sir," she responded. "I truly am grateful," she said, wiping a corner of her eye. She would not, could not, break down in front of these men. Regaining her composure, she straightened and looked him in the eye. "Might I know your name, sir? I see by your dress that you are of the nobility. I, too, am of good family,'' she said proudly.

Better and better, thought Feast Giver. If her family was influential, maybe he could get his sister released and humiliate Fighting Wolf publicly. Still, he didn't want to let her know too much, since they were in Fighting Wolf's territory. ''My name is Feast Giver,'' he said shortly. ''How came you to be by yourself, out in the middle of the sea, on a small island?''

''Oh, I was not alone, at first,'' she explained. ''I and my two old retainers were gathering flowers on my yearly flower-gathering expedition to this island. There were so many flowers I decided to stay overnight. The Kwakiutl attacked us and killed my slaves. They had other plans for me,'' she added wryly. ''They were going to eat me.''

''I suppose they were,'' said Feast Giver doubtfully, ''but they didn't look like they had a meal in mind when we arrived on the scene.'' Then he frowned. ''Gathering flowers? You risked your life to gather flowers, woman? That wasn't very smart,'' he said angrily.

Precious Copper was surprised at his tone. ''I always gather these particular flowers at this time of year,'' she said defensively.

Thinking sympathetically of what she had just been through, Feast Giver relaxed his stance a little. ''Never mind,'' he muttered. ''But if you were my wife, I certainly wouldn't let you go so far from the village with only two old slaves for protection.''

''I'm not married, sir,'' she replied demurely, eyes cast down.

''Oh, I see,'' answered Feast Giver, neutrally. She was certainly an attractive woman. Perhaps later when relations between their two families were esablished, he might . . . With an effort, he drew his thoughts back to the present. ''What is your name?'' he inquired.

''Precious Copper.''

''Hmm, that name sounds Kwakiutl.''

"It is. My grandmother was from that group of people. When I was born, she told everyone they would come to value me above all else. The Kwakiutl put all their wealth into those large pieces of copper that they give away at potlatches on special occasions. They have powerful names for those valuable pieces of copper and each piece has an illustrious history. My grandmother was very insistent and so the name stuck." She smiled at him, her dimples showing.

Even in the firelight, her smile lit up her face. Feast Giver could only stare for a moment. She really was very beautiful. But more than that, there was something kindly and honest about her that seemed to shine forth from her eyes and smile. Then, realizing he was staring rudely, he turned to his men and gave orders to make camp. "Can I lend you one of my cedar mats for a blanket?" he inquired solicitously. "We'll take you home in the morning. I'm sorry it can't be tonight, but my men are weary and we're new to this area."

She flashed her lovely smile and graciously accepted his offer of the blanket. "The morning will be fine," she answered. "I thought I'd never see my home again, so a short wait is no hardship."

She retired to the far side of the fire, and, seeing that the men respectfully gave her a wide berth, she rolled herself into the soft mat. She lay awake for a short while, reliving the events of the day. She shuddered as she realized anew how close to rape and death she had come at the hands of the vicious Kwakiutl. Then her thoughts took a pleasanter turn as she dwelled for awhile on her rescuer. He certainly was a handsome man, she thought wistfully. Had there been a man like that in her village, she would not have hesitated to encourage his suit! He seemed honorable, too, and concerned about what happened to her . . . On this note, she drifted off into a much-needed, dreamless sleep.

Precious Copper awoke to the smell of fish roasting in the hot coals of the fire. These travellers certainly ate well! In the daylight of the foggy morning, she noted uneasily how well-armed the men were.

Carefully straightening her clothes, she did her best to appear presentable. Her braids had come loose, so, using her fingers for a comb, she did her best to rebraid the long strands. Finally, she felt she was as neat as could be expected. She looked around. All around her, the men were busy with domestic tasks, cooking fish or sharpening weapons. Again she was struck by the vast weaponry they had.

She spotted Feast Giver standing alone, at a small distance from the fire. Folding the cedar mat carefully, she approached Feast Giver and handed him the mat. "Thank you for the blanket," she said politely. "I was very comfortable in its warmth during the night."

He smiled, pleased to see in the full light of day that he'd been correct. She was indeed beautiful. His voice reflected his pleasure as he answered, "I'm glad you slept well. After we've eaten, we'll paddle to your village and return you to your family."

She smiled. "Yes, my brother and uncle will be very pleased to hear how you rescued me."

"Don't concern yourself with that," he replied modestly. In the role of host, he offered, "Would you like some cooked salmon? It should be ready now."

At her assent, they walked over to the fire and he pulled a large piece of the succulent fish from the hot ashes and placed it on a broad leaf before handing it to her. She thanked him politely and sat down beside him. They ate breakfast in silence, both very hungry and somewhat shy. Neither knew what to say to the other as the silence lengthened. At last, Precious Copper broke the impasse. "I notice your men are all well-armed. May I ask why?"

Glad for an opening to talk about his mission, Feast Giver answered enthusiastically, "We're searching for my sister. She's supposed to be in this area. We've come to take her back home."

Precious Copper nodded. "Perhaps I, and my

family, will be able to help you locate her. Then you won't need to use all those weapons," she said, watching him out of the corner of her eye.

Surprised at her astuteness, he grinned balefully, "Yes, you may save us a fight."

"My family has much influence in this area," she said proudly. "Many people respect my brother and if he makes inquiries, they'll tell him honestly where she is. I don't want you to regret rescuing me," she added. "I'll do all I can to help you find her."

Pleased, Feast Giver asked, "About your brother . . . Just how influential is he? The man who took my sister is supposed to be very powerful, too. Maybe they know each other," he said speculatively. "Maybe your brother won't care to go against this man—"

"Oh no," answered Precious Copper hastily. "My brother is very honorable. When he finds out that you saved my life, he'll help you." She looked down at the sand before explaining shyly, "You see, I'm his only family. Our parents are dead and we have no one else."

"I see," smiled Feast Giver. "You're telling me you're very important to your brother. Well, I certainly won't turn down any offer of help." Then, in a lower voice, he confided, "It's like that for myself and my sister. She's my only close family, except for my father, who is ailing. I don't know how long he'll live," he concluded sadly. Then, seeing her look of sympathy, he added hastily, "But I did not intend to burden you with my problems. It's just that you are very easy to talk to."

Precious Copper reached out and patted his hand. "Allow me to help you with your mission," she said. "That's the least I can do to repay you."

Amazed he was so vulnerable to this quiet beauty, Feast Giver carefully changed the topic. "What's your brother's name? Perhaps I've heard of him, although I do come from a goodly distance."

"My brother's name is Fighting Wolf," said Precious Copper proudly, oblivious to the effect the name had on the Hesquiat.

Feast Giver started visibly, and his mouth dropped open for a moment. Quickly he recovered himself, glad to see she had not noticed his reaction. "He's the war chief of my people." She turned to look at him. "That's why I know we'll find your sister. Fighting Wolf has many warriors he can call upon to aid in a search."

Feast Giver was looking at her oddly. His eyes had narrowed and he did not look quite so friendly. Inadvertently, a shiver of fear ran through her. Hesitantly she asked, "Have I said something wrong?"

He looked at her for a long moment, then suddenly threw back his head and broke into loud gales of laughter. Startled, Precious Copper looked at him and then at his men for some explanation for his strange behavior. They appeared as surprised as she was. After his loud, mocking guffaws had died down—it didn't seem like genuine laughter to Precious Copper—he explained casually to his gaping men, "Her brother's name is Fighting Wolf."

Instantly, ten pairs of hostile eyes were upon her. Precious Copper wanted to shrink under their cold scrutiny. "What—? Why—?" she began. She jumped to her feet and demanded in a low, controlled voice, "Why are you all looking at me like that?"

No one answered, then Feast Giver got to his feet. Towering above her, he reached out and lifted her chin with one brown finger. Tremulously, she gazed up at him. "My sister's name," he explained softly, almost regretfully, "is Sarita."

The enormity of what he had said struck Precious Copper like a blow. "Sarita?" she could only repeat helplessly. Stunned, she cried, "Oh no! Oh nooo! Then, you—your men—are all—!"

"That's right," Feast Giver answered, a mocking smile on his lips. "We're Hesquiats. Your enemies!" He laughed, and it was not a pleasant sound. "But tell me," he continued, dropping his hand from her chin, "how you, the sister of Fighting Wolf, know the name of one particular slave so well?" He had a terrible suspicion as to why she immediately recognized his sister's name, but he wanted to hear the answer from her own lips.

"Why should I tell you anything?" she shot back. "As you just so clearly stated, we're enemies!" Her eyes were like burning coals, she was so angry. Caught! Again. Only this time was far worse, she feared.

"Let's kill her now," spoke up an older warrior. "My nephew died in that slaughter her no-good brother led. She must die. Now!" There were several grunts in agreement from the watching men.

Feast Giver appeared to consider their words, but only for a moment. He held up his hand for silence. "No, men. I have a better idea," he said. "We'll take her back to our village. She'll be our hostage. As such, her brother will be forced to ransom her. What better ransom than my sister, Sarita?"

Some of the men continued to mutter, and hearing them, Feast Giver argued, "That way, we'll get my sister back with no loss of men. We have too few men to risk right now. It would be disastrous to lose any more to that no-good Ahousat. And," he continued with emphasis, "think how shamed Fighting Wolf will be when others learn his sister has been captured and he's been forced to ransom her! It will take him a long time to live down that blow to his honor!" This last point made good sense to the men, and they finally nodded in agreement.

Precious Copper, however, caught the older warrior's intent gaze at her. He did not look at all pleased, and she knew she would have to stay away from him.

"Gather up our gear," ordered Feast Giver. "Let's head out. Now. There's no telling when her snake of a brother is going to come looking for her." He glanced at Precious Copper but she lifted her chin defiantly and turned away.

Thus it was a short time later than a war canoe with eleven men and one disheartened woman hostage paddled swiftly back up the coast to Hesquiat village.

20

Fighting Wolf was sitting in the longhouse of his uncle, Scarred Mouth. It was evening, and several people were gathered about the fire. The nights were starting to get colder now, but the days were still warm. Summer was on the wane.

Fighting Wolf relaxed as he chatted leisurely with his friends. His uncle had given a small feast to honor visitors from a nearby village and now the guests were being entertained with singing and dancing. While the musicians played, the audience listened quietly and gave its full attention to the performers.

At that moment, silence reigned. In the center of the house, all eyes upon them, several young women began a song of welcome. Dressed in their cedar finery, they looked like exquisite flowers swaying gently in time to the song. They shook wooden rattles to keep the beat and provide an agreeable counterpoint to the women's lovely voices.

Fighting Wolf had admired one of the rattles, earlier in the evening. Carved from alder wood, the rattle was shaped like a bird, hollowed inside and filled with small pebbles. The craftsmen had paid careful attention to detail and the bird, a duck, looked very realistic.

At the end of the song, the young women smiled and vacated the center, giggling and laughing softly as they ran to the side of the room and squeezed together onto a seating platform.

The next performer was a thin, attractive young man. He was accompanied by several other men drumming rhythmically with wooden sticks on a long plank laid across shorter sticks. His was a song of peace, and reassured the guests of the long-standing friendship between their peoples. The singer had a high-pitched voice that contrasted pleasantly with the deeper voices of drummers when they sang the chorus.

Next came a dancer. Clad in a cured deer hide with deer hoofs and pieces of bone dangling from the legs, he wore a carved wooden wolf mask on his head. Reddish-brown hair was attached to the mask at the crown and hung down like a mane. With every step he took, the hoofs rattled and clicked against each other. At intervals he would punctuate his dance by opening the painted wooden jaws wide and then snapping them shut. Throughout the dance, a shrill whistle pierced the air. The audience knew it came from the dancing wolf. He ended his performance with a flourish and swept dramatically out into the night.

The concert concluded with the young women returning to sing a farewell song. Graceful gestures accompanied the song as the women reminded the guests to return again soon. The girls again rustled off, giggling, to the sidelines, and the audience resumed their conversations.

One of Fighting Wolf's friends leaned over and playfully inquired of the war chief, "Why haven't we seen more of you lately? You've been leaving the gambling games early. I even noticed that you didn't stay long at old Birdwhistle's feast. And you were the inspiration for it! Are you just working hard or is there some secret you don't want us to know about?" His eyes twinkled.

The men sitting around listened curiously for Fighting Wolf's response. Many of them suspected they already knew the answer.

Birdwhistle, another nephew of Scarred Mouth, looked at Fighting Wolf through narrowed eyes. "I don't suppose," he began snidely, "that a certain slave woman, who shall remain nameless—" Here there was laughter at his witty pun on the woman's now tarnished family name, and his pretense of civility, as if he would not bandy the lady's name in public, "—that a certain slave woman has succeeded in captivating the captor?"

Fighting Wolf looked at him through fathomless eyes and answered, "Keep your suppositions—*and* your sick jokes—to yourself, Birdwhistle. It's none of your business where I go or what I do." Taken aback by Fighting Wolf's sharp retort, the others ceased questioning him and turned quickly to other matters.

Birdwhistle, however, could not leave well enough alone. While the others were caught up in an argument on the relative merits of this season's sea otter pelts, he hissed at Fighting Wolf, "Any time you get tired of her, let me know."

"I thought we'd discussed this, Birdwhistle," answered Fighting Wolf evenly. "I'm not giving her away nor trading her. Do you understand? Besides," he chuckled, but no humor reached his eyes, "I'd have thought that cold bucket of water she dumped over you would have discouraged you."

"Who do you think you are, reminding me of that shameful incident?" demanded Birdwhistle huffily. "You know," he went on, "I could demand her life for that little incident." Sharp black eyes regarded Fighting Wolf challengingly.

"You could," acknowledged Fighting Wolf. "But," he added, "should anything should happen to her, you'd better watch your back in the next raid we make. As your war chief, I tell you who and where to fight. Should you be so unfortunate as to meet with an accident," he shrugged carelessly, "I'll be the first to extend my condolences to your wives and children." He eyed Birdwhistle steadily.

Birdwhistle regarded the implacable stare before he looked away. "Enough," he said gruffly.

"We understand each other then," said Fighting

Wolf evenly. He watched, unperturbed, as Birdwhistle got to his feet and slunk out of the longhouse. The remainder of the evening passed without incident.

Later, some of his friends invited Fighting Wolf to a neighboring longhouse for a gambling party, but Fighting Wolf politely declined. The smirks on his friends' faces annoyed him, but not enough to make him stay.

He headed out into the cool night. Walking leisurely back to his longhouse, he paused to look up at the clear night sky. The twinkling stars overhead were silent and serene. He was content with his life. Things were going well. He quickened his pace, anxious to see, and to hold Sarita.

21

Sarita knew the time of the full moon was quickly approaching. She must find a way to meet Rottenwood, without anyone observing. Now, more than ever, she could not let Fighting Wolf catch her discussing escape plans with the slave.

She pondered the problem. Now that Fighting Wolf was coming to her bed every evening, it would be extremely dangerous to sneak away at night. Yet, she had to know when they were going to escape.

It could not be put off much longer. Every day, she watched the Ahousat women packing up their many possessions into cedar baskets and boxes. Soon they would be taking down the very house planks and leaving the naked frame of the house behind them as the whole village moved en masse into the interior of the land. There, along a river, or inlet, they would set up their winter village, safe from the cold winter storms that viciously lashed the coast.

She went slowly about the task of preparing breakfast. She had slept later than usual, indeed the whole house had, and she knew it was because Precious Copper, an early riser, had not been there to start the fire and wake the servants and slaves. Sarita wondered briefly where Precious Copper was.

Sarita's thoughts quickly reverted to the forthcoming meeting with Rottenwood. Perhaps one reason she was hesitant to meet with him was that she was ambivalent. She wasn't as eager to escape as she had been when she had first arrived at Ahousat village. No, now she found herself trying to think of excuses to put off the escape attempt. After all, what difference did another moon make?

With difficulty she forced herself to acknowledge that the real reason she did not want to leave yet was Fighting Wolf. Something was happening to her. Something that had never happened before with any other man. She couldn't wait to see him every day, to hear his voice, to feel his touch. And oh! how she looked forward to those warm, passionate nights of love! Never had she known that it could be so wonderful between a man and a woman. And the things he did to her! She blushed as she recalled the previous evening when they had lain entwined in each other's arms. No, she could not go just yet.

But—she caught herself. What was she thinking of? She had to go. She had to leave him, leave this place. Her spirits plunged. Her feelings towards him were so confused. She wasn't even sure what she felt anymore. She should hate him for the raid on her family and village. And for stealing her away from her people. And for ravishing her.

But now, after all this time together, the long nights of lovemaking, the protectiveness he had shown towards her, his strength, his consideration—all this made her love him. There, she'd said it. She loved him. She sighed heavily.

But what was it like for Fighting Wolf? Was she only a toy, someone to play with after a long, hard day of work? Never would he consider marrying her, she knew. Her status precluded that.

But the most important point now, and here her lips compressed together in a tight line, was that her children by him would be born slaves. The thought made her want to cry, and with good reason. She suspected she was pregnant. Her monthly courses were almost a month late.

She could not bear the thought of her son, or

daughter, condemned to a life of slavery. Would her children hate the mother who birthed them into slavery because she had been too much in love with her captor? What would they say to her should they ever find out she had had the opportunity for escape but had let it slip by? Would her avowals of love for them ring hollow in their ears when they were old enough to understand the lowly existence they were doomed to? Did she love Fighting Wolf so much that she was willing to stay with him and condemn her children to a lifetime of servitude? No, she sighed despairingly, she could not do that. Not to her children, and not to herself. No love should ask that of a woman.

Sadly she continued her morning chores, her thoughts returning again and again to her dilemma. As she brooded, she used the heavy wooden tongs to place fire-heated rocks into cedar boxes filled with water. Every morning she heated water this way, sometimes to wash in, but usually to cook vegetables or fish for the morning meal. As the last rock dropped with a splash into the water, she looked up to see Fighting Wolf striding towards her.

She blushed and looked down at the water. She did not want him to see the torment she was in. She knew he did not suspect her pregnancy at all. If she *were* pregnant, she would be gone long before she started showing and he would never know of his child. It was better that way, she told herself. She would bring up the child in her own village. Her father and brother would help her raise the child. The summer nights when Fighting Wolf had made love to her would be nothing but beautiful memories by then. Perhaps, later, she thought sadly, when she had forgotten him, she would marry another man. She ignored the tiny voice that asked how she was going to forget Fighting Wolf so easily when seeing his child every day would be a constant reminder.

Fighting Wolf approached her, his handsome face alight with a grin, his intelligent eyes piercing hers, the wide chest half-naked, his kutsack tied jauntily over one shoulder, and Sarita felt herself melt inside. Holding her breath, she gazed at him, her heart unknowingly in her eyes.

Fighting Wolf's intense gaze caught the soft look. He knew it was for him. And he knew its cause—warm memories of their passionate joining the night before. Pleased with her, he gently touched her face, his big hand caressing her jawline.

"You look very beautiful this morning," he murmured softly in her ear. He ran his hand possessively over Sarita's thick, glossy tresses. "Could it be that something very good happened to you last night?" he teased. Abashed, she turned away, not knowing what to say.

He smiled to himself at her reticence. Then, looking around he asked quickly, "Where's my sister, Precious Copper?"

"I don't know," answered Sarita just as quickly, glad to have something else to concentrate on besides him. "I haven't seen her at all this morning."

"Hmmm," he answered thoughtfully. "Unusual. It's not like her to absent herself with no word. I wonder—"

"Now that I think of it," murmured Sarita, "I noticed she wasn't here last night either."

Fighting Wolf grinned at her. "I'm surprised you noticed anything at all last night, little one. I thought all your attention was on me. I must be slipping." Sarita blushed effusively.

Catching sight of one of the older slave women who usually attended Precious Copper, he called her over. The woman hurried over. "Where's your mistress?" he asked briefly.

The slave woman cleared her throat carefully before answering. "I don't know, sir. I haven't seen her since yesterday morning."

"Yesterday morning?" he mused. "Hmmm. That's too long." He paused for a moment. Then, decisively, "Find her. Make inquiries of anyone who might know where she is."

Not even looking at the steaming platter of fern roots Sarita was holding out to him, Fighting Wolf strode off. "I'm going to get my men. We'll search the village," he called over his shoulder. Then he was gone.

Later, Fighting Wolf and several of his warriors and slaves were back, milling about the longhouse. A thorough search of the village had failed to turn up the missing woman. "Where can she be?" the women whispered to each other.

Finally, an old man extricated himself from the throng and made his way slowly towards the concerned Fighting Wolf. The old man's bones creaked as he bowed slightly before the war chief. "What is it?" demanded Fighting Wolf. "Have you news of my sister?"

The old man shrugged. "Perhaps," he answered philosophically. "My good friend Slug is missing. We have breakfast together every morning. This morning he was not there." The rheumy old eyes fastened unblinkingly on the impatient Fighting Wolf.

"And?"

"And the old woman known as Frog is also missing." He stood there patiently.

Fighting Wolf looked at him in exasperation. "So?" he answered. Then, "Do these two, Slug and Frog, often go off by themselves?"

"No sir," answered the old man slowly. "Can't say they do."

"Thank you for the information." Fighting Wolf dismissed the old man with a brusque gesture. Just then, he felt a clawlike hand touch his elbow. Turning, he saw the older slave woman he had first questioned. "What is it?" he demanded impatiently.

"I just remembered," she began. "It's usually this time of year that old Frog goes with the mistress to gather white flowers for dyeing mats and basketry. Old Frog was complaining to me that she didn't want to go this year. Her bones've been hurting her lately.''

"Did you see them go?" asked Fighting Wolf.

"No, sir, I didn't. But the mistress doesn't usually tell anyone. She likes to keep it secret. Myself now, I could probably find out from old Frog where they go. If I really wanted to know. If I wanted to, I could.''

Fighting Wolf was becoming impatient with the woman's ramblings, but so far, no one else had stepped forward with any information. "Do you know where it is they go?" he asked as patiently as he could.

"Me? Oh no, sir, they don't tell me that kind of thing.''

"Well, does anyone know?"

"Don't think so, sir. Like I said, your sister, she keeps it pretty quiet." She paused for a moment. "I do know they have to go by canoe," she added, almost as an afterthought.

Realizing he'd get no more information out of the slave, Fighting Wolf ordered his men to their canoes. He barked orders at them to search the local area and report back by sunset. Taking two men with him, he set off in a canoe for his own search, all else driven from his mind.

Late that evening, Fighting Wolf returned alone to the longhouse. Head bowed, he looked weary and saddened. Sarita had never seen him so disheartened.

Without a word, Sarita reached up and took his cloak from his slumped shoulders. Silently she guided him to his usual spot in front of the fire. He sank down on the cedar mat.

Sarita bustled about getting his evening meal. She handed him some smoked salmon she had saved from an earlier meal. She pulled four roasted fern roots out of the embers of the fire. Pouring a cup of cool, refreshing water, she placed it next to the ever-present bowl of whale oil, then she sat down next to Fighting Wolf.

"Did you find any sign of your sister?" she asked.

He shook his head wearily in reply. "Nothing," he

said hoarsely.

Sarita swallowed, her throat dry and scratchy, then swallowed once again as she watched him. True, he was her captor, but she realized she had grown to love him. It hurt to see him so forlorn. She ached to throw her arms around him and ease his pain away. Seeing his reaction to his sister's loss brought home anew that he was a man capable of great depth of feeling.

Her thoughts were interrupted as he reached out one strong arm and pulled her close to him. He buried his face in her hair and held her tightly. Sarita could feel the strong beat of his heart, smell the tangy sea smell of his skin. Relaxed in his arms, feeling protected, yes, even loved, she longed to ease his pain. Tentatively, she put her arms around his shoulders, half expecting a rebuff. Perhaps he didn't want the comfort she could give him? His arms tightened about her, and, encouraged, she hugged him back.

"I do so wish you could find her," she murmured. "Perhaps tomorrow—?"

He gave her another squeeze, then set her free from his embrace. Ill at ease, she got up and walked restlessly around the fire, then came back and sat a little apart from him. He sighed heavily. He began to eat his meal, all the while keeping his eyes on her face.

"How well do you know the slave called Rottenwood?" he asked.

Startled, Sarita flinched involuntarily. "Rottenwood?" she echoed. What had Fighting Wolf found out? Did he know she was planning to escape? Her heart beat rapidly. "Rottenwood?" she repeated, needing the time to think.

"Yes," he answered casually. "He came from your village." Fighting Wolf continued to watch her as he ate, his gaze unwavering. "We captured him at the same time we took you."

"Why do you bring up such a thing now?" she asked frostily, angry that he'd mentioned her capture.

She thought he missed nothing as he continued to

watch her. At last he answered, "I want to know if the man is honest. Can his word be trusted?"

Sarita thought for a moment. "I would trust him with my life," she said at last, gázing defiantly back at her captor. Why was she baiting him? She didn't want Fighting Wolf to guess her plans. She must be more careful, she warned herself.

He raised an eyebrow. "Strong praise, indeed, for a mere slave," Fighting Wolf responded. He added casually, "Rottenwood approached me tonight. He told me he had seen a canoe leaving yesterday about mid-morning. There were three people in it—two old people and one who sat very straight. He thought it was my sister." Fighting Wolf continued to gaze at her. "He told me it was headed south."

Sariata said nothing. "If, as you say," he went on, "this man is reliable and his word can be trusted, then tomorrow we'll search to the south."

Sarita's heart was hammering wildly. She felt weak with relief. She had been so sure he was going to accuse her of planning to escape. Instead, it was his sister he was worried about! She was voluble in her relief.

"Oh yes, Rottenwood is a very good man," she praised. "He's intelligent and I have the greatest respect for him. If he tells you something, I'm sure you can believe him. He has many skills, too: navigation, hunting, fishing—" She stopped, feeling Fighting Wolf's steadfast gaze upon her.

"Indeed?" he asked ironically. "And how do you know so much about this paragon?" Sarita blushed and looked down. Her hands twisted nervously in her lap. Frantically, she willed them to stop. Clenching her hands together tightly, she started to defend herself. "I—"

A loud shout outside the door drowned out her voice. One of Fighting Wolf's warriors strode in. Sarita sagged with relief at the interruption; Fighting Wolf appeared not to notice her reaction. He spoke calmly with the obviously agitated man who asked for his

directions of where to search tomorrow. The warrior
seemed anxious to start out at first light. After he had
departed, Fighting Wolf looked at Sarita and explained
wryly, "Another one of my sister's admirers."

He got lithely to his feet and stretched. "Come."
He reached for her and wrapped one brawny arm about
her waist. She entwined her arm about his trim waist
and together they headed for the little alcove.

In the privacy of the alcove, Fighting Wolf kept his
arms around Sarita and pulled her closer. They pressed
together, kissing, arms embracing. At last, Sarita broke
his hold and gently pushed him away. He sighed heavily
and sat down on the bed.

Slowly, he unwrapped his belt from around his
waist, carefully laying the knives to one side. Sarita
stood in the dull light of a lamp, watching him hungrily.
His bronzed skin gleamed, his thick blue-black hair was
tousled from the day's activities. She wanted to reach
out and touch the side of his chin. She couldn't take her
eyes off him.

He reached down and stripped off his kutsack. He
shook his thick mane of hair. That magnificent body
awed her. Muscular arms and thighs, a flat torso, his
body radiated a quiet power. She shivered slightly at the
thought of the power of that body inside hers. Her
glance went back to his face and she saw he was
watching her.

Fighting Wolf stretched out a hand to her. Still she
stood, watching him. His hand hung there in the air,
waiting. At last, she took hold, and let herself be led to
his side. Woodenly she continued to stand in front of
him, marvelling at the control he had over her.

Gently he tugged at the knot of her kutsack, tied
just under her chin. The knot gave way and he stood
Sarita between his knees as he pulled the kutsack up and
over her head. She felt like a small child being
undressed.

She shivered slightly. He turned her around to face
him. His black piercing eyes roamed over her

possessively. For a moment, she saw passion flare in those arrogant eyes. She wanted to pull away, to deny that she was his.

Instinctively, he pulled her closer, and a low growl came from his throat. She felt a frisson of fear run down her spine. It was always like this, she thought desperately. She was afraid of him, yet could not pull away. For she wanted him, too.

He ran his warm palms up and down the sides of her body, firmly and possessively mapping her flesh. Pulling her closer, he sat her down over one muscular thigh.

Yes, she was beautiful, this little slave, he thought to himself. He reached up and ran his fingers through her thick, loose hair.

"Your hair," he murmured. "Such an unusual color—" It was true, he had never seen a woman with comparable sable-brown, gold-highlighted tresses. "It makes you all the more valuable to me," he chuckled.

At his words, she shook with anger. He saw her as a mere possession! She struck his hand away. "Is that all I am to you?" she demanded. "Someone you own? Do you sit up nights and count out the value of each of your slaves?" She lowered her voice in an approximate imitation of his. "Hmmm, this one I could trade for two canoes, that one for only a small bale of dried fish. But Sarita, hmmm. That hair color. Very unusual. Should get a good price for her." She left off mimicking him. "Is that what you do, Ahousat dog?"

Fighting Wolf realized she was angry with him. The appellation "Ahousat dog" was the tip-off. But tonight he did not feel up to coping with her anger.

"I'll ignore your striking a chief, a crime punishable by death," he said in a low menacing voice that he had not used with her before. That brought her defiant chin up. His hand went to her hair and he gently stroked the back of her head. Suddenly he grabbed it tight and held her head immobile for a long moment as he looked into those beautiful golden eyes. He saw a flicker of fear flash in her eyes, then it was gone. "I don't feel like taking any of your insults tonight, little Hesquiat slave. So don't goad me. You won't like the results, I promise you!"

She winced as he drew her down onto the bed, his hand still clutching the thick mass of hair. In the face of his considerable anger, her own melted. It would be foolish to antagonize this hardened man any further in the mood he was in. She cast about for a way to defuse the situation. The sudden thought occurred to her, too, that he was especially upset because of his sister's disappearance. A wave of compassion rippled through her; she knew what it was like to fear for one's family. How ironic that it had been this man who had taught her that fear!

Still, she felt a curious stab—was it pity for him?—deep in her breast and she knew she could comfort him this night if only he would let her.

She reached up to gently touch the cleft of his chin, as she had been aching to do all evening. Her soft gesture caught him by surprise. For a moment, he continued to clutch the back of her head tightly.

Then Fighting Wolf relaxed his hold. Sarita's long arms reached up and entwined themselves around his neck. An almost seductive smile entranced him as she drew him down to her and softly rubbed her nose against his cheek, then his nose. As she rubbed against him, she murmured soft reassurances to him, reassurances that he was important to her, that he was a kind man, that things were good between them. Relaxing under her gentle ministrations, he felt his anger change to something else, a driving passionate need that could only be slaked by this woman.

Outwardly passive, he let her continue to cuddle against him as he felt himself growing unbearably hard and full. He needed her and the release she could give him.

With a low growl, he leaned over her and pushed her thighs apart with one strong thrust of his knee. Both his large hands came up under her buttocks, and positioned her for his entry. With one lunge, he was inside her. He watched through narrowed eyes as she squirmed and writhed, impaled on his strong lance. Her head thrashed from side to side; she was caught up in the physical rhythm of his thrusts. His eyes closed as he pushed into her warm, velvety softness, driving as far as he could go.

Sarita gasped at the force of his entry. Her whole frame shook. His powerful thrusts drove her into the furs at her back. At first, she tried to push him off, but looking into those hard eyes, she knew she would never get away from him. She swallowed in fear as she saw him watching her, masculine passion on his face. She felt herself relax. How could she fight him when she wanted him in any way she could have him—pounding into her like this or compassionate and gentle as he'd been on other nights. She was one with him now, no longer fighting him or herself.

Fighting Wolf strained against her, his seed shooting into her. Sarita felt him climax, and they went over the edge into bliss together. He felt her shudder under him as her muscles contracted around him. Sweet, so sweet, she thought dazedly, intense beyond anything she'd ever known.

Fighting Wolf's forehead was damp with sweat and he felt the prespiration on Sarita's breasts slick against his chest. He rolled off her and blew out the lamp that cast a dull glow over their panting, wet bodies. He leaned across her, his eyes heavy-lidded from spent passion. Sarita opened golden eyes and gazed up at him. They stared at one another, then she opened her arms and he came into them.

They lay that way for a long time, Fighting Wolf accepting her wordless comfort.

Her faint whisper came out of the darkness and awakened him. "Fighting Wolf?"

"Mmmm?"

Sarita swallowed nervously in the dark. "What do

you plan to do with me?''

There was a short silence. "Make love to you again,'' came the sleepy reply as one large hand inched towards her breast.

"Fighting Wolf,'' she began again, brushing him away. "I'm serious. What do you plan to do with me?'' He heard the tremor in her voice. "Keep me as your concubine? Trade me? Please tell me.''

More awake now, he answered, "Keep you with me, of course.''

After a long silence, she ventured, "Fighting Wolf, is your revenge against my people, against my family, satisfied now?''

He grinned into the darkness. "It most certainly is. Better than I could have ever imagined!''

Her face flushed crimson at his response and she was glad of the dark that hid her from him. "Do you keep me now as a reminder of how successful your revenge was?'' she asked, unable to keep the bitterness out of her voice.

He sat up. "Why the questions, Sarita? What are you asking me? If you're asking for your freedom, I'm telling you now you'll never get it!'' He slumped back onto the bed beside her, fully awake now. What was the woman up to?

She tried a different tack. "Fighting Wolf, what would you do if I—if I—became pregnant?''

"Why?'' he shot back. "Are you?''

"No, no,'' she answered hastily, anxious to reassure him. "I was just wondering what you would do if I were. Pregnant, that is.'' She waited, holding her breath.

There was a long pause as Fighting Wolf thought about her words. Then his answer came softly in the night. "Many slave women become pregnant. They have the baby, life goes on . . . What exactly is it you are you asking me, little one?''

Sarita let out her breath, shakily. "I want to know,'' she said at last, "what you would do with your child that was born of a slave?''

There was a long silence. ''Do?'' he responded casually. ''What could I do? Everyone knows a child born of a slave is a slave.''

''It doesn't bother you that your own child, your own son—or daughter—would be born a slave?'' she asked incredulously.

There was another long silence. ''I didn't say it wouldn't bother me. I said that a child born of a slave remains a slave. That's how it is in this village. That's how it is in your village. Of course, I would love my child, whether born in slavery or born free.''

That statement sounded like an afterthought to Sarita. ''Will you have children that are born free, Fighting Wolf?'' she asked wistfully.

''Someday,'' he answered. ''I'm a war chief. I must have heirs. I come from a good, noble family. I have many privileges, songs, dances and properties for my children to inherit. I must have many sons and daughters. Heirs,'' he repeated.

''And to have heirs, you must marry,'' she finished dully.

''Of course,'' he replied, amusement lacing his voice. ''How else will I have heirs?''

At that moment, Sarita felt something die inside her heart. Never had she felt so alone. ''What about me?'' she asked bitterly. ''I, too, come from a noble family. I too, have many privileges, songs and dances and territories for my children.''

''Had, Sarita,'' he corrected gently. ''You had privileges. Now you don't. Now you are a spoil of war.''

She turned to look at him, and he could see the glimmer of tears in her eyes. ''Yes,'' she said softly, ''You're right. Your revenge is complete now.''

Something in the way she said those few words made him feel strange, as if something precious had been lost. But he would not let her know her words had shaken him. ''Yes,'' he repeated, just as softly. ''My

revenge is complete.'' Again he felt that inexplicable
sense of loss.

Sarita gazed at him for a long time before she
turned away from him and faced the wall. He reached
over and pulled her close to him, his grip warm and
possessive. One hand lay over her breast, one leg over
her thighs. Unaware of the silent tears of despair
coursing down her cheeks, Fighting Wolf whispered
into her ear, ''You're mine.'' He held her tighter.
''Mine.''

22

Sarita awoke the next morning and reached out blindly for Fighting Wolf. The furs next to her were still warm from his body heat, but he himself was gone. Her spirits sagged as the memory of last night returned. Finally she dragged herself out of bed. Goosebumps dotted her skin as the cool morning air touched her with light fingers. She slipped into her cedar smock, wondering briefly when she would get a chance to wash it. It was the only robe she owned, except for her wedding robe. That was put away in a safe place. She must remember to take the beautiful dress with her when she escaped.

The thought of escaping buoyed her spirits. In the new light of morning, anything was possible.

Humming quietly to herself, she slipped from the alcove. Now she faced the most difficult part of her day—facing the knowing smiles and lewd winks of the serving women and female slaves who gathered about the fire as they prepared the morning meal. This morning, however, she saw that few were up. It was still early.

Fighting Wolf was nowhere in sight. Coughing discreetly to catch Sarita's attention, one of the oldest slave women tittered knowingly, "He's gone, you know. Left early this morning to look for that dear sister of his. But he'll be back." Her old eyes sparkled good-naturedly. "He won't forget you, slave. Ha ha!"

At this news of Fighting Wolf's departure, relief washed over Sarita. After last night's conversation, she did not want to face him for a long time, if ever!

Sarita's attention was drawn back to what the old woman was saying. That worthy leaned close and confided in a sibilant whisper, "Did I ever tell you that I was this here war chief's great-grandpa's favorite concubine?" At Sarita's astonished look, she smirked and said proudly, "Yep, his favorite I was. Why, he and I used to—"

"That's enough," cut in Sarita hastily. "I'm sure you have work to do," she emphasized with a pointed look.

"Don't give me orders," bristled the older woman.

"I didn't mean—" Sarita began, uncomfortably aware she had no right to tell another slave what to do. She just had not wanted to listen to the old woman's tales. Would that be her in several years? Boasting to the young concubines of how she'd been Fighting Wolf's favorite? She shuddered at the thought.

Head tilted to one side, the old woman's bright eyes regarded Sarita steadily. She reminded Sarita of a precocious bird. At Sarita's look of discomfiture, the old woman relented. "He said to tell you he may be gone for several days. Said he isn't coming back 'til he finds his sister. Yep, gonna take awhile—" She smirked again before shuffling off to idly pick at some dried salmon bits left over from the previous night's meal.

Strangely uneasy, Sarita went to the door. She had to get some fresh air. Outside, a low fog bank hung over the land, hiding the beach, the trees and the sea from her gaze. She could only see a short distance, and she wondered how the searchers would ever find Precious Copper in such thick fog.

Suddenly a twig snapped, the sound loud in the smothering silence of the fog. Poised to dart back into the longhouse, she was stopped by a hissing sound.

"Sarita, it's me!" She was barely able to make out the words. All around her the fog swirled, an eerie silence pervaded the land. "Sarita," the voice came again, a little louder.

"Who is it?" she whispered back, surprised by her own courage in answering. She should go back to the house, she knew. A shadowy shape loomed out of the shrouded trees. With a gasp, her hand flew to her rapidly beating heart. Before she could run, however, she recognized the dim figure of Rottenwood. "What do you want?" she asked, visibly shaken by the eeriness of his sudden appearance.

"Quickly," he commanded. "Come here. We must plan. Now!"

Clutching her cloak about her, she stepped forward, closer to the trees. "Yes?" she asked uncertainly.

Rottenwood looked down at her. "We're taking a great risk, meeting this morning," he began. "But there's no help for it. We must leave tonight!"

"Tonight!" gasped the girl. "But—"

"We have no choice," he hissed shortly. "We must leave while the warriors are away searching for the woman."

"You," began Sarita. "You told Fighting Wolf to search to the south. You said that so we could get away! Away to the north!" she exclaimed, her eyes widening as she realized his cunning. She stared at him.

He gave a low, husky laugh. "It's the truth," he vowed. "I swear it. It's true that I did happen to see the woman and her two old slaves paddling away that morning." He saw the uncertainty in her eyes. "I decided to use the situation to our advantage, that's all," he said flippantly. Seeing that she was unsure of him, he continued sullenly, "Enough of that. Believe what you will."

When Sarita continued to eye him with a fathomless expression, he changed the topic. "Are you still willing to escape? If so, we go tonight. We'd be fools to wait any longer!"

Sarita nodded quickly. "Yes," she agreed, "I must escape. I'll be ready. I've hidden away some dried food and skins for holding our drinking water."

He nodded. "Good. Tonight, after everyone is asleep, wait for me just inside the main door of the longhouse. Got that?"

She repeated, "Wait for you inside the longhouse, at the main door."

"Good. Once we're away from the house, we'll run to where I've hidden a canoe. If we can clear the harbor without being seen, we'll have a good chance of getting away safely."

Sarita nodded, her voice quivering with excitement. "Yes. I'll be waiting," she said eagerly.

But Rottenwood was gone, slipping away into the fog like a wraith. Sarita shivered as she turned back towards the longhouse. She had set foot on a trail from which there was no going back.

It was evening. A pall seemed to hang over Fighting Wolf's longhouse. Conversations were desultory or mere murmurs. On this particular evening, no one laughed and no one wanted to play the usual gambling games. No one was even singing. Everyone missed Precious Copper and anxiously awaited her return.

Sarita was very tense. Tonight she would escape! She tried to appear calm and relaxed in front of the others, but when one of the women accidentally dropped one large fire-heated rock onto another, a loud crack split the air, and Sarita's calm facade split just as easily. She jumped and gave a shriek at the sudden noise. Several of the other women noticed and laughed at her reaction. She wanted to lash out at them, to scream her fear and torment at them, but with great difficulty she controlled herself. No good would come of indulging in a tantrum, this night of all nights, she told herself. Still, she was glad when the occupants of the longhouse finally settled down to sleep for the night, and she relaxed a little as silence descended.

Sitting quietly in her alcove, Sarita took inventory of her possessions as they lay scattered over her bed.

The creamy wedding dress and beautiful blue trading
blanket cloak were folded neatly in a small pile, and tied
with cedar bark rope. She clutched the package to her
chest for a moment, stroking the soft material and
dreaming of what might have been . . . If it had been a
real marriage ceremony, she might now be happily
married to Fighting Wolf as a beloved, esteemed wife,
expecting his long-awaited heir. She sighed heavily. No
use dwelling on what might have been . . .

Her jewelry, the copper necklace and earrings, were
wrapped carefully in soft, shredded cedar bark. On the
floor squatted an ancient basket, its empty maw
waiting for Sarita's precious paraphernalia.

She was dressed in the same kutsack she wore every
day, and her long, thick hair was tied back. She had
managed to find a somewhat worn cloak to take. She
didn't think anyone would notice it missing.

Sarita fingered several packages of dried fish,
assuring herself that they would prove sufficient for the
journey. She had managed to secrete them away in
preparation for this night. Two large seal bladders
bulged with fresh water. Dewy droplets of moisture
running off the bladders pooled unnoticed on the bed
furs.

She went over every item one more time,
determined to remember everything needed for the
journey.

Listening carefully, she could detect no unusual
sounds in the nightly routine of the longhouse's
inhabitants. She crept stealthily from the alcove, her
paltry possessions crammed tightly into the old cedar
basket. She tiptoed through the large open space,
holding her breath.

Loud snores drummed occasionally through the
house, while outside she could hear a raucous chorus of
frogs. For one timeless moment, someone's sharp
hacking coughs froze her in mid-step. Sarita waited, her
heart beating loudly, until the coughs died away. At last
she reached the main door, the designated meeting

place, and waited nervously in the shadows for
Rottenwood. She crouched there quietly for what
seemed to be a very long time.

Once she peeked around the deerskin flap, and
could barely make out the dim outline of a man. That
Rottenwood! There he was, leaning against a tree mere
footsteps away when he'd told her to meet him inside
the longhouse. Now here he was outside, no doubt
impatient because she hadn't shown up yet! Sarita was
just about to step forward and reproach him for keeping
her waiting when suddenly he shifted position. That
blunt profile did not belong to Rottenwood. Who—? A
guard! Fighting Wolf had posted a guard.

Her heart beating frantically, she pulled back into
the deep shadows. She held her breath and made not a
sound. After a few minutes, nothing happened and she
relaxed a little. Rottenwood would come soon, she
reassured herself.

His sudden, silent materialization from nowhere
unnerved her. "Ready?" he breathed.

Urgently, Sarita pointed to the deerskin flap on the
door and, with agitated gestures indicated the guard
she'd seen. Nodding grimly, Rottenwood glided to the
edge of the doorway and peered out. Drawing back, he
reached soundlessly for a nearby war club, then he
slipped outside.

Sarita peered into the dimness. The moon was
hidden behind large gray clouds, leaving meager light to
see by. Her heart in her mouth, she watched as
Rottenwood crept up behind the unsuspecting guard.
Rottenwood lifted the war club high and brought it
down on the man's head with a sickening thud. The man
crumpled to the ground. Sarita couldn't believe it was
over so soon.

Turning to her, Rottenwood stealthily gestured for
her to follow him. She hurriedly obeyed, grasping the
basket tightly on one arm.

He was a barely visible, swiftly moving shadow in the
darkness just ahead of her. Her eyes strained with the

effort of keeping him in view as they slunk alongside the longhouse. They were about to round a corner, when Rottenwood halted suddenly and she bumped into his solid back. Annoyed, Sarita was about to reprimand him for his clumsiness when he urgently gestured her to silence.

Over his shoulder she could see another guard, lounging against the longhouse as he looked idly out to sea. Even as she watched, the guard yawned loudly.

Still carrying the war club, Rottenwood sidled up to the preoccupied guard. Knocking him on the side of the head, Rottenwood waited for the man to slump forward. Instead of falling unconscious, the man turned and, in one smooth movement pulled a knife from his belt. Rottenwood raised the war club to strike a second blow, but the guard sliced at him with the sharp blade. Sarita heard a grunt. Fear for Rottenwood spurred her into action. Dropping her basket, she bent down and groped about for a heavy rock. Quickly finding one, she hefted it and crept behind the guard.

The two men fought silently and viciously, oblivious to her movements. Sarita could see that Rottenwood was tiring rapidly. A slave was no match for a highly trained warrior.

Looming over him, the guard lifted his knife for the final blow.

Sarita struck with all her strength. The heavy rock slammed into the guard's head, and he pitched forward to lie immobile on the ground.

"Thanks," muttered Rottenwood tersely. "I was sure he was going to kill me."

For a moment Sarita was speechless, reeling from what she'd just done. "Is—is he dead?" she managed to quaver at last.

The man lay face down. His thick hair prevented her from seeing if his skull had caved in. A thin trickle of blood seeped past one ear.

"He's not dead," answered Rottenwood. "But you sure knocked him out."

Rottenwood knelt beside the unconscious victim. Using a leather thong that Sarita guessed had tied his own kutsack, Rottenwood speedily bound the man's hands behind his back. "In case he wakes up soon," explained Rottenwood, still breathing hard from his exertions.

Glancing about, he was reassured the struggle had not been overheard. Nodding quickly to Sarita, he urged, "Let's get out of here!"

He set off along an almost invisible forest path at a fast pace. Still trembling from the fight, Sarita hastily grabbed her basket and ran after him.

She struggled to keep up, but in the dim light, her footing on the trail was shaky. Several times she stumbled and almost fell. She could barely see his dark shape far ahead of her. At last, afraid she would lose him completely, she risked calling out. "Rottenwood, please wait!"

In an instant, he was there. "Silence, woman," he hissed, looming in front of her. "If we're caught, it's death for both of us!"

This brutal reminder subdued Sarita and she followed him carefully and as silently as she could. He must have taken her words to heart, however, for she noticed he no longer walked as briskly through the brush. She was able to keep up with him.

At last they reached a small cove. She recognized it immediately as the cove where the women anchored the large chunks of cedar bark in preparation for softening it up. She glanced quickly around, but could see no one.

Rottenwood bent over a small patch of bush and grunted as he tugged heavily at the dark form of a canoe. Rushing over, Sarita added her strength and together they dragged the canoe out of the brush and onto the gravel beach. Sarita took the bow of the canoe and Rottenwood the stern. Together they managed to pull and push the heavy craft into the shallow waves.

Suddenly Sarita darted back for her basket; she'd almost forgotten it in her haste. She flung it into the canoe, then hastily clambered aboard.

At the stern, Rottenwood had one leg in the canoe, and propelled the craft into deeper water with the other. They were off!

Sarita shivered with barely repressed excitement. "We made it!" she whispered exultantly.

"Silence," came the hissed reply. "Sounds carry over water."

Sarita refused to let the man's caution dampen her hopes. "Nevertheless," she insisted, "I know we've made our escape!"

She heard his deep chuckle in the darkness. "Perhaps," was all he said.

Sarita sat scrunched in the bow of the canoe, her arms dipping repeatedly as she pushed the paddle against the choppy water's heavy resistance. Her mind was intent on only one thing—paddling to freedom.

Had she cared to, off to her left she could have looked out over the vast gray water, where caps of white foam flicked across the rippled crest of each wave. Off to her right rose high, sheer mountains, covered by towering forests. In the early morning dimness, the mountains appeared as giant, charcoal-colored sentinels looming out of the mist. The usual thick fog was absent this morning, but Sarita neither noticed nor cared.

She hunched over, the jerky bouncing of the canoe making her nauseous. Salty spray drenched her face and hair. She felt sticky all over. Her hands were blistered, and her back ached from paddling in one position all night. Her legs had long ago gone numb—she'd kneeled the whole night through. Privately, she doubted she'd ever walk again.

As if taunting her with the insignificance of her problems, the vast morning sky began to blaze crimson, amber and magenta. Never had she seen a sunrise to rival this one, she thought to herself. And the knowledge that she was free added to the glorious beauty!

She stopped paddling to admire the dawn sky and savor her freedom. Never again would she take liberty for granted. She had worked too hard to recapture it.

She glanced back over her shoulder at Rottenwood. His eyes looked sunken in the dim light. She knew he was tired, probably close to exhaustion. "Would you like some more fish?" she asked solicitously.

He shook his head and kept paddling. He was determined to reach Hesquiat village and Spring Fern, but he knew if he stopped paddling now, he'd never start again. He suspected Sarita knew it too.

Sarita shrugged and took up the paddle once more. It felt heavier in her hands. She resumed paddling and they traveled without further conversation.

After a long while, Rottenwood's hoarse voice cracked through the stillness. "Over there." Sarita swung her gaze to where he indicated. "That point of land is part of a large island. We'll take shelter there. The Ahousats are far behind."

They headed for the point and a short while later they wearily dragged the canoe up on the gravel beach. Now that the sun had risen, she could easily see the huge towering mountains. The island they were on squatted at the foot of the giants.

They pulled the canoe up above the high tide line so it would not float away. Sarita stood staring dully as Rottenwood covered the craft with salal bushes. She guessed he wanted to be sure no passing travelers spotted it and came to investigate.

She was so weary. All she could do was watch as Rottenwood took the basket and deposited it under a large spruce tree. Spreading branches made a natural shelter, and soft needles padded the ground.

"We'll rest here," stated Rottenwood. "Then, when it's dark, we'll head out again."

Sarita nodded and headed back down to the beach. She started to collect pieces of driftwood for making a fire. Rottenwood stopped her. "No wood. No fire." Seeing her uncomprehending look, he explained,

"Smoke would give away our position. We mustn't be seen by *anyone*."

Sarita nodded again, too tired to say anything, and turned back to the sheltering spruce. She couldn't stay on her feet any longer, and she sank to the ground.

Thankfully Sarita accepted the piece of dried fish Rottenwood handed to her. Then, thirsty, she threw back her head and drank greedily from a bladder. Water coursed down her chin and dripped onto her robe, but Sarita did not notice. She was too tired. Finished eating, she lay down, clutching her cloak about her. Stretching her legs luxuriously, she sighed heavily. Soon she was sound asleep.

Rottenwood surveyed the beach once more before he lay down a short distance away from Sarita. Almost instantaneously, his eyes closed and he slept, snoring sonorously.

It seemed Sarita had only just fallen asleep before she was being shaken awake. She sat up and looked about her.

"Time to go," said her guide. Seeing her dazed look, Rottenwood added, "You slept the whole day. It's time to go. We've got a long way to travel."

Sarita got shakily to her feet, then bent low and stepped out from under the spreading tree. Stretching, she revelled in the feel of her body's new strength. She ran her hands over her face and through her hair. Salt had tightened her skin and massed the strands of her hair. Oh well, she sighed, she would be home soon and could bathe then.

She turned and caught Rottenwood watching her. His narrowed eyes slid away from hers and she wondered uncertainly what he was thinking. "What is it, Rottenwood?" she asked.

He swung back to her and stared intently for a moment. Thoughts of Spring Fern slashed through his head, the desire to see her again nearly overwhelming him with its intensity.

Sarita swallowed nervously. Rottenwood's gaze

held hers as he asked softly, "Do you intend to stand by your promise to free me when we reach your village?"

The question hung suspended between them. If she answered "no," Sarita knew she would not live long. He could either leave her marooned on this beach or kill her. Either way, he had nothing more to lose. If she said "yes," would be believe her? Or would he think she was lying to protect herself?

"Rottenwood," she began at last, "I owe you my life. Please trust me. When we arrive at my father's village, I'll do everything I can to see that you're freed." She gazed at him intently, her beautiful golden eyes willing him to believe her.

Spring Fern's alluring form beckoned him in his mind's eye. Finally, a small smile twisted one corner of his mouth, and his eyes shifted seaward as Rottenwood answered gruffly, "Come, then. Time is wasting."

Sarita's shoulders slumped in relief. For now, he believed her.

They dragged the canoe from its hiding place and headed into the rapidly descending darkness.

23

As the small canoe ground into the gravel beach, Sarita was already dangling one leg over the side, just above the water. She jumped out, the knee-high water shocking in its coldness. Eyes focused on her father's longhouse, she waded quickly to shore and dashed up the beach. Her heart kept time with her pounding feet.

She burst in the door. She looked about wildly. Fear of what she would find warred with elation at being home. Elation won out.

A banked fire glowed at the hearth. No one was in sight. Belatedly, Sarita remembered it was still early morning. "Nuwiksu! Nuwiksu!" she called. "Feast Giver! Where are you?" All the time she had been away, she had been afraid for them. Now, faced with silence, her fears resurfaced. They were dead! Where was everyone? Why did no one answer her call?

Just then, a sleepy Abalone Woman shuffled into the main living area. She stopped and gasped when she saw Sarita. "What—where?" she cried. "Sarita! It's you!" She ran to hug her stepdaughter fiercely. Feeling Abalone Woman's arms about her, a warm feeling stole over Sarita. At least some of the people in her previous world were still alive!

"My father, where is he?" cried Sarita through her tears of relief. Before Abalone Woman could answer, Sarita continued, "And Feast Giver! My brother! Please, please don't tell me he's dead?" Her voice rose on the last word. The question hung poised in the air for a frantic heartbeat.

"No, no," Abalone Woman hsatily reassured her. "They're here. They're both here. Alive." Sarita almost collapsed with relief.

"Where are they?" she whispered hoarsely. "I must see them!"

"I'll wake them," promised Abalone Woman. "However, you should know that your father, especially, is still weak. He's recovering from wounds that will take a long time to heal," she added enigmatically. Abalone Woman hurried away to fetch her husband and stepson.

Sarita squatted by the dully glowing embers, and stared unseeing at the gray mass. She heard a small noise behind her and whirled. "Feast Giver!" she cried and launched herself into his arms.

"Ho!" he laughed, knocked off-balance by her sudden action. He managed to catch her and steadied them both. "You're back! How did you get here?" he asked, his dark eyes sparkling with happiness at seeing her. "I thought I would have to go to Ahousat and rescue you!"

"Don't tease," she admonished him playfully.

"I'm not," he said soberly. "I'm serious. We were going to rescue you. In fact, I've already led a raid into Ahousat territory and captured—"

"Sarita!" her father's voice boomed out. "Daughter! We feared we'd never see you again!"

"Nuwiksu!" Sarita ran to Thunder Maker and hugged him tight. Her father's arms around her calmed her. She was home.

"But how did you get here?" continued the older chief. "Your brother was just about to start negotiating for you."

"Negotiating?" asked Sarita. "But what—? How?" She took a deep breath. "I escaped, Nuwiksu. With the help of the slave Rottenwood. We stole a canoe and paddled for almost two nights to get back here."

"Mmm," answered her father. "Very good. You're very brave, my daughter."

Sarita released her tight hold on her father and stepped back. "I'd like to reward Rottenwood for helping me escape. I would never have made it without him."

Her father nodded. "Yes, certainly."

"He risked his life to help me, Nuwiksu," explained Sarita. "I wish to have him freed." She paused, her wide eyes on her father.

"Freed! Isn't that rather extreme, daughter? We could give him a canoe, perhaps even a wife. But to free him? How will I keep my wealth, if I go about freeing all my slaves?"

Dismayed, Sarita asked, "Do you value me so little, Nuwiksu?"

"No, no, it isn't that," blustered Thunder Maker.

"Then what is it?" pressed Sarita.

"You've just arrived. This is a fine welcome we're giving you!" said her father in a louder, jolly voice. He lowered his voice to add, "Come, come, we'll discuss this matter later."

To one of his slaves, he shouted, "Rouse the household! Rouse the village! I'm giving a potlatch now that my daughter is safely returned to me!" The slave hurried away to do his master's bidding.

Sarita turned away, piqued with her father. Surely he was not so cheap that he would not free one slave! She resolved to bring the matter up again. And, she promised herself, she would settle for nothing less than Rottenwood's freedom. She struggled against letting her angry feelings overwhelm the joy of her homecoming.

Sarita caught her brother's glance and hurried over. "Feast Giver." Her concerned gaze took him in. "You look thinner than when I saw you last. Have you been ill? Were you wounded in the battle at my 'marriage'?" she asked bitterly. Now that she was home again, the humiliation of the Ahousat raid returned in full force.

She regarded her brother closely. New, fine lines were etched at the corners of his eyes and deeper grooves were carved between his nose and the corners of his mouth. There was a newfound seriousness about him. He didn't have that familiar look of laughter. She sighed, wondering what had happened to change her carefree brother into this stranger. Ruefully, she conceded that she, herself, was no longer so carefree, either.

"Yes," he answered. "I was wounded." He undid the knot on his kutsack and lowered it to his waist. A thick red scar between his ribs marred the fine brown skin. Sarita gasped.

"It's healing well, now, thanks to Abalone Woman," he reassured Sarita. "I was also unconscious for a long time. I took a blow on my head."

"Show me," she demanded, tight concern on her face. Obligingly he lifted one long wave of dark hair that had fallen across his temple. Sarita saw a thin white line, barely visible.

"Oh, catlati," she moaned.

"Enough of me," he responded. "What about you? You're the one that was stolen away. How were you treated, sister?" He frowned as he waited for her answer.

Sarita turned away. "I was treated like any other slave," she responded calmly.

Her brother grabbed her arm. "Did that bastard hurt you, Sarita?" he demanded.

"No, no." She shook her head. "He treated me well, after—"

"After what?" he growled.

"Can't you guess?" she cried. "'Do I have to say it?"

Feast Giver let her arm drop, a stricken look on his face. "I'm sorry," he muttered. "I know it must have been difficult for you. It must have been terrible living in the longhouse of our enemy." His face hardened. "But this I promise—you will be avenged."

Sarita looked at him. "What—?"

He continued, "I'm going to lead a raid on the Ahousats. Fighting Wolf will pay, and pay dearly, for what he has done to you and to our family!"

"Catlati," she began gently, "Go carefully. Before you lead this raid, I would have you know something. I carry—" She stopped suddenly.

There, walking slowly towards her was a small, slim woman, her thick, dark braids making her instantly recognizable. "Precious Copper!" Sarita cried. "What are you doing here?" She stared openmouthed at the petite woman.

Precious Copper walked up to her, a dimpled smile on her face. She laid a small hand on Sarita's forearm. But before she could say anything, Feast Giver planted a possessive hand firmly on the small woman's shoulder and stated, "Precious Copper is my hostage. I led a rescue party down to Ahousat territory, to find you. My men and I captured Precious Copper. I brought her back here intending to trade her for you. Now that you've returned, I'll have to think of something else to do with her."

Feast Giver gazed at his hostage speculatively. Precious Copper saw the look and examined the floor intently.

"Oh, Precious Copper," murmured Sarita. "I'm so sorry."

"Sorry?" responded Feast Giver in surprise. "Sorry? Whatever for? This woman is the sister of our enemy! Don't waste your pity on the likes of her!"

Sarita noticed that, despite his words, Feast Giver moved to stand protectively behind the diminutive woman, his big hands clasping each of her upper arms. Interesting, thought Sarita. Aloud she said, "I'll have you know that this woman saved me from a terrible life in Ahousat village. She protected me when others would have molested me."

"Did she protect you from her brother, Fighting Wolf?" sneered Feast Giver. Sarita's silence spoke volumes.

"Ahh, I thought not," responded Feast Giver.

"Nevertheless," continued Sarita evenly, "she made my life as a slave bearable. I will not turn against her now, regardless of *who* her brother is!"

Feast Giver's self-righteous attitude annoyed Sarita. Taking Precious Copper's hand, she started to lead her away. "And I intend," she stated firmly, looking back over her shoulder at Feast Giver, "to see that Precious Copper is well cared for and protected from, uh, unwanted advances."

Feast Giver frowned at Sarita. "She's *my* hostage," he warned. "I'll decide what's to be done with her. Not you."

"Yes, catlati," answered Sarita sweetly. "Weren't you just condemning Precious Copper because she couldn't protect me from her brother?" The question hung there between the three. Sarita seized the initiative. "Precious Copper and I have a great deal of news to catch up on!" Smiling, Sarita led the bewildered young woman away, leaving Feast Giver to stare after them, a thoughtful frown marring his handsome face.

24

That evening there was a feast given in honor of Sarita's return. It was a lavish banquet, and the whole village attended.

Towards the end of the dinner, just before the ceremonial dances and singing, Thunder Maker slowly got to his feet. He stood quietly, with dignity, as he waited for his guests' silence. A hush fell over the crowd as they listened respectfully to what he had to say. He began in stentorian tones. "Tonight I wish to announce that I will be giving a potlatch for my daughter, Sarita. This potlatch will be to restore her name and," here he fixed his audience with a steely glare, "my family's name now that she is free once again." The audience was reverentially silent. Highly edified, Thunder Maker added, "The potlatch will be held ten days from now and all are invited."

He waited patiently for the loud cheers to die down. When the happy cries finally stopped, he continued. "In addition," he announced importantly, "I will be sending invitations to neighboring dignitaries. All will know that Sarita is indeed a worthy Hesquiat woman. All will speak well of her after they see the wealth that I, her father, can give away on her behalf." With these parting words, Thunder Maker exited dramatically from the feasting area.

The Hesquiat people loved such theatrics and speculated happily amongst themselves about the forthcoming potlatch. Sarita, herself, was impressed with her father's dignity and leaned over to say so to some of her companions.

She sat with the women of her family. Spring Fern was in attendance on her right, Precious Copper on her left. Abalone Woman and Crab Woman sat nearby. Sarita noticed that the slave woman, Cedar Bundle, was seated next to Spring Fern. Sarita smiled at the woman, now having some understanding of how Cedar Bundle's life had changed since her arrival in Hesquiat village. The woman smiled shyly back.

Sarita sat quietly savoring the sights and sounds of her home. Replete after a satisfying meal of smoked fish, roasted fern roots, and fresh salal berries, served with the ubiquitous oil, she was content in her newfound freedom.

She had yet to speak at any length with her father, and so far had not mentioned her suspected pregnancy to anyone. She wondered how her father would take the news. Ah well, she had been through so much and survived; she would survive this too, whatever his reaction.

She idly surveyed the large feasting area. She was surprised to see how many young men were attending the feast. She wondered what brought them to her village.

She noted briefly that none of them were as handsome as Fighting Wolf. There he was again—creeping unbidden into her thoughts. Even now, surrounded by family and friends, she thought of him. Willfully, she purged him from her mind.

Her glance caught Feast Giver's as he rose from his place and walked over to where she was sitting. "Greetings, Umiksu, mother." He nodded respectfully to Crab Woman. "Umiksu." He nodded again to Abalone Woman. They murmured polite responses.

He squatted on his heels, beside Sarita, blocking her view of the activities. "Well, sister," he said. "Are you glad to be back home?" For a moment his grin reminded her of the old Feast Giver she had known, before the Ahousat raid had changed either of them.

She smiled back happily, pleased at being home, pleased at his present good humor. "I most certainly am," she replied. "But I was wondering about something. As I looked around I see many young men—warriors—that I've not met before. Where do they come from?"

"Aah, Sarita, your sharp gaze misses nothing. They're young men I've convinced to fight for me. Promises of wealth and fighting hold them."

Sarita lifted one well-shaped brow. "Oh?"

"Mmmhm," he went on to explain. "Most of these young men wish to join me in a raid on the Ahousats. For a share of the loot, of course."

Sarita glanced at Precious Copper. Her eyes met her brother's in a silent question. "No matter," he said lazily. "She can't warn her people of our impending attack. She only knows we will attack, she doesn't know when, or how. Even Fighting Wolf must realize we'll attack him eventually."

He turned his gaze to Precious Copper's. She met him unflinchingly, her chin thrust out. "Why don't you try for peace?" she asked. "Hasn't there been enough killing? Enough revenge?" Her musical voice was barely above a whisper. Sarita had to strain to hear her.

To Sarita's surprise, Feast Giver appeared to give consideration to Precious Copper's words. Before he could say anything, Sarita added, "She's right, catlati. In war, it's the women who suffer. Yes, I know what you want to say." She held up a hand to stop him. " 'It's the men who lose their lives. What can be worse than that?' I'll grant you, catlati, that to lose a life is terrible, but it's also terrible to languish in slavery for years, as is the lot of women. To see our children, whom we love dearly, grow up in that slavery, without benefit or knowledge of their rightful heritage!"

Precious Copper quickly followed Sarita's statement. "And revenge, Feast Giver." Here she was unaware that she touched his arm, as she looked sincerely into his eyes. "Revenge is a never-ending cycle that is waged between our peoples. Winning is only temporary. The victors congratulate themselves and parade around with their victims' heads. They lord it over their slaves, savoring their 'win.' Then what happens?" She leaned forward, intent. "They, the mighty victors, are attacked by the very people they had vanquished! The humiliated, desperate losers who will do anything to revenge themselves, anything to 'win.' The cycle of hate and murder becomes ever more ferocious and intense."

There was a brief silence after her words; all who heard her could not doubt her sincerity. Crab Woman broke the spell with a grunt. "Hmmph. Easy for her to say. Her people aren't the ones being slaughtered."

Feast Giver addressed Precious Copper as though Crab Woman had not spoken. "Why didn't you tell Fighting Wolf your wise words? He's the one who's after revenge. He's the one who's so ferocious."

Precious Copper dropped her eyes. "Please believe me when I say I honestly didn't know his plans. I only learned of them after he brought your sister back to our village." She looked at him again, earnest entreaty evident in her dark eyes. "But I can tell you this: I'll do everything I can to bring about peace between our peoples. There's been enough killing, enough families destroyed."

Crab Woman interrupted again. "Hmmph. She says that because it is *our* turn for vengeance! She's afraid for her precious brother!" Crab Woman spat; the thick spittle landed on Precious Copper's bare knee.

Precious Copper, disgust rippling across her pretty face, rubbed some dirt from the floor on the mess, then scraped it off her leg. She looked at Feast Giver, impatient for his answer to her pleas.

"Your words are well-spoken," Feast Giver conceded reluctantly. "I'm convinced you're sincere in what you say. However, Fighting Wolf is the one you must convince. You say yourself you didn't know of his plans for revenge. Obviously, he doesn't think the same as you on this subject. He is, after all, the one who started this war."

"Not so," disagreed Precious Copper. "He'd argue that your people, the murderers of his father, and mine, were the ones to start this war." She looked fully at Feast Giver, trying to gauge the effect of her words. Feast Giver was staring at her, anger flushing his countenance. Undaunted, she continued, "Fighting Wolf would argue that he's obliged to revenge his father's death. By the beliefs of my people, and yours, that's a noble thing to do."

"Enough!" roared Feast Giver. "First you sit with my sister and I, you eat our food, then you call us murderers! And all the while you defend that murdering worm you call 'brother'! Enough, I say! Get from my sight!"

"The ingrate!" added Crab Woman. "She should be made a slave. That will shut her mouth quickly!"

Precious Copper got shakily to her feet. Her whole body was trembling. But before she left, she was determined to finish her speech. Hurriedly, afraid Feast Giver would not listen to her words, she added, "I didn't intend to anger you. I was trying, ineffectually it appears, to point out that your people were not the only ones to suffer grief. I want to end this fighting, not add to it! If I, who have lost a father, can say 'no more fighting,' why can't you also put aside your revenge? You have your sister back from slavery. You have a father who's still alive!" Precious Copper turned and fled from his presence.

"Alive, yes," muttered Crab Woman savagely. "No thanks to her, or that Ahousat dog she calls 'brother'!"

Feast Giver turned his angry gaze to Sarita. "Too bad she didn't say such fine words to her bloodthirsty brother!" he spat. "I let her get away with too much."

Crab Woman nodded, agreeing emphatically. She grunted as Abalone Woman's sharp elbow jabbed her soft stomach.

"Just what is her status here?" interjected Sarita calmly. "Is she a slave?" Sarita did not want to anger her brother further. Whether to fight or not was such a complicated decision and she knew he would do what he wanted regardless of what she, his sister, had to say.

"A slave?" repeated Feast Giver, focusing his gaze on Sarita. "No. She's not a slave. More like a hostage."

"She should be a slave," snorted Crab Woman, still sitting behind them.

"Shhh," cautioned Abalone Woman, trying to keep the peace.

"What," responded Sarita, "are you going to do with her now that I've returned? You no longer need a hostage."

Feast Giver looked at Sarita. For a moment, he reminded her of a lost little boy. "I don't know," he answered at last. "When she isn't making me angry," he acknowledged wryly, "I like having her around."

Glancing at Crab Woman and Abalone Woman out of the corner of his eye, he added, "She's useful, too." He gestured around the main area. "See the new woven mats on the walls? Precious Copper did that," he said proudly. "She organized some of the slave women and made the designs herself." He paused. "In fact, she's been busy ever since she got here. Precious Copper's always helping Abalone Woman and Cedar Bundle with their herb and medicinal plant collection."

Another snort came from Crab Woman. "Hmmph. Poor designs. They look Kwakiutl to me. And she's not that busy. I had to tell her what to do and who to organize!"

"She plays with the children," continued Feast Giver, as if he had not heard Crab Woman's comments. "She's up early, lighting the fire, getting the household started. And she's always cheerful." He paused again. "Except when she's defending that foul brother of hers!"

"Come, Crab Woman,' said Abalone Woman

patiently. "You must be tired after organizing this lovely banquet. Let's leave these two to catch up on their news." With that, she got to her feet, followed by a grumbling Crab Woman. Spring Fern and Cedar Bundle got to their feet also, bade Sarita good night, and went to their respective quarters.

There were still people seated nearby, but Sarita knew that if she and Feast Giver kept their voices low, they would not be overheard. "Are you really not sure what to do with Precious Copper, catlati?" she asked softly. When he didn't respond, she added, "You could let her go back to her people."

"Let her go?" echoed her brother incredulously.

"I'm serious," answered his sister. "What good does it do to keep her? You have the young men you need to make your raid. You don't need her. You're too noble to make war on women and children. Aren't you?"

"No," snapped Feast Giver. "I'm not. I can't afford to be noble. Not after that treacherous betrayal of Fighting Wolf's. I have few warriors, dubious weapons and a long way to travel to engage my enemies. I need every advantage I can command. Fighting Wolf's sister is one such advantage."

Seeing she would get nowhere with her line of questioning, Sarita decided to drop the subject. "Whatever," she sighed. "All I know is that it would be terrible to condemn a beautiful woman like Precious Copper to a lifetime of slavery. I should know. I barely escaped such a life," she reminded him.

Feast Giver's only response was a grunt. Sarita rose quietly to her full height. "Well, catlati, I bid you goodnight."

"Good-night, Sarita. It's good to have you home," he answered softly.

Sarita smiled and headed for her sleeping quarters. Looking back over her shoulder, she saw her brother still sitting by the fire. He was staring into the flames, an unfathomable expression on his handsome face.

* * *

As they walked in the direction of their sleeping quarters, Spring Fern said to her companion, "Let's take a short walk on the beach before we retire. I want to clear my head after all that food and conversation!"

Cedar Bundle nodded her agreement and they stepped outside the longhouse. They meandered through long grass towards the beach.

It was dark, but a quarter moon glowed silver in the night sky. The gentle lapping of the waves on the beach added a sense of calm to the dark scene. A salty breeze blew onto the land, adding a slight chill to the night.

"Oh, look!" exclaimed Spring Fern, pointing to the waves. "See the little bits of light dancing on the waves!" The phosphorescence truly did dance, gleaming white against the dark waters. The two women stood entranced, gazing at the waves.

"It's so beautiful," said Cedar Bundle.

Spring Fern smiled, her teeth a white smudge in the dark. "It wasn't so long ago that you couldn't find beauty here," she said softly. "I'm glad that things have changed for you."

"So am I," responded her friend. "So am I." After a short pause she added, "I suppose I've accepted my new role. Thunder Maker treats me very well."

"I should hope so," said Spring Fern. "You're the cleverest of his women. And the prettiest."

"No, not the prettiest," said Cedar Bundle in a calm voice. "But surely the most desperate!"

The two women laughed, their soft voices carrying on the gentle night breeze. They walked along the gravel beach, crunching the small rocks underfoot. "Are you his only concubine?" asked Spring Fern shyly.

Cedar Bundle nodded. "He does have four wives to keep him busy, after all." She took a sudden interest in a large rock, probing at it with her big toe. "I guess it all started after he was injured. He needed so much nursing. Crab Woman didn't want to do it. Abalone Woman wanted to help him, but she had others who needed her medical skills, too. So it fell to me to nurse him.''

''And?''

''And that's how I came under his protection,'' explained Cedar Bundle hastily, obviously disinclined to say more. Spring Fern did not press her. After a short silence, Cedar Bundle commented, ''My sons are in a better position now. Thunder Maker ordered an older man, also a slave, to teach them fishing and hunting skills.'' She paused. ''It's not what they would have had if their father had lived. But, it's a lot more than many slaves ever get.''

''You're right about that,'' agreed Spring Fern.

''Enough of me. What about you? Do you see Rottenwood now that he's back?''

Spring Fern shook her head. ''No,'' she answered sadly. ''He avoids me. Perhaps he doesn't love me anymore. I thought he cared for me. Before he was stolen away, he told me he did. Maybe he found someone else in Ahousat village. Someone he likes more than me.''

''I doubt that,'' responded Cedar Bundle loyally. ''And if he did, well—! You deserve better, that's all!''

Spring Fern smiled, secretly gratified to hear the indignation in her friend's voice. It was nice to have someone on her side.

Together the two women strolled slowly back to the longhouse.

25

Sarita had been back in her home village for a number of days, long enough to catch up on several changes. She'd had time to observe her brother, as well. He had indeed changed. The new, somber Feast Giver was now to be found with the young warriors, instead of catching crabs down on the beach for the children. He and his men spent a long time each day practicing with their recently acquired muskets.

Sarita noticed, too, how Feast Giver's eyes hungrily followed Precious Copper whenever he thought she wasn't aware of him. But it appeared to Sarita that Precious Copper was very aware of him. Sarita watched the two with great interest.

She had time to chat with Spring Fern, and she was able to find out more of the changes in the village. Spring Fern was happy to tell her about the new weapons that Feast Giver had brought to the village. Sarita noticed, however, that Spring Fern was reluctant to speak of Rottenwood. Sarita knew that while Rottenwood had wanted his freedom, he also wanted Spring Fern. In fact, Sarita suspected Spring Fern was the main reason he'd returned to the Hesquiat village. That Rottenwood had not yet apprised Spring Fern of his feelings was inexplicable. Puzzled, Sarita decided to say nothing to Spring Fern.

One sunny day, Sarita wandered down to the beach to watch the children swim. Summer was on the wane, but the weather was still warm. Watching the screeching, splashing children brought back childhood memories. She knew that soon there'd be no swimming, not once the rainy winter weather set in.

Sarita found a large, warm rock on which to settle herself comfortably. She was near enough to hear the shrieks of the playing children, but far enough away to ensure some measure of solitude. One thing she had relished since her return was her privacy. Here there was no one watching her with lecherous intent, no one watching to make sure she did not escape, and most of all, no one watching to make sure she was working hard!

Since she had been back, she thought idly, dipping her long toes in the swirling, clear water, she had not done any work. She wondered at this lethargy, but she just couldn't make herself do any of her usual tasks. Usually she just wanted to sleep. Today, however, she had forced herself to get up and go to the beach. She had no idea why she felt so tired. Perhaps she should consult Abalone Woman, she speculated.

Her musings were interrupted by the deep voice of Rottenwood. She looked up, shielding her eyes from the sun, to see him striding towards her. She smiled and waved to him. He nodded coolly, squatted beside her and said nothing.

Feeling suddenly uncomfortable, Sarita broke the silence. "Are you pleased to be back, Rottenwood?" she asked politely.

He shrugged casually, his eyes on the children. "Slavery is much the same no matter what village I'm in," he answered.

Sarita felt the blood rise to her cheeks. "Yes, I know it is," she responded quietly. "Rottenwood, I—I haven't forgotten that you helped me."

He was silent, now ostensibly observing the sea, and waiting. "I've asked my father to free you," she went on. "He said we'd talk about it later." Her voice faltered.

"And have you?" he asked, swinging his eyes

around to meet hers.

She looked down into the crystal depths below. "No," she answered in a small voice.

He grunted, contemptuously she thought. Then he got up and walked away.

Sarita felt mortified. She had promised to free him, but she had not done so. She sat there, gazing into the water. Nothing, nothing had gone right since she had come home, she sighed. Her brother was obsessed with vengeance. Her father was distant. And she herself had given her word to an honorable man and then failed to keep it. Rottenwood had kept his word to rescue her. She would never have escaped without his help, she reproached herself.

She stared into the water as if seeking an answer there. Fighting Wolf too, had been in her thoughts lately. She wondered if he missed her, now that she was gone.

She threw a small pebble into the water and watched the widening concentric rings fade into nothing. He probably didn't even care, she thought self-pityingly. He would find someone else to warm his bed. That had been all he wanted her for, she thought, as she tossed another pebble into the cool depths.

While she was being brutally honest with herself, she might as well admit something else. She missed him. Missed his warm embrace at night, his laughter and teasing in the day. She thought of his beguiling eyes, eyes that could be stern and hard, or soft and understanding.

She wondered how Fighting Wolf would have treated Rottenwood, had he been in her position. With a start, she realized that he would have kept his word. Fighting Wolf wouldn't have let anyone keep him from doing what he believed to be right. His revenge, misguided as it had been from her perspective, was ample testimony to that. He had certainly believed in avenging his father, and had done it. If Fighting Wolf, her enemy, could act as his sense of honor dictated, despite the risks involved, then why couldn't she?

She considered herself an honorable person. She had always tried to be fair with herself and with others—until now. Until she had allowed her father to make her decisions for her. She resolved once again to confront Thunder Maker and have Rottenwood set free.

Rottenwood walked away from Sarita, the bitter taste of failure in his mouth. He should have known better than to trust one of the noble class, he thought sardonically. Now that she was home and safe, she didn't care what happened to him, or about keeping her word to him.

The tide was out and he noticed a long strip of sand. He was very angry and knew he had to do something to express that anger. He loped across the sand, his tight muscles glorying in the fast pace he set for himself.

For days now, he had avoided Spring Fern. What it had cost him to stay away from her, only he knew. But he had wanted to go to her as a free man, not as a slave. Already the other slaves had been talking about him, calling him a fool for coming back. One of the men had even taunted him in front of Spring Fern. With great difficulty, Rottenwood had held his temper in check. At that time, he had hoped that within a few days he would be a free man. Now he knew differently.

The bitterness he felt at the hopelessness of his position washed over him. Before, when he had had hope, he had daydreamed that he was a free man, allowed to come and go as he wished, even free to take a wife, if he so chose. But he wanted Spring Fern, and though she was a slave, she would surely not turn him down once he was free! He would be free of that lowly status and scorn in the eyes of himself and other men. He would be free to be a man!

But today, the depth of his disappointment was almost unbearable. Better never to have had the chance of freedom, never to have dreamed of it, he thought bitterly.

The taste of defeat, the destruction of his dreams, the lost chance at freedom, were agonizing. He wanted to scream his anger to the sky, to Qua-utz, the god over all living things. Someone should listen, must listen; someone should know the pain he carried. It was too heavy for him to carry alone.

Not since his capture as a young boy had the chains of slavery cut so deeply into his heart. It had been bad then, yes, but it was many times worse now, when as an adult, he had come so close to gaining his freedom.

His race across the sand slowed gradually. He had worked out some of his disappointment while running hard. As his anger gradually dissolved, he was able to think clearly again. He would not let this setback stop him, he resolved. He halted, poised on the sand, and raised his fist to the blue sky. "Before Qua-utz," he vowed. "I swear I will be free or die trying." His ringing cry lingered a moment, as did he, waiting for he knew not what.

At last he grew tired of the silence. He turned and walked thoughtfully back to the village, his back straight. He had taken a gamble and lost. Nevertheless, there would be other opportunities for escape, he was sure. He had done it once. He could do it again.

That evening, Rottenwood sought out Spring Fern. He had noted that she usually went for an evening walk with her friend, Cedar Bundle. He watched them saunter through the village, past the longhouses. He recognized Spring Fern's taller, slim form next to the shorter, fuller figure of Cedar Bundle. He leaned against the last longhouse, and after they passed by, he stepped between them and the village.

The two women gasped upon seeing a dark shape standing between them and safety. Spring Fern stood poised to run.

Holding out one hand, Rottenwood assured them that he only wished to speak with Spring Fern. At last, recognizing him, the two women held a whispered conference. He was relieved to see Cedar Bundle slip by him, back to the village, leaving Spring Fern alone.

Rottenwood approached her cautiously. Spring Fern made no move, neither towards him nor away from him. He could feel the tension in the air around her, a palpable thing.

"I'm sorry if I frightened you," he began. "I wanted to speak with you today, but didn't have an earlier opportunity to tell you."

Spring Fern nodded. "Say what you have to say," she answered briefly, turning her face from him. He had avoided her for days, ever since he'd been back. What did he want? she wondered.

"Not like this," he said. "Not here, with you afraid of me."

"I'm not afraid," she lied.

He took her arm, feeling her tremble beneath his hand. "Come," he coaxed. "Let's sit down by the water. It's a lovely evening, and I would have the music of the waves serenade us."

She let herself be led down to a large rock near the water. In the rock there was a natural hollow, scooped out by wave action. Spring Fern settled gracefully into the hollow. Rottenwood squatted on his heels next to her.

Gravely he looked at her. Though the moon was hidden behind clouds tonight, Rottenwood was close enough to see her face, and smell the faint scent of cedar about her. He smiled and his teeth gleamed white in the dark.

Spring Fern felt herself relax slightly. "Was it difficult for you in the Ahousat village?" she asked politely.

Rottenwood shrugged. "A slave is a slave, wherever he is," came the casual response. He elaborated, "Some people treated me better than I've been treated here. Some treated me worse." He paused.

"I wanted to see you tonight," Rottenwood began, "to let you know I hadn't forgotten you. I haven't been friendly since I've been back, but I wanted you to know it's not you or anything you've done."

She sighed. "I had wondered. I thought you were angry with me. Or that you'd found someone else." She dropped her gaze to the pebbles near her feet.

Rottenwood reached out and gently lifted Spring Fern's chin until their eyes met. "Never that," he answered softly. "No one compares with you, Spring Fern."

He turned away. "No," he continued, and his voice was harsher now, "I've been caught up in thoughts of freedom."

"Freedom?" she echoed, surprise in her voice.

Rottenwood turned back to her. "Yes. Freedom. I thought that if I helped Sarita return to her village, she'd grant me my freedom." After a lengthy pause, he said simply, "I was wrong."

"Oh, no! What are you saying?"

"Just that helping Sarita escape did not gain my freedom."

"Did she promise she'd free you?" asked Spring Fern.

"Yes. I made a bargain with her. I'd help her escape and in return she'd set me free—once we were safely back in this village. I should have known better than to trust her," he answered sardonically.

"That's odd," murmured Spring Fern. "It's not like Sarita to give her word and then break it." Spring Fern frowned. "True, Sarita is headstrong at times, but never deceitful."

"Well, it's over with now," Rottenwood answered calmly. "For awhile I had these marvelous dreams of freedom—"

Spring Fern touched his arm. "I feel so bad for you, my friend," she said softly. "If only your plan had worked. You'd be a free man."

"Yes," he sighed. Then, more forcefully, "But that's all in the past."

He reached out and drew her to him. Spring Fern went willingly, and relaxed in his strong embrace. He kissed her, gently at first, then with more passion, his lips forceful against hers. They pulled apart slowly.

"What would have happened to us, if you were free?" she whispered, curious. "Don't forget I'd still be a slave."

"You'd be my mistress," he chuckled. He felt her tense in his arms. "Maybe it's just as well I didn't get my freedom, eh? Since we're both still slaves, we can get married."

"Oh, do you mean it?" she cried.

"I've always wanted to marry you, Spring Fern," he answered gravely.

"Oh yes," she answered happily. Then, more shyly, "—and I've wanted to marry you, Rottenwood." She thought for a moment. "You know we'll need Thunder Maker's permission to marry. Perhaps Sarita will ask him for us. He wouldn't deny her."

"Huh," responded Rottenwood contemptuously. "Sarita will do nothing."

Spring Fern chewed on her luscious lower lip. "I know you think her deceitful, but I think she'll help us. She and I have been friends all our lives."

"Don't fool yourself," he snarled. "To her you're merely a slave. And don't be surprised if she agrees to get permission, and then you never hear of it again!" He sat there angry, wounded. "And I'll tell you something else, Spring Fern. I'll tell you this: someday I will be free! I will be free or die trying!"

Spring Fern hugged him to her. "Yes," she answered solemnly. "I understand this. I, too, wish to be free. I'll do all I can to help you obtain your freedom."

He returned her hug, his strong arms holding her tightly. "Together we can do it," he said fiercely. "Together we can overcome this blight of slavery that poisons our lives!"

"Yes," she agreed fervently, covering his face with little kisses. "Yes!"

26

The sky was overcast. Sarita sat on the damp beach, a warm cedar cloak tossed over her shoulders. She watched idly as the children combed the beach. They were intent on finding edible morsels for the next meal. A triumphant shout caught her attention as a small girl held up a reddish-brown, kicking crab. Keeping a tight hold on the crab's back legs, the girl avoided the grasping front pinchers that could wound so painfully. Sarita watched, amused, as the little girl happily chased her friends, her angry trophy waving its claws menacingly at the shrieking children as they scattered.

Sarita chuckled to herself. She could remember playful days when she, too, had caught crabs on the beach. One day, she though pensively, her child would do the same.

Sarita glanced down at her stomach. She could see a slight rounding when she was undressing for bed, but during the day, when she wore her kutsack, no one could guess her secret—except Abalone Woman.

Sarita had gone to Abalone Woman earlier that morning. After a series of pointed questions, Abalone Woman had confirmed Sarita's suspicion: she was indeed pregnant. Sarita had pleaded with her step-mother to keep the condition a secret, and that kindly woman had agreed.

The young noblewoman sighed heavily. She couldn't go much longer without telling her family. Her father, particularly, needed to be told. Shuddering, she

wondered what he'd say about an illegitimate grand-
child. Especially one whose father turned out to be
Thunder Maker's archenemy Fighting Wolf!

Precious Copper bent over the wet, floating mass
of shredded cedar bark. She poked it with a long stick
and swirled the shreds around in the salt water. Wading
out a little farther, she held up one edge of her kutsack
so it would not get wet. Sweat ran down her face and she
bent her head to wipe her brow on her upper arm.

She glanced at the three other women on the beach
where they busily sorted the cedar shreds. Precious
Copper groaned. Preparing cedar bark was hard work.
Back home she had always directed slaves to do the
messy task. Now here she was doing it herself. Slowly
and deliberately, she pushed the floating mass towards
shore.

The slave woman, Cedar Bundle, walked over to
where Precious Copper stood knee-deep in the water.
Cedar Bundle smiled as she lifted an armful of the
dripping wet mass and carried it up to where waiting
cedar mats were spread out across the beach. Placing
the wet bark on the mats, she began to sift through the
pulpy mass. The weak sun helped dry the bark somewhat and made the sorting task so much easier.

Precious Copper returned Cedar Bundle's friendly
gesture with a dimpled smile of her own. She had been
glad of the older woman's friendship in the past few
days. Precious Copper's status was doubtful; though
still considered a hostage, she often worked in the
company of slave women.

Cedar Bundle had been especially kind, lending a
hand whenever her own tasks were completed. But
Precious Copper was reluctant to take the proffered
help. She knew Cedar Bundle liked to spend her rare
free time with her sons.

The two little boys played nearby on the beach,
building mounds of gravelly sand and piling up rocks.
The smaller child's hair was a dark blond, the older

child's a gleaming jet black. Both boys were naked, their brown bodies healthy and well-formed. Precious Copper knew the pride Cedar Bundle took in her sons. And rightly so. The boys were good-natured and cheerful; many times Precious Copper had watched their doting mother laughing and playing with them.

A movement near the tree line suddenly caught Precious Copper's attention. Along the path opening onto the beach strode the tall figure of Feast Giver. Precious Copper bent over the shredded cedar bark, pretending to be deeply engrossed in separating the softer, inner bark from the tougher, outer bark. She kept her eyes studiously on her work as she heard the gravel scrunch underfoot. Only when his brown feet stopped in front of her did she risk a glance at him. Ah, Feast Giver, she thought, no man should look as beautiful as you.

Her thoughts must have registered on her face, for Feast Giver grinned at her confidently, his teeth strong and white. Precious Copper smiled hesitantly back at him. He squatted beside her, saying nothing.

Under his appraising eyes, her fingers grew clumsy. She pulled ineffectually at some of the cedar shreds, then looked at him. Cocking her head to one side, she asked in her musical voice, "Do Hesquiat warriors sort cedar bark now?" Her dimpled smile unwittingly took the sting out of her words. "I thought this was woman's work."

Amused by her challenge to his masculinity, he laughed and answered, "Yes, Hesquiat warriors love to sort cedar bark. It's an important part of their training." His ebony eyes twinkled at her. "Second only to mus-ket practice every morning."

Reminded of his plans for her people, Precious Copper turned away, suddenly intent on twisting the piece of cedar in her hands. "It's sad your people and mine can't live together peacefully," she said softly.

He grimaced, all humor gone from his face. "As I said before, tell that to your bloodthirsty brother!" He stood up. "Drop your work and come with me," he commanded.

Precious Copper was reluctant to leave the safety of the other women. She glanced at them. All three, including Cedar Bundle, continued their work, refusing to meet her eyes. No help there, she concluded.

Stepping lightly and gracefully over the large round stones scattered amongst the gravel, she padded along the beach after him. He headed back to the overland trail. She wondered uneasily where they were going.

As they walked along the trail, Precious Copper breathed the sweet forest scents. The dappled trail was beautiful in shades of light and dark green as they walked through a tunnel of alder trees. She followed silently, watching the muscles of his back and the smooth stride of his long, lightly tanned and muscled legs.

She wondered idly how it would be to love and be loved by such a handsome man. Then she caught herself. Reality was that she was here under precarious circumstances. Better not to have girlish dreams such as those. Better to find a way out of her predicament, she thought.

Her thoughts were interrupted as Feast Giver gestured to a smaller path leading off from the main one. He held some low hanging bushes aside to let her pass. Now she was walking in front, he following. The path was easy to distinguish, though only narrow enough for one person. Perhaps a deer trail, she thought idly.

Feast Giver's eyes narrowed as he watched the swaying walk of the diminutive woman ahead of him. Even now, as he watched her he could feel his body's responses to the sight of her, the warm, fresh smell of her.

He had watched her closely since bringing her back to his village. He knew he should be avoiding her; she was the hated Fighting Wolf's sister, but he could not stop himself. It was as if another man inhabited his body when she was about. A man who was not afraid to laugh, to relax, perhaps to love?

Feast Giver shook his head, shrugging off such thoughts. He wanted Precious Copper. He could not deny his desire any longer. Then why not take her? The fact that she was his enemy's sister made such action all the more fitting. But she was so dainty! And far more beautiful than any woman in his village, including Sarita, he mused. With Precious Copper's doe-like eyes, and thick plaits of black hair framing her delicate face, he had wanted her from the first time he had seen her—crouched in torn clothing, dead Kwakiutl warriors scattered around, her large dark eyes looking to him for protection.

No, the thought of seeing tears in those beautiful black eyes, tears that he had caused, perhaps by violent action, was loathsome. It wasn't in him to destroy someone so beautiful and gentle, despite her being an enemy. She was well-named, he thought ironically. She was very precious, indeed.

The trail they were following had begun to twist its way up a hillside. They were almost at the destination he had in mind. All at once they crested the hill, and came out of the thick forest to an open field that slanted down towards the village far below.

He heard Precious Copper catch her breath at the beautiful vista spread out before them. From where they stood in the thigh-high grass and shrubbery, they could look out over the trees below them to the village, to the beach and then, farther out, to the bay in front of the village. Far off in the distance the sea stretched into gray nothingness.

High white clouds drifted lazily across the blue sky. Leaves on many of the trees scattered throughout the broad vista were starting to turn to the bright yellow and bronze of autumn. The piercing, indefinable, smoky smell of fall was in the cool air. It was truly a beautiful place, and one he was glad he had chosen.

As Feast Giver walked over to a rocky outcropping,

he gestured to Precious Copper to follow. A small lizard, basking in the sun, blinked up at them before scurrying away into a rocky crevice. Birds called shrilly to each other in the surrounding woods, warning each other away from occupied territories. A rustling in the nearby grass marked the escape route of a garter snake, disturbed in its sun bathing by the two intruders.

Feast Giver sat down in a comfortable, cross-legged position on one of the flat rocks and stared out to sea. Precious Copper quietly sank to her knees on the long dry grass nearby. It felt good to rest after the long walk and arduous labors.

Feast Giver turned to Precious Copper and smiled disarmingly. She smiled shyly back. "Perhaps you're curious as to why I brought you here?" he asked, his confident, deep-timbered voice sending a shiver down her spine.

"Yes," she murmured, meeting his eyes with a quick glance before looking out to sea again.

"I wanted to show you the beautiful view from here." She could hear the smile in his voice. "Many times as a small boy, I came here and surveyed the village and beach and water. I pretended I was chief over all I surveyed." He paused, lost in memories. "I'd pretend that warriors from another tribe were attacking my village. But through valiant fighting, led by myself of course, my friends and I would drive the enemy away."

Sadly he added, "At that time I didn't think about the possibility of death, or injury—neither for myself nor for my 'men.' I didn't think about women being stolen, or of the shame of losing." He sighed heavily. "Now I've grown up."

They were both silent for a long while. "Why are you telling me this?" asked Precious Copper gently. "Your dreams? Your thoughts?"

"Don't you know why?" he returned.

Precious Copper looked down at the ground. In her low, musical voice, she answered quietly, "When I was a girl, I didn't have such wars to fight.'' She looked at him, the dimples deepening in her cheeks as she smiled. "When I was a girl, my thoughts were of all the young men I'd overwhelm with my beauty and talents. My father would have many suitors asking for my hand, but he would defer to my wishes, of course. And my wishes," she went on dreamily, "were that the most handsome and kind man, one I didn't already know, would be the one man for me. He'd be so smitten with me, he'd carry me away to his village, and we'd marry and live so happily together.'' She suddenly looked uncomfortable and turned her gaze out to sea. "Alas, I too have grown up.''

A slight flush covered her cheeks, Feast Giver noticed. "Do you think I might be that man?" he asked in a low voice.

She stared at him. "I don't know," she answered impishly. "I never got a good look at his face!''

But Feast Giver was not to be put off so easily. "It must be me," he said confidently. "I carried you away to my village. I even saved you from those rotten Kwakiutl slavers!''

Precious Copper looked down at the ground, embarrassed. "Yes, you did that," she agreed quietly.

"Of course," he added, "I realize that not all our childhood dreams can come true, but it seems to me that parts of them can." He smiled over at her. "I'd like to be the man you thought of when you were a child," he said gently. "I'd like to keep you with me always, for I'm deeply smitten with you, with your 'beauty and talents.' '' This last was said so softly, Precious Copper thought she hadn't heard correctly.

Feast Giver reached over and took her small dark hand in his, pulling her closer. One arm snaked around her narrow waist and clamped her to him. Precious Copper felt Feast Giver's lips against hers, ever so softly touching, then harder as his hold on her tightened. He slanted his lips across hers again and again.

She could feel herself falling into an abyss where

only he was real. The blood pounded in her body as he ran his hands up and down her small frame. Unsteadily she pushed against his chest, lifting her eyes to his face and gently touching her fingers to her swollen lips. "Ohhh," she breathed wondrously. Feast Giver looked at her, taken slightly aback. "I can do even better than that," he laughed.

"No, no," she cried. "Don't mock me." Still touching her lips, she said, "I—I didn't know people did this. That it could feel—"

He ran his hands lazily down her back, then pressed her into him. "They do even more, sweet Precious Copper," he murmured into her hair.

She tried to pull away from him, but he would not free her. He gazed longingly into the depths of her eyes, as if he would seek out her soul. "Let me love you, Precious Copper," he urged. "It will be so good. Let me love you," he repeated, nuzzling the hollow of her neck and her shoulder.

She lifted one shoulder, trying to stop the light, tickling touches of his lips on her sensitive skin. Again she tried to draw away.

"Don't you like me?" he asked at last. "Was I wrong to think you might care for me? Even a little?" His sparkling ebony eyes sent shivers through her.

"Oh, yes," she breathed. "I do like you. But—but I can't—It's not right—"

"It's right for us," he murmured, continuing his gentle assault on her vulnerable defenses.

Precious Copper closed her eyes for a moment and leaned into him. It would be so easy to yield to him. She had admired, respected, wanted, yes, loved him ever since he had rescued her from the Kwakiutl warriors. At last she could admit it to herself. It would be so easy to relax, to let their love culminate naturally here in this beautiful setting.

Then a cautious thought intruded. He might be toying with her—wanting only her body to satisfy his very masculine needs. The thought gave her added strength and determination. "Feast Giver," she said firmly, "please listen to me."

Feast Giver raised his head to stare at her and Precious Copper felt the full impact of his haunting ebony eyes. She forced herself to continue, "I don't know how you feel about me. I've told you my feelings, but what are yours?"

The pause between them grew, and her heart sank. At last he answered, "My feelings?" He snorted and pushed her away. Heedless of the brown grass and ferns he trampled underfoot, he paced the small area near the rock. "My feelings?" he repeated.

"Don't do this to me," she cried out in agony. "Don't torment me with your pacing, your mockery."

Feast Giver halted, then walked over to her. Taking her in his arms he said, "I don't know where to begin." He gazed into her eyes intently. "I've wanted you ever since the first time I saw you," he said in a husky voice. Precious Copper shivered. "When I found out you were the sister of my enemy I tried to harden my heart against you. I couldn't."

He raked his fingers through his hair. "Since you came to this village I haven't slept a night without dreaming of you. I haven't gone through a day without looking for you. I haven't thought of anything, anyone but you." His eyes impaled her. Precious Copper couldn't pull hers away from his tortured face. "Nothing, not even the raid I'm leading against your brother, can distract me from thoughts of you. It's like a sickness in me. I've got to have you!"

Precious Copper's eyes flickered with fear. They were alone on the hillside. Were she to cry out, no one would hear; he could do what he wanted. A tremor of fright shook her frame.

He grinned sardonically and ran his thumbs over the corners of her mouth. "Don't be afraid, Precious Copper," he said softly. "I wouldn't hurt you. I know what I want. I want you, it's true, but I want you willing. I'm not a Kwakiutl," he said harshly.

"Oh, my love," she cried out, throwing her arms around his neck. "I want you too. I haven't been the same since you rescued me. I haven't been able to keep my eyes off you, but I thought you didn't care for me. I was afraid, too," she admitted, "afraid you just thought of me as a hostage, someone to use." She broke off, wondering suddenly if this was a part of his plan.

He saw the doubt. "No, no. You mean far more to me than that. I don't need you as a hostage. I can make the raid without bargaining. But once I saw you, I couldn't let you go. I used the hostage bargaining as an excuse to bring you back and keep you here." They were silent for a moment, staring into each other's eyes. "I love you," he said softly.

"Oh, Feast Giver," she moaned, "I love you, too." They held each other, neither willing to let go. "What are we going to do?" she asked at last.

He hugged her tightly. "We'll work something out," he said confidently. "Now that I know you love me too, I'll do anything, anything at all, to make you my woman."

The fierceness in his declaration both scared and elated Precious Copper. He was so serious about her, about their love.

27

"Potlatches, hmph," muttered Crab Woman to herself as she sorted through numerous bundles of long, tangled roots. Cinquefoil was a favorite vegetable all year long, but it was especially tasty in the fall, when it was freshly dug. Each bundle was bound with a special, identifying knot, tied by whichever woman pried the roots out of the earth. "Waste of time. Just a lot of work," grumbled Crab Woman. "There are some blind fathers around here. That's for certain. Giving potlatches for worthless daughters. Hmmph. Worthless daughters who go and get themselves stolen by useless Ahousats."

"Now, Crab Woman," chimed in the voice of Abalone Woman. "If Sarita's name is cleared, then the names of all Thunder Maker's children will be without taint. Do you want your children taunted because their half sister is a slave?"

Crab Woman continued sorting in silence.

"I thought not," responded Abalone Woman with a lilt in her voice. "And neither do I. Thunder Maker is putting on this big potlatch for his entire family, not just for one daughter."

Crab Woman heaved herself to her feet. "I'm going to find some worthless slaves to dig the steaming pits for these roots," she said. She pointed to Cedar Bundle. "You there. Come with me."

On the way to the door, Crab Woman passed Sarita. "We're late moving to the winter village site, and it's all your fault. If we didn't have to put on this potlatch," she sneered, "we could've moved several days ago." Crab Woman paused, her face screwed up with irritation. "You'd better appreciate all the work we're doing for you."

Sarita looked at her and smiled. "I do, Crab Woman. I truly appreciate your efforts on my behalf." Sarita chuckled at the suspicious look on Crab Woman's face.

The older woman snorted, "Hmmph. I doubt that," and made her way out the door, Cedar Bundle trailing reluctantly behind.

Sarita followed them and added, "It's true, Crab Woman. I saw you save Feast Giver in that fight at my false marriage ceremony. You risked your life to hide him. For that I thank you."

Crab Woman stopped in her tracks and turned to gaze at her stepdaughter for a long moment. Crab Woman appeared disconcerted by the unexpected praise. "Can't you find something useful to do?" she asked gruffly. "This potlatch is for you. Get busy and help me dig the steaming pits."

Sarita smiled and nodded, falling into step again, behind Cedar Bundle. The three made their way in silence down to the beach, to where the pits would be dug.

The weather had remained warm and Thunder Maker insisted the potlatch be held in the open air. He expected many guests from other villages.

Sarita labored with several other women digging the pits deep into the sandy beach. Each pit had to be lined with rocks also. Tired, Sarita sat resting on the sand and watched as Crab Woman deftly started a fire in the bottom of a pit. Huge stacks of fern fronds and salal bushes were piled to one side, awaiting use.

Sarita knew the method of steaming cinquefoil roots. After the fire had burned all morning, and the rocks were red-hot, the fire was doused. A circular wooden post would be inserted in the middle of the pit.

Around it, layers of fern fronds and salal leaves were
spread over the hot rocks, followed by a layer of
cinquefoil roots. Additional layers of ferns, salal and
cinquefoil were piled on until the hole was filled to the
top of the post. Then several containers of water were
poured down the hole. The remaining fronds, packed
onto the pit, were covered over by cedar mats. To make
the oven airtight, sand was mounded over the mats and
the vegetables left to steam overnight. Sarita's mouth
watered at the thought of delicious roots awaiting her
on the morrow.

She was finishing her work at the steaming pits
when she noticed her father walking along the beach.
He was shouting orders to some of his slaves who had
been out fishing and were bringing in a huge catch of
fish for the potlatch.

Sarita hurried over to where her father was
standing. "Nuwiksu," she said breathlessly, "I haven't
had a chance to talk with you about the potlatch
tomorrow."

Her father turned to her. "Aah, yes," he said.
"It'll be a great feast. I'll be giving away many valuable
things—carved dishes, furs, blankets, too. I think the
guests will be favorably impressed by our wealth." He
smiled benignly at his daughter.

"I'm glad our family could call on our friends to
support us for this potlatch," Sarita answered politely.

"Well, they certainly did that. Our relatives came
up with some very fine items they must've hidden away
from me before." Then he said, more seriously, "I'm
doing this for you, yes, but also for our family name.
Our family has always been proud. My father and
mother, and their fathers and mothers before them,
passed on the most honorable name they could. With
that name came all our fishing territories along the river
and our right to hunt on Gooseneck Island." Sarita
nodded as he continued reverently, "Some of the dances
you'll see at the potlatch were handed down from my
grandfather. One of your grandmothers owned many

songs; I'll sing two of them tomorrow night." After a long pause during which Thunder Maker appeared lost in thought, he added, "It's because we have such a distinguished history that I can't stand by and see our name tarnished."

Sarita looked down at her feet. "I'm ashamed that our family has fallen so low," she said softly.

Thunder Maker continued as if he had not heard her. "This potlatch will show people that our illustrious name cannot be mocked. Our family is one to be reckoned with!" He stopped, noting the red flush on his daughter's cheeks. "There now, daughter. I didn't mean to embarrass you. It's not your fault the Ahousats attacked us and took you away. I shouldn't have trusted that devious Fighting Wolf," he said bitterly. "The humiliation of your slavery rests with me, not you. Your shame is mine."

Sarita cringed at the pity in his voice. She did not want his sympathy. She needed to be strengthened, not weakened. Her response was stiff. "As you say, Nuwiksu, after this potlatch no one will speak disparagingly of our name."

Sarita looked at her father with new eyes. She noticed for the first time that his hair was thin and gray, his once straight body now stooped. The past months had taken a terrible toll on him, she suddenly realized. "Nuwiksu," she began tentatively, "Rottenwood, the slave, helped me escape. Without his aid I could never have returned to you. I promised him his freedom. Will you grant that? For me?"

Her father looked at her assessingly. "Sarita, you can't make rash promises to every slave who helps you. What about Spring Fern? She makes your bed and cleans up after you. Next thing you'll be wanting to free her too. Where would I be if I freed my slaves so easily?" His gaze hardened. "No, I won't free Rottenwood. He merely did his duty."

"Didn't you just finish lecturing me about the honor of one's name? How am I supposed to be proud

of my family name if my own father won't help me keep
my promises?''

Stung, her father retorted, ''Promises to slaves
don't count.''

''Slave or not, that man risked his life for me.''

Thunder Maker stared at Sarita for a long while.
He was suddenly tired of all the trouble this daughter
brought him. What had happened to the happy little girl
he used to dandle on his knee? She'd grown up to give
him nothing but problems. He sighed resignedly. ''I'll
give him to you. He's yours. I'll present him to you
formally at the potlatch. Do with him what you will.''

Surprised at his sudden captulation, Sarita stood
stock still.

But Thunder Maker was not done. ''You've
changed, Sarita. Before you were taken from us, you
would never have made such a rash promise to a slave;
or if you'd made it, you wouldn't have seen fit to keep
it. You knew your place was far above slaves. Now
you're harder, more stubborn. Yes, you've changed,''
he repeated, ''and not for the best.''

Sarita stared at her father. Sadly she murmured,
''Thank you, Nuwiksu, for giving me the slave. As to
the changes you see in me, they're a part of me. I had to
change to survive.''

She turned and stalked back up the beach to her
father's longhouse. With grim insight, she realized her
father could never imagine what she had been through.
Sarita suddenly dreaded telling him of her pregnancy.
She had a terrible premonition that Nuwiksu would not
be as understanding as she had first thought.

28

On the day of the potlatch the weather was cool, clear, and crisply autumn. Smoke drifted upward from fires on the beach. At about midday Thunder Maker called his guests together for the first meal of the potlatch. Women worked around the fires, graciously handing out dishes of succulent fish and vegetables.

All morning there had been songs and dances to amuse and impress the visitors. There had been several contests; already three slaves and two sea otter furs had been given away as prizes. The air rang with the happy cries of children and laughing adults.

Sarita looked out across the crowd gathered in her honor. Now, she thought with satisfaction, her family's name would be restored. All the visitors were here to witness the great wealth and generosity of her father. She knew her father was constantly gathering costly items for his potlatches, but even she was surprised by the vast array he'd produced for this one. The goods piled up in his longhouse—furs, blankets, cedar mats, beautiful shells—were impressive in their magnificence. She imagined the visitors would be overwhelmed.

Thunder Maker and Abalone Woman approached, their feet scrunching the beach gravel. Her father laid a hand proudly on Sarita's shoulder. "Our guests look happy," he observed. Abalone Woman concurred with a murmur. "Hope you're ready for the ceremonies this evening."

Sarita smiled. "Yes, Nuwiksu, I am." She paused and inclined her head in the direction of a visiting chieftain. "Who's that man who stares so rudely?"

Her father followed her gaze and answered, "That's the great Kyuquot chief Throws Away Wealth. He's here today because he thinks I don't have enough bounty to share with everyone. He's hoping I'll be shamed and embarrassed when I pass out the presents. No doubt he's staring rudely because he thinks you, too, are about to be humiliated."

Sarita looked up, startled.

"Little does he know," continued her father, unperturbed, "that I have plenty of blankets and sea otter furs to give away." He chuckled. "Throws Away Wealth is in for an unpleasant surprise." Abalone Woman's laugh tinkled in the background.

"Why did you invite him?" queried Sarita.

"Unfortunately," her father sighed, "he has many young warriors at his command and your brother pressured me into inviting him. Feast Giver thinks they'll be useful allies in the fight against the Ahousats." He was about to say more when Feast Giver joined them.

"The potlatch is going well," complimented the younger man. Sarita looked around for Precious Copper. Lately Sarita had noticed that wherever Feast Giver was, so was Precious Copper. This time, however, the young Ahousat woman was nowhere to be seen.

"Where's Precious Copper?" Sarita asked her brother innocently. Abalone Woman was the only one to notice the twinkle in her eyes.

Her brother glanced at her. "She's away, for the present," he said casually. "I thought it best that our guests don't know she's here."

"Oh?"

"No sense stirring up trouble. I wouldn't want someone carrying tales to Fighting Wolf about where his sister is." Sarita arched a brow but said nothing.

Turning to his father, Feast Giver commented,

"I'm pleased that so many of the people I expressly invited are here today."

Sarita watched as Feast Giver's gaze strayed over to where the Kyuquot delegation sat. He rubbed his hands together in anticipation. "It won't be long now. Those Ahousats are going to be dead men."

Sarita involuntarily shivered at the thought of war between her family and the man she loved. Neither man noticed. Feast Giver continued, "Where did you get all the blankets and sea otter furs for this potlatch display?" He looked meaningfully at his father. "I thought we were poor. After that Ahousat raid—"

"I may not have many people left," interrupted his father wryly, "but I do have contacts in other villages. There were a few people who owed me favors. Don't concern yourself with where these goods came from." With a gesture, he dismissed the subject.

"Is it enough to satisfy the Kyuquots?" asked Feast Giver. "If we can't prove that we still control some wealth, they won't back us against the Ahousats. I don't trust Throws Away Wealth. I think he's only our ally for as long as he gets something out of it."

His father nodded. "He asked me about the muskets. Looks like he wants some for his own men."

Sarita froze at Feast Giver's next comment. "I'll make sure the Kyuquots fire the mus-kets at the Ahousats, not at us," he stated grimly.

He was determined to succeed in his vengeance, Sarita realized. The thought distressed her despite the grievances she held against the Ahousats. True, she had been their slave. They had stolen and killed her people. It was only right that her brother avenge such deeds. But somehow, the image of Fighting Wolf, vanquished and bleeding, lying dead, filled her with a great, numbing sorrow. No! He was too vibrant, too dynamic, too alive. On impulse, she blurted out, "Is it so important that you go off and kill Ahousats?"

Her brother looked at her strangely. She felt her father's questioning glance, too. Abalone Woman was watching, a frown on her face. "After all," Sarita protested, "there have been enough lives lost. There's been enough sorrow."

"Hesquiat lives, Hesquiat sorrow," stated Abalone Woman sharply.

Her brother interrupted harshly, "Do you fear for Fighting Wolf?" His question caught Sarita off guard. Was she so easily read?

Her father scowled. "Your brother must avenge our people. You can't ask him to give up his plans."

"Why not?"

" 'Why not?' Surely you know. We'd be the victims of every tribe on the coast. We'd be raided constantly if word got around that we didn't revenge ourselves!"

Sarita said quietly, "But if you kill—" she stopped. Images of Fighting Wolf, dying, flashed through her brain—Fighting Wolf, father of her child. Her hands clutched her stomach protectively. Abalone Woman saw the gesture and opened her mouth to speak. But Thunder Maker hadn't finished.

"You can't seriously expect that we'll just forget what the Ahousats did to us. You, of all people, should understand." He paused, watching her. "Have you no loyalty to your own people?"

"Yes. No. Oh, I don't know!" Sarita's anguish was very evident to the other three.

"What?" roared her father. "What are you saying? Have you no loyalty to us, your own flesh and blood? Your own family?" Sarita could see he was working himself up into a rage. Abalone Woman laid a calming hand on his arm.

Feast Giver was watching Sarita intently. "What's the matter, sister?" he asked suspiciously.

There was a long, uncomfortable pause. Sarita answered in a dull voice, "I'm pregnant with Fighting Wolf's child."

"You what?" roared her father.

"What?" echoed her brother in disbelief.

Aghast, both stood and stared at Sarita. Abalone
Woman was shaking her head, a reproachful look on
her face. Sarita nodded miserably. "I didn't want to tell
you this way, Nuwiksu," she pleaded.

She looked briefly into Thunder Maker's eyes, then
glanced nervously about. Everyone else was enjoying
the festivities. No one seemed to notice the drama
taking place in her corner of the beach. Was it just her
imagination that the day had darkened? There was an
awkward silence pulsating among the four. Sarita
looked at the ground, unable to bear the censure she
read in their eyes. "I was going to wait until after the
potlatch—"

"What difference would that make?" her father
asked bitterly. "People would still laugh at me."

Sarita darted him a glance as Abalone Woman
patted Thunder Maker's arm; obviously she was trying
to keep him calm.

Sarita slowly raised her head. "What about me,
Nuwiksu?" she asked in a suddenly stronger voice. "Or
do you care only about yourself? What about my child?
I don't want to be laughed at. I don't want my child
laughed at, either."

Thunder Maker looked at her in silence. His words
came out cold and clipped and condemning. "Your
child will be a bastard. Illegitimate children have no
place in our tribe. And they certainly have no place in
my family." He raised his arms wide, gesturing at the
people crowded onto the beach. "Look around you,"
he continued in that same deadly voice. "Why do you
think I've invited all these people to a potlatch? An
expensive potlatch, I might add." Sarita looked
helplessly at Abalone Woman, who shook her head,
warning silence. "I invited them so we could restore our
name." The words shot out of him, stark and terrible.
"And now you have, once again, succeeded in dragging
our name through the dirt!"

"Nuwiksu," pleaded Sarita. "It's not as if I
wanted this to happen. It was beyond my control. I

didn't plan to get stolen, to get pregnant! I never wanted to embarrass you."

Her father gave no sign that he heard her.

"Surely you must see, husband," Abalone Woman began softly. "She's not done this to spite you—"

"Silence, woman!" roared her father. People nearby looked up at the discordant sound. Thunder Maker lowered his voice. "Don't defend her. She's brought me enough grief. Well, no more!" His words sounded ominous to Sarita's ears. Thunder Maker looked at Abalone Woman. "You will prepare your herbs; you know which ones I'm talking about. Give them to Sarita."

Abalone Woman looked at him, not understanding. "Get rid of the bastard!" he hissed. Shock filled the women's eyes as they realized what he was saying.

"Nuwiksu! No!" Sarita could not believe it was her father saying this thing. He wanted her to kill her baby! He was condemning her child to death. Abalone Woman looked sick. Feast Giver silently stalked away, anger apparent in every step. Sarita turned back to her father.

In a hard voice he answered her. "Abalone Woman will give you something to get rid of the bastard. Take it!" With these words he marched away, leaving Sarita standing there, stunned.

Abalone Woman hesitated. "He's angry now," she whispered. "Later, when he's come to his senses, he'll surely see reason. He'll change his mind, I'm sure." But Sarita could hear the doubt in her voice. With tear-filled golden eyes, Sarita accepted the warm hand that Abalone Woman placed on her arm.

Sarita tried to speak, but for a moment, the words could not get past the lump in her throat. At last, regaining control of herself, she asked the older woman, "Would you actually—" She halted, unable to say the words. She tried again. "Would you actually do what he asks? Kill my little one?"

Abalone Woman looked down at the sand she as spreading in circles with her big toe. "He told me to prepare the herbs; I have no choice." She looked into Sarita's eyes. "I must do 'as he says. Please understand."

Sarita stumbled away, shaking her head. She could not think logically. Even Abalone Woman was against her. Knowing if she stayed on the beach any longer she would burst into tears, Sarita fled towards the longhouse.

Once inside, she threw herself onto her bed of furs and wept with great shaking sobs. The baby, now that his little life was threatened, became the most important thing in her world. He was completely dependent on her, his mother. He was a part of her, a part of her love for Fighting Wolf. She hesitated. She understood now; she loved Fighting Wolf. For a long while she'd thought she could forget him, but now she knew she could not, could never forget him.

She shook her head. He did not love her. He gave no thought to her, and knew nothing of their child. And now this child, the only part of Fighting Wolf that she had left, was to be ruthlessly destroyed—by people who claimed they loved her.

A long time passed before Sarita was able to sit up and dry her eyes. Her face was swollen from crying, her hair matted and wet against her cheeks. She shuddered with each breath, she was so spent from crying.

But inside Sarita a hard resolve was forming. She had survived captivity by the Ahousats. She had fled from the man she loved rather than see her children born into slavery. She had borne too much to meekly accept her father's will in this matter. No longer was she a girl who would marry as her father dictated, who would unquestioningly accept society's condemnation. No, Sarita was a woman. A woman who had survived. As her child would survive.

Sarita clenched her teeth, feeling her misery slowly dissipating. Her golden eyes narrowed. A new calm

settled over her. Her child would live. Nothing, and no
one, would destroy this child—not while there was still
life in her body.

By evening, with Spring Fern's help, Sarita had put
her tears behind her, and prepared for more potlatch
festivities. Bathed and dressed in fresh clothing, she felt
much better.

Spring Fern finished combing Sarita's glossy hair.
Standing back, Spring Fern tilted her head to one side
and pronounced, "That kutsack looks very attractive
on you. It's almost the color of bleached clamshells. I
like the soft sea otter border at the neck and hem, too.
The fur is such a rich black. Here, let me polish the
earrings one more time—" She worked in silence,
rubbing the turquoise abalone-shell discs. "There," she
said with evident satisfaction, "you look beautiful."

Sarita smiled and the two women glided off to the
section of the longhouse where the guests impatiently
awaited the evening's proceedings. Thunder Maker had
insisted that this part of the celebration take place in the
longhouse. He had no desire to watch a heavy rain
destroy his theatrical efforts.

As she and Spring Fern walked into the area
marked off for the festivities, Sarita noticed the blazing
fire in the center. Light from tall torches threw giant
shadows onto the walls. A wooden stage had been built
off to one side.

The large gathering pleased Sarita for her father's
sake. Thunder Maker had put a lot of effort into this
potlatch.

Sarita walked quietly to a place near her family.
Crab Woman and Abalone Woman sat on cedar mats
looking proudly out across the throng of guests. Sarita
kneeled behind them, leaning back gracefully on her
heels. The women chatted and gossiped while waiting
for the opening ceremonies.

Sarita noted the Kyuquot chief, Throws Away
Wealth, glancing surreptitiously at her several times.

She shifted uneasily and then forgot about him as a favorite welcoming song, long in her family, began to drift over the crowd.

After several minutes of the familiar chant, the Speaker entered. He strode to the stage and launched into his narrative. A great part of his speech dwelt on Thunder Maker's famous and noble predecessors. After droning on about the Hesquiat chief's wealth, his clamming beds, fishing streams, canoes and fishing banks at sea, the Speaker pointed out how strong the village was. After a lengthy summary on the recent fortifications built to defend the village, he launched into another topic. To Sarita's amusement, the Speaker assured the listeners of the extreme cleanliness of town and beach. He defied them to find garbage anywhere.

Clearly he thought cleanliness made up for strategic deficiencies, thought Sarita wryly. Lastly, the speaker traced the genealogy of Thunder Maker's family and tied it to every important guest that was present. Sarita marvelled at such a feat, the man had to go back several generations in some cases, and refer to mythological ancestors in others, but she realized that much of what he said was for dramatic effect. He was under strict instructions to solidify the tie between host and guests, and to ease the path for future political alliances. Reluctantly the Speaker ceased his oration and vacated the floor.

Thunder Maker himself appeared next. To a chanting chorus, the rhythm beaten on a hollow, over-turned canoe, he began a song Sarita had not heard before. After singing, he bowed in her direction and announced he had learned the song from his grandmother, and that she, Sarita, was the new owner of the song.

Sarita flushed when all eyes turned to her. She nodded her acceptance graciously, however. This procedure continued for several songs and dances. Thunder Maker then persuaded a few of his high-ranking relatives to sing some of their songs. He thanked the singers and gave them gifts of rain hats, cedar robes or basketry. Finally, noticing the audience's restiveness, Thunder Maker made a dramatic presentation of the slave, Rottenwood, to his beloved daughter. Sarita heard Spring Fern's gasp and watched out of the corner of her eye as the young woman sought to conceal her reaction. Sarita patted Spring Fern's hand protectively, but felt the slave girl withdraw slightly.

After Sarita's polite assent to her most recent acquisition, Thunder Maker signalled to several nearby young men. Leaping to their feet, they began to drag forth large cedar boxes. A low murmur of appreciation swept the crowd as the largesse of the boxes was held up for all to see. Hundreds of cedar mats, carefully woven by skilled weavers, were piled in the middle of the stage. Next, approximately fifty, very expensive, red and blue trade blankets were carefully laid out on top of the cedar mats. Gasps could be heard here and there in the crowd as it was realized the expense involved. Next were brought out yellow cedar robes so loved by the nobility. Sarita saw several of the senior guests eyeing the robes avidly.

At Thunder Maker's gesture, the young helpers began handing out magnificent gifts to the visiting chieftains. Sarita watched the pile of blankets in front of the Kyuquot chief grow higher and higher. She laughed at her father's clever planning. The Kyuquot looked embarrassed as he realized that Thunder Maker did indeed have enough wealth to satisfy the large, unruly Kyuquot delegation.

Not content with this triumph, Thunder Maker brought out kelp bulbs filled with whale oil. An expensive oil, it was always in high demand by his people. Thunder Maker strode around the area, personally handing out the kelp vessels to eagerly reaching guests. Lastly, he brought out fifty seal hair blankets and potlatched those to his guests. Satisfied murmurs could be heard around the room as the visitors gathered up their new wealth. Several visiting chieftains

stood up and took turns thanking Thunder Maker for
his largesse. The last one to speak was Throws Away
Wealth, and Sarita was secretly amused as he made his
speech. The Kyuquot chief shifted uncomfortably as he
faced Thunder Maker. A smug look crossed the host's
face as he listened to the flattering words of his shamed
guest.

"We are here today sharing your food, O Chief,"
began the disgruntled Kyuquot. "It is now evident to us
all that you are truly a great chief. You have much
wealth and you use it wisely to procure a strong name
for your beautiful daughter. I know you did not obtain
all these goods without effort. It is obvious that you are
very industrious and have many friends and relatives
you can call upon to help you. Include your Kyuquot
friends in their number. We are proud to be considered
your allies and to share with you the songs and dances
newly given to your daughter. This potlatch strengthens
the bonds between our peoples. Thank you for the
lavish gifts. We are truly impressed. Thank you, thank
you."

The Kyuquot sat down, wiping his sweating brow.
Sarita chuckled to herself as she guessed what his polite
acceptance speech had cost the proud man.

While the guests happily carted away their wealth,
Sarita rose to her feet and slowly followed the other
women back to their quarters. Her status restored, she
now had plans to make—plans for herself and her child.

29

Most of the guests returned to their villages over the next several days and once again the Hesquiat long-houses were quiet. Mottled gray sea gulls shrieked demands for fish and wheeled on invisible air currents above the cold green waters of the bay. The days were chill, and low gray clouds heavy with rain, their presence a constant reminder of impending winter storms, hung over the mountains. Nights were bleak; no stars brightened the sky. Autumn reigned.

The Hesquiat villagers bustled about preparing for the annual move to the winter village site. Sarita squatted on the beach, packing a large freight canoe with household goods. Her days were busy with preparations for the upcoming journey.

Precious Copper arrived on one of her numerous trips from the longhouse, her arms laden with baskets and bundles of dried foods. She passed a basket stuffed with dried herbs to Sarita. Sarita smiled her thanks, then found a corner of the canoe to stow the bulging basket. She and Precious Copper worked together companionably, disposing of the rest of the bundles. When they were finished, there was little room left for anything else.

"Let's rest awhile," suggested Sarita. "We've been at this all morning."

Precious Copper nodded and straightened weary limbs. "I brought smoked fish from the house if you're hungry. There's a few roasted cinquefoil roots, too, left over from the potlatch. The food's in that basket,'' she said.

Sarita replied, "Let's eat. Afterwards, we can go for a walk if you'd like.''

Again Precious Copper nodded. The two young women sat down to eat the delicious fish and vegetable meal. "Do you like staying with us?'' Sarita asked conversationally. "I know your status with us is rather vague, but have my people treated you well? Have you any complaints?''

Precious Copper waited a long moment before replying. "I've no complaints about the way I've been treated,'' she said at last.

Sarita detected the note of caution in Precious Copper's voice. She got to her feet. "Come,'' she said, gesturing further up the beach. "Let's take that walk now.''

The two women walked along, both lost in thought. At last Sarita broke the silence with a long sigh. "I know it hasn't been easy for you here. I hope Feast Giver hasn't made things difficult.'' She waited.

Precious Copper glanced at Sarita out of the corner of her eye, then replied lightly, "Your brother has made my stay most, uh, intriguing.'' Her dimples showed as she smiled at Sarita. "Really he has. He's behaved very well.''

There was no doubting the sincerity in Precious Copper's voice. "I'm relieved,'' answered Sarita. "I truly want you to enjoy your stay here. I don't know what my brother has planned for you, but if I can help you at all, I will. I'll never forget the kindness you showed when I was a captive in your village. If I can ever repay you, I will.''

Precious Copper reached over and patted Sarita's hand. "Thank you for your concern. I did my best to help you when you were in my village because, well, because I felt my brother was wrong to steal you. And at first he treated you badly, but later he changed.'' She looked off into the distance. "You know, Sarita, I'll also help you if it's ever in my power to do so."

Sarita squeezed the hand holding hers, then let it drop. "If only you could," she sighed ruefully.

"What do you mean?"

Sarita was silent as she came to a decision. "Precious Copper," she began, "I'm carrying Fighting Wolf's child." Sarita heard her companion's quick intake of breath.

"Oh, Sarita! What are you going to do?" The other woman's concern touched a responsive chord in Sarita. With little encouragement, she poured out the sad story of her father's reaction to her slavery and pregnancy; and her own determination to have her baby. Precious Copper listened carefully, nodding her head occasionally, but never interfering with Sarita's monologue.

At last, Sarita finished her tale and there was a long silence while the two women reflected on Sarita's dilemma. "I don't really know what I'll do," mused Sarita. "But I refuse to take the herbs Abalone Woman keeps offering me."

Sarita looked up in time to see Precious Copper give a start as she stared off into the distance. Sarita followed her gaze. "What are you staring at?" she demanded.

"Hmm?" Preoccupied, Precious Copper was silent a moment as she watched a canoe pull into shore. Even at this distance, two figures could be discerned in the small craft with distinctive white markings.

"Oh, it's—it's nothing." She turned swiftly to Sarita and smiled, her dimples deep in her cheeks.

"It's only a couple of visitors," said Sarita petulantly.

"Forgive me," implored Precious Copper. "I didn't mean to be distracted from your troubles."

"It's all right, I was finished anyway," sighed her friend. "Let's head back and finish the packing. We have to be ready for the big move within the next few days."

Precious Copper assented, somewhat too eagerly in Sarita's opinion. She felt chagrined that Precious Copper could dismiss Sarita's serious troubles so lightly. The two turned their steps to where the freight canoe lay on the beach.

They strolled past the visitors who were just pulling their canoe ashore. Sarita inspected them casually. The two men, one young and husky, the other older and wizened, carried the canoe farther up the beach. The men glanced briefly in the direction of the two women.

"Strangers," commented Sarita. "I wonder what business they have at our village?"

Sarita thought Precious Copper stiffened. The next moment she was sure she was mistaken as Precious Copper said enthusiastically, "Let's get that packing finished!" The two women quickened their pace, neither glancing again at the newcomers.

The rest of the afternoon passed quickly as the two loaded another large canoe. "We'll be ready tomorrow at this rate," said Sarita happily. Perhaps a change of scene would do her good. This village held too many unhappy memories for her.

"What?" answered Precious Copper. "Oh, yes. Yes, we should be ready by tomorrow."

Sarita looked at her friend for a moment. "Where are you, Precious Copper?" she asked softly. "You've been preoccupied all afternoon."

But her friend gave no sign that she had heard. A glimmer of uneasiness registered in Sarita's mind, but she shrugged it off.

The night was dark and eerie. A mere sliver of moon lit the sky. Clouds drifted past, frequently obscuring the weak light shed on the village that nestled far below. The black, shadowed hulks of packed freight canoes lay on the beach fronting the village.

Emerging from one of the longhouses, the dark shape of a small, graceful woman flitted through the night until she reached her destination: a disreputable dwelling at the far end of the village.

Quietly pushing aside the skin flap over the main entrance, she peeked inside. All was silent. A dying fire glowed in the center of the main living area. A loud pop from the embers startled her, but she relaxed when no one stirred.

Over to one side of the fire she spotted the man she was seeking. Creeping carefully towards him, past snoring lumps stretched out side by side, she hissed hastily into his ear, "Uncle, uncle!" The figure stirred, moaned. "Shhhh," she cautioned. When all was still again, she shook the figure slightly, "Uncle, uncle, wake up. Please!"

The urgency in her voice roused the rounded form. He sat up and looked cautiously about. The woman laid her finger across his lips, indicating silence, then gestured for him to follow her outside the longhouse. Silently unwrapping himself from the cedar mats, the older man got up slowly and together they silently slipped out into the night.

The woman exhaled in relief as she maneuvered the man towards a protected stand of trees. "Here we can talk in privacy, uncle," she assured him. They sat down on a wet log.

"What is it, niece?" asked the older man politely. He was not, in reality, Precious Copper's uncle, but a distant relative the same age as her father. She was entitled to call him uncle if she wished, and because she held the higher status—he was a commoner—he was pleased to go along with the closer kindship term. "I thought I recognized you earlier this afternoon, niece."

"Oh, uncle," she whispered, "It's such a long story. I can't tell you all of it now. I don't have much time." She hesitated. "I need your help."

"You have it," he responded loyally.

She hugged him. "Before I tell you, I'm curious to know why you're here, in this Hesquiat village."

He shrugged. "My eldest son and I are heading back to Ahousat. We were trading at Yuquot. Some nice things there. We stopped off here to visit some of my wife's relatives.''

"Don't your wife's relatives know about the fighting between the Hesquiats and our people?'' inquired Precious Copper apprehensively.

Again the older man shrugged. ''They know, but we're related. That's important to my wife's family. They won't betray their own kin.''

Precious Copper smiled. There were many such interrelated families up and down the coast. In fact, she knew Fighting Wolf often relied on this informal network of kin to warn him of impending raids on the Ahousats. ''Tell my brother, Fighting Wolf, that I'm safe here in the Hesquiat village.''

"Safe?''

She nodded. ''Feast Giver, the chief's son, brought me here. You see, he—he rescued me from a party of raiding Kwakiutls.'' Even now, memories of that horrible time scared Precious Copper when she realized how close to rape and death she had been.

"Your brother, and your uncle, Scarred Mouth, aren't going to like you staying here,'' warned the older man.

"I know. But surely they'll realize I had no choice.''

"Ah,'' he answered, ''so it's not quite as safe as you would have me believe.''

She looked into his wise old eyes, then nodded slowly.

"Come with us when we leave tomorrow,'' urged the old man.

Precious Copper shook her head. ''I can't. I'd only endanger you.'' It was true, she realized. Feast Giver would probably come after her and he would be angry. She couldn't risk this kindly old man's life, or his son's.

"Very well,'' responded the ''uncle'' crisply. ''I'll give your brother the message.'' He stood up to leave.

Precious Copper pulled at his arm to hold him back. ''And tell Fighting Wolf that Sarita—he'll know who I mean—has returned safely to this village and is now pregnant." The old man dutifully repeated this message to memorize it.

"Thank you," whispered Precious Copper. "And please, please get this message to my brother as soon as you can. It's urgent."

The "uncle" nodded. "We were headed towards Ahousat, anyway. My son—he's very strong—and I will paddle straight through. Never fear. Fighting Wolf will get this message."

Precious Copper was reassured by the quiet confidence in his voice. She exclaimed, "You'll be well rewarded for this, I promise you." She paused, remembering one other important item. "Oh, and tell him that this Hesquiat village will be moving up the nearby inlet to their traditional winter village within the next few days. Here," she said hastily, taking a delicately carved wooden bangle from her wrist. "Show this to my family. They'll know you speak the truth."

He nodded as he tied the bangle on a thong at his waist. "I'd better hurry back to my sleeping place by the fire. No one knows I'm gone. I'd like to keep it that way," he said.

Precious Copper agreed, and they parted quietly in the still night. As she walked through the silent village, Precious Copper wondered if Sarita would think she had betrayed her confidence. Well, it couldn't be helped. She, Precious Copper, couldn't let her family worry about her own whereabouts any longer. Also, she knew Fighting Wolf would be very interested in the news about Sarita—and his child.

30

Sarita walked along the shaded path towards the river. Ah, it was good to get away from the bustle and noise of last-minute packing in the village. All that remained to be done was removing cedar planks from the sides of the longhouses. The men would do that. As for herself, Sarita would have a very brief, but very refreshing bath. Carrying a soft cedar blanket to towel herself dry, she hummed happily as she strolled.

It was one of the occasional sunny days of autumn, and Sarita meant to make the most of it. She was pleased she had evaded her usual retinue of ladies. Somehow she just could not tolerate their prattle today. She wanted solitude.

Sarita noticed the usual sounds of the woods—the birds chirping, the squirrels chattering—were absent today.

At last she reached the woman's bathing area, pleased to find it deserted. Dropping her robe to her feet, she waded into the slowly flowing current. She ducked under the water and jumped up with a scream. It was cold! Laughing to herself, she splashed the freezing water over her skin. She fell on her back in the frigid liquid and scrubbed her scalp with a handful of herbs; the fresh, clean scent would linger in her hair.

Sarita was shivering now and hurried to complete her toilette. She stepped out onto the river bank and towelled herself dry. She slipped on her kutsack. Her skin tingled all over from the cold water and she felt so alive. She wondered if the baby could feel the cold water, too. Gathering up her things, she turned back to the trail.

She halted abruptly. There, leaning against a tree, his arms folded across his thin chest, stood Throws Away Wealth. Behind him stood two big henchmen. Fear coursed through Sarita when she realized how isolated the place was, but she refused to let the men see that.

"How long have you been standing there?" she demanded in her haughtiest, chief's daughter's voice. "What do you want?"

Throws Away Wealth leered at her. She counted three teeth missing in his wide grin. He looked her up and down and made a comment under his breath to his men. Their coarse laughter drifted through the stillness.

"My father will punish you for this. Now, leave!" They continued to watch her. "Insolent Kyuquot dogs," she spat. "Leave, or my father will have you killed!"

The men laughed outright at her statement. "I think not," said Throws Away Wealth in a nasal voice. Sarita waited. "You see," he continued, "your father has arranged for you to marry me." He watched her face for her reaction, his small eyes intent. He was not disappointed.

"What?" she shrieked. "My father what?" Regaining herself with visible effort, she said quickly, "You're wrong. I know nothing of this. And even if my father did promise such a thing, *I* will not be party to it!"

Throws Away Wealth shrugged and sauntered up to her. She refused to back away. She would not show this Kyuquot any fear. He halted in front of her and stared. When he spoke, his hot fish breath hit her full in the face. She blinked, then glared at him.

Unimpressed, he said, "What you want matters little. You *will* be my wife, my second wife," he boasted with satisfaction. "I'm an important chief. I shall have many wives."

He reached out a hand to grasp her shoulder. She shrugged away. "You're too sure of yourself, Kyuquot. I tell you I refuse to marry you! I'll speak to my father and—"

"Don't bother," he said laconically, his hand dropping to his side. "Your father needs an alliance with us. He begged me to marry you. Though I must say I'm surprised you aren't already spoken for—" His voice trailed off. "Of course that visit to Ahousat did decrease your marriage value somewhat, didn't it? Maybe your father didn't have quite so many suitors for your hand after that nasty little incident, eh?" he sneered.

His eyes dropped to her stomach. "And I wonder—" He raised his small eyes to hers. Sarita stared back, unable to look away from his malevolent gaze. "I wonder if there is a little one on the way," he said, poking her in the stomach. "If there is, I'll take care of it." He smiled, but his smile didn't reach his cold, small eyes. "I'll make sure it meets with an accident."

Sarita gasped and grabbed her stomach. From the tone of his voice he might have been discussing whether or not to toss a small salmon back to sea. No, he'd show more interest in a salmon, she corrected herself.

Throws Away Wealth tipped her chin up, his eyes roaming her face. "Hmmm," he murmured, noting her protective gesture. "So. I was right. Well, never mind, I'm sure we can entertain each other in the meantime." He chuckled and another whiff of fish breath caused Sarita to choke back a gag.

She pushed his hand away and retorted, "I will not marry you." Then she marched away, her head high.

Surprisingly, the two henchmen parted to let her pass. She walked calmly until a bend in the path blocked their view, then she ran as fast as she could back to the village. Her feet fairly flew along the path.

Thunder Maker had interfered in her life for the last time. She would find him and tell him so.

As Sarita approached the village, she slowed her

pace. Her father would consider her disrespectful if she ran to him with her hair hanging in wet strings. Drying it near a hot fire would give her time to plan what to say, she decided.

She wandered over to what was left of her father's longhouse. Already men had pulled down several of the planks at the far end. Several other longhouses showed similar dismantling. Women scurried about, gathering up children and clothes. They grabbed household items, stuffing them into baskets and bent cedar boxes. Sarita suddenly realized her village would be moving that very afternoon.

Quickly, she towelled her hair dry. There was little time to speak with her father, but she wanted things settled between them as soon as possible. Then he could tell Throws Away Wealth the marriage was off, and she could make her own plans for the coming child.

Hearing her father's booming voice, she followed the sound out the door and to the back of the longhouse. He was busy directing several of the commoners and slaves as they tore apart the house. Soon nothing would be left but the big corner posts and ridge poles on the roof.

"Over there," Thunder Maker shouted to one of the men. "Move those planks to that pile!" He turned as Sarita approached and wiped his sweating brow."

"Nuwiksu," she began, "I wish—"

"Not now, Sarita," he said impatiently. "I'm busy." He swung around to shout another order. "You! Take those boards and load them into Vast Capacity." Vast Capacity was the name of one of his large freight canoes. A slave nodded and went obediently about the work.

Sarita was feeling far from obedient. "Nuwiksu," she began again. "I must speak with you."

"Move, girl! Can't you see those planks coming this way? Now's not the time for talking. Later." With a gesture, he dismissed her and barked further orders at two slaves who were busy loading Vast Capacity.

Humiliated, Sarita stepped quickly to one side. The men ignored her. She realized she could not speak with her father while he was taking down the longhouses. Agitated, she walked over to where several women were diligently packing a canoe. She watched them until her anger and embarrassment had passed.

Well, there was no help for it. She'd have to wait until later, when things were calmer, and speak with her father then. He might think he could put her off easily, but she would not give in on this issue. She would not marry Throws Away Wealth. Of that she was certain.

Early the next morning, orders came to move out. Slowly the people filed into their canoes.

Soon the bay's smooth surface was covered with various sized craft. There were several freight canoes, some piled high with cedar planks, others with bulky bundles.

There were the sleek, racy, canoes used to hunt for seals. Shiny and black, these canoes were the most prized by their owners. Never were such canoes dragged across the beach, they were always carried.

There were small two-seater canoes paddled by one or two persons and filled with precious household possessions. Lastly, there were the small, rough craft, only big enough for a child and a basket of dried fish or clams.

The flotilla paddled out of the bay towards a nearby sheltered inlet. Sarita and Spring Fern paddled a finely crafted two-seater. Deep black on the outside, and deep crimson on the inside, it was Sarita's favorite canoe. When but a child, she had painted the interior red, first mixing red ochre and mashed salmon eggs under the watchful eye of her father. Then she had chosen a name for her vessel: Sea-Serpent. She had imagined it sliding as smoothly through the waves as its mythological namesake. Now an adult, it still amused her to keep the name—a happy memory of her childhood.

The tribe had to paddle for two days to reach the winter village, far up the inlet. After paddling all through this day, the one night would be spent camped on the same smoothly gravelled beach as always. Then another full day of travelling before they would arrive at the safe haven of the winter village.

Once there, the whole village had to be reassembled. Merely thinking of the work ahead exhausted Sarita. She knew it would be some time before her normal energy level returned. She felt so sleepy these days but she was relieved she did not have the morning sickness Abalone Woman had warned her about.

Sarita had avoided Abalone Woman lately by taking her meals at the fireside of her aunt, Rain-on-the-Sea. Her aunt appeared content with the arrangement, too. Perhaps she was less in awe of her powerful brother, Thunder Maker, than the rest of his family, thought Sarita. At least her aunt had shown no desire to press foul-smelling teas upon her, unlike Abalone Woman.

As she paddled, Sarita pondered her dilemma. Pregnant with Fighting Wolf's child, she was faced with two threats to her child's life: her father's order to abort the baby, and Throws Away Wealth's statement that he would kill the baby at birth. Her only hope of saving her baby's life lay in persuading her father to let the child live, and in impressing upon him that she would not, under any circumstances, marry Throws Away Wealth.

"Are you feeling all right?" Spring Fern broke into her thoughts.

"Yes," murmured Sarita, "I'm fine."

"Oh. I thought I heard you groan," answered the slave.

"No," answered Sarita tiredly. She sank back into her reverie. Never could she marry another man while her heart was filled with Fighting Wolf. For a moment, his image came clearly to mind, his strong arms holding her, his warm kisses thrilling her. What would he do if he knew she as carrying his child? she wondered. What would he do if he knew the threats to his child's life? Fighting Wolf would never let someone else tell him what to do with his child, Sarita realized.

Suddenly she felt hopeful. She would be strong, for her child's sake, and yes, for Fighting Wolf's sake, too, though he knew nothing of her struggle. She laughed to herself as she tried to imagine his uncle, Scarred Mouth, forcing Fighting Wolf into a marriage he didn't want. The war chief certainly wouldn't stand for such treatment. Neither would she.

The certainty that she must take control of her life calmed Sarita. No more would she be the pawn of her father, her family, or men like Throws Away Wealth. And neither would her child!

Perhaps someday Fighting Wolf would see this child, she mused. No, how could he? He would never know of its existence. Best to banish such thoughts from her mind, she told herself sternly.

But, unbidden, they crept back. Pensively, she wondered if she would always feel the loss of Fighting Wolf so deeply. For he was lost to her, as surely as if he were dead. Her family would never accept him. He would never accept her as anything more than a slave, and she, she would never again be a slave while there was breath in her body. She could not regret escaping slavery for the sake of her child.

She sighed. Her child. How would her child fare, being born illegitimate? Better illegitimacy than slavery, she thought. Would the child be a boy, handsome and strong like his father? Or a beautiful girl, like her mother? Sarita giggled to herself, amused at her own conceit.

"Are you sure you feel all right?" questioned Spring Fern.

Sarita stopped paddling and waved her hand in dismissal. "Quite sure. In fact, I suddenly feel better than I've felt in a long while, Spring Fern. A long while."

Spring Fern shook her head silently. The nobility had such strange ways.

31

"Why did you do it, Nuwiksu?" Sarita stood on a small knoll, her thickly woven cedar cape wrapped about her shoulders. A winter wind buffeted the sea otter trim. Beside her, Thunder Maker looked out over the village. The longhouses were assembled, his Hesquiat people had settled comfortably into their winter homes.

"It seemed like a good solution to your problems. When Feast Giver made the suggestion—"

"Feast Giver!" exclaimed Sarita. "What has he to do with marriage plans for me?" she demanded.

Her father gave a long-suffering sigh. "Sarita," he protested. "We didn't plan this to hurt you. We were trying to help you. Marrying you off to Throws Away Wealth seemed like a good idea. You'd get a husband, something you badly need," he added, looking pointedly at her stomach, "and we'd get a loyal ally."

"Next time, ask me before you 'help' me," she retorted bitterly.

Thunder Maker frowned slightly. "Keep a civil tongue in your head, girl," he warned.

"Nuwiksu," she said impatiently, "I'm being as civil and polite as I can under very trying circumstances. You don't seem to understand. I don't want a husband. When, and if, I decide to marry, *I* will do the choosing. Twice now you've interfered by trying to find me a husband. Please, don't interfere any more!"

"Sarita. Enough." His voice took on the angry tone she had come to recognize lately. "Where did you learn to talk to your father like that?"

"Stop making an issue of my manners, Nuwiksu," she said angrily. "My manners, polite or not, are unimportant compared to my future. We are discussing my future, are we not?" Irony tinged her voice.

Thunder Maker glanced at her and nodded. "It's your future I'm concerned with. Now that your noble position is reestablished in the eyes of our people, you have a chance to lead an exemplary life. You can be a fine example of what a chief's daughter should be."

"Oh, Nuwiksu," Sarita snorted. "I could not care less what the people think."

"Is that so? We've been over this before, Sarita. I care what the people think of you. I care that your name is beyond reproach."

"No, Nuwiksu," she replied tartly. "You care that *your* name is beyond reproach."

Thunder Maker was silent for a moment. "It's a wonder you survived slavery with that sharp tongue, daughter." Her answer was another unladylike snort. "As I was saying," he went on, "you now have a chance to lead an exemplary life. Such a life, however, does not include a bastard child."

"Nuwiksu," answered Sarita evenly, "I am keeping my baby. No matter what you say."

There was a long pause. "Very well," Thunder Maker responded at last, "if you want to keep your baby, the alternative is simple—marry Throws Away Wealth. You'll have a husband; your child will have a father."

"And you'll have your ally," finished Sarita.

"Your impudence is beginning to annoy me," he warned.

"I will not marry Throws Away Wealth."

"Why not? He seems like a good man."

"A good man? Do you know what he plans to do to my child when it's born?"

Her father looked at her, waiting, one eyebrow arched questioningly. Suddenly Sarita couldn't say the words. She had a terrible premonition that her father wouldn't believe her. She hesitated, then her shoulders slumped in defeat. "Never mind, it's nothing," she muttered. "But I do refuse to marry Throws Away Wealth." The words came out sounding sulky and weak.

"That's too bad," Thunder Maker answered casually. Instantly, Sarita was on the alert. Here it comes, she thought. "I've already promised you to him," stated Thunder Maker grimly, "and I will not, *will not*, go back on my word!"

"Nuwiksu," she cried in anguish, "haven't you heard me? I said I will not marry him!"

"I heard you," he answered, seeming unperturbed. "I heard you. Now you hear me. There are some things more important than your wishes. You will marry him. You'll be an obedient daughter and marry whomever I tell you to."

"Nuwiksu—"

"Enough, Sarita. You'll do as I say." His stern look softened. "Someday you'll thank me for this, I know," he said softly. "I want what's best for you, too."

When she was younger, such a statement would have melted her resistance. Now it merely inflamed her ardor to defend herself and her child. "I think not, Nuwiksu. I think not."

She turned her back on him and strode away, unable to look at the man she had trusted and called "father" since she was a tiny girl. Nothing he could do or say would convince her that he had chosen wisely.

No, now it was up to her to plan her own fate. But what to do? What to do?

Sarita walked slowly along the rocky beach fronting the winter village. The town sat poised on one side of a narrow inlet, the longhouses scrunched onto a lonely strip of level land. Rainclouds covered the backdrop of mountains looming behind the village. A narrow stretch of salal undergrowth and scraggly bushes feebly protected the village from the winds that swept down the inlet and flailed the houses.

Sarita braced herself against the buffeting wind and turned her back on the village. She gazed across the short stretch of saltwater. An impenetrable forest of evergreens rose straight up from the waterline. Over the forest the sky was glazed white.

She turned back to the village and looked at the cloud-covered mountain peaks behind. With the arrival of her people, it seemed as though the giant, rain-laden, heavy gray mantle rolled over the mountains to its winter site, too. She knew the clouds would stay there until spring winds blew them away. Where would she be, come spring?

Oh, why was she here? she wondered miserably. This place with its muted grays and dark greens looked as desolate as she felt. In previous winters, she'd thought the village cozy, nestled inland from the severe winter storms. She had loved its quiet, natural beauty. Now, it was only a cold, bleak place.

She knew what was wrong. She missed Fighting Wolf. Never had she longed so for another human being. If he were here with her, the winter village would once again look warm and welcoming. More and more she realized how deeply she loved him.

Sarita observed a lone figure walking along the beach towards her. As he approached, she recognized the wide-chested shape of Rottenwood. She reproached herself silently. Forgotten in all the turmoil of her personal life, he loomed before her now. She owed him her life, as complicated as it had become recently, she thought ruefully.

Smiling, she called him over. He greeted her, his face closed.

"I have some good news for you," she began.

"Oh?" His response was guarded.

"Now that you're my slave, I've decided what to do with you." She couldn't help herself, she was enjoying toying with him.

Again that guarded response.

"Yes," she went on, "I've decided to free you."

She watched with satisfaction as his jaw dropped, then waited until he recovered from his surprise. "You are now a free man."

"I—I—" He was overwhelmed by the news, she thought smugly. She was enjoying herself. Already things were looking brighter. "Thank you," he managed at last.

Sarita smiled, pleased. "I'll be giving a feast tomorrow night to announce your freedom to the rest of the village. After that, your life is your own." Rottenwood nodded, dazed.

"I'm standing by my promise to you," she pointed out kindly.

"Yes—yes, you are," he stammered. "Thank you, again. I hardly know what to say—"

"Then say nothing," she said, feeling generous. "I haven't forgotten how I longed for my freedom when I was a slave. If not for you—" she broke off. "Well, suffice it to say that I owe you my life. I trust we're now even?"

This last question brought a fervent response. "We most definitely are. I thank you, again."

Highly amused at hearing him repeating himself, Sarita waved her hand in a dismissing gesture. "I hope you'll find much happiness in your new status. I assume you'll continue to work for my family?" At his nod, she added magnanimously, "Now that you're no longer a slave, I'm sure you'll want new living arrangements. There is a vacant space on the wall of my longhouse. It's yours. Come, I'll show you."

Rottenwood bowed with as much dignity as he could muster, and followed her to freedom.

The next night, after the small feast Sarita gave in his honor, Rottenwood moved his few belongings to his new quarters.

The cedar bench looked bare without any mats to cover it. The fire pit was cold, the floor was littered with old shells and bones from the previous occupant. But Rottenwood noticed none of these things. He was too happy to have his own place, and more important, his freedom. He lay down, his stomach satiated with rich food, his mind spinning from the myriad plans he was weaving for his newfound freedom.

Lifting up on one elbow, he eyed his new accommodations. Soon, he thought, soon he would fix up these quarters. Or have someone do it for him.

He thought of Spring Fern. She had looked sad tonight. Sad and withdrawn. When she'd caught him watching her, she'd smiled shakily back. Poor thing. He hadn't approached her; he was unwilling to flaunt his new status at her. He knew she must feel awkward. Perhaps even questioning his commitment to her. Well, he'd let her know soon enough that he wanted her, that he loved her.

If only she, too, could be free . . .

32

Weary and disheartened, Fighting Wolf returned from the fruitless search for his sister. He had given up all hope of finding Precious Copper alive. He and his men had exhausted themselves scouring the local area. They'd found the canoe and the decaying remains of the two old slaves. The decapitated body of Slug told its own story. Warriors had done this. But warriors from where? Then Fighting Wolf's men found the Kwakiutl bodies, and the answer to their question. But they did not find Precious Copper.

Now Fighting Wolf feared the worst for his sister. She'd been taken captive, he speculated, by vicious men. Only vicious men would tangle with fearsome Kwakiutls and win.

His heart was heavy as he thought of his lost sister. Deep lines of sorrow were newly etched into his face.

He barely noticed the strange behavior in his household. Everyone was avoiding him. Fighting Wolf was too tired to wonder why. Grief and going without sleep for two days in the desperate search for his sister had robbed him of his usual vitality. After a hasty meal, he staggered to bed and slept through the next day.

Awakening in the evening, Fighting Wolf ordered a meal prepared and asked for Sarita. A hapless old woman was pushed forward from the small crowd of servants pressed around him. Hesitantly, she stammered the news that his female Hesquiat slave had escaped.

The old woman scurried away from the fury that leapt into his jet black eyes.

Slaves and commoners alike darted panic-stricken out of their war chief's path as he unleashed a ferocious roar.

"That bitch! How dare she! I'll kill her! Who let her go? She was supposed to be guarded!"

The two hapless guards were brought to him. He turned his furious countenance upon them. "Well?" he demanded. "How did she get away?"

Defensively, the first guard began, "I was standing watch, outside the longhouse as you'd ordered, when all of a sudden I was jumped from behind." He bowed his head to show the bruise and cuts on the back of his head. "Next thing I knew, I woke up and she was gone!"

The second guard chimed in, "That's right, sir. I was at the other end of the longhouse. A man attacked me with a warclub. I drew my knife to finish him off. That's the last thing I remember. When I woke up, my hands were tied." A leather thong dangled from his hand. "It took me a while to undo myself. Bound tight, I was. Anyway, once I was free, I ran to where my partner, here, was. He was just waking up. By then, of course, the lady—uh, slave—was gone." The other man nodded, confirming the story.

Even in his extreme anger, Fighting Wolf knew the two men would stick by their story and by each other. They doubtless were telling the truth, and they were brave men. That was why he had picked them for guard duty in the first place. "Is anyone else missing? Did she escape alone?"

The second guard shook his head. "Slave named Rottenwood's missing. He must have been the one with the war club. They've been gone for three nights."

Focusing his frustration and anger on the two guards, Fighting Wolf barked, "Is there any reason I shouldn't kill you both, here and now? Speak up!"

The two men stood their ground. "No, sir," they

replied in unison.

"I failed in my duty," acknowledged the first guard.

"Please, sir," begged the guard still holding the leather thong, "take care of my wife and children after I'm gone."

In disgust, Fighting Wolf turned away from the men. He couldn't afford to kill two brave men just because he was in a fury. "Get out of here!" he thundered at them. "I'll see to your punishment later!"

The servants, who had crept closer to watch the drama unfold, scattered anew like a flock of screaming sea gulls. His anger still high, Fighting Wolf strode out of the longhouse and headed towards the beach. Leaping into a two-seater canoe, he paddled swiftly out of the harbor, his fury evident in every paddle-stroke.

On the beach, the onlookers murmured and chatted amongst themselves. He was so angry! Surely he must love her very much, to be so upset at her disappearance. Love her? What nonsense, he didn't love her. He was just angry that a good bed partner had escaped. No, he was angry that one of those sneaky Hesquiat wenches had made a fool of him and then escaped.

Fighting Wolf plunged the paddle, time and again, into the gray, choppy sea until he was out of sight of the coastline. Gradually his fury abated.

His initial red-hot anger started to give way to a lethal calmness. Cooler now, he began to plan. The bitch wouldn't get away with this. Thought she could leave him, did she? Well, she wouldn't get far. He'd go to Hesquiat and drag her back by her hair if he had to. Then he'd tie her to his bed and rape her until she couldn't stand up. Let her know he was her lord and master! When he was finished with her, she'd be begging to stay with him. He'd see her crawl on her knees first—and then he'd laugh. After that, maybe, just maybe, he'd spare her worthless life!

"What are you going to do?" asked Scarred Mouth. Hearing the uproar in the village, he had lain in wait for his nephew. Standing onshore, he had watched as the war chief paddled calmly back to shore, ignoring the curious crowd.

Scarred Mouth eyed the younger man curiously. Who would have thought the young devil was so enamored of the little slave? True, she was beautiful, but to roar and shout and lose such face just because she'd escaped . . . Well, it just wasn't done . . .

"Do?" replied Fighting Wolf, seemingly indifferent. "What do you think I'm going to do? I'm going to bring her back!"

Many days went by, however, before Fighting Wolf was freed from village responsibilities and able to carry out his vow. The fall season was fast upon the Ahousat people. A move to the winter village site had to be made now, before the severe winter storms buffeted the open summer village.

His first priority had to be his people, reminded Scarred Mouth. After they were taken care of, then he could pursue his personal business. Reluctantly, Fighting Wolf conceded that his uncle was, for once, correct.

The move took longer than planned because of the early gale winds and rain sweeping the coast. At last his people were safely moved to the protected winter village.

The site was a new one. This was to be the first winter spent there. The village was situated on a large island surrounded by deep waters, at the head of a long inlet. The island had additional natural fortifications. Tall trees flanked the shores and large boulders scattered over the rocky beach prevented enemies from safely beaching their canoes in a night raid.

The fresh water supply, midway across the island, came from a small lake fed year-round by a bubbling spring. Fighting Wolf knew that on the mainland, a short distance away, hot sulphurous springs steamed in deep pools in the rocks. His people would have the

luxury of warm baths during the cold, rainy months.
Yes, it was a good site for a winter village. He hoped it
would prove satisfactory for many winters.

It had been a long while since Fighting Wolf had
bathed in the hot springs. A dip in the cold waters of the
inlet followed by a dash along the path to the springs
would rejuvenate his tired body and mind, he decided.

He paddled across the small channel from the
island to the mainland and beached his canoe. Although
the day was overcast, and rain was falling lightly, he
quickly stripped off the cedar kutsack he wore and
waded out into the cold salt water. He rubbed water
briskly over his strong body, unaware of dark brown,
sloe eyes avidly watching him.

His quick swim finished, he ran up the trail that led
to the hot springs. There, in a forest clearing, a fine mist
floatd over the surface of the tub-like depressions cast in
the solid rock. The springs were unoccupied and
Fighting Wolf sank slowly into the nearest one. He
heaved a great sigh. Sitting in the hot water, he felt his
body slowly relax for the first time in many days.

Leaning back against the rim of the small pool,
Fighting Wolf closed his eyes. Suddenly he opened
them. The forest noises had stopped. The silence was
overpowering. He looked around for his knife and
cursed himself. He'd foolishly left it on the beach with
the canoe. But unarmed though he was, he knew he
could still put up a good fight against any marauding
foe.

Without moving, his eyes searched the clearing. His
sharp ears detected a soft footfall behind him. Tensing
himself, he was ready to shoot out of the water when a
low voice called, "Oooh, Fighting Wolf, there you are.
I've been searching all over for you."

He relaxed. It was only Rough Seas.

"I think I'll join you," she said, mincing into the
clearing. "There's room enough for two in that little
pool." Seeing her disrobe in front of him surprised
Fighting Wolf, but did not arouse him.

Stepping gracefully into the hot water, she took her time folding her long legs under her as she sat down. "You've been so busy lately," she chided. "I thought you'd forgotten all about me."

"Oh?"

"Yes. Running all around searching for your sister and that—that slave." Noticing his frown, she added quickly, "I'm so sorry to hear about your sister."

Fighting Wolf merely nodded and leaned back again and closed his eyes. They sat like that for a few minutes, Rough Seas watching the resting man. At last, she leaned forward and touched his neck. He opened his eyes to find her puckered lips mere inches away from his face.

"What do you want, Rough Seas?" he asked lazily.

"To kiss you," she said coyly, her dark eyes wide.

"Oh?" Seeing her simper was suddenly too much for him. He stood up abruptly, the surprised woman falling back against the rim of the pool. "Let's not waste your time or mine," he said crisply. "I'm not looking for an affair."

"But Fighting Wolf, I'll marry you," she said eagerly. "I'm not looking for an affair, either. I've finally decided to settle down. No more affairs, no more husbands, just you. I'll marry you as soon as you want me to." Her raised arms beckoned him back into the pool.

"You misunderstand me," he answered evenly. "I will not now—or ever—marry you."

He jumped out of the pool and strode down the path, leaving the angry woman sitting in the steaming bath.

"Who wants you, anyway?" she screeched.

Fighting Wolf's taunting laughter drifted back to her, then she was alone in the silent forest.

As Fighting Wolf returned to the beach, he thoroughly scanned the inlet waters. As war chief, he was constantly on the alert. This observant habit was many times amply rewarded.

A two-seater canoe with distinctive white markings lay beached on the island. It had not been there earlier when he had gone to the hot springs. He easily recognized his old uncle's canoe.

Paddling quickly across the narrow channel, he moored his canoe and strode to the village. Heading towards his longhouse, he veered off when he saw a thin older man coming towards him.

"Uncle," he greeted. "I'm glad to see that two of the bravest men on the coast have returned safely. Very few men I know would travel all the way to Yuquot in a two-seater, no matter how sturdy."

The older man smiled. "My son did all the work," he answered modestly.

"That may be," returned Fighting Wolf, "but he had one of the best navigators on the coast to guide him."

The old man chuckled proudly. "I see you haven't forgotten all the lessons I gave you on finding your way around the inlets and bays."

"No, indeed. Many times on the sea, I've owed my life to the skills you taught me, uncle. And I'll be using those skills again, shortly. I'm taking a little trip north. I'll be leaving in the next few days."

Fighting Wolf stared bemusedly into the distance for a moment. Then he clapped a large hand on the older man's shoulders. "Come back to my longhouse and join me for dinner. We'll talk about old times."

The senior man agreed. "I'll gladly join you for dinner, Fighting Wolf, but I've some more immediate news to discuss with you—not just old times."

The ominous tone in his voice did not escape Fighting Wolf. He glanced quickly at the seamed face and nodded. "I'll make sure we have privacy," he answered.

Their dinner over, Fighting Wolf waved the serving women away. At last the main area was cleared of people and he turned to his guest.

"What are the immediate news you wished to discuss, Uncle?" Fighting Wolf leaned back on the cedar mat and waited. The older man reached for a cup of water and took a sip before answering.

"I bring you news of your sister." Fighting Wolf sat up quickly. "She's alive," assured the uncle, "and apparently well-treated. She said to tell you she's safe." The old man paused. "She's at Hesquiat."

"Hesquiat?" exclaimed Fighting Wolf.

Before he could say more, his uncle continued. "She told me that Feast Giver—"

"Thunder Maker's whelp! If he's so much as touched her, I'll—"

"That Feast Giver rescued her from a band of marauding Kwakiutl."

Fighting Wolf sat back again. "Continue," he said, his eyes narrowed.

"She didn't tell me the whole story, but my guess is that Feast Giver found out she was your sister and took her back with him." The older man added hastily, "For what purpose I don't know. She said she's well-treated, but when I pressed her, she admitted she wasn't free to leave."

"That bastard!"

"She gave me this bangle." The uncle untied a wooden bracelet from a thong at his waist and handed it to Fighting Wolf, who studied it carefully.

"It's hers, all right."

"She said to tell you that the Hesquiats were moving to their winter site. They'll be gone by now."

Fighting Wolf nodded. "I'll send out scouts right away. They can reconnoiter the area and report back to me."

"No need for that," chuckled the old man. "I can tell you where they're going." He took another sip of water. "Straight up that inlet from their summer village. They've been going there for years."

"That's right," responded Fighting Wolf. "You have relatives in that village. I'd forgotten."

"My wife has relatives," emphasized the older man. "But *my* relatives are here." His eyes twinkled. It was clear where his loyalties lay.

"Thank you for your help, old uncle. I'm glad to know my sister is alive. But with the Hesquiats—" He shook his head.

"Oh by the way," the older man added. "She did tell me one other thing. Said some woman has returned to the village. She said you'd know of her. Now, what was her name? Let me think . . ."

Fighting Wolf eyed his uncle intently. Could it be—?

The old man scratched his head and thought. "A strange name. What was it? S—S—Sarita. Yes. Sarita, that's it." He didn't notice how still Fighting Wolf went at these words. "Now there was something else, too. What was it?"

Watching the old man hesitate, then hesitate again, made the impatient Fighting Wolf want to throttle his old uncle. "Something about Sarita?" the war chief encouraged tautly.

"Mmmm. That's so. Now what was it? Oh yes," the old uncle beamed triumphantly. "I've got it! Sarita's pregnant."

That night, a determined Fighting Wolf led a huge flotilla of war canoes north. They paddled silently, steadily, their destination the Hesquiat winter village.

33

A violent storm whipped the rugged coastline for two days. Torrential rains and gale winds wrought havoc on land and sea.

Sarita sat by the fire in her father's longhouse. She was weaving a cedar mat. Nearby hovered two silent men, strong giants assigned to keep a close watch on her. She ignored their unwanted presence.

She had been housebound since the vicious storm began. In past years, she had enjoyed staying in the longhouse when storms passed through the area. This time, however, she had no enthusiasm for the usual rainy day occupations. Rehearsing a part in a play, singing, or practicing one of her family's dance steps held little appeal.

Overwhelmed by her personal problems, she wove carelessly, her thoughts and fingers flying.

"May I join you?"

She glanced up to see Precious Copper approaching. Smiling with relief, Sarita slid to one side of the mat she was sitting on so that Precious Copper could sit near the fire. Sarita noticed, out of the corner of her eye, that the two guards moved away, out of earshot. She was grateful for their unexpected tact. "I'd be delighted to have you weave with me," she answered Precious Copper.

Precious Copper indicated the slipshod piece of

weaving and said dryly, "Indeed. You really must teach
me how you do that. Someday."

Sarita laughed and said, "My weaving can't
compare with yours and you know it!" Her fingers
slowed down a little as she added, "Seems like I've
spent a lot of time with you lately."

"If you want some time alone, I can go elsewhere."

"No, no. I'm very glad to have your company. You
remind me of—" She stopped. "Never mind." She had
been about to say, "Fighting Wolf."

Precious Copper raised an inquiring brow, but
receiving no response, shrugged and sat down comfortably.

"My father is insistent that I marry Throws Away
Wealth," confided Sarita. "I told him I refuse, but it's
as if he's deaf." She indicated the two guards with a
slight inclination of her head. "Not so deaf that he can't
set guards on me, however," she added bitterly.

Precious Copper's glance flitted briefly over the
guards. She eyed Sarita sympathetically but said
nothing.

"And my brother," continued Sarita, "says
marriage to Throws Away Wealth is the answer to my
problems." She snorted. "Some answer."

"Did you tell Feast Giver that Throws Away
Wealth said he'd kill your child when it's born?" asked
Precious Copper.

"I told him, alright. It didn't do any good. He just
laughed and said Throws Away Wealth wouldn't dare
risk our family's anger like that." She sighed heavily. "I
think Feast Giver doesn't want to believe me. All he's
concerned about is making an alliance with the
Kyuquots."

"I know he wants that very much," acknowledged
Precious Copper. "Although I see Feast Giver
frequently," and here Sarita noticed a blush staining her
friend's cheeks, "he never says anything about his plans
to attack my people. Maybe he thinks if he doesn't
remind me, I'll forget we're enemies." She, too, sighed.

Sarita ·nodded. "He put off the raid until our village was safely moved to the winter site. Any day now, he and his men will be ready to raid the Ahousat."

"Oh. I thought he was putting it off because of dog salmon season."

"No. I know we need fish, but the dog salmon seem to be running late this moon. I think Feast Giver is hoping he can attack your people and still return in time for the big harvest of dog salmon." Sarita added worriedly, "I hope he doesn't miscalculate. We need those fish."

Precious Copper nodded. Then she asked, "Do your warriors always go on raids at this time of year?"

"No. We don't usually raid in fall or winter when the big rains and snows come, but Feast Giver is out for blood this time. He's going to lead a raid—and nothing will stop him."

Precious Copper was silent for a moment. "Feast Giver and I used to argue about that. Now, as I said, he doesn't mention it anymore," she repeated sadly.

Sarita patted Precious Copper's hand. "I know you simply want to protect your people. It *is* difficult when Feast Giver won't listen to you. Sometimes we women are so powerless," she mused.

"It seems so," agreed Precious Copper. "And yet, we can't give up—I can't. If I don't try and change his mind, well, I hate to think what might happen. He could be killed . . . My brother could be killed . . . Oh Sarita," she sighed. "What a mess men make of things!"

Sarita laughed. The two women continued their weaving, Precious Copper said casually, "I happen to know that Feast Giver thought he really was helping you when he suggested to your father that you marry Throws Away Wealth." She paused. "He knew how upset you were about your father's order to abort your baby. He thought this marriage would save your baby and your reputation."

"And provide him with a military ally," pointed

out Sarita caustically.

"Yes, too true," responded Precious Copper. After a short silence, she asked, "Do you think you could grow to love Throws Away Wealth?"

"What? That filthy little man?" shrieked Sarita. One of the guards frowned at her. She lowered her voice. "Never!"

Precious Copper kept her eyes intently on her work.

Sarita watched her in silence for a few moments, then said softly, "Precious Copper, I love Fighting Wolf. He's the only man I could ever think of marrying." She turned back to her work. She tried to keep her voice indifferent as she added, "I know he doesn't love me, or even think of me—"

"How can you say such a thing? My brother loves you more than he's ever loved a woman!"

Sarita looked at her sadly. "No, it's kind of you to say so, but I know he doesn't. He was just using me—"

"Don't say that, Sarita," implored Precious Copper. "Never has he been so cheerful and happy as he was with you. I could see a real change come over him after he brought you to our home. Why, whenever he was near you, he couldn't keep his eyes off you."

Or his hands, thought Sarita with a blush. Aloud she sighed. "Still, that doesn't mean he loved me."

Precious Copper opened her mouth to say something else, then stopped. Sarita was not going to be convinced, no matter what she said. Instead she asked, "When is the wedding between you and Throws Away Wealth to take place?"

Sarita looked down at the weaving in her hands. Then she began to slowly unweave a section she had just finished. Too loose, she thought. "Tomorrow night," she answered dully. "Nuwiksu says the groom won't give many gifts for me. It's supposed to be a quiet ceremony. Just close friends and relatives."

She was quiet for a moment. "Oh, Precious Copper," she sighed and Precious Copper heard the despair in her friend's voice. "For once, I don't know what to do. My father's forcing me into his marriage," she glanced at the two large guards, "and I can see no way out. After I'm married to that—that monster—my baby's life will be in constant danger. Perhaps mine, too." She stopped weaving, she was so distraught. "For once, I can't run away. I have nowhere to go."

Precious Copper softly touched her friend's shaking hands. "If only I could help you somehow," she said earnestly.

Sarita smiled sadly. "You've already helped me immensely, by being my friend and by listening to my troubles." She blinked back tears. "We still have several more cedar mats to weave. They have to be ready for tomorrow night," her voice quavered, "my wedding celebration."

"Yes, of course," responded Precious Copper briskly. The two women finished their weaving in silence, while in the background the two burly guards hovered restlessly.

For the first few days of his liberty Rottenwood did nothing remotely resembling work. When his slave friends questioned his laziness, he waved them away with a slow smile. "All my life I've worked for someone else," he explained. "Now I'm resting. Soon I'll work again. But this time it will be for me!"

The other slaves merely laughed or shook their heads enviously, but Rottenwood didn't care what they thought. He was the one that was free. He was finding, though, that freedom held a few surprises.

The first day or two he'd spent getting used to the idea that no one owned him any longer. He luxuriated in his new independence and spent the time roaming around the village, looking at houses, places and people with new eyes.

After that, he began to think about what he wanted out of his new life. He'd told Sarita in the first moments of freedom that he'd continue to work for her father

and now decided he could live with that commitment.
Thunder Maker was by far the best chief in the village,
as well as the highest-ranking. Rottenwood had been
pleased when Thunder Maker gravely welcomed him
into the longhouse as a commoner. He knew the crafty
chief wanted to keep hard workers in his longhouse,
workers who would contribute to his growing wealth,
but still Rottenwood was pleased that the chief had
taken notice of him.

Lately, however, his thoughts were consumed with
Spring Fern. During slavery, his overwhelming desire
had been to be free. Now that he'd attained his liberty,
other wants crowded in, but his desire for Spring Fern
eclipsed them all. He didn't know what to do about her.
When they'd both been slaves, marriage between them
had been a possibility—with Thunder Maker's
approval, of course. Now, there was no hope.
Commoners did not marry slaves.

While he wrestled with the problem, he threw
himself into hard work. The days of slavery had never
felt so good, he thought wryly, as he went to bed each
night weary from his labors at fishing or repairing
canoes.

Early one morning he decided to paddle out and
catch fish for Thunder Maker's house.

As he walked down the beach to where a small,
one-man dugout lay, he revelled in the fact that no one
called out to him with curt orders that he do some task
for them. No one demanded to know where he was
going. No one called him to account for taking the
canoe. He was free.

A few of the commoners nodded casually to him.
Pleased at this sign of acceptance, he nodded back.
When he was first freed, he had faced sneers and insults,
but not for long. He had defended himself vigorously,
both verbally and physically, and now found himself
respected by a growing number of his new class.

Late that night, he returned tired and sore, but the
five cod and four halibut he carried up to the longhouse

made up for his weary body. Abalone Woman took the
fish from him and thanked him politely for his efforts.
Rottenwood glowed inside. He gloated to himself over
the better treatment he received.

After a hasty meal and a bath to get rid of the fish
smell, he decided to seek out Spring Fern. She'd had
several days to accept the idea of his freedom, and he
wondered what she thought of him now.

He walked through Thunder Maker's longhouse to
the chief's quarters where Spring Fern usually spent her
evenings. Stationing himself in the shadows near the
door, he waited for a chance to speak with her. He
gazed hungrily at her as she hovered close to Sarita.
They were rehearsing a theatrical display with several
other women.

All evening long, Spring Fern stayed close to her
mistress as they practiced the songs and dance steps over
and over. Growing impatient, Rottenwood stepped out
of the shadows, hoping to catch Spring Fern's eye and
signal her to meet him outside. He thought she saw him
once, but she looked away so quickly, he couldn't be
sure. As the evening wore on, and she continued to
avoid his gaze, he realized she was indeed aware of him.

Growing annoyed with Spring Fern's behavior,
Rottenwood strode out the door into the night. A heavy
rain beat a constant tattoo against the side of the
longhouse. He decided not to stroll around as he'd get
nothing but a soaking for his efforts. Ducking under the
overhang of the roof, he leaned against the corner of the
longhouse and looked out into the darkness in the
direction of the inlet. He idly wondered how he was
going to talk with Spring Fern when it was obvious she
was avoiding him.

His speculations were cut short when she exited
from the longhouse and slipped quickly into the nearby
bushes. Moments later, as she ran back to the
longhouse, he called out her name.

Seeing her pause, he asked softly, "Are you
avoiding me, Spring Fern?"

His large hand clamped around her waist and Spring Fern felt herself being pulled firmly away from the door.

Rottenwood looked at her hungrily. "Why are you avoiding me? Don't you know how I want you?"

She looked at him, fear in her dark doe eyes. He saw it and didn't like it. "What are you afraid of?"

"You."

"Me? What have I done?"

She shrugged and moved away from him. He noticed the slight movement and reached out for her arm. She tried to shrug out of his tight grip. "You're hurting me—"

He let her go. "Sorry. I didn't mean to." He watched her rub the spot on her upper arm where he'd grasped her. She saw him watching her and stopped. She quivered slightly as he reached out and touched a dark tendril of her hair. "Remember when I asked you to be my wife?" he asked, his voice like a caress.

She nodded, her eyes turning to find his in the darkness. "Yes," she answered softly. "I remember." Then pausing to gather her courage she asked, "But since you're now free, I release you from your promise." She wouldn't let him know how much it hurt her to say those words. "Now . . . now that you're a commoner, I know you won't want a slave for a wife." She'd said them hastily, but the words lingered between them, cold and hard and honest, then faded away like the ripples on a pond after a rock is cast.

His hand paused in mid-air; his eyes narrowed. "I don't want anyone else for a wife," he said.

"But what can we do?" she cried. "You can't marry me—"

"True," he cut in in a brutal voice, "but I can make you my mistress."

She gasped, "You wouldn't!"

He growled back, "I would."

She looked into his eyes searchingly. "You would," she agreed dully.

He ran a brown forefinger slowly down her forearm. She shivered. "Don't you like the idea?" he asked.

She looked at him incredulously. "It's quite a fall from being asked to be your wife, to being told I'll be your mistress," she said bitterly.

"Yes, I guess it is," he acknowledged. His admission surprised her. There had been a hint of compassion in his voice.

"You don't like the idea any better than I do, do you?" she asked perceptively.

"No, I don't. But it's the only way we can be together."

"There's one other way—"

He looked at her. "What is that? I've gone over and over it in my mind. If there was any possibility of marriage—" His voice told her the hopelessness he felt.

"Let me ask Sarita," she said eagerly. "I'll ask her to help us."

"Sarita!" he snorted with contempt.

Spring Fern was astonished. "Why do you say her name that way? She freed you!"

"Yes," he agreed disparagingly. "She freed me. And took her time doing so, too. Before we left Ahousat, we made the agreement. But once she was back home she didn't need me anymore. She conveniently forgot our pact." He shrugged. "What can you expect? No one keeps their word to a slave."

"That's not true," flashed Spring Fern. "She kept her word. It was her father who wanted to keep you a slave. I heard Sarita and Thunder Maker wrangling over you many times."

Rottenwood looked at her. "Let's not argue about what she did or didn't say or do. I want to talk about us."

"So do I," shot back Spring Fern. "I just know that Sarita will help us get married if I ask her."

"Hmmph, why should she?" He paused, then asked, "And how can she go against a whole society?

Everyone knows that commoners can't marry slaves. What can she do about it? She has enough problems of her own." Contempt laced his voice.

"Please," coaxed Spring Fern softly. "Let me speak with her. At least let me try."

He stared down at her for a moment. Spring Fern was so beautiful and he wanted her so much. "All right," he conceded gruffly. "But you'd better come up with something soon. I hear she's going to marry some Kyuquot chief. After that, she'll be whisked away to Kyuquot." He added warningly, "I won't wait long. Only for one moon."

Spring Fern protested, "That doesn't give me much time."

Rottenwood smiled lazily. "Time enough. If she can't help us, we'll go back to my plan." He wrapped her in his arms. "I think you'd make a lovely mistress," he whispered.

She pushed at his chest gently. "Oh, I would," she murmured. "But I'd make an even better wife!"

With that she slipped out of his arms and ran back into the longhouse, leaving him chuckling in the rain.

34

The Ahousat warriors had started out late in the evening. Fighting Wolf noted the ominous cloud cover. He hoped the approaching storm would hold off for one more day, long enough for him and his men to get close to Hesquiat territory. They needed shelter until the storm passed. But a search of the inhospitable coastline proved fruitless. No sheltered cove or bay beckoned the weary men. Disheartened, they had to keep paddling north.

The storm lashed them with its mighty force the following morning, just as dawn was breaking.

Barely in sight of the coastline, the pelting rain obscured the men's vision and pounded against their naked bodies. Crashing waves threatened to overturn the bobbing canoes and dump the frantically paddling men into the depths of the rolling, gray sea.

It was the whipping wind, however, that really damaged the close formation of the canoes. Carelessly tossing them about as if they were toy boats, the wind blew them farther and farther off course, and farther and farther apart.

Fighting Wolf watched in anguish as the canoe closest to him was lost behind a wall of rain. It would take days to gather his men together again, that is, if they survived the storm.

The roaring wind assaulted the men's ears as ferociously as the rain pelted their bodies. Fighting Wolf cupped his hands over his mouth and yelled to

Otterskin, "There's a sheltered cove not far from here. We're heading for it."

Otterskin's shouted response blew away on the wind.

Slowly, the twelve aimed the canoe in the direction Fighting Wolf pointed. They paddled with all their strength. It was as if they stood still. Every time the canoe bounced up on the crest of a gigantic wave, half the paddles were out of the water. Then the craft was plunged down into a wave's trough, the nose of the boat thrust into an oncoming wave. Time and again the frail craft plodded onwards, only to be swept back, as though by a giant hand.

Fighting Wolf was thoroughly alarmed, but he tried not to let his men see his fear. Never, in his many years battling the sea, had he been caught in such a storm. He glanced quickly over his shoulder at the men. Fear was on every face. Several of them gazed, agonized, at him. He knew they were depending on him for the strength to fight the raging elements. Others were mumbling. Praying, no doubt.

Almost unconsciously, Fighting Wolf, too, found himself praying to Qua-utz. Interspersed with prayer were thoughts of Sarita, and the child she carried. Uppermost in his mind was the fear he would never see her again, never hold the woman he loved in his arms.

For he could no longer lie to himself. He loved her. Facing death, he was honest with himself, with Qua-utz. Tossed about like a leaf, he faced only the important moments of his existence. He had risked his life, and the lives of his men, in the pursuit of the only woman he had ever loved.

He raised his arms to the raging wind, the churning sky, the pounding rain, to Qua-utz. He chanted into the wind, his words lost to those around him. "God over all, spare my men. They did but follow where I led. It is true I pursue the woman, Sarita, to bring her back to my village. You have now shown me the foolishness of my decision. Spare my men, spare me, and I will cease my foolish quest. When you sent her into my life, you gave me a gift, a precious gift. One that I was too blind to see. You have shown me the folly of my actions. Spare my men from the results of my wrong actions. Should you also spare me, I will no longer seek to enslave her, but will cherish her as long as you allow me to walk the earth, and to paddle the seas."

Fighting Wolf squatted down in the tossing canoe, his only answer the howling of the storm. To trample on what he had had, to deny the powerful love he felt for Sarita, to make her a slave again, was terribly wrong. He realized that now. The whole world, the rain, the storm, the sea, were telling him that.

His thoughts were interrupted by a sudden lurching of the canoe. Thrown to one side, Fighting Wolf fell heavily against the gunwale. A wave lashed the boat sharply from the other side.

In the space of a heartbeat, Fighting Wolf felt himself hurtling through the rain into the cold, seething water. As the treacherous liquid closed over his head, he fought desperately for the surface. Gasping for air, another large wave swamped him. He inhaled water, and sunk under the waves. He opened his eyes in the dark water but could see nothing.

Suddenly he felt the lash of a whip-like tail sweep past his leg. A sea snake? A serpent? It slithered by him again. Aah, a cedar rope.

Bobbing once more to the surface, he lunged for the thin lifeline that sank under the waves. He almost reached it, but another wave sucked at him, pulling him further under.

With superhuman effort, he kicked back at the towering waves, his whole being concentrating on the one small, skinny rope that led to the canoe. Seizing it, he wrapped it around his fist and yelled. The yell came out as a gasp and he knew whoever tossed him the rope couldn't hear him above the roar of the storm.

He felt the line go taut, and slowly, slowly, he was pulled through the waves. Kicking again and again with all his might, he fought his way to the side of the plunging craft. Eager hands reached over the side and pulled him in, his body a dead weight, so exhausted was he from fighting the sea. He slumped to the floor of the lurching canoe, oblivious to its wrenching motion.

The quiet motion of the canoe awoke him. The storm had spent itself. Haggard, Fighting Wolf raised his eyes to the darkened sky and realized anew that his life had been spared. He lived, and would see those he loved once again. Sarita's face flashed before his mind's eye. Struggling to sit up, he surveyed the exhausted paddlers in his canoe. Weary they were, but all twelve were there.

His next thoughts were for the rest of his men. How many had survived the storm's rage?

He got slowly, wearily, to his feet. Standing at the bow of the battered canoe, legs planted apart, he raised his arms again to Qua-utz and chanted a prayer of thanks.

"Many times I thank you, God over all, for sparing the precious lives of these twelve brave men from the fury of the storm. Many thanks also for sparing my life. I pledged my word to You that I would cease my quest to enslave the woman, Sarita, and I will hold to my word. Thanks upon thanks for your mercy in the face of the storm."

He sat down again, his body aching and cold. He looked at his men. Bleary eyes stared back at him. Then, tired grins broke through the weary faces and Fighting Wolf knew they had rallied. "Who tossed me the rope?" he asked.

"Comes-from-Salish," came the answer.

Fighting Wolf looked over at the ex-slave. "If it were possible to set you free again, my friend, I would do it. My thanks for saving my life. I thought I'd never look upon a human face again."

Comes-from-Salish shrugged, embarrassed at the words of his chief.

Fighting Wolf saw the other's self-consciousness.

He laid a hand on the broad shoulder, and lowered his voice. "Nevertheless, I mean it. I thank you for tossing me that rope. If there's anything I can do to help you, any favor I can give you, you need but ask."

Comes-from-Salish looked at the floor of the canoe and mumbled, "There is nothing, my lord."

"Come," encouraged the war chief. "I want to repay you for what you did. Let me at least do that—"

Realizing that Fighting Wolf seriously did not wish to be beholden to him, the ex-slave said slowly, "There is one thing. My daughter, my youngest girl, will be coming of age soon—"

Fighting Wolf seized upon his words with alacrity. "Then allow me to make gifts in her name. I'd consider it a great honor to share in sponsoring her puberty potlatch."

Comes-from-Salish grinned tiredly. "It is I who am honored. I can't believe my good fortune. I was only a lowly slave. Now my children live in freedom and I'm about to give my daughter a ceremony—" Overcome, he choked on his words.

Fighting Wolf clapped him on the back once more. "You deserve such honors. Your bravery won them for you, my friend."

Fighting Wolf turned at last to his men. "Let's head for that point and light a fire. The others should see our beacon and come to us. *If* they survived the storm," he added grimly.

The weary Ahousats paddled slowly in the direction their war chief indicated.

Fighting Wolf and his men set up camp near some large boulders on the stony beach of the point. Fighting Wolf surveyed the men gathered around the large fire. Many of his straggling warriors had been beckoned to safety by the bright leaping flames. Several familiar faces were missing, but the storm had spared more men than Fighting Wolf had dared hope. Those men who had not shown up by now, well, he would just have to assume the worst.

There was much to do before they could push on to the Hesquiat winter village. Canoes had to be patched, food hunted, and the wounded tended.

Things were quiet for the moment, and Fighting Wolf relaxed, looking into the dancing orange flames as though in a trance. Ever since the storm, he had been unable to tear Sarita from his thoughts. He mused about what he would say to her.

He admitted again that he loved her. This time he felt more comfortable with the thought. No longer could he think of her as a possession, a woman to be used and thrown aside when another attractive female came along. Now he realized he wanted her, and their child, with him for the rest of his life.

Years suddenly stretched before him. Without her, there would be only emptiness. But with her, those years would be filled with joy and happiness. Oh, there would be angry times, he couldn't deny that, but he knew he loved her enough to accept those, if he could only have the good times.

He thought back over his treatment of her. He'd used her, he realized now. He'd expected that she'd always be there for him to come home to. That's why he'd been so angry when she'd left. Not only was his pride hurt that she could leave him, but he'd *needed* her to be there for him. When she'd gone, he'd felt sorely, savagely betrayed.

With her, he'd begun to feel alive again. He'd begun to love again, after that cold, dark period of his life when he'd been afraid to feel, afraid to love ever again. She'd brought him the gift of life, and he, in return, had walked on her pride, her love, and for what?

Revenge. He almost choked on the word. How paltry it seemed now. To sacrifice someone so precious, for an ideal like revenge. All his life he'd heard how he should revenge the wrongs done to his people, done to him. Since he was a young boy he'd been taught that vengeance against his enemies was noble, the correct and honorable thing to do. But the events of his own life proved how wrong such notions were. All those people who'd taught him—his father, his uncle, others—were wrong. He'd paid a high price for following their dictates so blindly. Vengeance had cost him the woman he loved.

Fighting Wolf hoped Sarita would understand his changed thinking. He loved her and wanted her back, but he couldn't blame her if she wanted nothing further to do with him.

He agonized over the possibility that she'd refuse to marry him. Surprised at the direction of his thoughts, he realized marriage was what he wanted. She would be his equal, honored and protected, walking with him through life. And, he added with satisfaction, in his bed at night.

His thoughts rested briefly on her child. His child, too. He had no doubt of that. He squirmed inside as he remembered the last night he had held Sarita in his arms. She'd asked him then if he'd allow his child to be born into slavery. He hadn't seriously considered her question. Now he realized he could never allow a child he loved—and he already loved this child—to be born a slave. To let his own flesh, a child of his own blood, be raised as anyone less than the noble he or she deserved to be, was an excruciating thought.

Otterskin approached. "Some of the men are asking if we're heading back to Ahousat. I've told them I'm awaiting your orders."

Fighting Wolf looked at his faithful lieutenant. "We'll be heading for the Hesquiat winter village."

"But, sir. Some of the men heard your chanting to Qua-utz—"

"And they heard me promise to cease my quest to enslave the Hesquiat woman?" finished the war chief, a glint in his eye.

The other nodded sheepishly.

"I may have ceased my quest to make her a slave, but we will continue on to Hesquiat. My business there is not finished," explained Fighting Wolf tolerantly.

"As far as the men are concerned, I have every intention of keeping my vow to Qua-utz." He paused, then ordered, "We leave in the morning. Tell the men, and make the necessary preparations."

Otterskin nodded, then turned away to carry out the orders. Watching him walk away, Fighting Wolf smiled to himself. Like his men, he had no wish to incur Qua-utz's wrath, either.

35

With dawn's first light, the Ahousat warriors paddled closer to their destination. They traveled quickly, their paddles dipping rhythmically. Heading into the quieter, inside waters, Fighting Wolf recognized the inlet described by his "uncle." Soon they would come upon the Hesquiat winter village.

The fjord-like inlet gradually narrowed, but the water remained deep. The weak morning light showed charcoal colored cedars rising from the rocky shoreline and melding into thick forests. Gradually, the damp mist muted the charcoal to a lighter gray.

Along the smooth surface of the water skimmed a kingfisher, searching out its breakfast below.

After several miles of journeying, Fighting Wolf signalled a halt. As previously planned, half the men paddled over to the narrow rocky beach on one side of the narrow pass. The war chief watched approvingly as they hid their canoes in the thick tree line, then melted into the forest. The last to leave was Otterskin. He waved to Fighting Wolf before he, too, disappeared silently into the thick undergrowth. Otterskin and his forty men were to sneak through the forest and silently surround the Hesquiat village.

Fighting Wolf was confident the hidden men would provide the protection he and his remaining men would need when they paddled openly into the Hesquiat village.

Should Fighting Wolf be attacked, Otterskin would

immediately storm the village. Should Fighting Wolf be greeted in peace, the hidden Ahousats would stay in the woods. The Hesquiats need never know they were surrounded.

There was a slight bend in the rocky shoreline. If his old "uncle's" directions were correct, the Hesquiat winter village should be just ahead. A loud yell went up as the Ahousats rounded the point. Fighting Wolf was surprised to hear the shouted warning. He hadn't expected the Hesquiats to post guards in such an isolated location.

Paddling slowly, his retinue of forty-two men arrayed behind him, Fighting Wolf approached the shore where the village sat perched against a backdrop of cedars. Standing up in the precarious canoe, he balanced himself evenly. One of his warriors sprinkled white eagle down over Fighting Wolf's head. The Hesquiats should realize from the gesture that he came in peace.

He watched, outwardly stoic, inwardly alert, as several Hesquiat warriors ran down to the rocky beach. Apprehensively, he noted they were armed with muskets. Someone, it looked like Feast Giver, ordered the men into a neat formation, their weapons pointing at the slowly approaching Ahousats. Behind them, stood a row of men holding sharp pointed wooden lances. A few men holding bows and arrows formed the last row.

"Formidable," muttered Birdwhistle. His voice carried across the water. Fighting Wolf did not reply.

He watched as the Hesquiats stood their ground. He grudgingly admired their disciplined ranks.

Feast Giver's shout broke the tense silence. "That's close enough, Ahousats! Any closer and we'll shoot!"

Drawing himself up to his full height, aware that he made an easy target, Fighting Wolf called back, "We're here to talk. We do not come to fight!"

"You lie, Ahousat! We know how you like to fight!" sneered Feast Giver.

Fighting Wolf heard his men mutter angrily at the

slur. They bitterly resented hearing their leader labelled a liar. Ignoring the animosity around him, he responded in a calm voice, "If we wanted to raid your village, Hesquiat, we'd come at night, not in the full light of day." He paused to let his words sink in. "Look at my men. Do you see any weapons?"

"Weapons are easily hidden, Ahousat!" snapped Feast Giver warily. "What do you want?"

First drawn by the sudden stillness in the village, then by the shouts, Sarita watched in disbelief as the Ahousats paddled slowly up to the rocky shale beach. Seeing Fighting Wolf standing proudly in his canoe, she felt tears gather in her eyes. She realized anew how much she loved him. Her breath caught as she heard Feast Giver shouting his questions at the Ahousat war chief. She couldn't bear to see Fighting Wolf shot down in front of her. Why, oh, why, had he come? She strained for his answer.

"I want to talk with you and your father."

"You can talk from where you're standing, Ahousat!" came back the hostile answer.

Drifting ever closer, Fighting Wolf raised an eyebrow. "Is that so?" He shrugged casually. "Well, if you really want to discuss personal details about your family in front of the whole village—"

Feast Giver shifted his glance to the men awaiting his orders. His eye caught his father's form coming out of the longhouse. It was obvious from his hurry that Thunder Maker had heard the last exchange. Pausing to speak in a low voice with his son, Thunder Maker then called, "You say you want to talk, Ahousat!"

"That's right," agreed Fighting Wolf.

"Very well. You can come ashore. Alone. Your men stay in their canoes, where we can keep them covered."

Fighting Wolf hesitated. If it was a trap, he would be defenseless, alone with the Hesquiats. On the other hand, his men could retaliate. They were armed. He'd had no qualms about lying to Feast Giver. The Ahousat warriors' weapons lay ready on the floors of the canoes.

"I agree to your conditions," answered Fighting
Wolf. "Provided we stand on the beach, where my men
can watch." Seeing Thunder Maker's nod, Fighting
Wolf continued, "But let me warn you. If you harm me,
my warriors will kill every man, woman and child in this
village!"

Satisfied that the Hesquiats thoroughly understood
his threat, Fighting Wolf stepped out of the canoe and
walked up the rocky beach, flanked by a belligerent
Feast Giver and a silent Thunder Maker.

Once out of earshot from the others, Feast Giver
halted abruptly. "Say what you came to say, Ahousat.
Then leave!" Thunder Maker remained silent, and
Fighting Wolf assumed he agreed with his son's words.

"I know you're holding my sister, Precious
Copper," began the war chief. He was rewarded with a
guilty start from Feast Giver.

"Lies," blustered the young man.

"No, not lies," replied the Ahousat evenly. "She
was seen in your village and I've come to take her back
home with me."

Feast Giver looked silently at the Ahousat, then at
his father. Thunder Maker maintained his silence.
Stepping into the breach his father refused to fill, Feast
Giver said, "Why should we give her up to you? Have
you any ransom to pay for her?"

Feast Giver was stalling, but he could not bear to
let the beautiful Precious Copper go. If she went back to
the Ahousat village, his chances of ever seeing her again
were negligible.

"No, I have no ransom with me," admitted
Fighting Wolf.

"Then what are you wasting our time for?"
scoffed Feast Giver. Maybe he could yet keep Precious
Copper . . .

"The matter of a ransom is a small one," stated the
Ahousat arrogantly. "I can easily send for whatever you
ask and have it shipped from my village."

"Not good enough."

Realizing they were at an impasse, Fighting Wolf mentioned conversationally, "I've also come for Sarita's hand in marriage."

For a moment, the two Hesquiats looked stunned. They both quickly recovered, however, and Thunder Maker spoke up first. "You what?" he asked, disbelief echoing in his voice. "After what you've done to her, to me, to my son, you have the effrontery to come to this village and ask for my daughter's hand in marriage?"

"I'm not asking, I'm demanding," cut in the Ahousat brusquely.

Thunder Maker was shaking his head. "This is too much. I cannot believe such insolence."

"Believe what you will, old man," responded the war chief. "But I've come to take my sister home and to take your daughter with me, as my wife."

Thunder Maker drew himself up to his full height. "The answer is 'no,' " he stated. "I want it clearly understood. You will not take your sister back with you. She will no longer be a hostage, but a Hesquiat slave." The older man did not notice his son flinch at the hard words. "She'll stay in our village and work for us."

Thunder Maker paused, impaling his opponent with a steely eye. He was gratified to note the flush of anger on the Ahousat's face. "As for my daughter, Sarita, I absolutely refuse to enter into any marriage negotiations with you."

"Why not?" bit out an enraged Fighting Wolf. He struggled to keep a calm facade.

"Because Sarita is going to marry the Kyuquot chief, Throws Away Wealth." Thunder Maker gloated to himself as he watched the astonished Ahousat digest these words.

"What?" demanded a now-furious Fighting Wolf, all pretense of calm forgotten.

"That's right," responded Thunder Maker calmly. He hugged himself in delight at being able to thwart the Ahousat's plans so easily. "She can't marry you be-

cause I've already promised her to the Kyuquot."
Seeing the Ahousat's fury, he added uneasily, "The
Kyuquot has many warriors."

The threat was not lost on Fighting Wolf. "That
dog! The Kyuquot is a cowardly fighter!"

"Oh? And how would you know that?" asked
Thunder Maker, his uneasiness intensifying.

"Because I fought him," sneered Fighting Wolf,
his thoughts racing. His initial burst of fury past, he was
busy plotting how he could still have Sarita. "I and my
men beat him soundly when he raided us last summer.
The cowardly Kyuquot ran back to his village with his
tail between his legs." It was plain from the look on his
face that Fighting Wolf relished recounting the victory
over the Kyuquot.

Thunder Maker coughed uncomfortably. "That
proves nothing, Ahousat," he said. "You're probably
lying . . . trying to intimidate me."

"Probably," agreed Fighting Wolf laconically. His
eagle eyes watched his prey. "Are you intimidated?"

"Not at all," responded Thunder Maker quickly.

Fighting Wolf noticed the sweat beading the older
man's brow. He smiled to himself. "Nevertheless," he
suggested smoothly, "I suggest you forget the
Kyuquot's marriage suit and entertain mine, instead."

Thunder Maker stared at him for a moment. "That
I refuse to do," he said stubbornly.

"Why not?" asked Fighting Wolf, curiously. He
was merely playing with Thunder Maker now. The
Hesquiat was a fool not to know the Ahousats would
make better allies than the weak Kyuquots.

"Need you ask?" snorted Thunder Maker. "I
don't trust you," he snapped. "After the last 'marriage'
we went through with you . . . well, just let me say that
I will not be victimized by such treachery again!" With
those words, he turned on his heel, obviously dismissing
the Ahousat war chief.

"Not so fast, Thunder Maker," said Fighting
Wolf. A determined note in his voice made the older
man turn.

A shiver passed through the Hesquiat chief as his eyes locked with the piercing ebony eyes focused on him. "What do you want? We have nothing more to say to each other."

"I want," said Fighting Wolf evenly, "my sister *and* Sarita."

"Are you deaf, Ahousat? I said no to both demands." The older man turned to walk away once more.

"You're in no position to defy my demands," shot back Fighting Wolf coolly.

"Watch what you say when you're in my territory," warned Thunder Maker. "This is my village. My men have mus-kets trained on you. One word from me, and you're a dead man. Now, if you'll excuse me—"

"Tell your father," said Fighting Wolf, turning to the ignored Feast Giver, "that unless he wants his village destroyed, he'll return my sister."

"What can you do, Ahousat?" sneered Feast Giver.

"My men have your village surrounded," said the war chief casually.

Feast Giver stared at him. "You're bluffing," he said softly.

"Am I?" smiled Fighting Wolf pleasantly. The flash of white teeth was gone in an instant.

"Nuwiksu," called Feast Giver, not taking his eyes off the war chief. "Come back here. There are a few more points to discuss."

Hearing the warning note in his son's voice, Thunder Maker reluctantly padded back to the two antagonists. "I'm waiting," he said, impatiently.

"The Ahousat has our village surrounded," said his son curtly.

Thunder Maker sized up the handsome face turned to him. "He's bluffing," he announced and started back to his longhouse.

"Can you afford to gamble your people's lives on that one guess?" asked Fighting Wolf politely.

Thunder Maker stopped and seemed to argue silently with himself for a moment. When he turned back to the two men, there was a look of resignation on his face. "All right," he said wearily. "Let's get this over with."

For a long while the two chiefs debated their positions while Feast Giver looked on. Finally, seeing that his father would not be swayed from his intention to enslave Precious Copper, Feast Giver spoke up. "I think you should both know," he began, "That I wish to marry Precious Copper."

As one, the two disputants turned to stare at him. "What?" they asked in unison.

Thunder Maker sputtered, "Of all the—"

He was cut off by Fighting Wolf's roar. "No! Absolutely not!"

When silence reigned once again, Feast Giver said with dignity, "I love her and I want to marry her."

"Impossible," responded Fighting Wolf. "I won't allow my sister to marry you. She can find a far better man."

"Now look here," began Feast Giver.

"Not only that," interrupted Fighting Wolf, "But I will not force my sister into marriage . . . no matter what you have done to her." His cold eyes left no doubt that he believed the worst of Feast Giver.

"I resent your implication," snarled Feast Giver. "If I've done anything, it's no more than what you've done to Sarita."

Fighting Wolf lunged at Feast Giver. Thunder Maker barely managed to hold the heavier .was chief back. "Please," he said nervously. "Let's discuss our problems. We're noblemen, not brutes." At this reminder, the two combatants reluctantly backed off. But Fighting Wolf was still angry and Feast Giver looked very hostile.

In the shadows of a nearby longhouse, Precious Copper looked at Sarita. "Shouldn't we do something?" she asked, wide-eyed.

Sarita nodded. "I can't just hide here and watch while they're out there fighting each other." Taking a deep breath, she stepped outside the door. "Are you coming?" she asked.

Precious Copper responded quickly, "I'm right behind you." Together the two women hurried across the rocky beach to where Thunder Maker had placed himself between the Ahousat and Feast Giver.

Fighting Wolf was the first to see the women approach. He looked up and relief swept over him as he saw his sister walking towards him. She looked rested and healthy.

Then his gaze swung to Sarita. He devoured her with his eyes. It had been so long . . . She looked as beautiful as ever. More so. He eyed her figure knowingly. The bulky kutsack hid the swell of her stomach.

Sarita's steps faltered as she approached the waiting men. She couldn't tear her golden eyes away from Fighting Wolf. Her heart beat furiously. So often she'd dreamed of seeing him again, and now he was here. Far more threatening in life than in her dreams. He threatened her heart, her life, her very soul . . . Unconsciously, her hand went to her stomach, as if to protect the new life there.

Fighting Wolf caught the gesture and smiled slowly. His eyes held hers. "Sarita," he breathed.

"Fighting Wolf," she acknowledged defiantly.

Thunder Maker watched through narrowed eyes as the two eyed each other warily. Sarita doesn't like the Ahousat, he thought. Perhaps, if the Ahousat is bluffing about his men surrounding the village, he may yet be put off from his plans to have her . . .

Precious Copper ran to her brother. The two hugged, then she stepped back, looking up at him. "It's so good to see you, brother."

"Have they treated you well? Tell me the truth. If they've done anything—" His fierce gaze rested briefly on Feast Giver.

"They've treated me very well," she assured Fighting Wolf.

"Oh? What about the chief's son, here? Has he bothered you?"

She flushed. "No," she answered in a quiet voice, looking down at the ground.

"Did you know," he addressed Precious Copper, but never took his eyes off Feast Giver, "he has the audacity to ask for your hand." Fighting Wolf laughed heartily, fully expecting his sister to join in. When she didn't, but continued to stare at her feet, the laughter died in his throat. He looked at her in angry surprise. "Surely you don't expect me to consider his offer seriously," he demanded.

Precious Copper raised her eyes to his. She glanced once at Feast Giver who was watching with troubled eyes.

"Precious Copper, it's not the way I would have told you," began Feast Giver earnestly.

"Stay out of this," ordered Fighting Wolf.

"How can I?" demanded Feast Giver. "I'm very much involved. I told you I want to marry her and I meant it." He turned to the dark-eyed woman, his heart in his eyes, and said softly, "I love you, Precious Copper. I want you for my wife."

The silence was broken by Fighting Wolf's snort. "Fine words, Hesquiat. But I'll tell you right now, you're not good enough for her. You have no name—"

"Thanks to you!"

"—And your wealth is nothing! Many of my sister's suitors come from families with many slaves, many furs. What do you have?" he asked contemptuously.

Feast Giver's hopes plummeted. What did he have to offer such a desirable woman as Precious Copper?

"She's only a hostage," inserted Thunder Maker. He spat on the ground, showing what he thought of that status.

Fighting Wolf ignored him. "No," he shook his

head at Feast Giver. "You just won't do."

"Brother, I must speak with you," interrupted Precious Copper urgently. "In private."

Fighting Wolf looked at her impatiently. He said nothing, however, and the two stepped out of earshot of the Hesquiats.

"Fighting Wolf," she hissed at him. "I want to marry Feast Giver!"

"What?" Caught off guard, Fighting Wolf could only stare at his sister. "You want to marry him?" He jutted his chin in the general direction of Feast Giver. "He's not good enough for you, Precious Copper. His family is poor now, they have no name—"

"Yes, yes, I know," she answered hastily. "I heard you before." She drew herself up to her full, diminutive height and looked her brother firmly in the eye. "Nevertheless, *he* is the man I want to marry."

While Fighting Wolf pondered this new development, she added, "Besides, his family is not that poor. They still control several fishing territories and rivers. The Hesquiats are still the most powerful tribe in this area. As for their name, it was respected until you pulled that 'marriage' trick on them. You have to accept responsibility for that."

Goaded, Fighting Wolf replied, "But Feast Giver?" He made the name sound synonymous with "worm."

"And another thing," continued Precious Copper. "He saved me. Kwakiutl warriors seized me; that's when I went missing from our village. They killed the two slaves I had with me., The Kwakiutl were just about to rape me when Feast Giver and his men rescued me." She touched his arm. Sincerity shone in her deep brown eyes. "Feast Giver saved my life."

"So you want to marry him out of gratitude?"

"No, it's not that. Since living here at Hesquiat, I've had a chance to get to know him. I—I love him, Fighting Wolf."

Fighting Wolf searched her countenance. He saw

that love displayed nakedly on her entreating face and
sighed heavily. He hoped Feast Giver was worthy of
her. "What do you want me to do?"

"Let me marry him. Convince the rest of our
family that it's a good alliance!" She paused. "Fighting
Wolf, I've never met a man like him. I would never be
satisfied with those other suitors you mentioned. I know
it. I want Feast Giver."

"I suppose I could convince Scarred Mouth that it
would be a good match," Fighting Wolf mused slowly.

"Oh, thank you, brother!" She hugged him.
"Thank you."

"He'd better treat you well," Fighting Wolf
answered gruffly.

She smiled. "He will."

They rejoined the three waiting members of
Thunder Maker's family. "My sister has convinced me
to reconsider Feast Giver's marriage proposal,"
announced Fighting Wolf.

He would not tell them yet that he'd agreed to the
marriage. He could use his assent to advantage later
with these wily Hesquiats. "In return, I wish to speak
with Sarita." Thunder Maker and Feast Giver looked
ready to deny his request. "Alone."

Surprisingly, Sarita stepped forward. "I'll talk
with you," she said briefly.

Her father looked about to say something, then
changed his mind. He nodded. "Very well."

"Follow me," said Sarita shortly.

Obediently, Fighting Wolf followed Sarita along a
path that led from the village. They walked along in
silence until they came to a small clearing. Sarita
approached a large boulder that was to one side of the
open area, and sat down.

She turned to look at him. "What is it you wished
to say?" Her heart was beating rapidly, whether in fear
or anticipation, she couldn't tell. But she was sure he
could hear it. Her tawny eyes met his unflinchingly.
Fighting Wolf stared back at her, drinking in her

beloved face.

"Are you happy here?" began Fighting Wolf cautiously. Perhaps if he could get her to relax first, he could find the right words to persuade her to return with him.

"You travelled all this way to ask if I'm happy here?" taunted Sarita.

His white teeth flashed in a grin. "Your happiness has always concerned me," he responded good-naturedly.

Sarita watched him for a moment, wondering where this bantering Fighting Wolf had come from. Certainly she'd seen little of him in the time she'd lived at Ahousat. "Oh? That's why you took me as a slave? So I would be 'happy'?"

"I did my best to keep you happy," he shot back. He leaned closer, his face near hers. "And succeeded, too. Especially at night." His grin told her he was remembering some of their more passionate interludes.

She flushed, and turned her head away from those mesmerizing eyes. His nearness disturbed her. "What are you here for?" she demanded. "To take me back into slavery?"

"No," he answered simply.

"I don't believe you," she spat.

"Marry me, Sarita."

For a moment, she was speechless. She stared at him. His eyes were narrowed as he watched her intently. She shivered.

She recovered quickly. "You don't mean that."

"I do," he answered softly.

She tilted her head and watched him, amazed at this new side of the man she thought she knew so well. "Don't play with me," she snapped.

"I want to marry you," he insisted. "I want to take you back to my village and keep you with me. I love you."

"Why?" she whispered. "Why are you doing this? Is it not enough to take my body? Must you take my heart, too?'' He was lying, all lies. He had found her one weakness so unerringly. To tell her he loved her . . .

"Are you here to complete your revenge?" she managed at last. "Is this the final step in your plans? Convince me that you love me so that I'll go back with you? Then, when I've fallen in love with you, when I've believed all your lies, you can cast me aside in a final, vengeful gesture?"

She stood up. "It's a fine plan, Fighting Wolf," she said, her heart breaking inside. If only what he said was true, that he did love her. Even now, she wanted to cling to that hope. "But it won't work. I won't come back with you and be your willing victim."

She stood very tall, very dignified. He couldn't help but admire her regal pride. She truly was lovely. He clenched his fists at his side.

"I want you," he said in a low voice. "I want you, and I'll take you any way I can get you." Forgotten were his vows to cease his pursuit of her. Forgotten was everything but her, and his overwhelming desire for her.

She shivered under the impact of his words. He looked so ruthless. "No," she responded shakily. "No!"

She took a step away from him, but it was too late. His arm snaked around her waist and held her in an iron grip.

"Let me go!" Sarita pounded her fists against his brawny arms, then, when he didn't flinch, against his hard chest. "Let me go!"

"Not until you say you'll marry me," came his reply, hot in her ear. He seized her hair with his free hand and held her head immobile, then his lips were plundering hers, his strong body molded against her softer one. His warm, firm lips demanded, then cajoled her response.

She struggled against him, but realizing his greater strength, she gave up her feeble efforts. His kisses were too strong, too potent, and too much what she had longed for those many lonely nights. How she wanted to be held in those strong arms and never let go.

Relaxing against him, she gave herself up to his demands, and her arms stole around his neck. One strong arm supporting her, he arched her body back.

Fighting Wolf's enticing masculine scent was strong in Sarita's nostrils. She could feel the hard length of him against her stomach. Eagerly she returned his kisses. As if drugged, she melted under his heavier weight and they sank to the mossy ground together.

"Oh, Fighting Wolf," she moaned. "It's been so long—"

"Too long," he murmured. His hand was under her kutsack, stroking the back of her knee, then sliding up her leg, pushing the garment out of the way. "You feel so good," he whispered. Callused palms were running across her slightly rounded stomach. She tried to push his hand away. "Let me," he breathed. "Let me touch you." His strong fingers were stroking closer and closer to her womanhood.

"Oh, yes," she moaned. His hands were doing wonderful things to her body. His harsh breathing in her ear told her he was as aroused as she was. She couldn't stop him now, even if she wanted to.

His hand was making lazy circles over and around her. He gently cupped her mound of Venus. Somehow they were both naked, then he was leaning over her, his thighs warm against hers. His kisses were more forceful now, matching the screaming desire in her. Parting her legs with one of his own, he was nudging against her. "Open your legs for me," his husky whisper grated against her.

She started to close her legs.

"No, it's too late for that," he chuckled deeply.

Frantic, realizing how close she'd been to surrendering to him, she struggled once more. His hands pinned her wrists firmly against the moss as he looked into her eyes. "I've got to have you," he murmured thickly.

"Please," she moaned, not knowing if she was

pleading for him to let her go or to take her. His knee was against her womanhood, her legs splayed open to him. Gently, firmly, he pushed, then he was inside her. She gasped at his entry, then they were moving as one in the ancient rhythm. She held his shoulders close to her, licking and biting him lightly. In response, he drove deeper into her.

His fingers were between them, touching, gliding in circles over her womanhood. She felt herself rising spirally. In a burst of sunlight, she clutched him to her, moaning his name over and over. A sweetness enveloped her and she cuddled him to her as though she would never let him go. Then he stiffened and cried out her name. She felt him shudder with his release.

They lay together afterwards, their arms wrapped about each other, breathing evenly at last. He kissed her gently on the forehead. "Well?" he asked confidently. "Will you marry me?"

Sarita froze. How could he pretend he wanted to marry her? After what they had just shared, why couldn't he be honest with her?

"Marry you?" Her voice was sad. "You don't want to marry me. You just want to trick me. You Ahousats are stronger than we Hesquiats, you have more men, you take whatever you want. Why keep up this pretense of wanting to marry me?" she asked bitterly.

"What pretense?" he asked, his voice dangerously even.

She looked at him, despair in her eyes. "You don't have to pursue your revenge, Fighting Wolf. Don't you see? You've already won. I love you."

She stood up hastily as she spoke, throwing her kutsack over her head and knotting it with fumbling fingers. Fighting Wolf rested on one elbow and watched her frantic movements.

"Fighting Wolf, I love you," she repeated defiantly. "That's why I won't willingly return to Ahousat with you. I will not be used and tormented by a man who doesn't love me—"

"But I do love you!"

She shook her head. "I know you will lie and cheat to get whatever you want." She was angering him now, she could see it in the ugly look that crossed his face, but she rushed on, heedless. "Yes, and even kill. But I refuse to go to a man who values his revenge above my love. Or who would leave his child in slavery!"

With that, she whirled and ran swiftly back along the path that led to the village. Fighting Wolf leapt to his feet, intent on pursuit. Her long, dark hair rippled as she ran like a deer from his sight.

He paused. Let her go, he thought. She can't run far—never far enough to flee from him!

36

Hair tousled, Sarita arrived breathlessly in the village. She glanced quickly at the beach before darting into her father's longhouse.

Everything looked much as when she'd left. The grim Ahousats were still sitting in their canoes, watching the wary Hesquiats who were lined up on the beach. Precious Copper sat apart from everyone, and waited patiently as Feast Giver and his father conversed nearby in low tones.

Quickly running a comb through her tangled locks, Sarita managed to get most of the snags and moss out. Straightening her kutsack, she went outside to join her family.

Her father appeared surprised to see her return alone, but words died on his lips as a Hesquiat scout rushed up, panting heavily.

"The village—the village—" The man could hardly get his words out, he was so out of breath. Sarita surmised he'd run at top speed for quite a distance. "Ahousats have surrounded the village!" he got out at last.

"Where?" demanded Thunder Maker. Hastily, the man told the locations where the enemy warriors had been spotted.

"I was right," moaned Sarita. "It was a trick. He never intended to marry me at all!"

Catching a strange look on her father's features, she turned away from the others only to come face to face with Fighting Wolf. It was evident from his cold expression that he'd heard the scout's report.

"So," challenged Thunder Maker. "You weren't bluffing."

"No," answered the Ahousat war chief curtly.

Thunder Maker cleared his throat. "My son and I have decided to reconsider your marriage proposal for Sarita," he announced in stentorian tones. Sarita swung around in surprise. What was her father up to now? she wondered.

Fighting Wolf stood there watching her, a taunting smile on his face.

Ignoring him, she approached her father. "What are you talking about?" she fumed. "I'm not going to marry this Ahousat."

"Sarita. Silence," commanded her father.

"No, Nuwiksu. You listen to me." She turned to face Fighting Wolf. "I will *not* marry you, and nothing you can say or do will convince me otherwise."

If she was expecting her words to devastate him, she was gravely disappointed. Fighting Wolf continued to smirk at her as he asked her father casually, "I don't suppose my warriors had anything to do with changing your mind?"

Thunder Maker coughed several times before regaining his composure. "It only seemed fair," broke in Feast Giver, "since you were reconsidering my proposal for Precious Copper."

Fighting Wolf turned to the younger man and saw the sincerity in his eyes. He felt a momentary pang of guilt at baiting the Hesquiats.

Before he could say anything else, Sarita interrupted sweetly, "Nuwiksu, what about the Kyuquot chief you were about to marry me off to? Have you forgotten?"

Her last hopes were dashed at her father's next words. "We'll potlatch him and send him away. He won't leave here empty-handed," he assured her.

"I don't care whether the Kyuquot leaves here

empty-handed," Sarita hissed at her obtuse father. "I care that I'm not married off to this—this—" She broke off when she saw the amused smile on Fighting Wolf's face. Words failed her in her anger. She'd had enough.

Getting a grip on herself, she stated through clenched teeth, "I have one last thing to say: I will not marry anyone! Can you understand that? Not the Kyuquot, because I loathe him, and not the Ahousat because I know he does not really intend to marry me!" With that, she stalked off to the longhouse.

Fighting Wolf watched her go.

"Ahousat," began Thunder Maker before Fighting Wolf could make a move in the direction Sarita had taken. "If you can't have Sarita will you attack this village?"

Fighting Wolf merely shrugged, wondering what the wily old man was up to.

Thunder Maker took his silence for assent. "Go to her, then," advised the older man. "Surely you can convince her to marry you. My people's lives are at stake and I won't fight for her."

Fighting Wolf looked contemptuously at the old chief. "Still ready to sacrifice your daughter for political purposes, aren't you?" The fact that he, Fighting Wolf, would benefit from the old man's maneuvers added guilt to the contempt.

"You'd make the same decision," responded Thunder Maker firmly, his wise eyes watching the Ahousat. "Being chief is not easy. Were I to order my warriors to fight a battle whose outcome is already decided—"

At Fighting Wolf's interrogatively raised eyebrow, Thunder Maker observed, "You and I both know that you have the superior military strength in this encounter. Why pretend otherwise?"

Fighting Wolf nodded his acquiescence to that factual statement.

"As I was saying, should I order my men to attack you, too many lives would be lost. It's better to let one woman go, than to lose more of my people. We're too few as it is.''

"I'm glad you see things my way," said Fighting Wolf smoothly.

"I do," responded Thunder Maker. "Besides there's something about you that reminds me of myself when I was younger." He shook his head. "The Kyuquot would never be strong enough for Sarita. She'd quickly have him on his knees, whimpering." Thunder Maker paused in thought, then added, "Go, my son. Take your woman and leave here."

Thunder Maker watched the younger man leave. He hoped he'd done the right thing for his people by giving in to the Ahousat's demands so readily. It angered him to surrender to the crafty war chief once again. The memory of that debacle of a wedding ceremony still ate at him.

He hadn't been lying when he'd told the Ahousat he reminded him of himself when younger. Only omitted that it was the ruthless, aggressive side of the war chief he'd identified with. Ah well . . . Thunder Maker was tired of the fighting, the revenge. It had almost destroyed his family once. He would not let it do so again. He sighed. Now it was up to Sarita. . . .

Fighting Wolf departed, grinning. He caught up with Sarita in the longhouse. Taking her hand gently in his, he asked, "Sarita, will you walk with me one more time?"

She looked at him suspiciously, hearing the coaxing note in his voice. "You never give up, do you, Ahousat?"

"No." He smiled ferally.

What would it matter to talk with him once more before he left? She'd never seen him again. She'd have only memories to keep her alive from this time onwards. Feeling she was making a mistake, but unable to stop herself, she weakened. "Very well. But we'll walk on the beach, in plain sight of everyone," she stated firmly. "I won't have you seducing me again." She flushed at her own reminder.

There was a twinkle in his jet eyes, but he said nothing as he led her out into the cool, gray day. She wrapped the cedar cloak more tightly around her as if for protection from the masculine threat at her side. He led her down the beach as far away from the grim, watching warriors as he could.

He halted beside an old, weather-beaten driftwood log that was protected by a gnarled, wind-twisted pine.

"Is this safe enough?" he asked sardonically. "Nearby you have the greatest of Hesquiat manhood to protect you." He shot a disparaging glance at the stoical Hesquiat warriors shivering in the cool wind.

"You said you wanted to talk to me," she reminded him bitingly. "Say what you have to say and get it over with. I want to go back to the longhouse where it's warm."

"I'll keep you warm," he said, reaching for her.

Nimbly, she backed out of reach. "I believe I'll survive the cold for the short time I'll be out here," she observed sarcastically.

Fighting Wolf's eyes narrowed, but he said nothing. Instead, he squatted down near the driftwood log and looked out across the narrow inlet. "What are you going to do about the baby?" he asked.

"Baby?" she repeated, caught off guard. "Baby? What baby?"

"Don't try and deny it, Sarita. I know you're pregnant."

"Me?" she scoffed shakily. "Me, pregnant?" Her voice ended in squeak. Then her shoulders drooped, and she asked in a leaden voice, "How—how did you know?"

He smiled. "I made love to you. Remember?" Seeing the stricken look on her face, he added, "Did you think I wouldn't notice how your stomach fits so wonderfully against my palm, how your breasts are fuller, how your—" Seeing her blazing eyes, he broke off. Gently he asked, "What are you going to do with my child?"

"Your child?" she snapped. "What makes you think it's your child, you arrogant bastard!"

His amused gaze focused on her face. "Perhaps it's the Kyuquot's, then?" he drawled.

"No!" she shouted vehemently. Her abrupt response to his taunt took them both by surprise.

"Sarita," he said softly. "I know it's my child."

She was silent, then answered slowly, "Precious Copper."

"What?"

"Precious Copper. That explains how you know, doesn't it? Doesn't it? She told you!" In her anger Sarita jumped up from the log. When he didn't deny it, she stated, "And I thought she was my friend! I should have known—"

"She is your friend," he soothed. "If it hadn't been for her, I wouldn't have known where to find you."

"That's being a friend?" snapped Sarita. Her irony was obviously lost on Fighting Wolf. "I don't see why you're suddenly so concerned about your child," she said, hoping to hurt him. "You were content enough to let him be born into slavery the last time we discussed his future!"

"At that time, you told me you weren't pregnant. That your question was only for 'curiosity,' I believe you said."

"I wasn't certain that I was pregnant." She sniffed haughtily. "Then." She smiled at him slyly. "Are you still willing to let your child be born into slavery, Fighting Wolf? Because that's what will happen if you drag me back to Ahousat."

"No," he answered. "I don't want my child born into slavery." The words were said so quietly that Sarita had to strain to hear them. In the silence that fell between them, Fighting Wolf turned to her and impaled her with his jet black eyes. "Sarita, I love you."

"Love me?" she echoed. "Oh, Fighting Wolf, if only I could believe you."

"It's true," he said. "I do love you."

"No," she shook her head. "You're only saying that so I will believe your lies and you can complete your revenge."

"Ah, yes. My revenge," he said thoughtfully. "My revenge was completed some time ago."

She looked at him, wishing his words were true. "Oh, Fighting Wolf—" she moaned, struggling against her fears that this was just another trick.

"You ended my revenge," he said solemnly.

"Me?"

"Yes. When I came back to Ahousat and learned you'd escaped, I was furious. I ranted and raved. My slaves were afraid to come near me for fear I'd kill them. I told myself I was so angry because you, a mere slave, had run away from me, a great war chief." He laughed shortly.

"When word came that you and Precious Copper had been seen at this village, I was greatly relieved that you were safe, but my anger was still very strong. I set out with my men to rescue Precious Copper, but my main intent was to drag you back to Ahousat with me."

"I knew it," Sarita exclaimed triumphantly. "I knew it!" She faced him defiantly. "Well, I'm not going!"

Fighting Wolf eyed her thoughtfully. "As I said, I was intent on dragging you back with me. Everything went well until my men and I got caught in that terrible storm. We were paddling close to a very treacherous cape when the gale struck." He shook his head. "The waves pounded at us, the wind blew us off course. I've seen a lot of bad storms in my life, come close to death once or twice, but this time—"

Sarita listened, her heart in her eyes. "What happened?" she asked weakly.

"I was washed overboard," he answered briefly. "I was sure my life was over, that I would drown right there. As I was going under the waves, all I could think about was that I loved you and that I'd never see you again." There was silence after his words.

Sarita didn't know what to say. Slowly she began to hope that he was telling her the truth . . . Did he love her? Oh, if only . . . !

He continued, "Then someone tossed me a rope. I grabbed it and was hauled back to my canoe. Never in my life have I had such a close escape." He shivered and Sarita could tell the memory still haunted him. She put her arms around him.

"Oh, Fighting Wolf. How terrible," she sighed tremulously. "I'm so glad you weren't killed."

He looked deep into her eyes and read the love reflected there. He held her tight. "It was then that I had to face the truth about myself. I wasn't hunting you to bring back an escaped slave, I was hunting you because I loved you and wanted you back with me. Without you, there would be only emptiness in my life. I want you, Sarita," he said softly. "Not as my slave, but as my wife."

She pulled back at these words. "I . . . I need time—" she began. He drew away at her hesitancy.

"Time?" he asked slowly, not understanding. "Haven't you had enough time? What do you need more time for?"

He was becoming angry, she realized. He'd probably been expecting her to fall into his arms, she thought. "I . . . I need to be sure," she began.

"Sure?" he bit off. With visible effort, he sought control of his temper. Finally, he was calm enough to say, "Sarita, I've told you my feelings. I've opened my thoughts to you in a way I've done for no other person, man or woman. If you can't, or won't have me, then I want to know. Now."

"But our child—?"

"What about our child? I've told you I want our son. I want him free."

"Do you, Fighting Wolf?" she asked bitterly. "Or do you use that as bait to drag me away from here?"

"Sarita," he said impatiently. "What more do you want of me?"

Sarita remained silent. She didn't know herself what she wanted. Too much was happening, too fast. He said he loved her. Why couldn't she believe him? At last she answered, "If you truly want your child born free, you'll leave here."

"Leave?"

"Yes. That will be the test, won't it?" she asked, desperately. "You can't take me away forcibly, or else I'll be a slave again, and your son will be a slave. So, if you truly want freedom for your child, you must leave me free."

"Or marry you," he interrupted quickly.

"Fighting Wolf," she said softly. She would call his bluff now. If he really intended to take her back into slavery, her answer wouldn't matter to him. He'd overpower her and take her. If, on the other hand, he was sincerely concerned for his child, and sincerely wanted her as a wife, he'd be willing to give her freedom of choice as far as his proposal went. "The answer is no."

He looked at her for a long moment, his jet black eyes trying to pierce her golden ones and read her very thoughts. At last he said bitterly, "Very well. I've told you how I feel about you. I cannot, I *will* not crawl."

With that he turned on his heel, and stalked back past the warriors who were standing around in various shades of alertness.

She watched him walk away, a huge lump forming in her throat. Fighting Wolf had let her go! Unbelievably he had let her go. He was abiding by her choice. She was safe, her child was free, but somehow she felt no triumph in her victory.

37

As she watched Fighting Wolf walk out of her life, an eerie feeling of emptiness passed over Sarita. She loved him and she was letting him go. Why? She'd already proved her point. If he was intent on dragging her back to Ahousat, he'd have been pulling her across the rocky beach even now and she'd have been kicking and screaming every step of the way. She gazed at his retreating back and thought once more of her child . . . no, their child. Did she really wish to deny the man she loved his own child? Suddenly she knew the answer.

Jumping up off the old log, she raced after him. "Fighting Wolf," she cried.

He kept walking. "Fighting Wolf," she screamed this time. Desperation laced her voice. Wind whipped the loose hair about her face, and carried her voice to him.

Halting, he whirled to face her. She ran towards him, both arms outstretched. He reached for her, a grim look on his face. She bounded into his arms and he caught her to him tightly. "Oh, Fighting Wolf," she moaned. "I do love you. I—I couldn't let you go, either."

Golden eyes looked up into jet black ones. A brilliant smile lit up her face as she entwined her arms about his neck. She leaned forward and rubbed her nose affectionately against his. "Yes," she whispered huskily. "Yes, I'll marry you." She paused and drew back to look at him. "That is, if the offer is still open," she said uncertainly, waiting for his reaction.

A grin spread over his handsome face. "It is," he assured her, kissing her heartily. "It is!"

Suspicious Hesquiat and Ahousat warriors turned to watch the two lovers walking hand in hand on the wind-torn stretch of rocky beach. Ignoring the many eyes upon them, the two soon slipped silently into Thunder Maker's longhouse, in search of the old chief.

They found him sitting, resting near the fire, while Cedar Bundle gently massaged his neck and shoulders. The old man nodded as they approached. "You have something to tell me," he guessed.

Feast Giver padded up silently from the shadows, Precious Copper in tow. His look was guarded as his ebony eyes darted from Fighting Wolf to Sarita and back again. Then he saw the two touching hands, and he relaxed his stance somewhat.

"Yes, Nuwiksu," began Sarita, addressing him politely. Her effort at manners was not lost on her father. "We wish to tell you that we want to get married."

Thunder Maker nodded. "I've already given my approval," he said.

Sarita looked at him in astonishment, then turned to the man beside her. Her eyes narrowed suspiciously as she asked, "I don't suppose you knew anything about this?"

Fighting Wolf looked guilty, but said nothing as he shrugged casually.

"Nuwiksu," Sarita cried exasperatedly, "Nuwiksu, you've done it again!"

"Done what?" asked that man, baffled.

"Married me off without my permission," she screeched.

"Sarita, your manners—" he warned.

Suddenly the ludicrousness of the situation struck her and she began to laugh. "Three times," she chortled, between gasps, "Three times that old man has tried to marry me off!"

Thunder Maker managed to look scandalized. "Have I succeeded this time?" he asked, anxiously.

Sarita could only nod, she was laughing too hard. "Just barely," she finally exclaimed.

"I convinced her that she would be better off with me than with the Kyuquot," offered Fighting Wolf smoothly.

Thunder Maker nodded. A wise choice. His daughter had more political savvy than he had thought.

Thunder Maker led the way out of the longhouse to the beach outside.

Surly Hesquiat warriors turned to watch the small party proceed down to the waterline. Mistrustful Ahousats eyed the Hesquiats warily.

"It is my great pleasure," crowed Thunder Maker in a loud voice, "To announce the marriage feast of my daughter, Sarita, to Fighting Wolf, war chief of the Ahousats. The feast will be tomorrow night."

Gaping in disbelief, the Ahousat warriors could only stare dumbfounded at the grinning Fighting Wolf. What was this? Another plot? Looking hastily at one another for answers, their confused murmurs reached the war chief's ears.

He strode forward. "It is true, men," he confirmed. "Sarita has consented to be my wife. I am very pleased. I hope you will join me in welcoming the Hesquiats into my family!"

There were a few halfhearted cheers, but the men were still wary. Fighting Wolf shrugged. They would soon realize he was sincere about this marriage.

The reaction of the Hesquiat warriors was little better. They too could only gaze in utter bewilderment at the smiling young couple. Feast Giver's keen ears caught disgruntled mutterings in which the word "trick" figured prominently. He went to his father and whispered discreetly to the older man.

Thunder Maker nodded, then held up his hand for silence. "I have a further announcement," he stated clearly. "Tomorrow at the same time, the marriage of my son, Feast Giver, to Precious Copper, sister of the

Ahousat war chief, will also take place.''

Fighting Wolf frowned, then looked at Precious Copper. The glow on his sister's face told him of her happiness. He decided he didn't mind that she'd accepted Feast Giver's proposal, after all.

At the second announcement, both groups of warriors broke into loud cheers. One marriage might be a trick by those wily Ahousats, but two? Not likely. The tension was broken as the Hesquiat warriors surrounded the two couples and vocally extended their congratulations.

The Ahousat warriors stood up and stretched their cramped limbs. Then, curious, they joined the others on the beach.

It was some time later that the happy couples managed to slip away from the crowd of well-wishers to Thunder Maker's longhouse.

Sarita was still holding Fighting Wolf's hand as they walked through the family's living area. She caught sight of Crab Woman, slumped over, asleep by the warm fire. The older woman's snores sounded comfortable, though a trifle noisy.

Sarita couldn't resist the temptation in front of her. "Crab Woman," she said slowly, standing over the woman. "Crab Woman, wake up!"

Crab Woman grunted and snuffled as she slowly woke up. "Get up, woman," continued Sarita in the same loud voice. "You have a feast to give tomorrow night. You'd better get started right away!" The older woman jumped, still half-asleep. When she peered up, she saw with surprise that it was her stepdaughter ordering her about.

"What . . . What's the matter with you, Sarita? Talking to your old mother like that?" she demanded testily.

Sarita laughed, never before having heard Crab Woman acknowledge such a close relationship between them. "Crab Woman loves to prepare feasts," she explained jocularly to Fighting Wolf.

"Who are you talking to? Who's that you have with you?" went on the older woman, blinking at the large shadowed figure behind Sarita. She gave a sudden yelp. "Watch out It's that Ahousat! He's back. Run, Sarita!"

She scrambled to her feet far faster than Sarita would have ever thought possible for such a bulky woman. Grabbing a heavy piece of nearby firewood, Crab Woman was about to swing it at Fighting Wolf's head when Sarita's shout stopped her.

"Crab Woman, it's all right!" laughed the younger woman. "He's my husband-to-be. Put that stick away." The old woman blinked owlishly at the two in the dim light. "He's the reason you have to prepare another feast," explained Sarita patiently. "We're getting married tomorrow night. Just a small ceremony, of course," she added.

Crab Woman appeared dazed, but quickly recovered herself. "Of course," she mimicked. "Would you like something like the last wedding feast I prepared for you?" she asked acidly. "I'm sure the bridegroom would be happy to supply the weapons."

"Not necessary," responded Sarita airily. "Oh, I almost forgot. Feast Giver and Precious Copper will be getting married at the same time." She smirked as Crab Woman gaped in surprise.

"Has everyone gone mad?" inquired the older woman. "Why does he want to marry that—that slave?"

Feeling Fighting Wolf bristle beside her, Sarita sought to defuse the situation. "She's not a slave. She's a high-ranking Ahousat noblewoman. And he loves her. That's why he's marrying her!"

"Oh, of course," responded the irascible old woman. "Are there any other marriage feasts I should know about?" she asked in a mockingly polite tone.

Her words gave Sarita a jolt. "Not at the moment," she managed absently. She tapped her chin gently with one long forefinger as her thoughts raced.

"I'll be sure to let you know in plenty of time should there be any other weddings."

"Hmmph," grunted Crab Woman. "Now will you get out of here? I can't start organizing everything with you two getting in my way. Out!"

Laughing in sheer good spirits, Sarita allowed Fighting Wolf to lead her back outdoors. She wondered briefly why Crab Woman's acerbic comments no longer bothered her. Maybe it was because she sensed that, under that gruff exterior, the older woman actually cared for her. Or maybe it was because now that she was in love, and loved, everything looked brighter. She certainly felt kinder. Which reminded her . . .

"I must speak with Spring Fern. Soon," she said to Fighting Wolf.

"Oh? Who's she? Another stepmother?"

"No, four are enough, thank you," Sarita laughed. "Spring Fern is my slave. I have something important to tell her."

"Really? Are you in the habit of confiding your marriage plans to your slaves?" he asked politely.

"Not my marriage plans," she smirked. "But wedding plans nonetheless." She refused to divulge another word, despite his questioning. But the thoughtful smile on her lips warned him she was up to something.

38

The Kyuquot war canoes circled the narrow inlet in the pouring rain. The sound of the men's chanting was blown away by the wind.

"What do you want?" asked a sleepy Sarita, as Fighting Wolf shook her awake. Still groggy from last night's celebration, she gradually woke up. Her golden eyes met and held his piercing black ones. "My husband," she said softly.

"That's right, wife," he responded. "I'm your husband. As of last night. Now we tell the Kyuquots."

"The Kyuquots?" She jumped up, reaching for her kutsack. "I'd forgotten all about them."

"Evidently they haven't forgotten about you," he said, an ironic tone in his voice. "They're here now." He didn't wait for her to dress, but headed for Thunder Maker's quarters. "I'll be back soon," he called over his shoulder. "I want to see if your father needs any help in handling the situation."

"Wait for me, Fighting Wolf," Sarita called, to no avail. It looked like she had some work ahead of her in this marriage, she thought ruefully. One of the first things she'd have to do was teach Fighting Wolf to obey her!

Hastily combing her hair and putting on her earrings and bangles and anklets, she rushed after him.

She needn't have hurried. The Kyuquots were slowly floating into the beach in their large canoes. Some of the canoes looked damaged, but most were piled high with goods. Wedding gifts, she thought guiltily.

She was about to run down to the beach for a closer view when Spring Fern's voice halted her. "Mistress, please. Don't go down there. You might be in danger."

"There's no danger," Sarita answered. "What can the Kyuquots do? Fighting Wolf has more warriors—and better ones, too."

"Still," her slave pleaded, "Don't risk yourself. Wait just a little while. Let the men work this out."

Sarita turned to her and asked gently, "Why are you so concerned about me?"

Surprised, Spring Fern answered, "I've always been concerned, mistress. I've always cared about what happens to you."

Her simple words left Sarita feeling warm. "You've always been a faithful friend," murmured Sarita. Turning away thoughtfully, she decided to watch the confrontation on the beach from a safe distance.

Thunder Maker and Fighting Wolf stood side by side, facing the approaching Kyuquots. Throws Away Wealth stepped daintily out of his canoe and walked cockily up to them.

"Who invited the Ahousats to my wedding?" he asked arrogantly. "Get rid of them, Thunder Maker."

Thunder Maker looked nervously at Fighting Wolf before answering. He cleared his throat. "I see the storm delayed you, my friend," he began carefully.

"Of course the storm delayed me," snarled Throws Away Wealth. "It was the worst storm I've ever been in. Lost twenty of my men. Did countless damage to my canoes. We even lost a few canoes that were overloaded." He added pointedly, "Overloaded with wedding gifts."

He rubbed his hands together to warm them. "The middle of winter is a damn foolish time to hold a wedding celebration, if you ask me."

"Yes, well, that's too bad about your men and canoes," offered Thunder Maker politely. "At least you've arrived safely."

Fighting Wolf raised an eyebrow at the older chief. Throws Away Wealth turned to him. "What are you doing here, Ahousat?" he asked belligerently.

"Fighting Wolf is visiting me as a guest," cut in Thunder Maker before Fighting Wolf could say anything. "He's welcome in my village at any time."

"Really?" asked the Kyuquot chief sarcastically. "That's not what you told me the last time I was here."

"Hmmph, yes, well—"

"What Chief Thunder Maker means," said Fighting Wolf smoothly, "is that he can't very well keep his daughter's husband out of his village."

"You've married off another daughter?" asked the Kyuquot jovially. "Didn't know you had so many marriageable daughters."

"He doesn't," said Fighting Wolf succinctly.

"You can't mean—" began the Kyuquot, anger beginning to flush his tanned face.

"Yes, he does mean that," stated Fighting Wolf triumphantly. "Sarita is now married to me."

The Kyuquot turned to Thunder Maker. "Is that true?" he cried.

"He speaks the truth," confirmed Thunder Maker neutrally. He shrugged uncomfortably. He didn't want to alienate the Kyuquots. They would be formidable enemies, despite what Fighting Wolf had said earlier about their fighting capabilities. He sighed. "I realize this must be a terrible shock—"

The anger on Throws Away Wealth's face surprised Thunder Maker. He hadn't thought the man valued an alliance with the Hesquiats so highly.

"You have insulted me *and* the Kyuquot people, by this action," began the Kyuquot chief stiffly. "You will not get away with treating our great tribe like this. Or me." He hit his own chest forcefully, then winced at the blow.

Fighting Wolf coughed to hide the snicker that sprang to his lips. "What are you going to do about it?" he asked in pretended concern.

"We'll take action," threatened Throws Away

Wealth, waving his arms about. The little man was almost hopping up and down in his anger. He hadn't realized how much he'd been looking forward to bullying Sarita. Now the haughty bitch was out of his reach.

"There's no need for that," said Thunder Maker soothingly. He shot a warning look at his son-in-law. "We would be very honored if you and your men would stay here as our guests. Even now, my wives are preparing a lavish feast for you."

Throws Away Wealth looked at Thunder Maker, then at Fighting Wolf. Lastly, he looked at his weary men. They'd been through a terrible time in their efforts to get to this worthless village. Let Thunder Maker go broke feeding them all, he thought. Besides, the Ahousats were too strong to challenge at this time. He remembered uncomfortably how his men had been soundly beaten on that summer raid . . . .

Throws Away Wealth nodded with as much dignity as he could summon in such humiliating circumstances. "Very well," he acknowledged icily. "We accept your kind invitation."

He turned on his heel and shouted orders to his tired men. Glad to have an evening's celebration and rest ahead of them, they emptied their canoes with alacrity.

Throws Away Wealth fell into step stiffly behind the taller Fighting Wolf and Thunder Maker. The three wound their way in silence up the beach to Thunder Maker's longhouse.

It was later that night, after the lavish banquet Crab Woman prepared for the disgruntled Kyuquots, that Sarita was at last alone with her beloved Fighting Wolf. Tired and relaxed, they cuddled together after making sweet, passionate love. "I love you," she murmured.

He turned to her half asleep, his eyes heavy-lidded. "And you're a wonderful lover," he answered.

She smiled. "You know, I didn't really think you

were going to go through with it.''

"What? I always finish any lovemaking I start," he responded, giving her a playful nip on her earlobe. "Almost always," he corrected. "There were one or two times in my longhouse—"

She laughed. "That's not what I'm talking about. I meant the marriage. I didn't think you were really going to marry me.''

"After all I went through?" he asked incredulously. "I fought my way through a storm for you. I fought your father for you—"

Seeing her quick look of concern, he added, "With words, my love. Only with words."

She sighed, reassured.

"I even had to fend off an angry Kyuquot suitor for your affections," he continued in a mock aggrieved voice.

Sarita giggled. "Still, I can hardly believe we're together—"

"Believe it," he cut in, moving slowly down her frame and laying his cheek gently against her stomach.

"I'm so happy," she sighed.

"So am I," he murmured.

"Fighting Wolf," she said after a moment.

"Mmm?"

"I'm freeing one of my slaves."

"Oh? Anyone I know?"

"Hmmmm-mm. Spring Fern. I'm so happy with you, I'm freeing her so she can marry the man she loves, and be happy too."

He opened his eye. Shook his head. "You amaze me," he said after a while. She smiled, content to take his words as a compliment. "She's going to marry Rottenwood.''

"Rottenwood? That name sounds familiar."

"It should," she answered with another giggle. "He helped me escape from your village."

Fighting Wolf was silent as he remembered his turmoil when he heard Sarita had escaped. Before he could say anything, however, Sarita said hesitantly, "Fighting Wolf?"

"Hmmmh?"

"I have something to tell you."

He raised his head warily. "What is it?"

"That night you caught me outside your long-house—Remember? You accused me of meeting a man?"

Fighting Wolf nodded, his face contorting grimly. "I remember," he stated. "All too well."

Sarita shivered at his barely suppressed anger. She hurried on, "It was Rottenwood I met that night."

"What?" shouted Fighting Wolf jumping up. Then he remembered she'd been a virgin when he'd first taken her. "And?" he asked through tight lips.

"We—we met that night to plan our escape. That's all." Sarita waited, holding her breath. The sincerity in her golden eyes was obvious in the lamplight.

"I believe you," Fighting Wolf answered at last. "I was furious," he acknowledged. "I was so angry that night that I went paddling for a long time. When I finally calmed down it was morning." He shook his head ruefully. "Even then I must have loved you and not realized it."

Then he gave a low growl and attacked her playfully. "Well, there'll be no more 'Rottenwoods' to help you escape from me, ever again," he said, a possessive hug reinforcing his words. "You're mine, now. And you'll stay mine."

"Yes, Fighting Wolf," she said meekly, a sparkle in her eye. "And you're mine."

The complete satisfaction in her voice was evident to them both, and they laughed joyously.

Epilogue

"She's beautiful," breathed Fighting Wolf, leaning over his wife to look at the baby cuddled in her arms. "She's got your eyes."

"My eyes," agreed Sarita, "and your nose."

"Poor thing," murmured her husband. He rubbed the firm bridge of his straight nose.

They both chuckled. The little girl was the delight of her parents. Indeed, Sarita at times thought her husband was, perhaps, overly proud of their daughter. There was the day she found him showing her off to a bored Scarred Mouth. At Sarita's pointed suggestion that Scarred Mouth had raised nine of his own children and probably had better things to do than admire babies, the old man had gladly escaped. He left behind a disgruntled Fighting Wolf. "But I was just about to tell him how alert and clever she is."

"I'm sure he can see that for himself," soothed Sarita indulgently. She was warmed by the memory.

Seeing her serene face, Fighting Wolf asked, "Did you want to show our baby to your father? She's old enough to make the trip safely now. We could paddle to Hesquiat in the next few days."

Sarita looked thoughtful. "That would give me a chance to see how Precious Copper is doing. She should be past the time of her morning sickness." She smiled. "Feast Giver was saying he wants a boy."

"Let him think he wants a boy. In this longhouse we want girls, don't we?" crooned the war chief to his tiny daughter. She smiled and curled her small fingers around his large one. "She's strong, too," he observed approvingly.

At that moment, a slim young woman bustled into the living area. "Spring Fern! I mean Sea Palm Woman." Sarita was embarrassed at the slip she'd made. "I thought you'd left for Hesquiat already."

Sea Palm Woman answered, "We're leaving now. Man Out of the Shadows wishes to return to your father's longhouse. I just stopped to say good-bye one last time."

"Thank you for all your help after the baby was born. I was so glad you could come to see me," Sarita's glowing face expressed her deep contentment with both husband and child. "We'll see you soon," continued the new mother. "We're heading to Hesquiat for a visit within the next few days."

Sea Palm Woman smiled, "Well, I'd best be going. Man Out of the Shadows hates to wait." She patted her flat torso. "He'll have to wait for this one, though."

"Sea Palm Woman! Are you—?"

"Pregnant? Yes, Abalone Woman confirmed it. Man Out of the Shadows is jubilant. He's happy his son will not be born into slavery. Thanks to you, Sarita," the woman said with tears in her eyes. "Thank you for freeing me, so I could marry Rottenwood—I mean Man Out of the Shadows." The two women hugged.

"There now. Hurry along," admonished Sarita, tears of happiness in her eyes, too. "You don't want to keep your husband waiting."

At Sea Palm Woman's departure, Fighting Wolf turned to his wife and said, "And you don't want to keep your husband waiting, either. Come to bed."

Warning him happily that it was the middle of the day, Sarita took his outstretched hand and hurried to the tiny alcove. Soon they were very busy making more beautiful babies.